THE GOLDEN GHETTO

THE

A NOVEL BY

PUBLISHED BY

AND DISTRIBUTED IN ASSOCIATION WITH

GOLDEN GHETTO

NOEL B. GERSON

M. EVANS AND COMPANY, INC.
NEW YORK

J. B. LIPPINCOTT COMPANY
PHILADELPHIA AND NEW YORK

FOR MARILYN

"Stella Ross, you are a mess!"

She pulled off her shower cap, dropped her bath towel over its rail and examined herself critically in the full-length mirror. What she saw belied her words: her breasts were still high and firm, her waist was small, and she had only a hint of a tummy. Her thighs, although solid, were shapely; her legs, as always, were her best feature. Her body, she had to admit, didn't look like that of a woman in her thirties.

Neither did her face. Her very short blond hair was tousled and youthful, and her blue eyes, even without make-up, were enormous. She imagined she saw lines at their corners and on her forehead, although they were invisible to anyone else. In spite of how she felt, she looked terrific.

But this morning Stella could not be satisfied with what she saw. Reaching for the shabby flannel dressing gown she wore when she spent the night in her own apartment, she stared at her reflection again, briefly. "Life begins at thirty-three, does it?" she asked aloud. "Max Berman, go to hell."

For a moment she stood motionless and dazed, vulnerable to her indecision. Then in a burst of resolution, she hurried into her small, modestly furnished bedroom and sat in the one chintz-covered easy chair. Again she hesitated, reaching for a cigarette before she picked up the telephone and dialed.

Margaret Lafferty's middle-aged voice sounded a weary, dispirited "Hello."

"This is Stella, but don't repeat my name if Paul is still home."

"He left fifteen minutes ago. He and Max had to meet at breakfast to talk about some new contracts. They're always busy these days," Margaret added bitterly.

"Are you free for lunch today?" Stella asked. "There are things I want you and Paul to know, and it's easier talking to you alone."

"Why don't you come upstairs to my apartment, Stella?"

"I'm not at Max's place. I'm home. But I've got to spend the morning at the office, and I have to talk to Max there anyway. So I thought we could meet for lunch."

Margaret's sigh was lugubrious. "I suppose I could make it to the Prince Consort."

Stella smiled. The wife of her co-employer ate lunch at society's favorite hangout every weekday of her life, no matter how much she complained about the food and service there, or the state of her own health. "The Prince Consort will be perfect."

"My regular table at twelve-thirty?"

"Would one be just as convenient? I have a rather complicated session coming up with Max this morning, and it may take me a little time to break away."

"Of course." For the first time Margaret heard the strain in the younger woman's voice. "Is something wrong, Stella?"

"Just about everything."

"Between you and Max?"

"Yes. I'll tell you about it at lunch." Stella replaced the receiver and went to the tiny kitchen to turn on the coffee.

Returning to her bedroom, she sighed as she went to her clothes closet. She usually made a point of dressing for work like any of the other cost accountants in the L & B Construction Company offices, but she couldn't wear an inexpensive blouse and skirt today. Lunch at the Prince Consort called for a more elaborate costume, perhaps one of her four-hundred-dollar suits. Preferably—for Margaret's sake, in the presence of all those rich-bitch females—a Paris import.

Today, Stella thought, she'd be playing the role of a prince's consort herself. The ambivalence of her position was beyond endurance, and it would be a relief, once she had settled matters, to be moving in just one direction.

If only she could hate Max. Just a little. It would make everything so much simpler.

They sat opposite each other at a gleaming oak table in the pine-paneled private dining room in the L & B Tower: two powerfully built men who, although middle-aged, still looked capable of taking care of themselves in a barroom brawl. Manhattan was spread out beyond the oversized windows, but the partners were too engrossed this morning to appreciate the view. Maybe after breakfast they would relax and enjoy the splendor of the city panorama beneath them, knowing they had created all this for themselves from nothing but their own brains and gut strength. But they might not have time for such pleasure this morning.

Paul Lafferty, finishing his eggs and toast, was immersed in a column of figures, which he read and reread with infinite care. Max Berman, his meal finished, was scribbling in the margins on his sheet of identical figures, pausing occasionally to stare up

9

at the ceiling and tap on the edge of the table with his gold pencil. "I shouldn't drink more coffee," he said aloud. "It gives me heartburn. Paul, I say we go ahead."

"I'll be satisfied if we put up the building at a fee and get out," his partner replied. "Why buy the property itself? Who needs more real estate?"

"It isn't a matter of needing it. We want it. Because we can show a thirty-percent profit by selling the whole package—land, building and all—when the construction is finished."

"We'll be extending ourselves again."

"Goddam," Max said. "We're already into the banks for eighty-five million credit. What's another fifteen million?"

"I don't like it. We've achieved a solid position by putting up good, solid twenty- to forty-story buildings. Nothing super-fancy. Nothing glamorous. Now we're spreading out all over the place. We must own a quarter of the East Side—at least on paper. We own eight hotels—no, nine, including that idiot resort in Puerto Rico that you wanted after you and Stella went there this winter. What do we know about the hotel business?"

Max reached into a special inner pocket of his London-made suit for his cigar case, and absently offered his partner one of the special brand made for him in Tampa. "We know absolutely nothing about hotels," he admitted with a grin. "Or theatres. Or department stores. When you were adding up our assets you forgot that two-store chain we bought."

"I call them liabilities," Paul said. "And I'm getting a little frightened."

Max lighted his cigar and relished the flavor. "Look, Paul. To run the hotels we've hired the best men in the business. The Goldberg brothers are on our payroll, operating the stores they sold us, and if I do say so, that was a master stroke. I'm interested in chunks of property—"

"I know. More and more we play Monopoly."

"Why the hell not?" Max demanded roughly. "We're smart, we know what we're doing, and we've created a real empire.

An Irishman and a Jew who started without a nickel between them. I don't know about you, but I have a pretty good opinion of Lafferty and Berman." He gestured with the cigar at the sheet of figures. "Without qualification, I want to go ahead with this deal."

"What does Stella think?"

"I never discuss these things with her." Max's mood changed, and he became irritated.

"Since when? Last year, when the four of us flew to Amsterdam and Copenhagen together, she knew everything about our plans."

"That was last year. Last month, even. Right now she's having one of her spells. She has to prove she's the independent working girl."

"She's a good cost accountant."

"The best we've ever had," Max said, then shrugged. "But never mind Stella. I'll handle her. Now, let's get this deal settled one way or the other. I've got a meeting in my office in fifteen minutes on a hotel we might be able to pick up. The ownership is shaky, and with a little under-the-table push, we might be able to get it at a real bargain. So you see, Paul, I'm still a bargain hunter at heart, and never mind the size of our portfolios."

It was cold in the bedroom of the townhouse on the Lower East Side, but Lance Balutis didn't mind, and purposely used only one blanket. His childhood in Whiting, Indiana, had been responsible, of course: a mother who had believed in fresh air and a large family so poor that no one would have dreamed of giving a boy more than a single blanket had made it impossible for him to sleep any other way.

Lance was grateful for that experience. A slightly numbing sense of cold, like any other heightened or exaggerated feeling, increased the individual's reaction to super-reality. Whatever talents he possessed as an artist and creator of cinemas had been God-given, to be sure, but his interpretive abilities, which set him apart from his peers, were the direct consequence of his sensitivity to super-reality, a state made no less valid by the fact that he had invented its name.

His eyes closed, one arm gracefully flung outside the blanket, Lance simultaneously enjoyed and endured the cold. Liquor and drugs were only moderately effective in deepening his insights, and he had discovered that both, taken in quantity, tended to blur the images he found essential to interpret the essence of modern life. His gift, as he had good cause to know, gave him a heavy responsibility as a leader of a movement that sought only basic truths. And, as always, the knowledge that he possessed that talent made him humble.

The day that stretched ahead would be frantically busy, but he had grown accustomed to spending all of his days in a frenzy of activity. If his parents could see how hard he worked, they would be sorry they had accused him of laziness when he was a boy. On the other hand, he reflected, their opinion of him probably would be unchanged. Knowing nothing of creative art or the problems encountered by those who were trying to help a floundering young generation understand itself, they would think him unchanged. It would have been beyond their ken to grasp the fact that hard work meant far more than the back-breaking physical labor in which his father had engaged. In fact, they undoubtedly would have regarded his hardest work as loafing.

Restless, eager to continue his experiments with light and sound on film, Lance threw back the satin sheet, slipped his feet into his monogrammed velvet slippers and stood. His silk nightshirt felt good to the touch, and so did his cashmere dressing gown. All of the senses had to be utilized, constantly, to enable him to maintain his grasp on super-reality.

So many of his close friends, even Bobbie Wayne, refused to sympathize with him, insisting that he pampered himself, and the inconsistency of their attitude infuriated him. A four-poster bed, for its own sake, would have been an affectation. But as an aid in creating and maintaining a mood it was worth its weight in marijuana. His efforts—and the profits he made—were proof of that.

But his accomplishments to date were just the beginning. His patrons had of necessity been people of wealth, but he needed more than they could offer now. Only a multimillionaire of Max Berman's stature could finance the long-range projects that were forever spinning in his head.

From the outside the Prince Consort looked like dozens of other restaurants in the East Sixties. Its canopy was faded, the doorman wore a dark uniform almost indistinguishable from that of a chauffeur, and the entrance was inconspicuous. The uninitiated would have found the interior equally unimpressive.

A few chairs, settees and tables in the eighteenth-century-English style were scattered around the blue-carpeted lobby, where no one ever sat except an occasional elderly lady waiting for a friend. The bar, a separate room that opened off the lobby, was dark, almost murky, its mahogany tables and chairs blending with matching walls and the bar itself. At noon, only the heavy drinkers frequented the bar, and not until the dinner hour did it come into its own. Then three waiters were needed to help the bartender, late arrivals who crowded into the room stood against the walls or in the narrow aisles, and strangers or tourists were politely asked to leave.

There was a hint of grandeur, but no more than that, in the cream-colored eighteenth-century main dining room. Beneath the neoclassical chandeliers set in the high ceiling the tables were placed sufficiently far apart to discourage all but the sharpest-eared eavesdroppers. The cream-colored carpet muffled the usual restaurant sounds, and the frock-coated waiters were so

13

expert that dishes rarely clattered. Even the busboys learned decorum before they were permitted to work in the main dining room.

But the real glory of the Prince Consort was its clientele. No one, including the shrewd proprietor of Italian descent who had inherited the restaurant from his father, cared to recall that it had been a speakeasy forty years earlier, one of the East Side's more notorious drinking establishments. The food had always been good, however, and over the years a myth had been created and maintained: the Prince Consort was an establishment which catered exclusively to the ultra-elite.

The generosity to society gossip columnists, who were always guests of the house, had paid handsome dividends. The hard core of patrons were ladies and gentlemen whose families had taken their presence in the Social Register for granted over the course of generations. Visiting royalty usually stopped in for a meal or two, and several expatriate former monarchs and their wives had regular tables when in New York.

Inevitably, show business was represented, too. The president of a large motion-picture company which made its headquarters in Manhattan ate lunch there on Mondays, Wednesdays and Fridays, and so did a prominent Broadway theatrical producer. Only those actors with genteel backgrounds—or those with pretensions to gentility—cared to bother, however. The other stage and cinema stars were bored by the surface calm, and preferred livelier inns.

Café society, that odd mixture of the Four Hundred and celebrities, claimed representation in the years immediately following World War II, and was succeeded by the slightly coarser, more democratically based jet set. Now that group had given way to still another, to which it was related, the Beautiful People. Money, residence on the East Side and some type of distinction or notoriety qualified an individual for membership in the amorphous association of Beautiful People. Regular mention of one's name in the newspaper columns was a requisite, to be sure, and was aided by the press agents hired by businessmen and play-boys, well-to-do housewives and higher-priced call girls.

The refinement of the Prince Consort, combined with the presence of several columnists, made the restaurant a natural gathering place for the Beautiful People. And their presence was creating a subtle and gradual but definite change in the aura of the establishment. The Social Register ladies still wore simple dresses or suits by Mainbocher, complete with pearls, or, by way of variety, something by Chanel. With great reluctance they had raised their skirts to an inch or two above their knees, but made no secret of their discomfort. Their escorts were attired in suits by Madison Avenue tailors that made the wearers look totally inconspicuous, which was their aim. But such diners were in the minority these days.

Miniskirts and boots had long been the uniform of the Beautiful People, and the Prince Consort had fought a hard battle against pants on women and either turtlenecks or scarves on men. Ladies wore skirts, the management had insisted, and gentlemen never sat in the main dining room without cravats. But the tide had been irresistible, and a patron who had been away for even five years would have shuddered at what she now saw at noon in the staid Prince Consort.

Sandra Tilstrom, her shoulder-length red hair gleaming beneath the crystal chandeliers, wore green corduroy elephant pants and a blouse of the sheerest jersey. Some of her dearest friends, scattered around the room, considered her far too flamboyant. But she was an internationally acknowledged fashion leader, thanks to the thousands provided by her indulgent wholesale-produce grocer husband, who was earning money faster than she coud spend it. Her money and her flair were, as she well knew, her prime assets, and she had made the most of them, carving a position of prominence for herself within the social-art scene. She gave money to artists so they could go on with their work, and they, in turn, paid court to her as a famous personality. And she became famous. Even within her own elite group people were jealous of her because, as Sandra herself would tell you, she was a woman in her late thirties who didn't look a day over twenty-five.

Sandra's luncheon companion was the only woman in the room who outshone her. Barbara Howe, known to millions of gossip-column readers as Barbie, was actually twenty-five, but looked somewhat older. Her black hair was piled high on her head in the distinctive style that had made her the darling of the fashion magazines and had started a new trend. She, too, had an indulgent husband, Morris Howe, who owned a large string of second-hand automobile sales lots, and her clothes reflected real daring as well as wealth.

No longer a sensation because of her hair style and doll-like features, Barbie believed in extremes. Her sliver of a microskirt was the shortest in the room, but the ultimate, spectacular touch was her man-tailored shirt of almost transparent voile, slit to the waist.

"I wonder if you and Morrie would like to drop over next Tuesday night," Sandra said, knowing the Howes rarely spent an evening together.

Barbie hesitated, her too-perfect features trying to indicate an attempt to remember her social schedule.

"I'd love to come, darling, but I don't know about Morrie—"

"Tell him that Marty is working up a card game. Usually Marty goes his own way, but he's insisting we have some husbands and wives this time. The poor dear wouldn't know what my friends are talking about, so he'll organize a pinochle or poker game before the party is a half-hour old. Depend on it."

"He doesn't know yet that there'll be a card game?" Barbie giggled inanely.

"Hardly. He—" Sandra broke off. "Where's Hal Harper going?"

Both stared surreptitiously at the mild, inconspicuous little man who wrote one of the world's most widely syndicated gossip columns.

Barbie stiffened when she saw the columnist join two women who had just come in, one grey-haired and the other, who was much younger, a short-haired blonde. Both were expensively but conservatively dressed, and she had no interest in either. The mere fact that Hal Harper thought them important enough to greet effusively, however, piqued her curiosity. "Who are they?"

Sandra studied them through lowered lids. "Not our crowd, darling. The old one is Mrs. Paul Lafferty, the building tycoon's wife. She comes here all the time, although God knows why. The Consort is wasted on her sort. I think the other is the mistress of his partner, What's-his-name Berman."

"Max."

"That's the one. But I'm not sure, because they never hang out in the places anybody goes. I hear he's some kind of a nut."

"He can afford to be whatever he wants." A hint of avarice showed on Barbie's doll-like face. "He could buy and sell Morrie with the loose change in his pocket, and Morrie has plenty of bread, believe me."

"She's attractive enough." Sandra peered harder. "But dull. Really dull."

On the far side of the room Stella Ross was uncomfortably conscious of the interest being shown in her by the bizarrely dressed women, both of whom she knew from fashion-magazine and tabloid photographs. But she tried to concentrate on the unexpected visit from Hal Harper, whom she met only a few times previously.

"You're looking well, Mrs. Lafferty," the columnist said, automatically launching into his standard opening. In his youth he had wanted to be a playwright or novelist, but had drifted into newspaper work. Now, wealthy and powerful, he was forced to stifle his natural sensitivity in order to fill the daily void demanded by his column. Ordinarily his approach was second nature to him, but when people were somewhat reluctant to see him, as these women were, he regretted the brashness that his vocation required.

17

"I'm down in the dumps, Mr. Harper," Margaret replied, smoothing the jacket of her Chanel suit.

"Nothing serious, I hope." His smile was solicitous.

"The usual. But I refuse to talk about it, just as I refuse to see any more doctors."

Harper remembered that Margaret Lafferty was something of a hypochondriac, so there was no story in her illness, and he lost interest in her. But he was careful to say something soothing to her before turning to Stella. "You're a real stranger, Miss Ross."

"Oh? I live and work right here in town, Mr. Harper."

"I mean, we never see you and Max Berman around town."

Stella's smile was noncommittal.

"Where does he keep himself?"

"I suggest you ask him."

"I'd love to. I've been dying to do a column on him for years, ever since I heard he prefers crummy little restaurants and delicatessens."

"So do a lot of people," Stella said.

Harper laughed. "Sure, but they aren't Max Berman! I suppose if you own half the good eating places in town, you don't feel like eating there yourself. Is that it?"

"I can't put words into Max's mouth for you, Mr. Harper."

"Maybe you could set up a date with him. I could make it any time—"

"You'd have to call his appointments secretary for that, I'm afraid." Stella saw his incredulous expression and added, "I'm just a working girl who has a job at L & B. That's all."

"You and Max aren't seeing each other any more?"

"We see each other at the office," Stella said firmly. Harper chatted a bit longer, then drifted away when the waiter brought two glasses of sherry to the table.

Margaret sipped her wine and looked at the younger woman over the rim of her glass. "Have you and Max broken up?"

"I guess you could call it that. Just now, this morning. That's why I wanted to see you, Margaret."

18

"Did you also want Hal Harper to know? Because you told him."

"I didn't mean to." Stella looked stricken, then shrugged. "Not that it really matters. They're always saying things in print about Max. That isn't what's important."

Margaret continued to watch her. "Is it your doing?"

Stella took a cigarette from a jeweled gold case that Max had given her, and tapped it nervously before lighting it. "I'm afraid so. It shouldn't be hard for you to guess why."

"You've been gnawing at yourself ever since you went back to the Church."

"Being a Catholic is part of it. But the reasons I've gone back to the Church are all tied up with why I can't go on with Max any more." Stella took a deep drag, then blew out a thin column of smoke. "It's all so complicated. I gave Max eleven years."

"He gave the same to you."

"He gave me too much of too many things. My jewelry and furs and clothes. It's been overwhelming, Margaret. And all that travel."

"You brought him good luck, Stella," Margaret said.

"Oh, I'm grateful to Max. He doesn't understand that, but I hope you do. It's just that—well, I'm not the mistress type. For eleven years I've been living a lie. And even when things have been at their best, and I've loved it all, I've hated myself. Does that make sense?"

Margaret smiled thinly. "Just because we're wallowing in money doesn't mean I've lost my middle-class sense of morality. Of course you make sense. I must admit, though, that I've always thought of you as Max's wife, not his mistress."

"Except that I haven't been, and that's the difference. When one of us wanted to marry, the other didn't. And now I've got religion all mixed into it. The whole thing is such a mess that I've had to make a clean break so I can start over. At my age I'll find somebody else—maybe. At the very worst I'll always have my career."

"Are you leaving L & B?"

"Max says he won't let me. I have a contract."

Margaret was silent for a few moments, watching the younger woman taste her sherry. "Do you want advice?"

"It's all done." Stella hesitated briefly. "What would you have told me?"

"To do what your conscience dictates. Paul would say the same, I'm sure."

"Thanks." In a single, quick motion, Stella drained her glass of sherry.

"How did Max take it?"

Stella slowly shook her head. "You know Max."

"I'm so sorry. For both of you."

"Under the right circumstances," Stella said, "Max would make the perfect husband. Rich or poor, it wouldn't matter. He has all the qualities that a sensible woman wants in a husband. That's the real hell of it all!"

"Stella Ross, go screw yourself. Up a tree." Max Berman, alone in his car, spoke aloud, his voice bitter, a hint of wistfulness behind the angry words.

His black Continental sedan surged forward. He had just crossed the New York line onto the New England Thruway, accelerating to seventy-five miles per hour. Then, all at once, Max slowed to sixty. Connecticut troopers were certain death on speeders, particularly those who carried New York license plates, and that kind of trouble Max didn't need. As he had so often told Stella, a man older than forty-five who drove too fast was in his second childhood and deserved to have the book thrown at him.

Stella. He wished to God he could get her out of his mind. Taking one of his special Tampa-made cigars from the inner pocket of his jacket, he ripped off the aluminum case. But he waited until he slowed down at the Greenwich toll before clipping off the end and lighting it. Then the sudden thought that Stella had given him the gold clipper on his last birthday spoiled the taste of the cigar.

The telephone in the back seat rang, and Max cursed the inconvenience, cursed himself for giving the chauffeur the weekend off, cursed his stupidity in not having taken the Mercedes convertible, and, for good measure, cursed Stella again. Pulling to the shoulder of the road, he climbed into the back seat.

"Well?" he growled into the telephone.

The L & B switchboard operator was understandably nervous. "Your call to London just came through, Mr. Berman, and you said to get you wherever you—"

"Is Franklin on the line now?"

"Yes, sir."

"Then put him on, for God's sake! No wonder we have such high phone bills!" Max chewed on the cigar, oblivious to his surroundings, suddenly relaxing when he heard a series of clicks at the other end of the line. "Dave, how are you?" he asked, his voice jovial.

David Franklin, executive vice-president of the L & B Hotels, replied in the same spirit. "A little tired, Max, and a little wet. But otherwise great."

Max forgot his injunction about wasting money on the telephone. "Bad weather there?"

"The usual. How is it at home?"

Max glanced out of the car window at the sky. "A great day," he announced. "You're calling late, Dave."

"I've just this minute come out of the meeting with the Whitstable group. And we're in. They'll take six million for the property, which is a steal, and another eight million for the hotel."

"How much of a down payment?"

"Three million in securities, and they don't care if it's in sterling."

"Not bad," Max said, and paused to light his cigar. "What's the hotel actually worth?"

"Our team has been looking at it under microscopes for the past week, and we concur with the previous estimate. Seven million."

"So they're holding us up by a million, huh?"

"We're more than making up the difference on the real estate itself, Max. And we're about four million under our original estimate of what we'd have to lay out."

"Never mind that," Max said, his voice becoming cold. "Haul them down that million."

"How much room for maneuver will you give me?"

"Two hundred and fifty thousand," Max said promptly.

"It may not be enough," Franklin said, and his anxiety carried clearly across the Atlantic.

"Nobody else can match our offer, and those Englishmen know it. They may sweat you for a day or two, but they'll settle on our terms." That settled the issue. "Any change in your estimate for repairs and redecorating?"

"No, Max. We can do it easily for seven hundred and fifty thousand."

"Go ahead, then. I'll tell the bank to cable you authority to draw the whole down payment, so you can write a check for it Monday morning. Wave a check for three million under those English noses, and they'll break their old-fashioned fountain pens, they'll be so eager to sign."

"You're probably right, Max. You usually are. Anyway, I'll keep in touch."

"Do that. And one thing more, Dave. When you get a chance, try that little restaurant in Soho. Take it from an expert, you won't find better knishes in heaven."

"When I come home I'll bring you a box of knishes on the plane."

"I'd like that," Max said, and felt enormously pleased. "Dave, I hope nobody knows you're over there."

"The Whitstable crowd knows, and—"

"I mean the press."

"No, not yet."

"See to it they don't." When Max gave an order, his voice invariably hardened. "Keep it quiet until midweek, Dave. It's important. We don't want any stock fluctuations before then. Paul and I have something cooking in L & B Common, and there would be a real flurry if the London deal leaked out prematurely."

"It'll be kept quiet," Franklin assured him.

"Good. And don't forget my knishes."

Chuckling, Max returned to the front seat and snapped on the engine. Then, as he remembered Stella, the laughter died in his throat.

What in God's name was wrong with her?

Maybe the fault was in him, not in her.

Abstractedly, he began to assess his personal assets in an effort to assure himself that they were considerable. Aside from an occasional touch of heartburn, a small roll of flesh around the middle from good food and *schnapps,* and his recent need of reading glasses, he was in first-rate physical condition, as strong and healthy as he'd been when he'd come to the States from Austria as a boy. If necessary, he could still heave sandbags and walk on girders, and if Stella didn't want him, there were plenty of others who would. Throwing his hat onto the seat beside him as he left the turnpike and headed down the tarred, winding road that led to Long Island Sound, he unconsciously ran a hand through his thinning, sandy hair.

By anyone's standards he was very rich, even though most of his personal funds—and the company's—were tied up in the speculative ventures that Paul considered so risky. What's more, he'd continue to rake it in for a long time to come: for one thing, he had a real feel for expansion projects; for another, there were no better builders in New York than Lafferty & Berman, Contractors, a tough Irishman and tougher Jew who had started from scratch, and, as Paul Lafferty was fond of saying, "built a business out of a hole in the ground."

He'd seen it coming with Stella for a long time, and shouldn't have been surprised. Repeatedly during the eleven years of their affair she'd refused to marry him, and now, suddenly, she had broken off completely, insisting that she hadn't found someone else. Maybe, maybe not. Anyway, the facts were plain. He'd been good enough to keep her, and from the time she was twenty-two, she had been so stylish that people stared at her wherever she went. Eleven years of staring had gone to her goddam blond head, maybe.

"Good-bye, Stella, good luck, and I hope you choke," Max said.

His spirits rose, as they always did, when he caught a glimpse of the house through its screen of budding oaks and maples. His house, sitting on a knoll overlooking the Sound, built by Lafferty & Berman, a solid house that wouldn't deteriorate in fifty years, or a hundred. Slowing to a crawl as he nosed into the long driveway, Max inspected the property with a critical, professional eye. The gardener had come at least twice, once to clear away the winter brush and once to seed the lawn, and a new layer of prime gravel covered the driveway. The storm windows hadn't yet been removed on the upper floors, and the blinds were drawn, but the husband-and-wife cleaning team he'd hired would show up at noon, and by evening the place would be in shape after the long winter of sitting empty and idle.

A white convertible sports car was parked beyond the bend in the driveway, and Max, pulling up behind it, was surprised. He'd never yet met house cleaners who drove expensive foreign imports, but these days you couldn't tell. However, they couldn't get into the place until he unlocked it for them, and he looked around, but saw no one. He wandered toward the side of the house, then halted abruptly beside an open window that led into the library.

Burglars usually didn't drive sports cars, either, but a prudent man took no chances. The neighborhood was lousy with well-to-do adolescents who tried anything for kicks. Retracing his steps, Max quietly unlocked the front door and let himself in. Braced for trouble, he moved with a quiet grace surprising in a big man, and listened intently.

Faint sounds came to him from the library, and he made his way toward it, both fists clenched. The door was open, but the drapes had been shut inside the open window, and he waited impatiently for his eyes to become accustomed to the darkness.

Someone appeared to be stretched out on the couch of dark-green leather that Stella had selected for him when he had furnished the house. At virtually the same instant that he realized his uninvited visitor was unclothed, he heard sounds indicating there were two people on the couch, making love. Their heavy breathing, the man's occasional grunts and the woman's soft, protracted moans told him they were achieving the climax of sexual intercourse.

A year or two earlier there had been rumors that youngsters in the neighborhood occasionally broke into unoccupied summer houses for that purpose, and Max went to the window, pulled up one of the heavy silk drapes and turned.

The pair were still locked in an embrace, the man grasping the buttocks of his partner pinned beneath him, the girl's long legs wrapped around the backs of his knees. To Max's astonishment they continued to perform the sex act for another thirty seconds or longer, the girl emitting a sustained, whimpering sound as she obtained release.

Max was irritated, but tried not to be too harsh with them. "Kids," he said gruffly, "go down to the beach, and if it's too cold there, rent yourselves a motel room. I don't care where you go, but get the hell out of here."

They parted at last, and the male rolled over, raising himself to a sitting position. Another surprise awaited him. The face that twisted in his direction was that of an adult in his late twenties, not a boy. The man's hair was cut like that of a god in an ancient Greek statue, so black that the sunlight streaming in through the opened drape brought out blue highlights.

His physique was magnificent; his disciplined body tapered down past almost nonexistent hips to powerful thighs.

He was blocking a view of his companion, except for her legs and several strands of unusually long dark-brown hair that were hanging over the side of the couch.

The young man blinked in the sunlight, his clear, exceptionally bright blue eyes trying to focus, and wiped a film of sweat from his forehead with the back of a hand. "What a time to interrupt." He spoke pleasantly, in a voice that reflected neither panic nor anger.

Max could feel his temper rising. "Get out!"

The young man stood, his movements sinuous, and held out his hand. "You must be Max Berman. I'm Lance Balutis." His tone indicated a belief that his name meant something.

The girl raised herself to one elbow, no more embarrassed than her partner, although considerably younger.

Max, in spite of his rage, noticed her beautifully rounded breasts and thighs.

"This is Muriel," the young man said, not bothering with her surname. "Muriel, meet Mr. Berman."

"Hi," she said cheerfully, and waved a hand on which the fingernails were filed flat and left unpainted.

Their complete lack of concern over their nudity, much less being caught in the act in the house of a total stranger, was as bewildering as it was infuriating. "Leave in the next two minutes with no fuss," Max said, "and I won't call the police. Give me back talk and I'll throw every charge in the book at you. Breaking and entering. Lascivious carriage. And if you don't know about Connecticut's lascivious-carriage law, you can spend six months to a year in jail."

Lance Balutis' broad smile was engaging. "You've got us all wrong. We're not housebreakers."

"You got a new name for it?"

"I came out from New York to see you. Your office said you'd be here today, and gave me the address. Muriel came along to keep me company, that's all."

"Some company." Max knew he was stronger, in spite of the young man's athletic physique, and wondered whether to throw him out before he dressed. But he rejected the idea almost as quickly as it occurred to him. His high-society Protestant neighbors would be delighted if the Jew who had built his house in their midst became involved in a juicy scandal, and in no time at all they'd be insisting he had been master of ceremonies at an orgy.

"We came inside," Lance said, "because we got tired of waiting in the car. And one thing led to another. You see?"

"No," Max said. "And for God's sake, put on your clothes."

Lance looked around for his underpants, and when he donned them Max noted they were expensive silk. He also noticed his hand-sewn English moccasins. Whoever he might be, he was no pauper.

"Harvey suggested I see you," Lance said. "He thought we ought to get together."

"You know my nephew?"

Lance exuded charm. "Obviously."

Max's eyes narrowed. "He's your pal, huh? He's such a good pal you don't even know the government sent him to Ceylon last year."

"He wrote me from his base at Foul Point. Gorgeous name, isn't it?" Lance climbed into old, paint-spattered dungarees that, when new, could have cost no more than a few dollars, and pulled on a hand-tailored silk shirt.

Max hesitated. His nephew *was* stationed at a place called Foul Point in Ceylon, and he remembered how he and Stella had laughed at his first letter.

"I have his note with me, if you'll give me a minute to find it." Lance moved to an oval mirror to don an ascot, and then began to search in his jacket of heavy tweed, ignoring a long rip that extended from the side of one pocket.

The silent girl sat upright, swinging her legs to the floor.

"Find my dress for me, Lance," she said plaintively, her voice childlike.

He grinned, and, going to her, ran a hand across her bare breasts. "Maybe we'll make you stay in the raw while you serve us some drinks. The ultimate super-reality of art in action. If there's anything better than a topless waitress, it's one who is bottomless, too."

Although Max was outraged by the calm assumption that he would offer them his hospitality, he was dumfounded by the girl's reaction. The suggestion, made to any woman he had ever known, would have caused a reaction of insulted anger, but the girl called Muriel merely giggled.

"You're wicked," she murmured.

"You know it." Lance produced a battered envelope from the inside jacket pocket and handed it to the older man with the air of a magician.

"She should get dressed, too." Max looked as nervously irritated as he sounded.

Lance shrugged. "It's your house. But stand up for a minute, Muriel." He pulled her to her feet, and turned her around, slowly. "You'll notice she has a better than ordinary figure, not spectacular, but good." His tone was serious now, but impersonal. "What gives her an erotic appeal is her tail, which is out of proportion to the rest of her body." He caressed her buttocks, then squeezed them. "If she takes off a few pounds in the rear, the focal point of interest is lost, and she becomes a complete nonentity. She's reduced to the level of ordinary reality, which is commonplace. Since only a heightening of the senses produces an effect other than the mundane, that level of reality is similarly reduced, and becomes static. That's what I believe and preach, and I try to live accordingly."

"Not here you don't!" Max's voice became hard. "I don't like naked girls running around my house!"

Again Lance shrugged. "It was just an observation of interest

28

—in passing." He found the girl's dress on the floor, near the desk, and threw it to her.

She pulled it over her head, and it occurred to Max that she had been wearing nothing else. The skirt was very short, and, he saw, fitted tightly over her behind. Apparently she accepted her companion's dictum that she should show off her rear.

Max continued to watch her as she pulled on a pair of knee-high boots, then sat down to run a comb through her waist-long hair.

"Harvey's letter," Lance said.

Annoyed with himself because he had been caught watching the girl, Max snatched the envelope. The communication itself was brief: *"Dear Lance: I was surprised to hear from you. The State Department is reluctant to give out addresses, but I suppose you have connections. By all means, see my uncle, provided he'll see you. And if you want to tell him we met at a couple of weekend parties at Bimsy Grant's, that's all right with me. Sincerely, Harvey M. Berman."*

Harvey had been polite, Max thought, but by no stretch of the imagination friendly. Max knew that Bimsy Grant was a food-chain heiress renowned for her many parties, a generous contributor to political campaign funds, one of the smugly styled Beautiful People and a favorite of the tabloid newspapers, which gleefully recorded her numerous marriages and divorces. Harvey, who was sober and ambitious, cultivated such hostesses in order to help his career.

More to the point was Lance Balutis' acceptance in Mrs. Grant's circle. Nobodies, of course, were automatically excluded from her parties, which meant he was rich or talented, famous or notorious. Still on his guard, Max returned the letter.

"Before you ask," Lance said, smoothing his long hair into place, "I wrote to Harvey for a specific reason."

"That's plain." Max glanced in the direction of the girl, who was spreading a shiny, colorless substance on her lips.

Lance wanted no interruption. "Muriel," he directed, "go use the bathroom. Where's the nearest john, Mr. Berman?"

"Down the corridor, second door on the left." It was incomprehensible to Max that any girl would be so obedient, and he watched Muriel depart, handbag swinging from her shoulder, her hips swaying.

"See?" Lance laughed, pleased with himself. "Nobody can resist looking at her tail." His manner changed, and became confidently quiet. "I assume you're familiar with my work."

Max hated to admit ignorance. "Should I be?"

"Most people are." Lance was not putting on an act; his self-confidence was monumental.

Stella was Max's principal link between the outer world and his realm of steel and cement, bulldozers and labor unions and construction schedules. "I don't talk business here, only at my office in town. But you can tell me what you want, so I'll know if it will be a waste of my time—and your time, too—for you to make an appointment next week with my secretary." Max's brusqueness was habitual.

"I want to suggest a cooperative deal that won't cost you a penny." Lance looked older, and the dark circles beneath his eyes were suddenly more noticeable.

"But I'll clean up. I'll make a fortune. Go ahead; say it. I've heard it all before." Max began to compose a letter to Harvey, who certainly ought to have known better than to burden him with this cheap promoter.

"No," Lance said. "You won't make a penny."

"But you will, of course." Max instinctively reacted badly to cuteness; especially in business.

"That's unlikely, too, but if I did, I'd certainly be willing to cut you in for a fair share. What I really need right now is another prestige jolt. It's more important than money in a profession as competitive as mine."

Max glanced at his watch, saw that the morning was gone and decided to send the pair on their way as soon as the girl returned. Unless he called the movers soon they wouldn't be able to come for Stella's belongings as soon as he wanted them to, to rid him of every last reminder of her. "If you want to try a business where you spend your apprenticeship cutting throats, try putting up office buildings, or apartment houses."

The girl returned, her expression unchanged.

Lance jumped to his feet. "If you'd been much longer, I was going to push you off the throne!" He paused at the door and grinned at Max. "I'll be back in a second."

He was gone before Max could reply.

Muriel made herself comfortable on the couch, indifferent to the fact that her skirt had risen perilously high, and rummaged in her handbag for a pack of crumpled cigarettes.

"Quite a fellow, your boyfriend," Max said.

The girl appeared indignant. "Lance is hardly my boyfriend!"

"You barely know him, maybe?"

"He helps me," she said earnestly.

"To do what?"

"Find myself." She laughed with the ingenuousness of a little girl. "You heard him before. He really thinks I have a jazzy bottom, and I'm sure he's going to use it."

Max bit back the obvious retort that Lance had already used it effectively. "How?"

"In his next picture. Sometimes he teases me and says he's just going to use my bottom, but he can't, I mean, without using me, too."

"Oh, he'll use you, all right." Max's irony was a bit too heavy. "So. He's a photographer?"

She was shocked. "You must be kidding."

"I'm such a joker I'm thinking of giving up my business to become a comedian. On television. Special rates for weddings and bar mitzvahs."

She scarcely heard him. "Lance Balutis is the best film producer in New York, and a lot of people think there's no one like him anywhere!"

31

All the parts of the puzzle fell neatly into place: Balutis made movies, and the girl gave herself to him in the hope of winning a role in his next picture. "I didn't realize we were really talking about art when we were talking about your rear end."

Muriel did not find his remark amusing. "If Lance says I have a career ahead of me, then I have. Look at what he's done for Bobbie Wayne!"

That name meant nothing to Max. "Finish school. In the long run you'll appreciate it."

"I spent three years studying fashion design, and I loathed every minute!"

Obviously she was older than he had thought, and he calculated rapidly. If at least three years had passed since she had been graduated from high school, it was possible she was of legal age. "Have it your way. Be an actress."

"Not really. Just for kicks." And to emphasize her meaning she wriggled slightly, managing to inch her skirt a fraction of an inch higher.

Max felt uncomfortable. She was still a child, stupid and not his type, but she was making no secret of her availability, and the best cure for his break with Stella might be a roll in the hay, even with a promiscuous young tramp.

"Everybody chummy with everybody?" Lance returned to the room, enveloped in an aura of cologne from the guest bathroom.

Max felt ashamed of his brief desire for the girl. "You have your brand of chumminess, I've got mine."

Lance's long forefinger was pointed at the girl. "Muriel, don't move!"

She obediently froze.

"This is fascinating, Mr. Berman. If only every woman could instinctively and unconsciously make use of her most potent attribute the way Muriel does. If Muriel had been blessed with a perfect mouth she would pout and smile. Or if she had perfect breasts, she would slash all her dresses to the navel. But look at Muriel! A girl with a perfect ass! She sits with half a rump heaved into the air, and a skirt hitched to show it off. Marvelous! And how the critics will secretly feast on what I shall offer them!"

Muriel made no attempt to shift her position or pull her abbreviated skirt over a partly exposed buttock.

Max's guilt gave way to fresh irritation.

"Next week," he said, "call my office, and we'll make an appointment."

His tone made it obvious that he'd be out when Lance Balutis' call was announced, but Lance's smile was unwavering. "Never fear, I'll be in touch." He held out a hand to Muriel, and, as he pulled her to her feet, added casually, "Maybe we'll drop in at the end of the day, around the middle of the week."

He was an offensive bastard, Max thought, holding out the girl as bait. But he wasn't as clever as he imagined. Max's moment of temptation had passed. And when he was ready, he would get his own woman. He was attractive enough. And virile enough. He was a bit square. But as a cute little typist recently told him, "Square men can be very sexy, Mr. Berman."

The warm afternoon breezes had vanished, and the chill of a spring evening had descended on the city as Max approached his Park Avenue apartment. It was more than his apartment. It was his building and Paul's, on which they had lavished extra touches that weren't in the contract with the realtors. After all, when builders were going to live in a place, they wanted it to be right.

In the years before Stella had come into his life, and for brief periods since that time, Max had been convinced that a bachelor's freedom was infinitely preferable to the burdens a married man carried. But, he had to admit, he had cause to envy Paul Lafferty. Tonight being a Sunday, the Lafferty maids were off, and Margaret would be doing the cooking. She was not only a good wife, but a damn fine cook as Paul well knew, no

33

matter how much he bitched about her at the office.

One of these years he'd be bringing young Paul into the business, and with luck, his daughter Janet's husband, when she married. Max, however, had no relative other than Harvey, and he could not imagine his nephew surviving in the rough atmosphere of the construction game.

Max Berman was alone. He had wasted eleven years on the wrong woman, and that was that. Ordinarily Max enjoyed twilight in the city, when the huge buildings, including those he and Paul had erected, blended into the night. But a lonely man felt worse when he thought about beauty, and Max retreated farther into himself, barely acknowledging the greeting of the doorman to whom he turned over his car.

He punched the elevator button, stared with unseeing eyes at the sandalwood walls of the cage, and reached into his pocket for his keys.

Lights were burning in the foyer and the sunken living room beyond it, and for the second time in one weekend Max was surprised by uninvited guests. In this case, a single guest. A glance at the woman's suede jacket lying on a foyer chair told him her identity. He made his way through the apartment quickly, and found her in the bedroom adjoining his, removing clothes from a closet. She was so intent on what she was doing that she didn't hear him, and he paused at the threshold to look at her.

When Stella Ross wore slacks—which Max loathed—and no make-up, she looked like a kid. Yet Max knew, as did no one else, that she was the most feminine of women, not only in her sexual responses, but in her attitudes, which could be maddening.

It surprised him to discover he wanted her, and he didn't mean in bed. She needed protection from the world and herself, and a wave of unexpected tenderness swept over him. Yet he couldn't express it and when he greeted her there was an invitation in his voice he hadn't intended.

Stella jumped. "I didn't hear you come in."

34

She had a dress, coat and negligee over one arm. "I assumed you'd be staying in Connecticut until tomorrow morning, so I was getting my things out of here tonight," she said.

He couldn't admit to her that he had found the country house unbearable without her. "I have an early meeting in the morning," he said gruffly.

Her eyes told him she knew the truth, although she accepted the lie. "I can come back tomorrow. I'll give you my key now, and you can leave word so Michael can let me in."

"You're here," Max said. "You might as well finish doing what you came for."

Stella turned back to the closet without a word. She began laying out a pile of clothes on the bed. "Here," she said suddenly, taking a white mink cape from a hanger and thrusting it at him. "You may have some use for this."

To Max, the fur had been a concrete symbol of love and possession. It meant "I love you, Stella." And it meant, in the most deeply felt, most substantial old-fashioned way, "Stella, you are my woman." Stella's gesture right now was, for all of those reasons, like a punch in the stomach.

"I can tell you exactly how many times you've worn it, Stella," Max said, in an effort to reach her. "On board ship the last time we came back from Europe, and to the Catholic Charities ball with Paul and Margaret."

"Without you I won't be traveling first class to Europe, or going to two-hundred-dollar-a-plate dinners."

"It won't look as well on me as it does on you," Max said.

"You're somebody who needs a woman, Max. More than one, maybe, and anyone would appreciate a cape like this."

A vein pounded in his left temple. "Since I'm not a Christian, that kind of charity leaves me cold. This cape was a gift. From me to you, with no strings attached, like everything else I ever gave you. If you don't want it, burn it or give it away, but you can't hand it back to me like—oh, for God's sake, Stella. You ought to know me better than that."

"This is why I didn't want to see you. I didn't want to get into a—a whole thing with you. I'm not very good at putting things into words, and when I try to talk to you, I get mixed up."

"Try, Stella." He was gentle but unyielding.

She patted a few stray strands of the shingled hair at the back of her neck, a gesture of bewilderment and fear that he remembered from the first day she had started to work in his office, fresh from secretarial school.

"Max. What have you eaten today?"

"I had breakfast with Paul," he said defensively.

"What did you have for lunch?"

"I didn't get around to lunch. I thought I'd stop off on the drive into town, but I forgot. What difference does it make? You're the one who's always telling me I ought to watch my weight. Besides, who the hell cares?"

"So you didn't have dinner either." Stella dropped the mink cape on the bed and left the room.

Max made no move until he heard sounds emanating from the kitchen. He was unable to fathom this newest, inexplicable shift in her attitude, but, always a pragmatist, he followed her.

Salami was frying in a pan, and she was breaking eggs into a bowl. "Your drink is on the counter," she said, not looking at him.

Max picked up the glass, and thought it ridiculous that only she could fix a simple drink the way he liked it: the glass filled to the top with ice, bourbon poured over it, and no more than a splash of water added. "How about you?" She rarely drank except when they went out, but often, on Sunday evenings, she unbent and took a single highball.

"Not tonight," Stella said.

He decided not to push his luck. He took two cigarettes from a box on the counter, and handed her one.

She knew where to reach for it without turning. And she lit it herself before he could complete the ritual.

"Rye toast or pumpernickel?" she asked.

"I'm easy."

"Pumpernickel, I think. Take a loaf from the freezer, will you?"

Delighted to comply with the demand, he placed the bread on the counter.

Stella added frozen chopped onions to the eggs, measured a small quantity of milk into the bowl and started to beat the mixture.

Max moved to a chair at the kitchen table, sipped his drink and, trying to hide his tension, spoke in what he hoped was a normal voice. "I had the damnedest experience when I got out to the house," he said, and told her about the couple he had found in the library.

She made no comment until he had finished the story. "Did you find out their names?"

"Didn't I mention that part? The broad was somebody called Muriel. If she has a last name, I didn't hear it. He's Lance Balutis, he told me."

Stella laughed. "That explains it."

Max stared at her, his eyes narrowing. "You know him?"

"Not personally, but I've read a lot about him. I suppose one reason I've been interested is that Balutis is a Lithuanian name."

"I see." She had been Stella Riusas before she had Anglicized her name, and was proud of her Lithuanian heritage. "Should I know who the hell he is?"

"I guess not. You never read the gossip columns. Or the art news and movie reviews."

"Then he really is a movie producer? He's such a cocky, good-looking bastard that I wondered if he was a con artist, or an actor."

"Lance Balutis," she said, "is nearly as famous as Picasso or Dali, and since he's been making movies, some of the writers say he's another Eisenstein."

"I've heard of Dali and Picasso," Max said, "but who is Eisenstein?"

Stella smiled. "All I really know is that Balutis made his reputation as the green-pea man."

Max stubbed out his cigarette. "The last couple of days I haven't felt much like kidding."

"I mean it. He produced a huge painting of a can of green peas, tipped part-way over, and then he pasted hundreds and hundreds of paper peas on his canvas, so they looked like they were spilling out of the can."

"Why didn't you say he was crazy?"

"I'd like to be that crazy," Stella said. "He got more orders for his 'Falling Green Peas' than he could make copies, and he was paid real sock-it-away-in-the-savings-account money every time. He was one of the leaders of the Pop Art movement."

"Who'd want that kind of trash?" he asked scornfully.

Stella slid a spatula under the omelet. "Rich, important people. Not just here, all over the country."

"I'm in the wrong business."

Max went to the percolator and poured two cups of coffee, adding saccharin to both and a little milk to Stella's. "I can't imagine anybody putting junk like that on their walls."

"I don't know how much he's earned, but he's invited to every big party, and he's become even more in demand since he's been making movies."

Max carried the coffee cups to the kitchen table, then went off to a cabinet for paper napkins and cutlery. "It's better that I don't ask what kind of movies."

"I never saw one, and I just glance through the reviews, but I know they're very arty, and they've been kicking up a real storm." With great deftness she rolled the omelet, cut it and slid the portions onto plates before joining him at the table.

"I suppose this Muriel kid is famous, too. As a dope peddler, or a professional witch, would you say?" Max tucked the paper napkin into his belt and, for the first time in forty-eight hours, was ravenous.

38

"I don't imagine she's anyone special. Lance Balutis has more girls hanging around him than he knows what to do with."

Max chuckled. "With this one, he knew."

"When there's an important art exhibit, or an opening night at the theater, or a big fashion show, Bobbie Wayne usually goes with him."

"You keep the gossip columns in business, Stella." Max never tired of his little joke.

Stella ignored it. "She's from the Philadelphia Main Line, and she's the star of most of his movies. She's really gorgeous, Max. You see her picture in *Vogue* and the *Bazaar* all the time."

"You do, not me." He ate in silence for a short time. "Paoli is a suburb of Philadelphia, and Mad Anthony Wayne came from near there. Maybe she's descended from a great Revolutionary War general, huh?" His adopted country's history had long been an avocation, and he was proud of his knowledge.

"Bobbie Wayne never showed me her pedigree," Stella said. "All I know is that she's got everything—looks, class, style, sex, you name it."

"I'll take you," Max said, and knew he made a major error.

Stella stiffened and sat upright, her food forgotten.

He wondered whether to manufacture more idle talk, but decided to face the issue. "Stell."

"What?" She was looking steadily at one of the decorative plates she had put up on the wall opposite her.

"Tell me."

"What is there to tell?"

"You and I don't play games. I'll drop it if you're coming back. Are you?"

"No."

"Then I have a right to know. After all, eleven years—"

"You've said it all yourself, Max, in two words. Eleven years."

He waited.

"Eleven years, and what is there to show for them? More clothes than I can wear, furs I don't need, and my rings and the brooch that make me so nervous I ought to keep them in the safe-deposit vault."

"You've earned them."

"On my back."

"If you were anybody except you, I'd push your teeth down your throat for that kind of crack. We've lived together because it's what both of us wanted."

"Let's face it, Max, you've kept me."

"Get it through your stupid head that you've earned your keep." His voice rose, and he shoved away his plate. "You know damn near as much about the business as Paul and I do."

"I've been grossly overpaid."

"Is that why Sullivan Brothers offered you six thousand a year more a year or so ago?"

"Seven thousand."

"Or why Kronlik will let you name your own salary?"

"They hope I'd tell them the inside of what goes on at Lafferty & Berman."

"Bullshit. They know you're honest, and they also know you're efficient. Paul and I don't pay you a penny more than you're worth."

Her right hand appeared under his nose. "This emerald," she said, "cost you as much as you pay me in a year."

"More, but that has nothing to do with your work. I give you presents because you and I—oh, for God's sake, Stell."

"I'm willing to admit the truth, even if you aren't. You've been keeping me, Max."

"If your conscience is kicking up again, go to confession, and get it over with," he said in disgust.

"I'm not blaming you, and I'm not blaming me," Stella said carefully. "Not any more. It was my fault I wouldn't marry you all those times you asked me."

"Because I'm Jewish."

"*No,* Max!" There was desperation as well as anger in tone. "You and your damn Jewish sense of inferiority."

"I'm not inferior to anybody!"

"Precisely what I've always said! But what you won't understand is that your being Jewish wasn't my reason for not marrying you. I couldn't have done it if you were a Protestant, either. Only if you were Catholic."

"You're as lousy a Catholic as I am a Jew. You don't go to Mass, I eat bacon. You—"

"This week," she said quietly, "I went to see Father Klimas. He suggested it at my mother's funeral. I think I told you."

Max nodded slightly as he studied her.

"We had a long talk, and then I went into the church with him so he could hear my confession. The first time in eleven years. This morning I went to Mass, and took Communion. I'll be going regularly now."

He was too sensitive to jeer or question her, and continued to stare at her.

Conscious of his scrutiny, Stella stroked the back of her neck, pushed her short bangs to one side of her forehead and then rose, turning away from him as she went to the counter for another cigarette.

"Me, too," Max said.

She brought two. "What else do you want to know?" She became defensive again.

"Plenty. Most of all, I want to get everything straight. You turned me down every time I proposed to you because it would hurt your mother. The couple of times I met her I was sure it was hurting her worse that we were living together, but we'll let that pass."

"We will *not* let it pass—because it isn't true. Sure, Mama hated it that we were living together, but it would have shredded her if I'd married you!"

"Even though it makes no sense to me that some Catholics think like that, I'll accept it." Max's voice was soft, almost caressing. "I always had the feeling your mother and I would have gotten on fine if we'd known each other better. But we didn't, so that's that." He paused, then became belligerent. "What I don't get is this crap you're pulling on me now."

She steeled herself. "It isn't crap."

"If you're tired of me, tell me you're bored or hate my guts, or whatever. But don't work religion into it."

"I could never hate your guts, honey. And I'm not bored. But after Mama died, all of a sudden everything changed. I knew how much she wanted me back in the Church—and, well, it's what I want."

"So what I said a while ago is completely true!" He viciously stubbed the cigarette. "I'm a Jew, so screw me."

Stella tried to control her own temper. "How many hundreds of times have we slept together? You're trying me make me out to be anti-Semitic—"

"You wouldn't be the first Lithuanian."

"When you talk like that, Max, I could kill you." Her cigarette rolled from the ashtray onto the table, but she failed to notice. "I've loved you for a long time. I know it. And you know it. And I'd marry you tomorrow. In church."

He put out her cigarette, then reached for her.

Stella shrank from him.

"All the way from here," he said, with all the sarcasm he could get into his voice, "I can see how much you love me. You love the Church! Not me! You want me to get down on my knees in a Catholic church? You want me to drink the wine and eat the wafer?"

"No, Max. Father Klimas would marry us in front of the altar rail. You wouldn't be expected to take Communion. Hundreds of thousands of non-Catholics have been married in church."

"But there's a catch. Isn't there, Stella?"

"You'd have to agree that our children would be brought up as Catholics. And I know you wouldn't. Which is why I wanted to avoid this whole discussion in the first place. What's the use?" She rose, went to the counter and poured herself another cup of coffee. "Do you want some?"

"As it is, I'll have a hard enough time sleeping. Stell, I can't swallow that line. For years now you've been using the pill, and don't tell me you'd stop because you've gone back to the Church. I wish I had a dollar for every Catholic woman who uses some kind of contraceptive, especially the pill. I'd have ten times as many securities locked away in my safe."

"I'm not interested in what other women do!" Stella's voice sounded raw.

"Okay. Your mother dies and you want to go back to your religion. That's natural. But nobody can convince Max Berman that all of a sudden Stella Riusas wants to be a saint so bad she'll throw away her prescription for the pill."

"How many years do I have left, after wasting eleven of them? I want a normal family life, which isn't asking too much in this world!"

Max was stunned by the realization that she wanted children.

"You're entitled to that," he said. "But I can't help wondering. Suppose I went back to Judaism and insisted my kids be brought up as Jews. You'd scream and bitch like crazy. It's all right for Catholics to get promises from the people they marry, but when the shoe is on the other foot you get corns on every toe."

"It's not as though you ever go inside your own church."

"Temple. Synagogue. Not church."

"What would be so terrible if our children would become baptized as Catholics, take religious instruction and be confirmed in the Catholic Church?"

"Only a *shiksa*," Max said, "could talk this crazy. Fact number one—in all these years she turns down my proposals of marriage so many times I stopped asking her. Fact number two—always she uses the pill, and before the pill—"

"Stop it, Max!"

"Fact number three—now she moves out, and doesn't even do me the courtesy of trying to work things out the way it should be when two people love each other. I'm not walking out, you are. I'm not setting impossible conditions, you are."

Stella pushed back her chair and stood. "It would have been much better for both of us if I'd packed my things and left before you came home. We'll suffer less if we don't see each other again."

"Two years ago I insisted you sign a five-year contract with Lafferty & Berman so you'd be protected if anything happened to Paul and me. Now it turns out it's the company that's going to be protected, and don't waste your money trying to get out. We have the best lawyers in town. You'll work out your contract."

"Is that fair?"

"Fair, shmair. I don't know five price estimators better than you in the construction game, and being a woman you see all kinds of things men miss. Like the time we nearly put up the Quality Products Building without women's toilets." Max began to laugh uproariously.

"We'll go mad if we see each other every day, Max."

"For years now you've reported to Paul, not me, and we won't change the routines. And I'll stay out of your way, Stell. Seeing I've been kicked in the can once, I'll stay out of your way so you can't do it again."

"You'll never know," she said wearily, "how much I hoped we could separate without hatred."

Max was silent, drumming on the counter with two fingers. "I'll help you pack," he said at last.

"First," Stella said, "I'll do the dishes."

The partners occupied adjoining offices in the tower suite of the L & B Building, and, as Max had remarked the day they moved in, "The President of the United States doesn't need a place this fancy. But he doesn't have to put up our kind of front. He doesn't buy and sell real estate like poker chips or build as we do. Sometimes I wonder how many tens of millions we have to be worth to impress those goddam bankers. They sure can't afford offices like these!"

Each room was large, light and comfortable in an expensive-but-lived-in style. Both men used heavy leather furniture and old-fashioned desks, but Margaret Lafferty had brought in a decorator to "tie things together" with custom-designed pieces from Italy. Each of their secretaries had her own huge office, and these were decorated too. Beyond the offices was an enormous plush antechamber where visitors waited, and on the walls were photographs of L & B properties: the hotels and other real estate they had acquired, and some of the solid buildings they had erected. And huge plate-glass windows looked out on their empire: New York City.

"The glamour skyscrapers aren't for us," Max was fond of saying. "Not that we'd turn down a job to build one, but we've never even tried to bid on one. We like the bread-and-butter jobs, and we've stashed away enough bread and enough butter to keep us from starvation for a lot of years. Let's never forget that we're contractors, not designers."

Paul Lafferty had collected so many photographs of his wife, son and daughter that he had been forced to place them on a small table behind his desk, on which he kept his telephone, while the desk itself was a wild jumble of blueprints, plans and cost sheets. He alone could reach into the pile and unerringly produce a needed paper, and his secretary had given up all attempts to keep the desk in order.

A tall, burly man of almost fifty, Paul and Max resembled each other so strongly that strangers, meeting them for the first time, frequently asked if they were related. They themselves were amused, but it was Margaret Lafferty's theory that their similarity wasn't accidental. They were both physically powerful men who had become construction workers, and their ambitions had led them to night school, where they had met. They had both known extreme poverty, fought bigotry and achieved success because of similar aggressive drives and a willingness to work cruelly long hours.

They wisely knew their limitations, too, and in their partnership achieved a remarkably harmonious balance. Intellectually and emotionally they complemented each other. Max was volatile, Paul phlegmatic. Their basic personal values had remained unchanged, even though they had become wealthier than either had dreamed in the early days of their partnership. Both lived comfortably, but not flashily, and their tastes were as quiet as their pleasures. As Margaret so often told them, their personal outlook was middle-class, and they had no desire to live up to their means.

"Sure," Max sometimes remarked. "We got money. But for what? So we can become the biggest reality owners and operators in the city's history. That's solid. That's real. But yachts and big estates in Georgia we don't need. We're shirt-sleeves men, not *machers*."

Only on rare occasions did they disagree on business principles, and when they did, their secretaries closed the outer doors of their offices and urgently advised staff members to avoid them. Those outer doors were tightly shut near the close of the business day, and the employees of L & B were conspicuously absent from the anteroom of the tower suite, seventy-two hours after Max's return from the first weekend of the season at his Connecticut house.

The doors between the two offices were wide open, however, and Max restlessly paced from one to the other, a sheaf of cost analyses in one hand. "Every damn time we have to use outside architects," he shouted, "we operate on a margin of profit that a few little mistakes can wipe out. Three times in the last two years we've lost on projects for that reason. If your memory is so bad that you can't even remember how we got creamed on the monstrosity we put up for Score Magazines, Incorporated, send down to the accounting department for the books!"

Paul, balding and with a paunch somewhat larger than his partner's, remained tranquil behind his desk. "I have an elephant's memory," he said calmly. "We were nicked for about two hundred and seventy thousand."

"Two hundred and seventy-eight thousand, six hundred!" Max thundered. "And we stand to take a worse shellacking if we sign for this job. Maybe this kid architect's ideas are sound, but if he's off the beam, we'll go down by a hundred grand, at least."

"I think we're reasonably safe. Our own architects can't find any flaws. Even you admit his ideas seem sensible. The chance of going into the red is very slight." Paul methodically stuffed a pipe.

"I say we turn down the job." Max stopped pacing long enough to glare at his partner. "Look at what we'll make on the London deal. Sometimes I even wonder if we should give up the construction end of the business. Especially for jobs like this."

"After we won the bid? What the hell kind of a reputation does that give us?"

"For every man in the business who says we're stupid, there will be two who'll figure we have our private reasons, which we have. And since when are we so sensitive to what the industry thinks? Our record speaks for itself."

Paul Lafferty showed a trace of annoyance. "How do I get it into your thick head that we're committed?"

"How do I get it into your thicker head that we have lawyers on a juicy retainer who'll get us uncommitted?"

"I talked to them this afternoon, I told you. We're stuck with the job."

"Then I absolutely insist," Max said, "that we get some option-escalator clauses in the final contract to protect us if the architect's plans turn out sour. The way this thing stands now, our margin of potential profit is too small, and our risk of loss is too great."

47

"Stop dreaming," Paul said. "If we wanted to stick with our house architects, we shouldn't have bid. We knew Scanlon was going to insist on using the wonder-boy he discovered. But we did submit the bid, and we're not going to get the extra protection clauses. No client in his right mind would hobble himself that badly."

"The trouble," Max said, throwing the analysis sheet on his partner's desk, "is that our original estimate gave us no breathing space. None. It was a stinking job."

"It was Stella who prepared the original estimate," Paul said.

"I don't give a goddam who it was. It was full of holes that should have been obvious to somebody brand new at cost estimating!"

"Be fair, Max. You and I each went over the estimate, separately, and both of us approved it. If the margin is too tight, we have nobody but ourselves to blame."

"You're wrong, Paul. This estimate was sent up to us in the middle of the busiest month we've ever known. You and I had other things on our minds."

Paul stood, and walked around to the front of his desk. "If you're going to tear off the roof over every job Stella does, it would be much better to give her notice."

"The hell we will!" Max shouted so loudly that the secretaries in the outer office could hear him.

"She'll have no problems. All she has to do is make a couple of phone calls, and a dozen contractors will want her."

"She'll live up to her obligation here. To the last comma and period of her contract!"

Paul put his hand on Max's shoulder. "Let her go."

Max lowered himself into an overstuffed chair and slumped there, gazing at his shoetops. "God help me, I can't," he said morosely.

"Give her the chance to stand on her own feet. Let her find somebody she can marry, if it's possible. She's talked to Margaret about this—"

"Yeah, Margaret told me. She thinks it's what Stella really wants. I don't agree.

"Because it isn't what you want."

"Of course it isn't!" Max snapped. "But I'm also convinced Stella doesn't really know her own mind."

"If that's true, she'll find it out for herself. Meanwhile, all you can do is gamble, Max."

"Once I stopped off at Las Vegas. About four or five years ago, remember? In one lousy night I dropped seventy-five hundred dollars, and it made me sick for a week. It wasn't so long ago that I could have lived for a year on that kind of dough. When there's hard, real property at stake, I'll take risks. Otherwise I'm just not a gambler. Most of all when it comes to Stella."

"Do you have any choice?"

After a long, strained silence, Max finally said, "No."

"Find another woman, and after you've been laying her for a few weeks, maybe you'll forget Stella."

"At the age of almost forty-seven," Max said, "it isn't easy to find somebody you want to take to bed. More than once, I mean."

"Monday night," Paul said severely, "you had dinner with us. By nine o'clock you were back in your own place, and what did you do? Don't tell me, I'll tell you. You had a drink or two, and you sat up until early in the morning, feeling sorry for yourself."

"Also," Max said, with dry self-deprecation, "don't forget to mention I had a glass of milk for heartburn before I went to bed."

"Last night you probably stopped off at that stinking restaurant downstairs on your way home—"

"It's convenient."

"—and then you did exactly what you'd done the night before, which was nothing. You've got to start going out again. Mix with people. Kick up a few storms. It's the same advice that Margaret and I gave Janet when her romance at art school went bad. And it worked."

"Janet is twenty-one, and I just finished saying that I'm—"

"Age has nothing to do with it. You've never in your life played solitaire, Max. You need people."

Again there was a silence, and Max finally mumbled, "I know."

The buzzer intercom sounded, and Paul flipped a switch. "Yes, Carol?"

"I know you're busy, but Joan says to tell Mr. Berman that a Mr. Lance Balutis is here. He insists he has an appointment, although she doesn't have it on her calendar. Does Mr. Berman want Joan to get rid of him?"

Paul glanced at his partner.

Max was annoyed, not only by the interruption, but by the assertion of the brash visitor that he had an appointment. He started to speak, checked himself and struggled to his feet. He leaned toward the intercom. "Tell Joan I'll see him," he said, and, smiling wryly at his partner, returned to his own office.

His secretary, flustered and obviously aware of the unexpected visitor's identity, opened the outer door, and Lance Balutis sauntered in, exuding charm and an aura of strong cologne. His blue-black hair was combed in deep waves, with a curl carelessly falling onto his forehead, and again his attire was unusual. His immaculately tailored slacks were stuffed into scuffed cowboy boots, and his thick cable-stitch turtlenecked sweater was obviously expensive, but the leather jacket he had thrown over it was soiled and paint-smeared.

The combination was startling, and, Max suspected, deliberate.

Lance carried a flat, newspaper-wrapped package under one arm, and a jeweled ring blazed on the index finger of his right hand when he extended it. "Your guardian out there was persistent, but I knew you hadn't forgotten our date."

Max saw nothing to be gained by disputing the alleged appointment. "How are you?" he asked mechanically.

Lance did not reply, and slowly looked around the office, shaking his head. "I was right! I had a Balutis hunch—I'm sometimes considered psychic, you know—so I made this for you as a little gift." He began to tear off the newspapers, throwing them carelessly onto the floor. "This office needs a brighter touch. What do you think of it?"

Max stared at the strangest painting he had ever seen, an oddly distorted study of his lawn and a portion of his house, with the library dominating the scene. Several touches made the picture unusual: real bark had been pasted onto the trees, and small swatches of silk similar to his library drapes protruded from the painted representation of an open window.

In spite of himself, Max grinned. The fellow had *chutzpah,* but there was no denying he was clever and endowed with a sense of humor.

Lance surveyed the room, removed a chart from a wall and hung the picture from its hook. "This is good enough for now," he said, throwing the chart onto a table. "Later we can clear the whole wall to give it the attention it deserves."

His nerve was so colossal that the startled Max grinned more broadly instead of becoming angry.

"Muriel had a date down in the East Village," Lance said, dropping into a leather chair and draping a leg over the side. "But she can meet us in an hour or so, if you'd like."

Max quickly sobered. He hated to be beholden to anyone, particularly a person who wanted something from him. He still didn't know the young man's pitch. But he was already the recipient of a painting, and now he was being offered a girl. "I can live without Muriel."

"Oh, it's easy for breast and leg men," Lance said, "but you'd be surprised how ass men flip over her."

Max had no desire to discuss Muriel's charms. "You produce

movies, and you want to make a deal with me that won't cost me any money," he said firmly.

Lance continued to smile, but his very blue eyes appeared to harden slightly. "I don't suppose you've seen any of my films."

Max's shoulders rose and fell. "When I go to the movies, I relax. I don't know these people, so I pay no attention to the credits on the screen."

"A couple of mine have just started showing in commercial theaters, but I can't take any bows for the underground breakthrough. Warhol takes those honors. Most of mine have stayed underground, and are shown in lofts, large apartments, makeshift movie houses, almost anywhere."

Max had never seen an underground movie, but felt no sense of loss. Glancing at his visitor's expensive slacks and sweater, however, he did feel mildly curious. "You can make a living out of that stuff?"

Lance had the ability to look like a naïve eighteen-year-old when he laughed uninhibitedly. "I survive."

"Then you really don't want any money from me."

"I'm after something much more important, Max." The young man used his first name without self-consciousness. "I'm a missionary, if you want to call it that. I'm one of the leaders of a movement—and I say it with some modesty—not just in art, but in *all* the arts. Times are changing, as you must know—"

"I've been told," Max interjected dryly, but refrained from saying that he had no use for the changes. If he stayed away from the wild parties, the expense-account restaurants and the fashionable discothèques, it was because he could not feel at home in a world of phony glamour.

"— and we're giving that change direction. We aren't allowing it to drift helplessly, to bog down and fall apart. The arts have always provided the spearhead, the thrust for a change." Balutis ran his hand through his dark hair, and it was impossible to doubt his sincerity now. He was tense, almost rigid, and his surface attitude of casual flippancy was gone. "Do you realize that never in all history have the artists—the painters and authors and musicians—consciously worked together to provide a direction that would unify and clarify men's fundamental thinking?"

"I guess," Max said, "it never crossed my mind. I've been busy."

"There's no need for a businessman to be aware of these trends," Lance replied, and did not mean to sound condescending. "That's the function of the artist in society. But I can promise you that when our concept of super-reality has been established, you'll be among the first to benefit."

"It'll buy me a new building, maybe? Or a hotel off Madison Avenue I've had my eye on?"

"Not directly, no," Lance said patiently. "But here's what it will do. First, a new school of architecture will develop, the super-real. I have some ideas on that subject, but I'm no architect, and I don't want to stick my neck out. New buildings will have a grace and beauty that will be unique. A new public appreciation of that beauty will flower. And as a result more people will *want* to be in those new places."

"How soon is this miracle going to happen?" Max glanced at his watch, then picked up the telephone. "Carol," he said, "call Howard at the bank and tell him we're going ahead with that binder. The law office is drawing up the forms, and I'll bring them along when I go over to the bank for lunch." He replaced the instrument in its cradle. "Like I was saying, Mr. Balutis, how soon?"

"How long has it taken for a new generation to develop in a way unlike any that's gone before us? Are we the product—or the rejection—of all previous generations? Or have we done our thing overnight, so to speak, and on our own? I can't answer your question, Max. I'm no seer. I do know that the potency of super-reality is beyond belief, and is spreading faster than I'd have dared to hope a few years ago. Whether it will materialize in a new hotel that you build or buy in a year, or five years, or ten years, even, is anybody's guess."

"At least you're honest."

"Why shouldn't I be?" Balutis countered.

"Most people who come to see me want to sell me something."

"I don't want your money."

"What, then?"

"I'm anxious to get your cooperation, and there's nothing at all you yourself will have to do. You're doing that new forty-story building uptown—"

"Forty-two."

"—and I'd like to use it as a set for some scenes I'm very eager to shoot. That's all there is to it."

"Only the skeleton is done," Max said. "We haven't put in the floors and walls above the eleventh story yet."

"That's exactly why I want to use it. You have a marvelous, huge cage elevator, and some sort of work platform on the top story. They're what I need."

"There's some elegant construction work being done in this city," Max said. "The World Trade Center is unique. In all the world there's nothing like it. And I can think of three new ones right here in midtown that have glamour, unusual design—what the bright boys in our trade call the exotics. Why should anybody want a solid nothing for a movie set? It looks exactly like a hundred other solid nothings."

"A friend of mine lives a couple of blocks away, and I've watched your building grow. That's what gave me my idea. For one thing, it overlooks Central Park, which will give me a background of spaciousness, of floating in space. The cage is big enough to shoot in, and the platform on the top story will be superb for my climax scenes."

Max raised a thick hand. "Wait. A building under construction isn't safe for a swarm of amateurs. Your electricians, camera crews, all those people might hurt themselves. And when you get hurt forty-two stories from the ground, it's permanent. There aren't any guard rails or that kind of thing up there."

"If there were," Lance said, "I wouldn't be interested. It's the sense of freedom that I love."

"In a mob, somebody is sure to lose his footing or stumble. L & B is responsible under the law, so I couldn't permit it. Also, our insurance agent would have a stroke."

"My production staff, camera and sound crews, technicians and helpers are all one person. The producer-director. Me. And I'll be using a cast of two people. That makes a total of three of us."

Max's concept of movie-making was shattered. "It doesn't seem possible."

"I don't squander money," Lance said.

Max began to consider the suggestion seriously. "Well, it could be done, maybe, if you and your actors would sign releases that relieve L & B of any obligation in case of accident."

"Of course. We'll sign any legal document you think necessary."

Max had to concede that Balutis could be crisp and business-like, but felt some lingering doubts. "Even with just three of you, something could happen if you started chasing around the skeleton. It's one thing to see people racing around on girders, and something else again to try it. I couldn't permit anything like that."

"I give you my word, we aren't suicidal." Lance, secretly amused, helped himself to a cigarette from a box on the desk. "Besides, my films aren't like the flicks of the thirties you see on television. I try to achieve the realistic penultimate, which is unattainable, so I must sometimes paint a series of abstracts, and leave the final realism to the imagination of my audience. Some of my competitors claim they have different goals, but they're fast enough when it comes to copying my techniques."

The explanation was gibberish to Max, but he sympathized with what he understood. "In every trade," he said, "there are thieves."

Lance flicked a long ash onto the carpet. "They can copy me until they drop dead. I'm always ten paces ahead of the pack. Once I've made this film, every unfinished building in New York will be a target. By the way, I want to shoot at night."

"Then I'm sure it can't be done," Max said. "Without electrical crews you couldn't possibly work at night."

Lance stubbed out his cigarette on the heel of a boot, and threw the butt in the direction of a wastebasket, but missed. "There'll be a full moon tomorrow night—and an almost full one the next. Tomorrow is going to be clear, and I need no other light."

"You'll make a movie in the dark?"

"Once you've seen my kind of work, you'll gain a better grasp of my style. I'd like to shoot tomorrow or the next night—tomorrow, preferably. For two or three hours, beginning around ten o'clock. I'm anxious to put this film in the can quickly. To be truthful, I've already scheduled a tentative showing for this coming weekend."

Max had been under the impression that movie-making was a long, tedious process, but perhaps he was mistaken. Stella would know what was being done these days, but he could no longer ask her.

"Come with us, why don't you?" Lance made the invitation sound spontaneous. "We'd love to have you. And you can tell us where we can go and where we can't."

"Well I sure as hell wouldn't let you up there by yourselves," Max said.

The idea of spending part of an evening with a young movie-maker on the skeleton of a new building was preposterous, but Max knew that if he didn't accept he'd go home and brood, as he had done the previous two nights. Remembering Paul's suggestion that he find something to occupy him, he decided to agree. If nothing else, the experience would be novel.

Lance spoke excitedly. "It's settled! We'll go to dinner, round up the cast and my equipment, and be on our way."

"I'll have to meet you there," Max said hastily. He could not imagine walking into any restaurant he knew with a companion in high-heeled cowboy boots and a jacket, no matter how expensive, that was smeared with paint. And besides, Max was shrewd enough to realize he had been conned. But what he had to lose he could not yet figure out.

The master's den in the East Side townhouse of Martin and Sandra Tilstrom was an unusual room. Originally intended as a library, the name of the chamber had been changed by its owners because it did not contain a single book. It was paneled in pine, with indirect lighting that, according to Lionel Green, the black poet, made it look like an osteopath's waiting room. There the resemblance stopped, however. The desk that filled one corner was leather-topped, and allegedly had belonged to Thomas Jefferson. Regardless of whether it was a genuine antique, it was impressive, and Sandra had paid six thousand dollars for it.

Dominating the room was a circular card table, purchased directly from a manufacturer who supplied the gambling houses at Las Vegas and the Bahamas. Forming an outer circle behind the players' chairs was a bar, each section of which contained its own liquor stock and ice. So a man playing cards could half-turn in his chair and mix himself a fresh drink at his pleasure. Consequently, as Martin often said, "Everybody I know finds it a pleasure to play poker at my place. All a wholesale grocer or anybody else needs to get along in this world is a little creative imagination."

Eight men, all in their monogrammed, tailor-made silk shirt-sleeves, were immersed in a game of poker, and without exception the entire group took the entertainment seriously. There was good reason for the silent tension at the table: the cheapest

57

chips cost five dollars, the most expensive fifty. A man could drop thousands in a single evening.

Martin Tilstrom, a man with blond, curling hair and thick features, clamped his teeth on his cigar and grinned bloodlessly as he dealt. "How it hurts me to take dough away from you silly bastards."

His friends made no reply, but Morris Howe, the only member of the group who wasn't a regular, could not refrain. "You look brokenhearted," he said, patting his balding head for luck.

Martin glared at him. He couldn't remember what it was Howe did for a living, and knew only that his wife, Barbie, was one of Sandra's chums. He should have known better than to let somebody from that crowd into the game, no matter now well-heeled he might be. "If you want to cut out because the stakes are too high, nobody will blame you, Morrie."

Howe reached for a cigarette. "I'll hold my own, thanks. Just because I had a little crappy luck so far won't send me to the cleaners." Glancing at his cards, he reached behind him for a stiff belt of Scotch.

Martin shrugged and called for bets. After he had called for discards and re-dealt, he discovered that he and Howe were the only ones out of the game, so he decided to probe a bit. It took the fun out of poker if somebody was really hurting. "I wasn't kidding, Morrie," he said.

Howe bristled. "You don't like the way I play, Marty?"

"Sure, sure. I was thinking of your wallet, that's all."

"I'll make it back—and more." Howe peered at his host through thick-rimmed glasses. "You think I'm not good for it, maybe?"

"No offense meant," Tilstrom said.

"None taken. I inherited a mint, and I've more than doubled it in the market. That satisfy you?"

"Look, you stiff-necked bastard," Tilstrom said, "all I know is Sandra is a friend of your wife's. And I've met so many phonies and deadbeats in that crowd she runs around with—"

"Now I get it." Howe laughed loudly, coarsely, and took a swallow of his drink. "Christ, I can't blame you. But if I was one of them, I'd be in their party, not here. Now I'm the one who means no offense, but the only reason I came along tonight is because Barbie bugs me about never taking her anyplace, she always has to get other escorts, all that crap. See what I mean?"

"Perfectly." Tilstrom grinned and poured some Scotch from his own bottle into the other's glass. "It looks like we're in the same league."

Howe laughed again. "No broad is as expensive as Barbie."

"I'll match you, dressmakers' bills, decorators' bills, the works." Tilstrom sobered. "Not that I bitch about what Sandra spends."

"What the hell. Barbie can do what she pleases. Just so she shows up from her arty-farty parties early enough that nothing gets in the papers."

"What I mean," Tilstrom said soberly as he reached for the cards the others had thrown down and began to shuffle them, "is that Sandra is pretty terrific. Look, I got no high-society background or anything. I sell onions. Wholesale. But Sandra's got this place fixed up great, she dresses great, and she's worked us in with a class of people who are something. Do you know Elmer Bates is in the other room right now? I didn't read that last book of his, but everybody at a fancy charity fashion show we went to the other night was talking about it. And Lance Balutis—"

"Bates. Balutis." Howe jeered. "They're nuts. I pay for Barbie's singing lessons so she can sing in Balutis' movies. Big deal. The lessons cost me more than she makes, and they show the movies in somebody's attic or somebody's broken-down theater that you'd get fleas if you sat in one of the seats."

"Don't fool yourself about the power of people like Balutis and Elmer Bates," Tilstrom said, dealing a new hand. "The oldest names in the Social Register are their chums. I tell you,

Sandra may be a pain in the ass sometimes, but she knows what she's doing."

A total stranger, unfamiliar with the social customs of New York's East Side, might have doubted the validity of that statement had he looked in the Tilstroms' "den." There Sandra was entertaining, as usual, and there her guests lounged on the marble steps of her sunken tropical garden, which occupied the entire center of the room under a huge skylight. Gardenias, camellias and orchids bloomed, and the entire chamber was dominated by a far-larger-than-life statue of Sandra, cast in bronze, around which flowering bushes had been planted.

Lionel Green, in black-satin lounging pajamas, held a long cigarette holder in one hand, a gardenia in the other, and paid no attention to the conversation swirling around him. Like two or three others he was smoking a cigarette of a coarse substance that smelled strong and sweet, and his thoughts were elsewhere. In fact, as he stared fixedly into space he seemed unaware of the presence of anyone else.

Chuck V. Chalmers, a star of television soap operas, was attired in a rough woodsman's shirt, hunting pants and fringed boots, and was trying to impress a vapid brunette, dressed in an identical outfit, with his erudition. "It's much simpler to contrast super-reality and existentialism than it is to compare them," he said. "I'll grant you they're both trying to extend man's grasp of the finite, but I'd be reaching, if you'll forgive the pun, if I found any other similarities."

The girl giggled. "Your shirt is open lower than mine. Three buttons."

Chalmers' features, which had enabled him to earn an exceptionally good living as a male model before he had become an actor, remained unchanged.

"Mine is only open two buttons. But I guess I can do what you can do." She opened another button.

A glance told him she was wearing no brassiere, but he would wait a few moments before showing his appreciation, and he continued his analysis.

Most of the guests were listening to a monologue delivered by Elmer Bates, who spoke in a voice drained of all emotion. "Study the actual election figures, state by state," he said. "Not the interpretations by the so-called experts. The figures themselves. And if you're honest, I defy you to say I'm wrong when I insist, as I did in my recent magazine series—you've all read it, I assume?—that the principal function of the White House is as a museum. It evokes memories. Just as a visit to JFK's grave. But inside each there is a corpse."

A young woman in harem pants, a Cossack blouse and no make-up glowered at him. "Elmer, you really turn me off!"

"Don't give Hilda any more grass to smoke," Bates said austerely. "It makes her overresponsive.

"The super-reality of the White House lies in its plumbing system," Bates continued sententiously. "Even though new plumbing was installed during the Truman Administration, it's positively archaic."

"When did you last use the White House plumbing, Elmer?" Lance Balutis, in a ragged old shirt and jeans, lounged on one elbow, his smile sardonic, and asked the question quietly.

Barbie Howe, seated beside him, laughed. "I think that's a real gas," she said.

Lance waved her silent. "When, Elmer?"

"The President's dinner for creative artists, on the fourteenth of last month, as if you didn't know. You're just jealous because you weren't invited. You've never had my talent for respectability. Isn't that so, Lionel?"

The poet, taking another drag of his marijuana cigarette, was in no condition to discuss White House dinners or plumbing. His eyes were becoming glazed, and he slumped limply, the gardenia falling from his hand.

"Now, Elmer," Lance said, smiling, "let me see if I can ex-

61

plain something to you. A privy on the White House lawn would be a symbol of super-reality. Not the plumbing, no matter how bad."

"You're really impossible," Bates said with amused superiority. "That's why I've had to attack your new film, *Song of Solomon,* in a review I've just written for the *St. Mark's Place Echo.*"

"Your by-line is a guarantee that nobody will read it," Lance said.

"That's my movie." Barbie was hurt.

"I'm not criticizing you, Barbie," Bates told her soothingly. "You were very cute and pretty, and I'm sure anybody who pays to see the film will go to see you."

She was mollified, and smiled at him.

Bates had no desire to flirt with her, however, and began counting off points on his fingers. "Why Barbie instead of a real singer, Lance? Somebody with professional pzazz? And why sit her naked in front of your camera for two solid hours?"

Lance became angry. "My message is clear to a twelve-year-old!"

"I'm thirteen."

"It had to be Barbie. The half-trained quality of her voice is what gives the film its bite. A rounded, perfect voice would have provided too smooth a flow."

Bates gulped a glass of champagne. "I hate to admit you might be right, Lance," he said thoughtfully, "but you do have a point."

"More than that. I *am* right, and I'll prove it. A costume, any kind of clothing, would have made the film a mockery. Barbie, come closer."

The girl obediently moved nearer to him on the steps.

Balutis lifted her sweater and exposed her breasts. "This is my rationale, Elmer, and I need no other. The mammary gland. The most painted, photographed, written-about, extolled object on the face of the earth. For thousands of years. Why?"

With the exception of Lionel Green and one or two others,

62

everyone in Sandra's den was staring at Barbie's breasts, but she showed no embarrassment. If anything, the sudden attention pleased her.

"Assuming your question isn't rhetorical," Bates said, "it's the symbol of universal motherhood. Naturally."

"Therefore, in essence, a sex symbol," Balutis said.

"Hell, yes. *The* sex symbol."

"My principle, Elmer, is that of stripping away *all* pretensions."

"Then you're claiming that only the erotic exemplifies pure art!"

"That's what I've been preaching," Lance said. "A few heretics like you are still holding out, but you'll soon swing into line. It's inevitable, particularly as I'll soon be in a position to enlarge my whole campaign."

Howard Christianson, Jr., surveyed the private dining room of the North Atlantic Bank and Trust Company from the vantage point of his private luncheon table in the corner, and turned to his companion. "Max," he said, "no matter how we slice it, the salami will go just so far."

Max Berman was red-faced and defensive, but did not lose his smile. "It's first-class salami, Howard. Not much of the stuff is being made these days, but all you boys in this dining room are growing fat on it."

"Of course." The bank's senior vice-president removed his glasses and polished them. "Banks never go on diets. You'll be the one who starves or suffers indigestion."

"What I don't understand," Max said, "is why you pick this particular time to wave the danger signals. L & B has never been in a better position."

"That's what I thought. Until I made the quick survey just before you came in. You're stretching your credit too thin, Max.

63

You're borrowing from one project to pay for the next, and if you come a cropper on a big one just once, the whole house of cards will tumble."

"L & B doesn't build card houses. We put up buildings that last."

"So you do, and you'll never find North Atlantic refusing you capital for an L & B construction project."

Max looked around the high-ceilinged room, with its cream-colored walls and conservative décor, and sighed. "But you're closing the door on any more property purchases."

"No, I merely said I intend to advise our board that we must study each proposed loan to L & B with greater care hereafter."

"Is it the deal for the English hotel that makes you so nervous, Howard?"

"I think this new acquisition increases your risk beyond the safety point."

"But why? We'll earn back our investment within two years, and then we'll unload. With the hotel shortage getting worse over there, and tourist travel still climbing, we can't help but make a few million on our sale."

"You're assuming the upward, inflationary trend of the past few years will continue."

"A few years? Ever since the end of World War II, with a few pauses."

"Suppose there should be one of those pauses within the next year or so," the banker persisted. "What contingency funds have you provided?"

"I'm betting there won't be a recession that'll upset us."

"If we and the other banks should be forced to call in your loans, Max, you'll be in trouble. Your liabilities would outweigh your assets by almost thirty million."

"Paper liabilities, a lot of them," Max said stubbornly.

"Some paper assets, too. North Atlantic doesn't want to see you getting into trouble, Max. Not only has L & B been a good customer for years, but you and Paul have been our personal friends."

"Sure." Max smiled, but kept his thoughts to himself. For years he had told Stella that the boys at North Atlantic, from Christianson down, were the type of office friends who entertained a man at lunch but never invited him to their homes. Secretly, he believed, they were vultures who wanted him to fail so they could pick the bones clean. "We're your friends, too, Howard. That's why I'll speak frankly to you. Every time L & B has made a big move you've advised against it. But we've become one of the world's biggest realty holders, all the same. And we intend to become bigger. If North Atlantic won't finance us, we'll go elsewhere. Strangers will advance the capital where friends won't. But nothing will stop our growth!"

Stella Ross studied the photographs on Paul Lafferty's desk. "I was asking Margaret about young Paul the other day. How does he like Oxford?"

"If he enjoys the rest of his year as much as he has the first couple of months in England, it'll be a great year." Paul rubbed his jowls and grinned. "You haven't come up to my office to discuss my son, Stella. Sit down."

She lowered herself into the nearest leather chair and tugged at the hem of her skirt. "I knew Max had a meeting scheduled at North Atlantic this noon, but I didn't think he'd appreciate my butting in. Not that it's any of my business, Paul."

Lafferty did not reply, but his grin was eloquent.

"My own ledgers," she said, "have had me wondering for the past six months when Christianson would step in and call a halt to the loans."

"He hasn't gone that far. Yet. Today was a warning."

"The English deal kicked him off?"

Lafferty nodded.

"I knew it! I told Max last month. But he's never listened to me." And now, she told herself, it was too late.

"He's convinced we'll show a good profit on that turnover, Stella."

"But the risk is so great!" She checked herself, then hesitated. "Why does he do it, Paul?"

"Shouldn't I ask you the same question? You know him better than I do."

"I thought I did, but I don't really know him at all. Those first years, I thought the construction business satisfied him, as it does you."

"We're good at it."

"That's what I mean."

"We're also good at juggling real estate. At least, Max is," Lafferty said.

"So far."

"Now you sound like Christianson."

She flipped back the blond bangs that drooped over one eyebrow. "Here's the way I see it, Paul, and I don't mean to sound like a psychiatrist. Just a woman, who has spent eleven years studying a man. Max is still insecure. His childhood in Europe, and then being a refugee, and all. He can't be satisfied owning a solid, money-making company. Being big and strong isn't enough. He's got to be the biggest—and the strongest. He's living the old-fashioned American dream. He personifies it, Paul."

"You can't fault a man for his ambition."

"We don't live in a Horatio Alger era, and you know it better than I do. I have no right to lecture a man in your position—"

"Lecture away. Margaret and Janet do it all the time. You're practically a member of the family. So don't feel inhibited."

Stella smiled, then grew tense again. "There are so many forces at work trying to drag a man down. The higher he climbs, the harder they tug. It's different for you, Paul. You have two things Max lacks. A family. And a perspective. If L & B took a beating, you'd survive."

"So would Max. He's pretty tough."

"But he isn't! Behind all that tough front he's sensitive. And sweet."

"You still love him, huh? Even though you walked out on him."

"My feelings have nothing to do with this, Paul," she said in anguish. "It's just that I know, better than anyone, how vulnerable Max is. He's ripe for trouble, and I'm so afraid he's going to be badly hurt."

By the time the taxi drew up at the construction site, a few minutes before ten, Max was thoroughly sorry he had consented to the idea. He should have taken his time, made a thorough investigation of the insistent young producer and then assigned someone from the office to supervise the project. It was absurd for a man of his age to be a participant in make-believe late in the evening, and he decided that if Balutis and his companions were late he'd leave at once.

As he paid the cabbie, however, he saw Balutis and another young man deep in conversation near the padlocked wooden door set in the high fence that had been erected around the construction site. A sixteen-millimeter camera and a sack of film were over Balutis' shoulder, and in his other hand he carried what appeared to be a tape recorder.

As he and his companion turned, Max took an immediate dislike to the other young man, whose shaggy brown hair was as long as a girl's. He seemed too slender, almost dainty, in hip-hugger pants, an elaborate sweater-shirt open at the throat and tasseled moccasins of green alligator. It was something of a shock to observe that he was wearing eye shadow and that his lips glistened.

Balutis started forward, and Max saw, behind him, a girl who had been staring at the construction site through the "superintendents' peephole" that had become obligatory in almost

67

every construction fence. She was stunning, and Max's bad humor lessened when she turned toward him with a smile.

Her tousled platinum hair was much shorter than Stella's, and, Max realized, only a fraction of the length of the actor's. Her eyes were dark—he later discovered they were violet—and her mouth, although small, was that of a sensualist. By way of contrast, her bone structure was patrician, her face finely molded, and she had the long, graceful neck he admired. She was exceptionally tall, very slender, and moved marvelously as she drifted toward him.

Her figure, in a close-fitting miniskirted dress of thin, white wool, was breathtaking, and momentarily drove everything else from Max's mind. She had a small but high bosom, well-defined hips, and long legs that were in a class with Stella's, the highest praise he could offer. This one, Max thought, is my type.

"You're right on time," Lance called cheerfully. "Max Berman, meet Gerry Jarvis, our leading man, and Bobbie Wayne, my favorite star."

It did not surprise Max that the actor's handshake was limp, while that of the girl's was firm. She looked like an aristocrat, he thought, but it disturbed him slightly when she looked at him for only an instant. He wondered if she was having trouble trying to focus. Yet he could detect no odor of liquor on her breath. Perhaps he was imagining things.

He opened the door, locking it again behind him, and Bobbie Wayne kept pace with him, striding beside him as he led the way to the supervisor's trailer, past a huge concrete mixer and two of his new cranes. The ground was pitted, and there were lengths of steel and planks underfoot, as well as rocks and other debris that had not been cleared away. She seemed surefooted and unconcerned. Only her eyes were made up, and she wore no lipstick or facial cosmetics, which made the actor's appearance all the more incongruous. Her earrings, large metal disks, gleamed in the moonlight, and she exuded an aura of healthy exuberance to which Max immediately responded.

But he would not let himself forget that he was responsible for the two men as well. Balutis and Jarvis were finding it more difficult than Bobbie to pick their way across the site, and Max called over his shoulder, "Watch your step, and be especially careful you don't trip over power cables."

A strong, naked light bulb provided the illumination in the supervisor's trailer, and Max produced liability-release forms, which each of the trio signed. Trying to make conversation, he asked, "Is most of this movie finished?"

They laughed, and Lance said, "What we shoot tonight will *be* the film!"

"You make a whole movie in one night?"

"I always shoot consecutively. That's what gives my work cohesion. Oh, I'll admit I do a splice job occasionally." Lance looked around carefully as they emerged into the open again, Max extinguishing the light and locking the trailer door behind them. "But I'm certainly *not* creating an anti-art form, no matter what the conservatives say. What I do is art in the purest post-Aristotelian sense."

Max shrugged. "The cables. Don't break your neck on them."

"Is there always this dampness around a new building?" the girl asked.

"Usually. The ground is damp, the vacuum sucks in moisture from the air around us, and in mixing concrete we use water. Also, Miss Wayne, this is a damp season."

"Bobbie. I hate formality, Max."

Apparently no one in the younger generation bothered with surnames. Bobbie Wayne's age was somewhere between that of his nephew Harvey and of his partner's daughter; Max guessed she was around twenty-three or twenty-four.

Lance halted and, while a faint breeze riffled his hair, inspected the site. "If I have enough film, I'll take fifty feet or so down here after we're done. Then I can either use it at the end or push it up to the opening, depending on the need for atmosphere."

Max was indifferent to the problem. "Do you need a hook-in for that recorder?"

"No, I find a portable more convenient for location work. For interiors I usually shoot sound on film, using a standard camera with the sound built in, but for locations the battery-powered portable tape recorder and a silent sixteen double-m are more sensitive to the nuances that my audiences are being taught to expect as my trademark."

Max unlocked the heavy metal cover of an electrical power board, pulled several switches and nodded in satisfaction when a generator began to hum softly. "Once we get above ground, you won't hear this noise."

"It adds authenticity," Lance replied. "I don't mind it in the least."

They walked to the cage elevator, and Max tried several keys on the heavy lock.

"You keep everything battened down, I see." Bobbie was amused, and her patrician Philadelphia drawl became more pronounced. "Are you afraid someone will walk off with your precious elevator?"

Max found no humor in anything relating to construction. "No. But some jackass might get into the grounds some night, or over a weekend, and kill himself in this thing. This gets rid of headaches without the aspirin." Opening the elevator door, he hooked the lock onto one of the metal bars, then snapped it shut.

"Very neat," Lance observed.

He missed very little, Max thought. "Standard procedure for operators. We don't lose locks, and we save time. Union pay-scales are high, so we try to eliminate any carelessness that might be expensive. You'd be surprised how much you can get behind when a crew loses ten to fifteen minutes at a clip."

The filmmakers were as unimpressed as he had been by the explanations of Balutis' artistic goals.

"This is just huge," Bobbie said, walking across the rough floorboards of the cage.

Gerry Jarvis spoke for the first time. "It's just adorable."

Max removed the lock and chain that had held the elevator's operating levers in place.

"Could we use those as props?" Lance asked him. "We might have some fun with them, and I give you my best Boy Scout oath we won't misplace them."

Apparently these people improvised on occasion during the shooting of a movie. Handing Balutis the long, heavy chain and padlock, Max switched on a very weak, hooded light over the controls. "This is all the light I'm going to use," he said. "Even at this time of night a crowd would show up if they thought something was happening here."

Lance was crouching at one side of the cage, motioning his companions toward the other end so he could see them through his finder. "It may be a little dim until we move outdoors, but that can give us another dimension." He sounded pleased. "Bobbins, you need no instructions. Gerry, do whatever feels right. Max, could we make a stop on the tenth or eleventh floor—or wherever the concrete flooring is in?"

"Sure, I guess so. But the flooring is still rough."

"That doesn't matter in the least." Lance checked his recorder and suspended a microphone above the heads of his players, looping its cord around an overhead cage bar. "One thing more, Max. Any time you feel like talking, go ahead. It'll lend verisimilitude to the whole performance, if you see what I mean."

Max didn't. "I'm not an actor."

Balutis grinned, and Bobbie laughed aloud. "Let me do the worrying," Lance said. "Ready, children?" He snapped on the tape recorder and pointing the camera, began to film the pair opposite him.

Max had not yet closed the door of the cage, and it shut with a crash so loud that he thought they'd have to start again.

"Marvelous!" Lance declared, not caring, apparently, that his own voice was being recorded. "That could have been a dungeon door, or the last escape hatch of a Turkish torture cage. Or the door of a bird cage," he added, slightly surprised at the notion.

He made no sense, and Max concentrated on the levers. They, too, made grinding noises, but at last the huge cage shuddered and started to rise.

"We're barely crawling," Bobbie said, looking out through the bars.

"It's fast enough for me," Gerry replied. "I don't mind telling you I'm frightened half to death."

"I think we're safe." Bobbie looked at Max and smiled blithely, her rows of even, white teeth shining in the dim light.

"Nothing ever bothers you, angel." Gerry sounded sulky. "You wouldn't mind walking a tightrope across the Grand Canyon."

"Ah, what a groovy trip," and she laughed, then turned to Jerry with her pretend-baby voice. "I suppose I'd have to learn tightrope-walking first."

"Not you." Suddenly the young actor gasped and took a backward step, away from the bars. "It really is scary, looking out there. Admit it!"

"I feel as though we're flying under our own power. Or holding almost still, like a bird treading air. I wonder if that's the right way to say it? You tread water, so why not tread air?"

Gerry inched still farther from the bars.

It occurred to Bobbie that he was genuinely frightened, so she went to him, kissed him lightly but tenderly, and began to stroke his long hair. "There, there," she said. "Mama won't let anything naughty happen to you."

"I prefer solid sides on these things." His voice shook a bit. "You really aren't any safer, but you can't look out, so you think you're safe. Absurd, I suppose." His laugh was unconvincing.

Bobbie continued to stroke his hair, and with her other hand held him for a moment, then, on what seemed to be sudden impulse, patted him reassuringly on the behind. An expression of speculative pleasure crossed her face, and, completing the re-

72

versal of male and female roles, she caressed his buttocks, running her hand along the surface of his tight, hip-hugger trousers.

Gerry evidently found the sensation soothing, and relaxed for the first time since the elevator had started to move.

"Mmm," Bobbie said. "Cute and cozy." Her caresses, although delicate, became more insistent.

Max watched them in astonishment. Every word of the nonsense they were speaking, every move they were making, including the girl's somewhat vulgar gestures, was being recorded on film and tape. And Lance, busily running the camera, was smiling in a smugly satisfied way. Max was amazed that these people were not working from a prepared movie script, but were saying and doing anything at random. Never had he seen a movie like the one they were making, and he became irritated when he began to wonder whether he was wasting his time on rubbish.

The cage approached the eleventh floor, so he brought it to a halt, level with the concrete that had been poured about a week earlier. Then, at Balutis' eager signal, he opened the door.

Bobbie stood for a moment, then dashed into the open, Jarvis following her reluctantly, not trusting the flooring beneath his feet.

Balutis flicked off the recorder, and followed them, the camera still whirring.

Max pondered for a moment, then locked the levers with the chain and padlock before he, too, went out onto the unfinished floor.

The mood of the young couple being photographed had changed drastically, and they were leaping around the concrete flooring like a pair of ballet dancers, laughing breathlessly as each tried to outdo the other's intricate steps.

Max cupped his hands. "Stay away from the edge!" he shouted. "There are no walls or rails!"

Gerry Jarvis obeyed instantly, moving closer to the center of the vast floor, but Bobbie paid no attention to the warning.

"If she isn't more careful," Max said, "you'll have to stop right now, and we'll call off the whole thing."

She heard him before Lance could call out to her. Halting suddenly, she glared at Max with a fury that astonished him before her mood changed again and she resumed her dance.

Max was reminded of two mindless children, each absorbed in a private world, each pretending for the sheer joy of make-believe.

Lance sensed something, too. Removing the used roll of film from his camera and inserting another in a few, deft movements, he said in a low voice, "I'd appreciate a great favor, Max. Get the recorder for me, will you?" He aimed the camera and began shooting again.

Max could see himself comfortably stretched out on a couch in his own living room, and was tempted to end the farce. But his sense of fair play, coupled with his curiosity, made him decide to wait a little longer. By the time he returned with the tape recorder, however, the pair were whirling, leaping and kicking so energetically that he became alarmed.

"The flooring isn't finished!" he roared. "You'll break your goddam ankles!"

They stared at him, both panting for breath, and Lance flipped on the recorder just as they began to giggle. "Tag, you're it!" Gerry said, beginning to hop on one leg. "I broke an ankle."

"Me, too." The girl hopped in pursuit.

Their game, played with variations, seemed endless. But the camera and recorder continued to make permanent impressions of their infantile sport, and Lance, sometimes moving closer for close-up shots, sometimes sprawling on the concrete floor and once climbing a wooden ladder that was leaning against a steel upright, finally finished a second reel and started a third.

Max, utterly bored, chewed on an unlighted cigar, stared out across the rooftops of the neighboring apartment houses and tried to shut out the sounds of the inane shrieks and laughter. Anybody who paid to see this movie, he thought, would be cheated,

74

no matter how low the admission charge. He was startled, when he glanced at his watch, to discover that the pair had been cavorting for more than forty-five minutes.

At last Balutis intervened. Beckoning, he backed toward the cage, camera in one hand and the recorder in the other, and the couple followed like two obedient youngsters.

"Now we'll fly up into the sky!" Bobbie gasped as she leaned against the bars.

Max closed the elevator door, removed the chain and padlock and started the machine on its ascent. Suddenly he saw that the girl was smoking. "Put out that cigarette!" he commanded.

She looked at him, smiled and insolently took another puff.

Indifferent to the whirring camera, he reached out, snatched the burning cigarette and carefully extinguished it with thumb and forefinger, stamping out the sparks that landed on the floor. "Not only are there city laws," he said harshly, "but on one of my projects *nobody* smokes. When the building is finished, it'll be fireproof. Right now we're using wooden equipment. The floor of this elevator, for God's sake! Don't try anything like that again. Your stupid games are bad enough, but you don't take chances of this sort. Not on one of my projects!"

Suddenly Max realized that Balutis had turned up the recorder volume while he had been speaking, and the moviemaker looked immensely pleased.

Bobbie's reaction was startling. Her eyes softened, her expression became melting and she looked like a girl desperately begging for love.

Max thought she was putting on an act, but, when the frightened Gerry Jarvis reached out to touch her, his terror mounting as the elevator rose higher, she grasped the back of his head with both hands, and started to kiss him with a frenzy that could not have been simulated.

Balutis was overjoyed, and moved in for a close-up in the dim light.

Max was convinced that all three were mad.

The girl stepped back, reached down for the chain and padlock, then swiftly wrapped the heavy links around her partner's arms, pinning them behind him until she snapped the padlock. His panic became worse when he found himself unable to break free, and she laughed huskily. It was a taunting sound, unadulterated sexual sadism of the most blatant sort, and Max knew she wasn't acting. She was exhibiting her real feelings, and was obviously enjoying the experience.

The elevator crept higher in a world of girders, the lights and silhouettes of the city visible beyond them, and Gerry's terror mounted. Moving his feet apart to brace himself, he began to plead with his tormentor. "Let me go. Please. This—isn't funny. Please."

Bobbie laughed again, and paid no attention. She unbuttoned his sweater-shirt, then began to run her fingertips across his bare chest, and he moaned.

"Don't tickle," he whispered. "I—can't stand it."

The girl grinned and deliberately began to tickle him, occasionally jabbing a finger into his side.

Slowly, against his will, he backed against the bars of the cage. Then, seeing the open spaces yawning beyond the steel, he closed his eyes, his face bathed in sweat. Unable to resist looking again, he peered out a second time, and opened his mouth to scream, but was unable to make a sound.

Max was simultaneously revolted and fascinated.

All at once Bobbie's mood changed again. Perhaps she felt genuine compassion for her victim, or else the game had grown boring. For whatever the reason, she caught hold of his hair, pulled his face close and kissed him soothingly. "Mama won't let anything happen to you," she murmured.

"Jarvis," Max interrupted, "back toward me. Slow and easy. That's it. Slow." Manipulating the levers with one hand, he opened the padlock with the other, trusting no one else with the key. Tugging so hard the young actor winced, Max pulled the chain free.

Max held the heavy chain like a weapon. "Stop your camera, Balutis, and turn off that goddam sound machine."

Lance hesitated for a moment, but thought it wiser to obey.

"Now, all of you," Max said. "We'll have no more of this crazy stuff. There's no danger up here when people behave themselves, but you're carrying on like you belong in a nut-farm. I can't reverse this machine while it's moving because I might strip the gears. But as soon as we hit the top, we're going down again. And that's the end of it."

There was a silence, punctuated by the creaking of the cage and the faint whistling of the wind through the bars.

Then a white-faced, contrite Bobbie Wayne took several uncertain steps toward Max. "I'm sorry," she said. "I didn't mean to be a bloody fool, but I got carried away. It was very stupid of me, Max. Mr. Berman. I've abused your hospitality, and I've jeopardized you as well as my friends. I have no real excuse to offer, and I can't even expect you to accept my apology." She spoke primly, shame in her eyes and voice.

"I give you my word, Max," Lance said earnestly. "that there will be no more adolescent irresponsibility. Bobbie will do nothing stupid, and neither will Gerry. The future of our film is in your hands, and I can only ask you to reconsider. What I've shot so far will be meaningless unless I can do a climactic scene at the top, and everything I've filmed so far will be wasted. Give us a break, and I swear to you that you won't regret it."

Bobbie continued to plead silently, with an intensity even greater than Jarvis had demonstrated when chained.

There was an almost hypnotic sexual magnetism in her steady, unblinking gaze, and Max felt uncomfortable.

The cage shuddered to a stop at the heavy platform of oak planks that had been erected at what would become the forty-second story of the newest L & B building.

77

Unwavering, Bobbie continued to look at Max. It was difficult for him to think, but he wanted to be fair. "All right," he said at last. "You're kids, you've got high spirits, you carried a joke too far. I'll let you out here, but I'm setting the rules. Break them just once, and I'll not only throw you into the elevator, but I'll beat the living hell out of you after we get back to the ground. You understand?"

Bobbie's eyes were shining, and she appeared spellbound as she nodded.

"You're the boss," Lance said crisply.

"I've had enough scare to last me forever." Gerry's voice was thick with emotion.

Max breathed easily, and couldn't help wondering whether the girl might be seeking a man who would master her. "Here's how it'll be," he said. "The work platform is fifty feet by forty, and very solid. On every other story there's a corrugated steel form that will be the beginning of a floor. So you can't drop too far. But it wobbles, and there are holes in it that have been cut by the electricians and plumbers and heating men. Even men who spend their lives in construction treat that flooring with respect. They should. And somebody like you, Jarvis, who has vertigo, could be in trouble far from the elevator. So nobody will go more than five feet. You'll do no more jumping around and dancing. Sit down—no more than five feet from here, remember, and I'll tell you when to stop. Enjoy the view, enjoy the feeling of being in the open on the roof of the world. There's nothing like it. Then we'll go down again. I'll have no discussion or arguments. Accept my rules, or that's the end of it."

"We accept unconditionally," Lance said. "And we're grateful to you."

Gerry weakly muttered his assent.

Max, still angry because he had been drawn into a situation unlike any he had ever known, felt a need to challenge the girl. "You're the troublemaker," he said.

"I wouldn't dream of breaking your rules, and I thank you."

She murmured so softly he could scarcely hear her above the rush of the wind. "It was one of the Prophets—in the Old Testament, I mean—who said that only the strong can afford to be generous."

Obvious flattery usually antagonized him, but he was pleased. Locking the operating levers with slow, deliberate care, he opened the door and stepped out onto the platform. "Stay there until I tell you." His control reasserted, he stepped out into the world he loved.

The full moon had risen high overhead, lighting the city and turning the Hudson and East rivers into bright ribbons. Tiny, moving lights blinked far below in the theatrical district's late-evening jam, and a few cars moved on Fifth Avenue, in Central Park and on the drives that bounded Manhattan on the west and east. Wall Street, to the south, was dark and deserted, its towers showing no lights, the cliffs of the Palisades across the Hudson showed faintly, and several large ships were anchored at their berths.

The camera and recorder were operating again, and, when he beckoned, Lance slowly backed out of the cage. Bobbie and Gerry followed, hand in hand, probably because the young actor feared the height, and both gazed in silence at the city spread out below them.

Max had known others who had reacted in the same way. No matter how familiar they might be with New York, the view from the top of an uncompleted skyscraper was far more immediate and compelling than that enjoyed by a casual visitor to the Rainbow Room at the top of the RCA Building or the observation roof of the Empire State Building. Only here was it possible to feel the full impact of the great towers and canyons that had been made by man, and Max gloried in the quiet knowledge that he had contributed his share to the architectural wonder of New York.

Lance halted obediently at the spot Max designated, the girl and the actor sat down a short distance from him, and he trained the camera on their faces, then swept the horizons with it so his audience could see through their eyes.

All three were subdued, and Max was relieved. It was too late now to blame himself for the evening, and he salvaged what he could, in his own way. No one but a builder could share his elation, his sense of well-being, and, although he remained alert, he put the trio out of the forefront of his mind.

Moving away, he gazed down at the ships lying at their berths in the Hudson, and without difficulty recognized the long, trim S.S. *France*. Memories of the voyages he had made with Stella on the ship engulfed him, but he made an effort to shake them off. It was ridiculous to wallow in the sentiment of a past that was ended, and he told himself, harshly, that he was young enough to enjoy the future provided he put Stella out of his mind.

Catching sight of a slight movement, he turned to see Bobbie Wayne and the actor locked in an embrace, stretching out on the hard planks of the platform. Gerry was stripped to the waist, and the girl, running a hand over his torso, seemed to be in command. She had a quality that excited him, Max thought, but was too aggressive for his taste. However, she might be more malleably feminine if the right man made love to her. The notion was intriguing.

Another reel of film went into the camera as they kissed, and Max shook his head. It became boring, after a time, to watch a static kiss, and from what he had so far seen of underground movie-making, an audience could easily be bored to death. A single embrace could sometimes last as long as five minutes, with neither partner stirring, but Lance made no demands. He allowed the couple to remain passive and permitted his camera to run on, only occasionally shifting his angle as he focused on them.

They themselves eventually became cramped, sat up and stretched. Bobbie started to straighten a sleeve of her dress that had become twisted, and Gerry, on impulse, reached behind her and pulled down her neck-high zipper. She made no attempt to fend him off as he hauled down the dress, stripping her to the waist, but she did not help him, either.

As Max had suspected, she was wearing no brassiere. Her breasts were small but perfectly formed, and were firm, high and pointed. She showed no sign of embarrassment, and actually looked a trifle bored as the camera concentrated on her body.

"I'd love a cigarette," she said as Lance moved his camera higher, lower and from one side to the other, shooting her bare breasts from every conceivable angle. "Oh, I'm sorry. I forgot." She showed emotion for the first time as she glanced apologetically at Max.

Remembering Muriel, he wondered if all of Balutis' female friends were completely lacking in morality.

"You had a real gas in the elevator," Gerry said to the girl, a feline smoothness in his voice. "Well, I know your hang-up, so I have my own way of getting even."

Max braced himself, ready to intervene in the event they had forgotten his injunctions.

Gerry's hands moved toward her breasts a fraction of an inch at a time, in an exaggerated form of slow-motion.

Bobbie could have escaped, brushed his hands aside or pulled up her dress again, but she seemed paralyzed, incapable of helping herself or getting away. For an instant an expression of anger appeared in her eyes, but it was replaced by a fleeting eagerness that, in turn, gave way to resignation.

The camera was busy now, the lens pointed at the young man's hands, the girl's breasts and, finally, her face.

Max gaped at the trio, too bewildered to know what he was thinking.

Bobbie's face registered shock as the actor's hands closed over her breasts, and she slowly sank onto her back on the rough boards.

The camera was focused only on her face now, and Lance held it directly above her.

She closed her eyes as Gerry began to fondle her breasts, then opened her eyes again and stared unseeing at the sky overhead when he gently brushed the nipples with his fingertips.

Bobbie was aroused and becoming more agitated, but her arms stayed limply at her sides, even when Gerry laughed. The venomous glee in his voice was startling, but she took no heed.

Suddenly he bent down to kiss her breasts, and she moaned. Occasionally a deep sigh or strangled sound emanated from Bobbie's parted lips, but she did not speak as Gerry stepped up the pace of his delicate love-making. Her desire was evident on her face, and after a long time she started to writhe, finally clutching the actor's head to her breasts.

All at once Lance's voice broke the quiet. "I've run out of film," he said. "Maybe it's just as well. We'll end on an existential note."

Gerry moved away from the girl at once, seemingly unaffected by his love-making.

Bobbie recovered more slowly. Her nipples and breasts swollen, she remained on her back for some moments before dragging herself to a sitting position. Then she energetically rubbed her bare arms before struggling into her dress. "What a tricky little bitch you are," she said.

"I must admit you're right," Gerry said smugly.

Max saw no reason to linger on the platform. Relieved that the film-making had ended, yet still disturbed, he said hoarsely, "Get back into the elevator. We'll go down now."

Lance and Gerry went to the cage at once, but Bobbie lingered, looking around slowly at the city and then the sky. "I envy you," she said. "How marvelous to spend your life up here —like an eagle." She seemed unruffled by the knowledge that Max had witnessed the intimacies to which she had been subjected.

"Once or twice, maybe, I come up to the temporary roof. I spend my life fighting with sub-contractors, dealing with city inspectors all day, making sure everybody stays on schedule. In the summer it's hot, in the winter it's cold."

She had formed her own image, however, and not listening to his protest, bestowed a dazzling smile on him.

He discovered his temples were throbbing as he followed her into the elevator. He glanced at his watch, saw it was almost two o'clock in the morning. He had spent approximately four hours with the unconventional young moviemakers.

"How much of what you took will you use in the final movie?" Max asked as they began the slow descent.

"All of it, naturally," Lance said. "One minute of the film time is the equal of one minute of real time. Once you've combined that principle with the techniques of cinéma-vérité, you can understand what I'm doing."

"Not me," Max said.

Bobbie moved closer to him. "Cinéma-vérité is a type of film-making. The camera is always held on the shoulder or in the hand, and the cameraman moves very quickly from one subject to another. It's a technique that creates a sense of urgency. Your audiences are actually present at the scene."

Her explanation meant nothing to Max, and he didn't care. What he had seen was indecent as well as insufferably dull, and all he really wanted to know was how an aristocratic young woman from Philadelphia could have become involved in such degenerate stupidity.

"It sounds easy," Bobbie said, "and there's so much of it at the film festivals these days that you gag. Even the Czechs and Poles use it all the time. But most directors and photographers lack the sense of balance that makes cinéma-vérité either great or ludicrous, and most of them just bore you. Lance is just fantastic, and not even Andy Warhol has his impact. His understanding of super-reality is so much greater than anyone else's. Dig?"

Max had the uneasy feeling she was secretly laughing at him, but saw that Balutis looked pleased.

"My best press agent," Lance said. "Lover, for that, you get anything you want tonight."

"I need plenty, believe me!" Bobbie was emphatic. "If there's anything I hate it's being abandoned half-way up the mountain."

"If you think I'm going to apologize," Gerry Jarvis said, "you can forget it. An hour of hard work up in the middle of nowhere isn't my idea of a blast, but you girls are all alike, and someone has to put the brakes on you."

Lance's laugh was tolerant. "You'll get what's coming to you, too, lover." He saw Max glowering, and said to him, "They get jittery without a follow-through. Who wouldn't?"

Max merely grunted. He would have believed they were talking for effect had he not seen them in action.

His unresponsiveness turned Lance back to his companions. "If we'd known what it would be like tonight, we might have brought someone else with us. Muriel flips when you just mention our friend here. She'd have loved it."

"Ugh." Bobbie was contemptuous. "I get so sick of the way she expects everybody to swoon when she flaps that fat can."

Gerry's laugh was shrill. "I suppose you prefer Bev."

"Any day, any night," Bobbie said.

Max shut out the sound of their chatter. If Jarvis was a homosexual, which he believed probable, everything he had witnessed was even more obscene than he thought. And Bobbie Wayne, who was unique in his experience with women, was beyond his ability to analyze.

Lance was aware of Max's withdrawal, and when they finally reached the ground, he said, firmly, "Take off your seat belts, children, and run ahead."

Gerry needed no urging to escape from the building site, but Bobbie was in no hurry to obey.

"We'll catch up with you," Lance said. "Wait for us at the door that leads out into the street." He did not speak again until they complied, and then he fell in beside Max, who headed toward the construction trailer. "I'm afraid I've repaid your kindness by subjecting you to all sorts of things you don't dig."

Max looked at a bulldozer nearby, but did not make the obvious retort; weary, out of sorts and feeling unclean, he was in no mood for further conversation.

"The *art* of film-making aside," Lance told him as they went into the trailer, "I'm in a business, just as you are."

"Some business," Max muttered.

"There's none better, provided your key man has the talent. It takes you a year and a half to two years to put up a building like this, right?" Lance paused for no more than an instant, continuing when there was no reply. "I read somewhere that this place is costing fourteen million, and if I remember what I learned in art school—we had to take several courses in architecture, including one in construction financing—the stockholders of your company will show a profit of about two hundred and twenty-five thousand. After taxes and overhead. Provided that everything jells, that you maintain all your schedules, and that the costs of raw materials and labor don't go up more than the fifteen percent margin you've probably allowed."

He was remarkably well informed, Max thought grudgingly.

"Since you probably won't mesh in everything, your actual profit will be about half of the potential. Let's call it one hundred and twenty-five thousand over two years. Still assuming you're lucky as well as efficient. Depending on how many stockholders will share the pie, and on how much of your own time you've got to give to this project, your cut won't be worth staging a parade down Fifth Avenue."

It was none of his business, Max thought, that he expected to earn about fifty thousand from the erection of the building, not including the capital he put back into L & B, and that the enterprise occupied about one tenth to one fifth of his work time.

"I've spent one evening making this film," Lance said. "The preparations took a half-day. What with developing film, putting in an opening, arranging distribution and so forth, let's say the whole thing is wrapped up in a week. Jarvis cost me five hundred, and I'll pay Bobbie her usual thousand, although she'd be happy to work for nothing. Even if I don't hit the commercial theaters, and there's no way of guessing in advance whether I will, this film will bring me ten thousand. Take out the cost of my cast—I won't even add in the price of film and tape—I'll show a profit of eighty-five hundred for a single week's work. How many people do you know who can match that kind of income?" The question was rhetorical and, expecting no answer, he fished a cigarette and gold lighter from a pocket. "I hope to God I can smoke now." Not waiting for an answer, he flicked the lighter.

Max couldn't imagine a market for the senseless vulgarities he had seen, and made no attempt to hide his skepticism. "Suppose you earn as much as you claim," he said, carefully putting away the various keys he had used, "I hope you save your money. You may have to live on it for a long time before you sell another." He didn't care what Balutis earned, but resented the young man's condescending attitude.

"The demand," Lance said gravely, "is unlimited."

Unable to believe anything so preposterous, Max shrugged. Making a last quick check to ensure that nothing was out of place on the desks of his project supervisor, resident engineer and the city inspector assigned to the building, he snapped off the main light.

Lance hovered close beside him as he locked the door and tried it. "I'm giving a screening a week from tonight," he said, "and I hope that you—"

"I'll be busy," Max cut in.

"Too bad." Lance ignored the obvious rebuff. "But I'll set up a private screening for you, any time at all you can make it."

Max skirted a large pile of the special steel tubing used to reinforce concrete. He found it easier to say nothing.

Bobbie Wayne and Gerry Jarvis were waiting inside the door set in the fence, and reached for their own cigarettes when they saw that Lance was smoking.

"I'll say good night to you," Max said stiffly when they reached the street.

"I've got my car right here," Lance said, "and the least I can do is give you a lift. You'll never get a taxi at this hour."

Bobbie did not wait for a response and, linking her arm firmly through Max's, led him toward the white sports car he had first seen in the driveway of his summer house. "We always have a party at my place after a film shooting," she said. "Why don't you come with us?"

"Do you know what time it is?"

"Time is a man-made invention. I wonder how I can tempt you. Food. Booze. Entertainment. Me."

It was possible, Max thought, that she was literally offering herself to him. After what he had seen tonight, nothing would surprise him. "I have a hard day of work ahead of me," he said, his tone unexpectedly gentle.

"Then I won't insist." Bobbie became the complete lady.

They halted at the car, and Lance unlocked it.

Peering at the leather-upholstered interior, Max shook his head. "I don't think you could get the three of you in there, much less me as well."

"Just you watch," Lance said. "Gerry, turn yourself into a jackknife in back. Do as I say," he added sharply as the young actor looked dubious.

Max would have insisted that he find himself a taxi or walk, but Bobbie was clinging to his arm, a sensation he found he enjoyed.

Gerry climbed into the narrow space behind the bucket seats, and Lance, who had gone around to the driver's side, moved behind the wheel. "All for you," he said to Max, patting the other seat.

Max reluctantly entered the car, and no sooner had he seated himself than Bobbie landed on his lap, curling an arm around his neck. At best there was little room, but he knew there was no need for her to press her body so tightly against his, and he became disconcerted when he felt one of her breasts up against him.

Instinctively he tightened his grip on the girl as the car started

87

off and rapidly gained speed in the silent, deserted streets of the city.

Bobbie responded by snuggling still closer and moving back and forth in his lap almost imperceptibly.

She was depraved, Max knew, but so was he. It was a shock to discover that, even with two others in the car, he wanted her.

"Bobbins," Lance said, "our friend here can't make the screening next week, so we'll set up another for him."

"At my place. I insist." She opened a button beneath Max's necktie and slid a hand inside his shirt. "You were so sweet to some nutty brats that I want to be the one who makes with the hospitality bit."

"I'll set it up with him later in the week," Lance said, "and I'll let you know, Bobbins. How does that sound?"

"Lovely," she said softly.

The car pulled to a halt, and, as the girl opened the door and disentangled herself, Max saw they had reached his apartment building.

Lance thanked him, and although Gerry remained sulkily silent, Bobbie more than compensated for his rudeness, giving Max such a warm, prolonged hug that he was relieved the night doorman had temporarily gone off duty.

Rumpled and, in spite of his weariness, physically aroused, he made his way into the building. It had been obvious to him for hours that Bobbie Wayne was an amoral slut, but not until he reached his own apartment did it occur to him that, perhaps, her ministrations had a purpose other than her own sensual pleasure. He had not mentioned his address, yet Balutis had driven to the building, so it was plain that the young moviemaker had gone to the trouble of finding out a great deal about him. It was likely, too, that Balutis had turned the girl loose on him after he had refused to attend the screening of the idiocy he had seen filmed.

Why? What was Lance Balutis' reason for pursuing him? Judging by the movie that he had shot tonight, the background of an uncompleted new skyscraper had been of minor importance; that kind of trash could be shot anywhere. It was obvious that Lance was interested in his money.

He undressed quickly, and made his decisions. He would take Bobbie Wayne to bed, and prove to her that it was dangerous to toy with a real man. And he would make a thorough investigation of Lance Balutis.

David Franklin wearily rubbed the stubble on his chin. "I've had no chance to shave—"

"To hell with shaving." Max rose from his desk, went to the connecting door to his partner's office and opened it. "You better drop whatever you're doing and come in here," he said.

Paul looked up slowly from correspondence he was signing, scowled and then reluctantly came to the other room, his features growing brighter when he saw Franklin. "Dave! This is a nice surprise."

"I expected to be talking to him in London in an hour," Max muttered. "Instead he's here."

"My plane landed at Kennedy less than an hour ago, and I came straight here. We hassled all night, and I caught the nine A.M without going to bed." He fished in a leather envelope briefcase. "Here. I wrote this out while I crossed the Atlantic."

"Tell us in a fifty-word summary," Max said.

"I'll do it in four," Franklin replied grimly. "The deal is off."

Paul sat heavily in a leather chair.

Max's fist crashed on the desk. "Goddammit, I knew it! I had a hunch something would go wrong. What was it, Dave?"

"I thought you might know. The Englishmen turned chilly last night. For hours they kept changing the contractual terms. Everything that had been agreed earlier. Finally they said the deal was off, no matter what terms we met."

"Sabotage," Max muttered.

"I can't say I'm heartbroken." Paul actually looked relieved.

Franklin breathed a little more easily. "Neither am I, really. We'd have been spreading ourselves thin. Too thin."

"That English property is the juiciest I've found in three years," Max said vehemently, "and I'm not going to let it slip away without putting up a fight."

Franklin blinked, fighting his exhaustion. "I'd have stayed on in London, but there was nothing to fight. It was the end of the ball game, and they just took their ball and goalposts—and went home."

"In the long run," Paul said, "this could be the best thing that could have happened. A London hotel is too far from our base of operations to administer as part of a chain. It becomes a separate unit, practically independent."

"That's why I never liked the idea from the start," Franklin declared.

"What's more, with money tight these days, I'd rather not have that heavy a fresh obligation added to the other burdens."

Max was smoldering. "Who says money is tight?"

"Howard Christianson at North Atlantic, for one," his partner told him.

Max grimaced. "Dave, do you have any reason to suspect North Atlantic might have been behind the English walkout?"

"I hate to accuse without proof, but they must have been responsible. One minute London was all set to close the deal, and I know we were the only bidders. No one else was in the picture. The next minute we were out in the cold. Somebody must have been tipped off that North Atlantic might not give us one-hundred-percent backing."

"We'll never know." Paul shrugged.

"Like hell we won't!" Max again pounded the desk. "Carol," he told his secretary, picking up the phone, "get me Christianson. I'll hold. Goddammit, Paul, if North Atlantic doesn't want to support us, let them tell us direct, not the crowd we're dealing with. That's worse than *chutzpah*. It's unethical."

"Easy, Max," Paul said. "You don't actually know that's what happened. You're just guessing."

"I'll find out fast enough. What, Carol? I see, I see." The telephone crashed into its cradle. "I'm right, gentlemen. Christianson isn't in."

The others saw nothing unreasonable in the situation.

But Max became still angrier. "For twenty years we've been dealing with him, and for twenty years he's always in his office after lunch. When he makes outside appointments, they're always in the mornings. You know that's so, Paul."

"Well, yes. But any one of a thousand things could have happened. Just because he's out of his office right now doesn't prove anything."

"He's there," Max said, "and he's trying to duck me. But we'll have a showdown. Immediately." He went to his clothes closet and took out his hat and coat.

"You're not going over to the bank!" Paul was perturbed.

"Where else? I'm calling North Atlantic's bluff."

"I think this is a mistake. We owe them too much to get tough with them."

"We own or control some pretty damn valuable properties, and if North Atlantic wants to cut bait, a dozen other banks, just as big, will jump at the chance to do business with us!" Max struggled into his coat, jammed his hat on his head and stormed out.

He was in such a rage that, as he swept through his secretary's office, he almost bowled over Stella Ross, who was coming in the opposite direction. As it was, he jarred her, and a folder she was carrying fell to the floor.

Max immediately became contrite, stooped and picked up the folder, which he handed to her with a stiff, old-fashioned bow. "In a million years you wouldn't believe this," he said with a tight smile, "But I didn't bump into you on purpose. As much as I've been tempted, I've never yet hit a woman." He turned on his heels and was gone.

Stella looked after him in bewilderment.

Paul stood in the entrance to his partner's office, silently beckoning to her, and meanwhile Franklin, to avoid embarrassment, went into Paul's office, closing the door behind him.

"What's that all about?" Stella wanted to know when she and Paul were alone.

He told her, briefly, what had happened.

She handed him the folder. "This says the same thing. It's my monthly analysis of the corporate financial situation. We're overextended, and I recommend that we sit tight for a few months. We might even be wise to consolidate some of our holdings and reduce our indebtedness by about ten million. But that's a decision for management to make, not me."

"It's what I'd like to do," Paul said, "but without you to help me persuade Max, he won't retreat. He's always insisted we bull through our crises, and each time we've come out stronger."

"But there's never been a situation like this one," Stella said. "It makes common sense to retract for six months to a year. He can resume the expansion program again when the gold dust settles."

"You tell him, Stella."

"It's all in here." She tapped the folder, which he still held.

"Reading it won't be enough."

"There isn't a chance he'll listen to me, Paul," she said wistfully. "We're barely on speaking terms, and he'd think I was attacking his masculinity if I urged him to adopt a more cautious policy. I can't speak to him as frankly as I once did."

"Speaking from the company's point of view," Paul said, "I can't help wishing you hadn't broken up with Max."

Howard Christianson's office on the second floor of the North Atlantic Bank and Trust Company was as impersonal and remote as the bank's senior vice-president himself. His carpets and drapes were neutral, and his furniture, although expensive, looked as though it had come from one of the sitting rooms in a conservative men's club. There were no photographs or other personal mementos on his desk, and even the paintings on the wall were antiseptic, slightly washed out examples of still life at its most drab.

Christianson himself was unruffled as he regarded his angry visitor. "You can hardly expect me to admit I was trying to avoid you, Max."

"Okay, don't." Max had thrown his hat onto a chair, but still wore his coat. "If I was trying to shovel dirt onto an old and valuable client, I might be too embarrassed to talk to him, too. That isn't important. What I want to know is how much of a hand North Atlantic played in the pullout of the English crowd. And don't deny you know the deal is off. It's no surprise to you."

Christianson meticulously polished his glasses. "We give the head of our London office a free operational hand, as we do with all of our major branch vice-presidents. We set policies, and the branch head implements them as he sees fit."

"Let's get down to brass tacks," Max said grimly.

"Foster in London knew that we're reviewing our whole relationship with L & B, and that we haven't as yet reached a final decision whether to extend additional credit or establish a cut-off point. So, under the circumstances, he didn't feel justified in granting as much credit as your projected hotel purchase there would have required."

"Then I'm right. North Atlantic did pull the rug out from under us."

"The sensible thing to do," Christianson said, ignoring the immediate issue, "will be for you and Paul, with your lawyers, of course, to sit down with our credit committee and me for an over-all review. We'll need a number of meetings to make a thorough survey, but at the end we should know—all of us—

93

where we're headed. Your piecemeal acquisitions are going to get us into trouble if you keep snatching up properties in a haphazard way, Max."

Curbing his anger, Max realized the situation was becoming too serious to be solved by an explosion. "Sure, we'll talk," he said. "I'll sit down with you and the bloodsuckers on your credit committee as often as you like. But one thing I can promise you, Howard. North Atlantic approval or no North Atlantic approval, L & B isn't going to sit still."

"That can be dangerous."

"I hate veiled warnings," Max said. "Lay it on the line, Howard."

"Even on the L & B level, there can be no such thing as unlimited credit."

"We have enough collateral. And you know our system. When it's necessary, we sell a property so we can have working capital to buy a better one."

"Exactly. You're at the mercy of the sellers' market," Christianson said.

Max gestured impatiently. "We rode out recessions when we were much smaller."

"The larger you become, the more complex your position becomes. And I'm not necessarily thinking in terms of a recession, Max. Potential buyers don't line up in the street for properties worth anywhere from five to twenty million. If one of your trades fails to come off—"

"It hasn't happened yet!"

"But, if it should, L & B could collapse. I'm not trying to frighten you, Max, but you've got to be alert to at least the possibility that you might face bankruptcy."

Janet Lafferty came to the door when Max rang the buzzer, and, as always, he was struck by her appearance of extreme youth. Although she was twenty-one, the long, brown hair that streamed down her back, the absence of any cosmetics except pale lipstick and the simplicity of her attire, a loose-fitting sweater and faded jeans that had been stuffed into boots, made her look much younger. Or, perhaps, it was the clean-cut innocence he saw in her face that made it difficult for him to realize she was more than fifteen.

"Uncle Max!" she cried as they embraced. "I've been wondering when I was going to see you."

He kissed her lightly on the cheek. "When did you get home, Jan?"

"This afternoon. I'm here for a week, and then I go back for graduation."

"I'll be there, and before then we'll have to discuss what you'd like for a graduation present."

"I don't want a thing."

"Since when do I have to listen to such foolishness?" he demanded severely. "We'll talk later, privately, and if you're coy, I'll really buy you something useless."

"And expensive. You shouldn't spoil me, Uncle Max."

"There's nobody I'd rather spoil. Are your parents home? I— uh—was reading, and all of a sudden I felt like a little company."

"Of course," she said, "come in."

She led him to the sunken, high-ceilinged living room, with picture windows that provided a fine view of the city at its most sparkling. Paul and Margaret Lafferty rose at once to greet him.

Max stiffened when he saw Stella Ross sitting on a divan, near the after-dinner coffee service.

Margaret Lafferty was a sufficiently accomplished hostess to bridge the awkward moment swiftly and smoothly. Extending both hands to Max, she kissed him. "I'm so glad you dropped in. We were just talking about you."

"I can imagine." He glanced at Stella, and nodded stiffly. "I didn't know I was interrupting something. I'll come back another evening."

"Don't make an issue out of nothing," Paul said. "Sit down and I'll get you a glass of *schnapps.*"

"Hello, Max." Stella seemed remarkably calm. "Please don't run away on my account. I won't bite."

Janet stepped into the breach. "I've brought most of my paintings home from school, and if you're very good, Uncle Max, I'll show them to you."

Max thought it better to give in as gracefully as he could rather than create an even more awkward situation by leaving. "To see your paintings, Jan, I'll stay. How many honors are you walking away with at graduation?" He looked at no one else as he lowered himself into the chair that Margaret always said she had bought for his exclusive use.

"No *cum laude,* Uncle Max." Janet brushed back a strand of her long hair. "Universities are very stuffy these days, and they won't give you honors unless you keep up an average. Which I couldn't do in political science and calculus and all sorts of horrid courses."

"But she's won the prize for portrait painting," her mother said proudly.

"A gold medal," her father added.

"A certificate, Daddy!"

"—and one thousand dollars in cash," Paul continued.

Max was delighted. "From the time you were in kindergarten, when we were all living up in the Bronx, you could draw better than any child I ever saw. I'll match the thousand for graduation, and that'll give you a start setting up the studio you've wanted."

Janet and her parents simultaneously protested.

Stella unexpectedly entered the conversation. "Let him," she said. "He thinks as much of Jan as he would of his own child."

All three members of the Lafferty family were momentarily silenced.

"Here's your *schnapps,*" Paul said gruffly. "It's a new brand from Holland I thought you could try. Young Paul bought it for me. As a gesture, I assume, that he still loves us even though he never seems to be around any more."

"Coffee, Max?" Margaret sat poised over the silver pot, ignoring her husband's remark.

"I wish I could, Maggie. I've tried it again the last few nights, but it makes sleeping more impossible than ever."

For an instant a flicker of concern appeared in Stella's eyes, but it vanished again before Max could be certain he had seen it.

"Here's to you, Jan, and to the most successful portrait painter of the younger generation," Max said.

Her father lifted a snifter of brandy, while Margaret and Stella raised their coffee cups.

The girl suddenly showed her immaturity. "I wish I were a tenth as good as all of you think."

"Jan," Stella said earnestly, "the day isn't far off when I'll be bragging to all my friends that I've known you. For years."

"Stop," Janet said. "I get so nervous about what I hope to do that I feel queasy when anybody even mentions it."

Max spoke when he realized how uncomfortable Janet had become as the unexpected center of attention. "Were the steel support struts delivered this afternoon, Paul? I forgot to ask you before we left the office."

"Yes," his partner declared, grinning because his wife had glared at them. "But you remember Margaret's rule about talking business in any room here except my study."

Max tried his best to look apologetic. The women picked up the slack, and resumed an earlier discussion of the clothes they intended to wear to Janet's graduation ceremony.

Max sipped his *schnapps* very slowly. His insides were churning. It was torture to refrain from looking at Stella, who was wearing a two-piece dress of thin, blue wool he didn't remember seeing before. It matched her eyes.

At last the women stopped talking, and Max turned back to Janet. "Jan," he said, "have you ever heard of a crazy man named Lance Balutis?"

Janet exchanged an amused glance with Stella. "Who hasn't heard of him? Why do you ask?"

"Until a few days ago, I didn't know who he was, which shows you what a no-good, uneducated bum I am." Max briefly told the girl the story of the making of the underground film on the uncompleted skyscraper structure. Then he reached into an inner jacket pocket and took out what looked like a gold cigar case on one side and a leather wallet on the other. He handed it to her.

"He designs this himself," Janet said. "I was reading not long ago about all kinds of things Balutis designs." She opened the flat side and saw the inscription, *To Max, my partner in crime.*

In appreciation, Lance. "Isn't this gorgeous." She passed it to her father, who sat closest to her on her other side.

"I just got it late this afternoon," Max said, refraining from mentioning that it had been delivered by the girl with the large and provocative rear end, Muriel, and that it hadn't been easy to get rid of her.

"The guy looks like the worst kind of nut from the one glimpse I had of him," Paul said, "but he must be loaded. This is eighteen-karat gold."

"He's loaded," Stella said.

"No artist in the country, practically, is making more than he does," Janet declared in almost the same breath.

Margaret looked at the case briefly. "Lovely."

Stella took it from her and inspected it with care, running a fingernail over the chased surface of the flat side, studying the inscription and, finally, opening the wallet to run a finger over the pliable sealskin lining. A card fluttered onto the divan beside her, and, picking it up, she glanced at it surreptitiously, trying to satisfy both her curiosity and her idea of propriety.

Max felt a small surge of pleasure, hoping the card would make her jealous. "Read it," he urged. "I've got no secrets."

Stella complied. "It says, 'I hope you'll come up for a little celebration Friday evening. See the film or not, as you please, but *I* hope to see *you*.' It's signed Bobbie Wayne."

Paul and Margaret looked blank. Janet, who recognized the name at once, added for her parents' benefit, "She's a glamour girl model who stars in Balutis' movies. May I?" She took the card and inspected it. "Well, she lives in the East Seventies, Stella, only a block or so from you."

"It won't make me move out of the neighborhood."

Max was sure she felt a pang or two. "Jan," he said, suddenly inspired, "since you know so much about all these hotshots, maybe you'd like to come to the party with me."

"I'd love it, Uncle Max!"

Stella laughed quietly.

Max raised an eyebrow. "Was that funny?"

"I haven't heard anyone say 'hotshot' in years. Your slang is dated, that's all," she said.

Remembering what Max had told him about the making of the film, Paul felt uneasy. "I'm not sure a party with those people is suitable for you, Jan," he said.

"I've been away at school for four years, Daddy!" the girl flared. "And I'll bet I've seen more than you—"

"Don't upset your father, dear," Margaret murmured.

"Relax, Paul, and have another brandy," Max said, suddenly feeling expansive. "Maybe some of Balutis' friends aren't our kind, but Jan will be as safe with them as she is right here. She'll be with me, so what could happen to her?"

The apartment building in the East Seventies had been built to last, and was solidly, expensively impressive. Max looked at the uniformed elevator operator, at the antiqued gold walls of the cage that was carrying them to the penthouse, and then glanced at Janet, raising an eyebrow. He hadn't known how Bobbie Wayne lived, but he certainly hadn't expected to find her in such splendor.

Janet nervously touched her false eyelashes to make sure they were in place. She tried to look relaxed and at ease but she was too apprehensive to be conscious of anything but herself. And she didn't hear anything Max was saying to her.

They emerged into a small foyer, decorated with a tapestry that filled the wall, a monk's refectory table and a pair of carved wooden benches. The uproar emanating from the apartment on their right indicated the scene of the party, and Max pressed the button beside a gold nameplate that said, "Wayne."

Chimes sounded inside the door, but the noise was so great that, apparently, no one heard him ring. He tried a second time, then a third, and was about to give up when the door suddenly opened, revealing a man in his early forties, with shaggy hair, dressed in pale-green silk shantung jacket and matching trousers, shoes and shirt, with a large, contrasting ascot in pink.

"Welcome to the pseudo-revels, dear friends," he said, bowing them in with an exaggerated gesture.

Max thought he had been prepared for virtually any reception, but hesitated. It was obvious that the strangely attired man, although in control of himself, had consumed large quantities of liquor.

"Don't be bashful, dear friends. Benjamin Harrison Henry, at your service whenever you need me." Turning away vaguely, the man wandered off into the inner reaches of the apartment.

Janet hugged Max's arm in excitement. "Do you know who he is?"

"Some drunken fag," he answered.

"He owns the Benjamin Harrison Henry Galleries on Fifty-seventh Street, Uncle Max! He's the king. Once or twice a year he puts on a one-man show for somebody new, and just like that, the somebody becomes famous overnight."

"Why?"

"Because he's had a show at the Henry Galleries!" Impatient, Janet tugged at him. "Let's go in. This is even better than I'd hoped."

Max sighed and followed her into a drawing room, furnished in conventional, very expensive Louis XV, that was jammed with chatting people from one end of its thirty-five-foot length to the other. All were drinking and smoking; all seemed to be talking simultaneously in loud voices, and the din was overwhelming.

Pausing with his partner's daughter to take stock, Max was surprised to see that at least half were conventionally dressed, the women without exception wearing the latest styles. Mixing with them, apparently on terms of easy familiarity, were long-haired people of both sexes, some young and others considerably less young, as well as a few girls with very short hair. Miniskirts were shockingly short, bell-bottom pants and maxiskirts reached the floor, and the varieties of boots, belts and heavy necklaces seemed endless.

No one paid any attention to the new arrivals until Max heard heard a shout and was enveloped in a bear hug. "Maxie!"

Almost gagging on the scent of strong cologne, Max extricated himself from the surprisingly strong grasp of Lance Balutis, whose sweatshirt and pants looked like a basketball player's warm-up uniform.

"You just missed a showing of the film in the library," Lance said, "but I'll run it for you again, a little later, when the rest of the crowd gets here."

"Don't rush," Max said. Then, as an afterthought, he reluctantly presented Balutis to Janet.

Lance managed to take in every detail of her appearance at a glance. Janet was flustered, but put up a brave, sophisticated front.

"Get these people a drink!" Lance snapped his fingers under the nose of a man in a tailor-made suit. "Bourbon and water for the gentleman, and the young lady looks like vodka and tonic to me."

"How did you guess?" Janet asked with a smile.

"I'm a genius, honey." His smile was genuine, too.

Max realized Janet was old enough to drink but wished he had cautioned her to be careful.

"Lance, darling!" A redhaired woman in her thirties was waving frantically from the far side of the room.

She was handsome, Max thought, but her attire was too freakish and young for her age. Boots and very short miniskirts belonged on girls like Janet—if anyone. A mature woman approaching forty looked like somebody dressing up in the clothes of her daughter.

Granted that he knew virtually nothing about women's styles, so it was possible he was completely mistaken in his belief. But, he thought, he couldn't help being influenced by the relative conservatism of Stella's dress. She was only a few years younger than this redhead with the heavily made up eyes, yet she had infinitely more dignity.

It was wrong to compare every woman he saw or met with Stella, and he realized he was making himself miserable again, deliberately miserable. With a great effort he put Stella out of his mind and tried to concentrate on the redhead. She had sex appeal, to be sure, and he supposed someone might find her attractive. In fact, most men might be drawn to her. He just didn't happen to feel that way. She wasn't his type—or something.

Unfortunately, no one but Stella was his type.

"Lance!" Sandra Tilstrom waved again.

Lance glanced around, and muttering something under his breath, appeared to wince as he returned the woman's wave. Then, slowly and with obvious design, he turned his back to her and again devoted his full attention to Janet and Max.

The woman, Max noted, was annoyed, and promptly left the room.

"Bobbie is around somewhere," Lance said. "She'll suddenly appear in front of us as soon as she finds out you're here."

Max looked up at a painting over the broad hearth, a portrait of a stern-faced old gentleman in turn-of-the-century attire who seemed to be glaring at the crowd beneath him. "I'm surprised," he said, "that she lives in a place like this. Somehow I got the idea that she has an apartment downtown."

"She does." Lance grinned amiably. "This is the co-op she and her mother jointly inherited from her grandmother. Bobbins can't bear the place, but we find it convenient whenever we put on a big bash like this."

The man reappeared with two drinks, and Lance, taking the newcomers by the arms, piloted them around the drawing room, introducing them in a haphazard fashion to anyone who came within shouting distance, then suddenly darted away.

Max and Janet found themselves standing with two conservatively dressed attractive men. The younger of the pair, subtly

103

effeminate, kept repeating, "I know I'm stubborn, but I have a Jackson Pollock hang-up. What artist of today has made art nearly as great as his greatest paintings? No one." He, it developed, was an art critic who wrote for magazines.

The older man, who mumbled in a deep monotone, was a newspaper art critic, and from the little Max could hear of his long diatribe, he was attacking present-day Abstract Expressionist painters, yet saying at the same time that they alone could save watercolors from extinction.

Totally lost, Max shifted his weight from one foot to the other for a quarter of an hour. Someone handed him a fresh glass, and he saw that Janet took another drink, too. "Let's look around," he suggested to her, and breathed a sigh of relief when they moved away.

"If anybody had told me a week ago that I'd be talking with Yates and McIntyre, I wouldn't have believed it!" Janet looked radiant.

"They're that important?"

"They make and break reputations, Uncle Max."

He guided her through the crowd toward a terrace, where he hoped they might get a breath of air. "I couldn't understand anything the old one was saying."

She giggled. "I understood what I could hear. Which wasn't much."

They moved out to the terrace, where a high hedge cut off the view. Two small table lamps provided a dim light, and several couples were dancing—shaking their bodies to the deafening beat of a psychedelic rock group. Max looked at the young musicians. They were outrageously dressed in wild-colored flowered shirts, striped pants, beads and bells, and Cavalier-like feathered hats. The leader wore tight black leather pants, and was naked from the hips up except for a large wood-and-metal primitive symbol that hung from a leather strap around his neck; he was singing a song of trial by fire. Max would have judged the theme inappropriate for dancing, but he was too stunned to feel capable of judging anyone at the gathering.

The sight of a bench in the shadows at the far side of the terrace reminded him that his feet ached, and, suggesting to Janet that they sit for a few minutes, he started toward it. When he drew near, however, the sight of a couple in a violent embrace halted him.

Before he could withdraw they parted.

The embarrassed Max was dismayed when he recognized Muriel, and was horrified when he realized her shirt-sleeved companion was another girl.

"Darling!" Muriel jumped to her feet. "I waited and waited when I heard you'd be here, but I gave you up for lost!" She took a tentative, drunken step forward. "Let's go find ourselves some privacy. Bev here," she added, indicating her companion, "will entertain your little friend."

Max muttered something and retreated rapidly, dragging Janet with him.

She freed herself from his tight grasp and looked at him with amusement. "Apparently you do get around, Uncle Max."

"I'd like to get out of here." But instead they reentered the apartment and he realized they had come in through the wrong door.

They found themselves in a handsome library, its walls lined with sets of leather-bound books, and the atmosphere offered a startling contrast to the mood elsewhere. Perhaps a dozen people were sitting in the room, several of them on the floor, and all were remarkably subdued. They spoke softly, with long pauses between brief snatches of conversation, and no one even glanced at the new arrivals.

Max's discomfort increased, and rather than risk seeing Muriel on the terrace again, he led Janet to a far door, which opened onto the dining room, where an overflow crowd from the drawing room chattered and posed.

"Well," Janet said when they closed the library door behind them. "Wasn't that something?"

"Was it?"

She laughed. "I'm not sure which of us is the chaperon tonight, Uncle Max. Didn't you realize that that was a pot party? Oh, you're really such an innocent."

"I realized. I'm afraid it left me unimpressed. Have you ever tried it?"

"I've done some growing up in these past four years," Janet said. "I've smoked a couple of times and I have a lot of friends who turn on all the time. But I didn't particularly like it, so I don't do it. It's that simple."

"Your own thing?" Max suddenly looked adorable, Janet thought, and she bent over to kiss him.

She and her generation were incomprehensible to Max, but he didn't find that a matter of great concern. He enjoyed young people. He liked youth, as a quality in itself. What it stood for in any generation was a matter of philosophy. And Max didn't care much for philosophical debate. Max's own philosophy, however, was a subject he was always happy to discuss. He had a firm grasp on it; it was easy for him to define. If you asked him what he stood for, Max would tell you, smilingly, "I'm an old-fashioned man of the world."

"Take it easy with the booze, Jan," Max warned. Paul and Margaret would never forgive him if she was tipsy when he brought her home.

She darted away from him to peer in fascination at a painting on the dining room wall. "This is a Watteau, Uncle Max," she breathed when he joined her. "An original."

He saw a portrait of a plump, pretty woman preparing for her bath. The painting pleased him, and he said so to Janet.

Suddenly she moved to another in a gilt frame, a portrait of a woman with a low-necked gown, wearing an elaborate hairdo and feathered hat. "And this one. A Renoir! And nobody here notices them or cares about them!"

106

"I do." Lance Balutis materialized beside her. "I saw your expression when you walked up to the Watteau, and wished I'd been carrying my camera."

Janet was ill at ease, but made an effort. "Do you really like these, Mr. Balutis? I mean, your own work—"

"Lance to you, Janet. And what I do doesn't make me incapable of appreciating the brilliance of an earlier period, does it?"

"Certainly not, but I'm surprised to hear you say it."

"You've probably been reading some of the publicity that's put out about me. Don't believe it. You know something about art, I take it."

"Well. I've been studying—"

"I thought so." Lance lowered his voice slightly, although Max could still hear him. "I'll tell you something. If an artist is going to be any damn good, he's got to study and understand and appreciate everyone who went before him. Manet. Rembrandt. All the old masters. Right back through the medieval artists who painted on wood to the cave dwellers who drew with chalk and a stone chisel."

Janet looked at him in open, obvious admiration.

Lance turned to Max. "Bobbie was searching for you in the living room a second or two ago. She wants to say hello to you."

Max nodded, and waited for Janet to join him.

"I'll look after Janet," Lance said. "Go ahead."

Max started to protest.

"This is an apartment, not a den of iniquity," Lance said, "and some of us aren't totally depraved, you know."

Janet felt humiliated. "You don't have to hold my hand, Uncle Max. I've managed to survive rather nicely these past few years, you know."

Realizing he had been too obvious in his attempts to protect her, Max couldn't blame her for bridling. It wasn't easy for him to remember that she was no longer a child. "I'm glad you found somebody you can talk to about art, Jan," he said.

Forcing a smile, he began to move through the crowd to search for his hostess.

Bobbie was standing on the far side of the drawing room, a glass raised to her lips, and he saw her at once, even though twenty to thirty people stood between them. Of all the attractive, imaginatively dressed women present, Bobbie Wayne was by far the most spectacular, and Max gaped at her, admiring her courage if not her taste.

She was wearing a low-cut, cloth-of-silver brassiere that resembled a bathing suit top, and, beneath a bare midriff, a floor-length skirt of the same material.

Bobbie waved to him and drained her drink, grabbing another from a tray as she came toward him. It occurred to Max that her eyelids and fingernails were painted silver, too, and when he caught a glimpse of her feet it amused him that her open sandals and toenails were silver.

"I'm devastated," she called to him. "You've been here at least forty-five minutes, and you haven't said hello to me."

"I've been looking for you," he replied, irritated by his own defensiveness.

"You can make up for it now." Bobbie curled her arms around his neck, spilling a little of her drink onto the carpet, and, pressing close to him, kissed him full on the mouth. When her lips parted, Max responded automatically, instinctively, before trying to withdraw.

Bobbie, however, had no intention of allowing him to escape. Holding one hand at the back of his head to prevent him from moving it, she rubbed against him, blithely unmindful of the people standing less than an arm's length away.

"The sample was pretty good," she said.

"This is quite a party."

"The usual freeloaders. I'd intended to give a quiet little bash at my own place downtown, but the list grew and grew. This is what usually happens when we have a showing of one of Lance's new films. You should have heard them, darling! They were ecstatic, all of them."

The guests, Max thought, even those who looked intelligent and sensible, obviously didn't care what sort of rubbish they watched on a screen. "I'm no judge of movies," he said.

"Mama will be your teacher, and you'll be astonished how much you'll learn." Bobbie's expression indicated that he could interpret her words as he pleased, and that, in any event, she was referring to matters more significant than a film.

Max became uncomfortable when a woman consistently played the role of the aggressor. "Maybe I'm happy the way I am."

"You'll change—when you find out how much you're missing." She seemed to be laughing.

Her trouble, he thought, was that she was too attractive, too rich and too sure of herself. Men, many of them, had been buzzing around her for a long time, and she took their attentions for granted. What she needed, perhaps, was a cuff across the side of the head from someone who would take her firmly, almost brutally, without catering to her whims. On the other hand, it was possible she would relish just that sort of relationship.

Unable to fathom her, he could only tell himself she was unlike any other woman he had ever known. Why, then, was he drawn to her? He had been celibate ever since he and Stella had parted, but Bobbie seemed to be making herself available, which was, in itself, a more than adequate reason for his feelings.

Watching her as a newly arrived couple came up to greet her, he noted, without surprise, that she permitted familiarities from both without showing even the faintest sign of distaste. In fact, she seemed indifferent to the embrace of the man, almost unaware of it, but smiled with what appeared to be genuine pleasure when the woman slid an arm around her bare waist, squeezed her tightly and, before releasing her, caressed her bottom. If her abandonment—the total disregard for conventional morality that she had displayed in varying degrees on the two occasions he had seen her—were responsible for his fascination, he would be wise to keep his distance from her.

As a younger man, when he had bought his pleasures, he had been on safe ground, always knowing where he stood with a professional prostitute. But it was bewildering to find the same attitudes, at least on the surface, in a girl of obvious breeding and wealth. An affair with her was a temptation. But beyond the temptation Max sensed bewilderment for which, at the moment, he felt totally unprepared.

"Shame on you," she teased. "You put up huge new buildings—with your bare hands, don't you?—but you can't even match me drink for drink."

Max refused to rise to the bait. "What are you drinking?"

"One-hundred-proof vodka with a chunk of ice in it." She raised her glass, then drained it. "It's what I always drink at my own parties, except when there's champagne, and that's something I wouldn't serve to all these thirsty hyenas. Now let's go someplace where we can talk. It's impossible in here."

"I've got to leave soon. The young lady I brought with me is my partner's daughter, and I've got to get her home."

"I saw her. Very pretty. Does she have a curfew, for God's sake?"

"No."

"Then don't fuss like an old hen. You don't look like an old hen." She looked up at him, her face close to his. "You have a strong face, Max. I think you must be a very virile man."

"I think you'd be good for the virility of any man," Max said.

"Darling, what a sweet remark. Thank goodness you're not hopeless after all. Listen, I really do want to have a talk with you. It's more important than you know. Has Lance spoken to you yet?"

He shook his head. "What about?"

"Not in front of this mob of eavesdroppers." Bobbie surveyed the room. "Come with me."

Moving through the crowd with Bobbie, Max saw Janet, still with Lance. They were talking animatedly. Janet was enjoying herself, and Balutis was behaving like a gentleman, so there was no immediate cause for concern.

"Every time I throw one of these parties, I swear it's the last," Bobbie said. "We'll head down the corridor, and no matter who speaks to us, we won't stop."

She was carrying two filled highball glasses. One, judging from its color, was a double bourbon, and the other appeared to be a very long vodka and ice.

At the end of the corridor, she leaned a shoulder against a door and it opened. "Hold these," she said, handing him the glasses, and took care to lock the door behind them.

Max saw they were in an exceptionally large bedchamber, part of which had been furnished like a sitting room.

"This is where my grandparents slept," she said, "and although I wouldn't have believed it possible, my mother and her brothers are proof they made love occasionally. Quaint, isn't it? I was going to get rid of the furniture and start all over, but I finally decided all this junk is just too campy-precious to throw out."

The four-poster bed was large and solid, and so were the other pieces of furniture. The only modern thing in it was Bobbie.

The girl moved to a chaise longue and dropped onto it, stretching with the sinuous grace of a cat. "Ah, that feels better. Hand me my drink, will you, darling? And get me a cigarette from the box on the table over there."

Max silently obeyed, thinking himself ridiculous for waiting on someone young enough to be his daughter.

"The worst of these parties is that my feet get tired." She accepted the cigarette from him and sipped her vodka. "That's why I'd have been a failure as a whore. I mean it, darling,"

111

she added when she saw his startled expression. "A couple of years ago I had an enlightening chat with a couple of street-walkers who were at the table next to mine at a sidewalk café in Paris. They told me the worst part of their job was spending so many hours on their feet every day. I just couldn't do it. In six months I'd have varicose veins. Of course the more success-ful French whores are like the German girls. They cruise around town in their cars, looking for pickups. That makes more sense. But the young ones just starting out can't afford cars, and the old bags are usually dead broke. I wish you'd stop standing there, with that disapproving stare. Sit down, darling, and get to work on your drink before the ice melts."

Max lowered himself into the chair opposite her. "I've had enough whisky for one night, thanks," he said.

"Don't tell me you're afraid you'd lose your self-control if you got bombed."

"I'm like anybody else in this world. If I drink too much, I feel it too much. And I don't like being sick the next day."

"I can give you three sure-fire cures for hangovers. They aren't cute little recipes. They really work."

"So does mine. I stay sober."

Bobbie raised herself and rested her weight on an elbow. "You're a coward, Maximilian A. Berman. The reason you won't drink any more is because you're afraid you'll make love to me. Why do I scare you so much? And what does the 'A' stand for?"

"You've already answered your first question. You scare me so much because I am afraid I might make love to you. I'm afraid because I think it might turn out to be a bad idea. For both of us. Number two, the 'A' stands for Adolf. I don't much like the name since it also belonged to a man named Hitler. In case you're not up on Hitler, he killed most of my family."

"Don't be furious with me." Bobbie bounded to her feet, went to him and landed in his lap. "I can be such a bitch. I'm sorry, darling." Holding his head with both hands, she kissed him, first biting his lower lip hard, and then, when he reacted, thrusting an exploring tongue into his mouth. An instant later she was on her feet again, moving back to the chaise. "In spite of all that gruff-bluff, you're very human, Maxie. And I'm going to find out whether my hunch is right."

"What hunch?" He realized too late that he had fallen into a trap.

"That you're a tremendous lay," Bobbie said calmly.

"What was it," he asked brusquely, "that Balutis wanted to talk to me about?"

"I've decided not to go into all that with you. Lance prefers to handle his own affairs in his own way. Let's just say the early crowd flipped over our skyscraper film tonight. Don't even tell Lance I hinted at anything, or I don't know what he might do."

Liquor, their intimate proximity and a sense of restlessness spurred Max. "What could he do to you that he hasn't done already?"

"Touchdown!" Bobbie laughed, started to sit up and suddenly became dissatisfied. "These long skirts," she said, "can be a real pain in the ass." She fiddled for a moment with snaps and buttons, and then removed the skirt, which she dropped to the floor.

It was almost too much for Max to look at her, clad now only in a silver bikini.

"It's so friendly and quiet in here that I hate to go back out to those clowns." Bobbie was enjoying herself at his expense. "What'll we do now? I know. We can play word games. In a single sentence and not one syllable more, what's the difference between freak out and cop out? Replies must be written on plain paper, and the contest isn't open to employees of the corporation or their families."

Unable to restrain himself any longer, Max took a long sip of his drink, and went to her.

Bobbie extended her arms full length as he joined her on

113

the chaise, wrapping them around him and pulling him to her. "Don't smear my eye make-up, darling," she murmured. "It takes forever to put on this damn silver gook."

The warmth of her lithe body aroused Max, and he held her tightly while kissing her. With one hand, he began to explore her body. He reached for the hook at the back of her silver bra and when he unfastened it, she lifted her arms, helping him slip the bra off her. Then she lay back and he saw that her stiffened nipples were painted silver. Had his desire not been so intense, he might have laughed.

Together, they rose from the chaise and moved toward the four-poster bed. They tumbled onto it, and Bobbie gasped as Max's hand closed over her small, firm breast. Then, all at once, she went limp.

Max looked at her, stopping his love-making for a moment, convinced she was playing still another teasing game with him. Her eyes were closed and she sprawled motionless on the bed, remaining inert when he touched her again. Finally he realized she was unconscious—she had passed out. He was still fully dressed.

His erotic desire ebbing, Max didn't know whether he was more disgusted with Bobbie or himself. The bourbon he had consumed had given him heartburn, and a nagging worry told him he had neglected Janet for too long. Wearily dragging himself to his feet, he noticed that some of the silver makeup Bobbie had daubed on her breasts had smeared his palm. Angrily, almost viciously, he wiped his hand on the satin spread.

Refusing to glance in the direction of the sleeping girl, he unlocked the door, but took care to close it behind him. Bobbie was at the mercy of any wandering guest, yet he couldn't be concerned. He had an idea that if she awakened and found someone making love to her, it wouldn't much matter who it was.

With no one to blame but himself for having been drawn into

114

that ludicrous and abortive scene, Max stormed down the hall, determined to leave the place at once, even if he had to drag Janet away. He went to the dining room, but she and Balutis were no longer there. His heart sinking, he searched the living room, then the terrace. Strangers merely smiled and either shook their heads or shrugged when he asked if they had seen the couple. Several servants in the uniforms of a catering firm that had provided an elaborate buffet looked blank, and there was no sign of either Janet or Balutis in the library.

Thoroughly frightened, Max steeled himself and went through the entire apartment, looking in each of the bedrooms without bothering to knock. In one room he interrupted a naked couple. Eventually he returned to the master bedroom. Bobbie was still alone, and snoring.

Curbing the panic that welled up in him, Max tried to think clearly, but the combination of liquor and fear was numbing him.

Stella, it occurred to him, lived only a short distance away. Stella, as always, would know what needed to be done, and he felt no hesitation about casting aside his pride. Hurrying to a telephone, he dialed her number, praying she was at home.

The sound of her familiar voice at the other end of the wire made him feel weak inside, and he began to tell her what had happened, speaking so rapidly the words blurred.

"At your age a man has to be careful he doesn't have a heart attack," Stella said. "They're here."

He continued to pour his explanation into the telephone for some moments before the significance of her words began to dawn on him. Then he halted, took a deep breath and demanded abruptly, "Who?"

"Janet and the artist. The movie man." Stella sounded remote and faintly amused.

Asking no questions, Max dropped the telephone into its cradle and bolted for the door. He elbowed his way through the crowd. Someone tried to clutch his arm and he recognized Muriel, but he brushed past her. He hurried to the elevator, where he stood with his finger on the buzzer.

When he reached the street he started to run, but the habit of city dwelling asserted itself, and he slowed to a rapid walk. It was far better to arrive a few moments later than to be stopped and questioned at length by a suspicious patrolman.

Max reached for his key-chain as he entered the apartment building, before remembering he no longer carried a key to Stella's apartment. Angrily he jabbed at the bell beside the mailboxes and when the buzzer sounded, permitting him to open the outer door, he stalked through the lobby to the self-service elevator, his heart pounding and his clammy shirt sticking to his back.

It was anticlimactic to find the apartment door open and to see Stella, Janet and Balutis standing together in the entrance. It was even more disconcerting to find all three smiling.

"Hold the elevator, Max," Lance called. "I'm just leaving."

Feeling more foolish than at any time he could remember, Max kept the elevator door open.

"You're a good kid, Janet," Lance said, "and I hope you'll remember my offer to look at your work. My advice may not be worth much, but I love giving it."

"You're sweet," Janet said, and shook hands with him.

They were being so pleasantly civilized that Max felt like cringing.

Lance turned to Stella and they took one another's measure.

It infuriated Max to see the way Balutis looked at Stella, even though he couldn't blame the man. She was worth a dozen Muriels and Bobbie Waynes, and had probably indicated that she was unattached.

Stella said something, and Max realized she was speaking in Lithuanian.

Balutis smiled, and replied in the same tongue. Then, grinning, he came to the elevator. "Thanks, Max, I'll do the same

116

for you some time." He lowered his voice and still grinning, asked, "How'd you make out with Bobbie?"

"If you're going back to the party, you'd better look after her. She knocked herself out cold with all that vodka she was drinking."

Lance groaned. "I might have known. Now I'll have to be both host and hostess. God damn." Before the elevator door closed he managed to become more cheerful, however, and shouted, "I'll call you this week!"

Max made no reply, and, walking grimly into the apartment, saw Stella and Janet exchange the swift, inscrutable glances that were a major method of feminine communication in the presence of men. He saw that his photograph no longer graced the table between the two windows at the far side of the room, and he became even more upset.

"You gave me the scare of my life, Jan," he said, looking accusingly at the girl. "I looked all over for you. How was I to know you'd left the party?"

"*You* were scared," Stella cut in, motioning him to a chair. "Tell him what happened, Jan, but first, from the way he looks, I'd better give him a drink."

"The last thing in the world I want is a drink." Max moved to the chair that had always been his favorite.

"You don't want a drink, it's too late at night for you to have coffee. So that leaves tea." Stella quickly went to the small kitchen which adjoined her living room, leaving the door open so she could hear the conversation.

"I'm sorry, Uncle Max," Janet said. "But things just—well, sort of happened."

"What things?"

"Lance doesn't act like a famous person, except when he's talking about art. And does he know it inside and out. The critics who attack him should hear him. He's forgotten more about conventional art than they've ever known—"

"He could be another Leonardo da Vinci for all I care," Max said. "Never mind about the art!"

"Well, that's what we were talking about. For a long time, anyway." Janet, perched on the edge of Stella's small couch, became defensive. "Then, it's like I said. He's just like any other fellow."

"What she means," Stella called from the kitchen, "is that he's what my generation would call a Handy Andy."

Max muttered angrily under his breath.

"You're as bad as Daddy," Janet said, forcing a smile. "A girl expects that sort of thing. Every boy makes passes."

"Balutis isn't a boy."

"All right, every man."

Stella emerged from the kitchen, carrying a steaming cup of tea, which she placed on the table beside Max. "In fact," she said lightly, "we're insulted when they don't make passes. Isn't that so, Jan?"

"Pretty much." Bolstered by the presence of an ally, Janet became less nervous. "He's pretty slick, though, and I realized I was out of my depth. I wanted to find you—" Janet broke off as she glanced at Max, then at Stella, and back at Max again. "He said you were—busy. Anyway, I hardly knew where to look in all that crowd. So I handled him the smart way."

Stella laughed. "A woman's instinct always saves her if she can think fast enough."

Max glared and remained silent, still reserving judgment.

"I told him I wanted him to meet Stella," Janet said. "I told him she works for you and Daddy, and I know he's trying to impress you, or something, Uncle Max. So I laid it on thick. I gave him the idea that she's the secret power behind the throne at the company, and that she makes all the final decisions. I don't honestly know if he was just curious, or if he had other reasons, but he seemed eager to meet her."

"So Jan called me," Stella said, "and they came over from

the party. You took care of a delicate situation very neatly, Jan, and I'm proud of you."

Max sipped his tea, "She's lucky. Suppose you hadn't been home."

"But I was," Stella said firmly.

"It would give me a good feeling," he muttered, "to break that punk in half."

"No, Uncle Max!" Janet was vehement.

"How can you defend him?"

"Because he really was sweet and attentive. Mostly we were just rapping—"

"Just what?" The tea was soothing, but Max hadn't yet become calm.

"Talking. I keep forgetting you and Daddy don't understand the new slang. I certainly don't blame Lance for trying to make out with me, and he's sharp. He got the message when I brought him here, so he won't try it again."

"Until next time." Max inhaled the aroma of the tea before draining his cup. "Except there won't be a next time if I can help it."

"A girl of twenty-one," Stella said, "doesn't need a guardian angel looking over her shoulder and telling her what to do. Especially a guardian angel who disappears at the one time she'd like him to be in the neighborhood."

He winced inwardly, and could make no reply.

Satisfied the blow had landed squarely, Stella softened. "A girl enjoys being acquainted with a celebrity. I'm not saying Lance Balutis will ever call Jan, but if he does, I'd hardly blame her for going out with him."

"Well, I would!" Max insisted. "She's already had a good indication of what he's like."

"I wish you wouldn't be so dense, Uncle Max!" the girl said. "I loved every minute of it! And I don't want you influencing Daddy."

"Why shouldn't I influence him, if I can?" Max wanted to know.

"For more reasons than you can imagine." Apprehension made Janet defiant. "For one thing, I want my own apartment when I come home to stay."

"What's wrong with where you live now? There isn't a better address on the East Side, your father and I put up the building ourselves, and there isn't another in town as solid."

Janet glanced in exasperation at Stella. "I might have known you wouldn't understand, Uncle Max!"

"What is there to understand? It's one thing to be away at college, even to go off to school in England, the way your brother has done. But there's nothing wrong with your parents' apartment. There aren't many girls lucky enough to live in a place that has fourteen rooms."

"Janet doesn't care about that," Stella said quietly. "They aren't her rooms."

The girl indicated her gratitude.

Max would not listen, however. "In a place of your own, you'd be entertaining all kinds of people. Suppose you went back there with a Balutis, instead of bringing him to Stella's, where you'd be safe. Then what would you do?"

"That was a bad example, Uncle Max," Janet said. "Lance isn't a beastie. A word or two, and he'd get the pitch fast enough. Besides, I'm old enough to live my own life—"

"You couldn't do that in your parents' house?"

"—in my own way."

"When I tell Paul about your experience tonight, if I have to tell him, that will settle the hash of any separate apartment. After what Balutis did—"

"Your father will take my word, even if Max doesn't," Stella said, "that Lance Balutis will treat you the way a gentleman should treat a lady. Whenever he sees you."

"You're the great expert?" Max raised an eyebrow. "Since when?"

120

"I know a little something about men," Stella said. "And I happen to understand his type very well."

Max wearily pulled himself to his feet. "This has been quite an evening, Jan. I'll take you home now."

The girl raised no objection. She embraced Stella and expressed her gratitude.

As Max moved toward the door he was struck by the emptiness of his own strange relationship with the woman who had meant so much to him. Only recently both of them would have taken it for granted that she would accompany him when he took Janet home, and then would spend the night at his apartment. Now, instead, there was a wall between them.

"Thank you for the tea," he said stiffly. "It hit the spot."

"You're very welcome." Stella was equally strained.

Max paused with a hand on the doorknob. "I know it isn't any of my business, but what were you and Balutis saying to each other in Lithuanian when he left here?"

Stella's sudden laugh was as hearty as it was genuine. "Many times you've given me advice, even when I didn't want it, right? Well, now it's my turn. Never ask a woman that kind of a question until you've wiped the smears of another woman's lipstick off your face."

"This is the last sub-contractor's bond," Paul Lafferty said, handing an envelope across his partner's desk. "Donovan is short of cash these days, so instead of the usual check he's given us seventy thousand in negotiable bonds."

Max grunted, opened the envelope and leafed through the documents of stiff parchment. "If they're all right with you, I have no complaint. Donovan wants the same securities back, no doubt, after he finishes his installations."

Paul nodded and held out his hand.

"Why take them to the bank?" Max rose and crossed his office. "It's easier to keep them right here in the safe." He bent low and twirled the dials of the heavy steel box set in the wall.

"Sometimes," his partner said, "I wonder why we have safety-deposit boxes in the vault."

The tumblers began clicking into place.

"I even wonder why you don't take all your own stocks and bonds home with you every night and sleep with them under your pillow."

"Go ahead, laugh." The door opened, and Max carefully placed the envelope in a cubbyhole. "I'm putting them in the second row on the left side, at the end." He closed the safe and straightened. "A burglar couldn't get in here any easier than he could break open the bank. Right?"

"I'm not getting involved in the old argument with you, Max. Not again." Paul wandered to the board on which the daily progress sheets in construction schedules were pinned, and examined them for a few moments. "Not bad."

"Damn good. If the heating and air-conditioning people don't let us down, we'll be finished five full weeks ahead of time, with a big bonus for everybody."

"With more than one hundred thousand for you and me. What'll we do with it, Max? Throw it back into the pot, or split it?"

"I hate to count on bonuses until we get them."

"I'm assuming this will work out."

"Then I'd rather leave the decision to you," Max said. "I'm not blowing money these days, but you have family expenses. Strictly on my own, I'd plow the bonus back into the business."

Paul strolled to the window and looked out at the city. "We don't have to decide now. What I have in the back of my mind is whether we bid on the hotel and office building complex in Philadelphia next winter."

"Why not?"

"Because it will tie up all our spare cash."

"Construction challenges don't scare me any more."

"You've been losing interest in construction ever since we

started buying up real estate," Paul said. "I've seen it coming."

"Right now," Max told him, "it's true that I can't work myself into a sweat over Philadelphia." He perched on the edge of the desk and grinned. "What would you say if I told you I've arranged the complete financing for the London deal?"

"Behind North Atlantic's back?"

"It's none of their business, the way I see it. They didn't want any part of the affair, so we're free to go elsewhere for the money."

"I suppose." Paul frowned. "Let's hear the rest."

"I tried a half-dozen places, and our credit is solid everywhere. Boston offered us the money with less red tape—and slightly better terms—so I've reached a tentative agrement with them." Max reached into an inner pocket for some papers, which he handed to his partner. "The law office is going over the duplicates. If they approve, and if you agree with me, Dave Franklin can be on his way back to London tomorrow. It's that simple and easy."

"If you and the law office think the terms are right, I won't fight them," Paul said. "But I'm worried about North Atlantic."

"Are they our keepers?" Max demanded.

"No, our major creditors. Howard Christianson may be a mild-mannered guy, but I don't want to rub him the wrong way."

"Screw him," Max said.

"And give him the excuse to pull the trap door on the seventy million we owe them? We'd have hell's own time trying to scrape up seventy million in a hurry."

"It's been done."

"Not by us. We'd be scraping the bottom of the collateral barrel."

"If we had to," Max said flatly, "we could do it. But it won't come to that, so don't panic, Paul. North Atlantic is in so deep with us they're practically our partners. They're trying to put the squeeze on us right now—"

"Obviously, but why?"

"It seems to me they don't want us to get too big. Another fifty to seventy million in basic assets, and we become too independent. They lose their basic control over us, and it becomes harder for them to protect their loans."

"You always said it was a mistake to rely too heavily on any one bank. North Atlantic controls almost seventy percent of our current indebtedness, according to Stella's latest tally."

"I haven't seen her breakdown, but that's approximately right. Anyway, the Boston loan is a step in the right direction. I'll be happier when we can work North Atlantic down to about forty percent of the over-all indebtedness."

Paul nodded. "This London deal has been your baby all along. I won't stand in your way, Max." Suddenly he chuckled. "Listen to us. A couple of punks who couldn't afford to buy themselves a decent meal twenty-five years ago have the nerve to be throwing around tens of millions. Sometimes I wake up scared in the middle of the night."

"I used to," Max said, "but not any more. Not for a long time. Our roots are firm, Paul, so we won't stretch ourselves too far. Here, if you want a laugh, let me show you something you won't believe, any more than I did."

Paul watched him as he went to the small clothes closet and took something from the inner pocket of his coat.

"This is a real laugh. I think." Max handed him a slip of paper.

Paul Lafferty examined it curiously. "A check for two thousand dollars, made out to you and signed by Lance Balutis. Is this a gag?"

"Apparently not. It came this morning in the mail, and when I telephoned him he insisted it was for me."

"Is it good, Max?"

"I don't know, and I don't care to find out. He says it's my share in the profits—so far—of the movie they made on our superstructure, but I don't like getting involved with him. I

124

agreed to have dinner with him tonight, just to shut him up, and I'm returning the check to him."

Paul was silent for a moment, studying the check before handing it back to his partner. "I think you're crazy to turn this down."

"He and his friends are a dissolute bunch. I've seen just enough of Balutis to know he never does anything without a reason, and when he sends me two thousand dollars in return for nothing at all, I'm afraid there are all kinds of strings tied to this check."

The Maltese Cross was the strangest restaurant Max had ever been to. As he sat at the bar waiting for Lance, he realized that "the Cross," as the regulars called it, was the perfect name for it: this place was some sort of mad coming together of all the disparate elements making up New York's Beautiful Scene.

The Cross was unobtrusive from the outside, sitting on one of New York's most beautiful and most expensive streets, but inside was another world, and upon entering one was struck by a rush of energy coming from the people, the sounds, the art works, the decor. An enormous piece of junk sculpture sat on the floor near one end of the bar. Max looked at the shining mass of battered tin, and wondered to himself how anyone could call this piece of junk "art."

He turned his attention back to his drink. Next to him stood two young men in almost identical tattered brown-leather jackets and faded blue jeans. They both had long, rather messy blond hair, and their fingers and nails showed traces of shiny, bright-colored paint. They looked like some farmer's sons from Nebraska and Max felt certain they didn't live on the Upper East Side. He was right. The Maltese Cross was in fact the only place uptown that the downtown crowd ever bothered to travel up for. What struck Max as even stranger was the presence of the very elegant sexy young woman who stood with them, obviously charmed by their Midwestern manners and earthy dress.

At the same time Max noticed an extremely beautifully gowned woman and an exceptionally well groomed man walk in. Immediately he recognized them—the man was one of the wealthiest and most respected brokers on Wall Street, and both he and his wife were so socially prominent that they didn't even have to go to the "right" places. But here they were.

Max knew that in a million years he never could have dreamed up a restaurant business like this, and that even if he could, he would never have imagined it would be such a fantastic success. Max had to give credit to the proprietor—he was obviously some kind of genius. The Maltese Cross had been open for only a couple of years, but from the beginning was a smash, the place to be. The food was known everywhere for its superb quality and exorbitant prices. It was always crowded, and Max noticed that even in the short time he had been there a unique excitement of the place kept building up.

As he sat for another few minutes watching some of the most gracious and most outrageous people in all the city walk by to the blaring hard-rock sounds from the juke box, Lance arrived impeccably dressed, to Max's astonishment, in a tailor-made suit.

They entered the dining room. It was quite pretty, and, in spite of himself, Max liked it. Tiny little jars of colored flowers sat next to a candle in the middle of each white clothed table. Paintings covered the walls. He recognized a Green Pea painting, and figured it was Lance's. There was a black painting, which Max thought was a joke; a brilliantly colored bull's-eye target on a square canvas, and by this time Max fully imagined someone from the bar might come and shoot an arrow at it; a painting of stripes, which reminded him of the awning at the Country Club; and a large picture of all different glowing colors that seemed to float in and out of the canvas. Max couldn't quite focus on that one, and stood abruptly still for a second looking at it. "So this is today's art?" he shrugged. "Well, it doesn't do anything to me." Lance smiled and led him to the table.

There were no waiters at the Cross—just waitresses, lovely young things dressed in teeny black skirts and matching tops. The two men ordered dinner and began to chat.

Lance played the role of a gentleman to perfection. An entertaining host, he told a number of anecdotes about his boyhood in Indiana, and demonstrated an unsuspected ability to make himself the butt of his own wry humor. Even though he was repeatedly interrupted by brief visits from other diners, he never lost the point of a story, and picked up his narrative smoothly as soon as he and Max were alone again.

Max was fascinated by the stir Balutis created. Most of those who stopped at his table were attractive women, but a number were men of means, and all treated Balutis with friendly respect, apparently accepting him as an equal.

It seemed odd to Max that someone whose art made no sense and whose motives apparently specialized in showing half-clad young people should have acquired status in a moneyed crowd. But he was forced to conclude that, regardless of any personal opinions he had formed, Balutis was universally accepted by those whose own credentials were impeccable.

At one point Max competely forgot his food, the atmosphere and his companion. A young woman with dark, upswept hair came in, accompanied by two expensively dressed young men, and after being seated she threw off her sable-collared mink cape. She was attired in a gauze-like silk blouse, under which she was wearing nothing.

As he gaped at her, she exchanged a warm greeting with Lance.

"You know that dame?" Max asked.

Lance concealed his amusement. "That's Barbie Howe—Mrs. Morris Howe—a young lady with fourteen-karat credentials on both her side and her husband's."

Max had done business with Morris Howe on occasion, and was doubly surprised, but refused to change his opinion. "So she has a pile of money. Does that make her less of a whore?"

"I assure you she isn't," Lance said. "I happen to know her fairly well because she's done some singing in a film of mine. Barbie is a lady."

"Dressed like that?"

"Why not?" Lance persisted. "The way people dress—Barbie included—has nothing to do with their morality, Max."

"Then human nature has changed."

"No, it hasn't, which is half my point. What people are doing these days is ridding themselves of their inhibitions."

"She sure doesn't have any." Max found it difficult to stop staring, even though he realized no one else seemed to be paying any attention to the young woman. "Which one is her husband? I know him only on the phone."

"Oh, Morris isn't here. He rarely comes to the better restaurants and places."

"But he lets his wife run around?"

"I know Barbie's escorts," Lance said. "They wouldn't try to make out with her. They happen to be more interested in each other."

"The Grand Marnier soufflé here is marvelous," Lance said. "I recommend it."

"I've had enough food for one night," Max replied, patting his paunch.

"What about a little Camembert cheese, then, before we order brandy?"

Max shook his head. "I'm a fellow who climbs around on the skeletons of buildings. Which I couldn't do if I spent my life eating cheese and drinking brandy."

"I insist you try a snifter of Cordon Bleu cognac." Lance

summoned the table captain, gave the order and turned back to his guest. "Now," he said, "let's talk."

"I've been waiting for nearly two hours," Max replied calmly.

"In the first place, I refuse to permit you to return that check to me. The film is doing better than I'd hoped, and has made more than twenty thousand so far. And that's just the beginning. You'll have to let me express my thanks in my own way."

"Couldn't you use the money yourself?"

"Of course, but—"

"Then it's a hell of an expensive way to thank somebody," Max said.

Lance grinned at him. "Oh, I have an ulterior motive."

The man's candor was as startling as his *chutzpah,* and Max couldn't help smiling. Every time he convinced himself Balutis was a phony, the fellow surprised him.

"I'm doing exceptionally well," Lance said. "I'm earning more money than I ever thought I could. But I'm ambitious, as you may have gathered. I want to earn far more than I'm making, and for that I need capital."

Max busied himself stirring the coffee the waiter had just poured for him.

"I want to make bigger films," Lance said, "and that will raise my production budgets. I also want to start cracking the commercial theater market. As I guess you know, it takes money to make money."

"Yeah, sure. But what has all this to do with me?" Max demanded.

"I want to offer you the opportunity to invest in my future projects," Lance said. "I'm not thinking in huge terms. What I have in mind is something in the neighborhood of one hundred thousand, and your lawyer, your accountants—anyone you please—can go through my books and my future projections. I'll guarantee that you'll more than double your money in a year to eighteen months."

129

"A great, solid gold investment," Max said. "With a return so good that only an idiot would turn it down. And guaranteed, too, so I couldn't lose a nickel. What's the guarantee?"

"Why, my word, of course. And my ledgers."

"Uh-huh. And why am I elected? Because I'm such a marvelous guy? Or because somebody told you I'm a sucker? Now I can see why I've had all the build-up, right from the beginning. But you picked the wrong sucker. If you told me this was a gamble, and I'd stand a good chance of losing my money, I'd have respect for you. But I don't go for this big talk about an investment."

Lance lost some of his poise. "I'm sure some slick operators have tried to get money from you over the years, so I don't blame you for being conservative. But this is a legitimate offer, honorably made. Investigate me legally and financially, as I told you a minute ago, and you'll discover there isn't a better buy."

"If that's true, why aren't investors beating at your door, trying to shove money at you?"

"Because I haven't put myself on the open market," Lance said quietly.

Max tried to exercise patience. "That Wilfred Hendon over there, who came to talk to you with his wife who uses a sunlamp—"

"They own a place down in the West Indies, and she spends half her time there, water-skiing."

"Whatever. He's a senior partner in a private banking house, which everybody knows. And I happen to know something about what his outfit is worth. He can buy and sell me. So why not go to him? Why come to me?"

"Every business has its own mystique—"

"Tell me in plain English."

"I'll try," Lance said. "I'm a salesman. The products I sell are my films and my paintings. They're worth more than unused celluloid and canvas only if the buying public think they have a value. Wilfred Hendon has become an important collector of Pop Art in the past few years. He's worth thousands to me every year. Why? Because I represent glamour to him. If I made him my business associate, I'd be no more glamorous to him than the electronic space gadget corporations his company subsidizes —businesses you and I think of as exciting. And I'd lose a client."

Max grunted, admitting to himself that the argument made good sense.

"When one goes, they all go. And I'm not fooling myself. The wealthy are fickle, and anyone who depends on them—a fashion designer, a restaurant owner, me—can lose favor overnight. When just one of them yawns in your face, you're dead."

"It could be," Max said cautiously, "that you're right."

"I am." Lance looked across the room at the same moment that auburn-haired Mrs. Hendon glanced at him, and he poured charm into a brilliant smile. "In this particular case, there are complications. Linda Hendon is a dangerous bitch. She's years younger than her husband, she has nothing to keep her mind occupied, and she'd leap at the chance to force me to star her in some of my films. As it is, she's always hinting, and she'd be nothing but trouble if he became one of my backers. She wouldn't be satisfied to pose in the nude. She'd want to be filmed directing an orgy."

Max half-turned in his chair to peer at the redhead. Either his education had been neglected or times were changing more rapidly than he had believed possible, but he hadn't known there were so many females in the world anxious to prance naked in front of a movie camera.

"This brings up another reason I've come to you," Lance said. "You're the first person I've met in a long time who has no interest in my work. You haven't bothered to see a film that couldn't have been made without your help, and my paintings mean even less to you. I'm in this business because of something I want, and I'm not talking now about money. I have articulated a philosophical concept, something I call super-reality. Of course, super-reality exists in actuality with or without me. It always has. But very few people have ever been conscious of it. Today, however, we are entering a New Age, an Age of the Mind. And people, young people, are ready to see super-reality. What I want is to bring about an awakening, to create an awareness of super-reality, and that's what I'm doing, Max, through my art and my —what you might call my life style."

"I'm even worse at trying to understand new-fangled philosophy than I am modern art. My head is filled with the figures you add and subtract in columns."

"Precisely. You'll never be a convert to our way of thinking, and neither will most members of your generation. As much as I respect you and all you've accomplished in the world of finance, Max, you couldn't grasp the essentials of the super-real as opposed to the artificial. You proved that a few minutes ago when we were talking about the way Barbie Howe chooses to dress."

"Let's not start that again."

"I have no intention of it. I don't want to reach you or anyone else above—roughly—thirty-five. But I *am* leading a crusade. And at the same time I'm pleased to say I don't have to starve while I'm doing it. I make plenty of money. I'm the artist with a head on his shoulders."

Max was amused, and wondered if he should invest in Balutis' enterprises, just for the hell of it. The money at stake was minor, and it would be a laugh to make a profit on something so nutty. Beyond that, with Stella no longer in his life, he did need more than a very occasional diversion. It was worth thinking about.

"I'm not trying to shut you out intellectually," Lance said. "So don't get me wrong. The films and paintings are available, if you want to learn. If not, I can sympathize with your reluctance. Super-reality simply isn't your bag."

"Correct. You don't understand real estate or construction, I know nothing about art. Everything evens out."

"I'm not complaining, Max! Just because you put some money into my films you wouldn't try to interfere with the artistic product. You'd stay out of my hair and let me do my own work in my own way. You wouldn't interfere, and the films wouldn't suffer."

"You've made it clear why I'm good for you. The question is, are you good for me?"

"There's no need to decide tonight," Lance said easily. "Send your accountant around to look at my books, and I'll visit your lawyer whenever you want to set up a date for me. After you've studied my financial setup you'll know what to do. Meantime, don't lose sight of the fringe benefits."

Max raised an eyebrow.

Lance's smile broadened. "Bobbie says she owes you an apology for the other evening. I don't know the details and prefer not to know them, you understand, but when she heard I was seeing you tonight she insisted I tell you that she hopes you'll let her apologize—in person."

Stella Ross's small office was dominated by a machine, sitting on a table beside her desk, that, she sometimes said, could do anything but fry eggs. It could perform any arithmetical calculation, and was equipped with several auxiliary mechanisms that made it something of a computer. When Stella fed figures into the machine, it replied promptly and accurately, enabling her to interpret the results and tell her employers whether a project was on schedule, whether enough materials were on hand to do the job, and whether enough men were assigned to the task.

Stacks of ledgers and building schedules filled the better part of her desk, and only a rose in a vase near her jar of pens and pencils indicated that the cubicle was the office of a woman. But Max, pausing for a moment at the door, told himself that when Stella was present, no other reminders of femininity were necessary.

133

He cleared his throat loudly.

Stella, who had been absorbed in a chart, looked up in surprise.

"Could I come in for a minute?" He waited at the entrance, taking care not to step inside until she replied.

Stella recovered and concealed a smile. "You pay the rent," she said. "And my salary."

"This isn't exactly a matter of company business. But," he added hastily, "it's business."

She cleared a pile of papers and blueprints from the straight-backed chair at one side of her desk.

Max glanced around the room. "A year ago I told you that you needed more space. You need it more now. Put a few more ledgers in here, and you won't be able to turn around."

"I like this office," Stella said.

He realized it was pointless to revive what had been a futile argument. The last time they had discussed the subject, she had insisted there would be a chain reaction if she moved to a larger office, that five or six employees senior to her would have a legitimate reason to feel they had been slighted.

"According to my latest projection, the heating and air-conditioning sub-contractor will be finished in time for us to get the bonus," she declared.

"Good. Because it looks like I may have a need for my share that I didn't know about until recently." It is absurd, he thought, to feel so nervous. "Would it bother you if I smoked?"

"Has it ever bothered me, Max?"

"A woman might decide that a cigar stink in an office wasn't her idea of heaven. Who knows what a woman thinks from one minute to the next?"

Stella accepted the rhetorical question with a smile.

Max took his time removing a cigar from his gold case, clipping off the end and lighting it. "I want to tell you something confidential," he said.

134

There was no need for her to assure him that she would betray no confidences, so she merely nodded.

"Also, I want to ask a favor of you." He smiled. "I want your advice." He took a deep breath, then told of the offer to invest in Lance Balutis' films.

She made no comment.

"I don't sound to you like a jackass for even thinking of doing it, Stell?"

"How much does he want you to invest?"

"One hundred thousand."

"That's a lot of money," Stella said.

"Too much. If I go into this thing, I'll start with fifty thousand." He frowned and puffed on the cigar. "I had an independent CPA go over his books. You'll find everything in this report." He took a sheaf of papers from a folder, and then rummaged through others. "I've also got a lawyer's report, and some information that Balutis got together for me from commercial movie theater owners who say they'll start showing his pictures if he makes them bigger. Which means more expensive."

Stella took the papers and began to leaf through them. "You want my opinion of these reports, Max?"

"I want your opinion of everything connected with Balutis' movies."

Stella hesitated for an instant. "All right," she said, "let's start at the beginning. Why are you doing this, Max?"

He shrugged and chewed on his cigar.

"It isn't the money involved."

"Hardly."

"It isn't a secret yen to get into the movie business."

Max laughed. "If that's what I wanted, I wouldn't do it on Balutis' level. I'd buy into one of the major companies."

"Why, then?" she persisted.

He was reluctant to tell her the whole truth. "You know the London deal is on again. With another bank. This time we'll close it, and add the London hotel to the L & B chain."

135

"So I've gathered."

"Then you also realize there will be an explosion at North Atlantic when Christianson finds out."

"I can imagine," Stella said.

"There's a chance—not a very strong one, but a chance, all the same—that North Atlantic will call in its loans."

"Oh, Max!"

"Yeah. Tremendous fireworks. I'm not expecting it, but I get a little nervous, sometimes. I wouldn't admit that to anybody else," he add quickly.

"Right now," Max continued, "I'm counting on the boys at North Atlantic wanting to serve their own best interests. I'm counting on it that they'll put those interests ahead of any anger they'll feel toward Paul and me, and that will be plenty of anger, believe me."

"I can imagine."

"This is a long-range gamble, and I'm not really a gambler at heart. If I win, L & B will be so big and so solid that not even an earthquake could destroy us. We might even be able to sell the construction end of the business and concentrate completely on the real estate. If I lose the gamble, it'll be the other way around. God knows how much of the real estate North Atlantic might take away from us by threatening bankruptcy. Then we'd be left with only the construction business. And glad of it, I suppose." He smiled bleakly.

"How soon will you know?"

"A man like Howard Christianson never acts in a hurry. Two months, maybe. Four months, six. Who knows? I'm thinking of using this business of Balutis to take my mind off my own worries. I've tested myself a little, and so far it works."

"What do you want me to do, Max?"

"I'd like you to make your own investigation for me, starting from scratch."

"I should have a breather next week, unless you or Paul come up with some new work."

"I've talked to Paul, and he won't bother you. Neither will I." Max hesitated, looking embarrassed, and then stared at the rose as he said, "Naturally, since this isn't strictly company business, I'll pay you extra for it. A flat sum, a daily fee, any way you want to work it."

"I wouldn't dream of charging you, Max!"

"You'll be paid one hundred dollars a day if the job takes three days or less, which it should. Or a flat five hundred if you take longer." He placed the folder in front of her. "It's settled, and I'll expect a report from you as soon as you can get it in shape." Feeling somewhat better, he left the office.

Stella leafed through the papers again, wondering if she would ever be able to achieve the complete break with Max that she had told him she wanted.

"Mother, I wish you'd try to understand!" Janet Lafferty was deeply distressed as she followed her mother into her parents' bedroom. She had wanted to hold this talk on the relatively neutral ground of the living room, but had lost that round.

"This just isn't like you, Jan." Margaret Lafferty sounded hurt rather than angry.

"I don't believe you know me at all, Mother."

"Oh? Have you changed so much?"

"I've grown up. That's all I mean, so don't read more into it, please." Janet tugged at the hem of her sweatshirt, started to stuff it into her jeans and then changed her mind. She had chosen inappropriate attire for the occasion, knowing how much her mother hated sloppy clothes, but it was too late now to change into a dress.

"I simply don't see why you want an apartment of your own. Daddy and I place no restrictions on you here. You can entertain here all you please." Margaret lowered herself onto her chaise, then looked up at her daughter, her eyes bright. "Unless, of course, you have friends you know we wouldn't approve of."

"I'm not ashamed of any of my friends," Janet said wearily. "But on principle I don't see why I've got to submit advance lists for your approval and Daddy's!"

"I wish you wouldn't shout, dear. I'm getting a headache."

Janet felt a surge of pure hatred, even though she knew she was winning. Her mother always fell back on sick headaches to end a discussion, after all else had failed. "Look," she said. "All kinds of friends used to come to my room at college. You didn't even know they existed, did you? And Daddy didn't know. But I survived, intact."

"The world," Margaret said with finality, "isn't a college dormitory, Janet."

"All the more reason for me to live my own life. And try to earn my own living."

"That brings up another aspect." Margaret closed her eyes and sighed. "You always become furious when I say this to you, but you'll have to listen to it again. You're no ordinary girl, Janet."

"I know. I'm a Lafferty. *The* Laffertys of Park Avenue. Well, screw that. I'm me."

"Janet!"

"Maybe," Janet said, her voice suddenly ragged, "I want to get out of here because I'd like to be an ordinary person for a change. Maybe I'd like to find out if I can make it on my own, not as Paul Lafferty's daughter. Maybe I'd even like to have friends who don't see dollar signs in front of their eyes when they look at me!"

"My head is splitting." Margaret pulled her peignoir around her more closely. "We'll have to finish this another time."

Lance Balutis had transformed the lower floors of the brownstone house in the East Village into living quarters that suited the public image he had created. Several rooms, with his own offbeat paintings and psychedelic works dominating the scene, were furnished only with mattresses and Oriental prayer stools. Others, done in what he still called high camp, were filled with massive Victorian furniture or early experimental modern, principally ugly free-form tables and somewhat grubby, low-slung canvas chairs in metal frames.

Only his studio, which occupied the entire top floor, indicated that a man of serious purpose worked here, and was efficiently, almost coldly impersonal. Daylight filtered through a skylight roof covered with the usual Manhattan grime, which reappeared within twenty-four hours of the time it was washed away. The whitewashed walls were bare, and their monotony was relieved only by a stack of painted theatrical sets, some of them no more than huge sheets of colored paper, pasted together, with each held by a bamboo frame. These had been propped against one wall.

Recording equipment, movie cameras and special lenses were hidden away in a large, locked steel box, which a dusty shawl and two faded velvet pillows tried unsuccessfully to conceal. Two still cameras stood on tripods beneath batteries of overhead lights, including a half-dozen baby spots. Unlike some of his colleagues, Lance scorned the use of strobe lights, which some photographers found essential, swearing he obtained better results. Although he did, in fact, sometimes use strobe lights, it was his boast, often recalled in print by newspapers and magazines, that he would not buy new lighting equipment until he could utilize a modification of the laser beam.

In one corner was his darkroom, completely sealed off from the studio, and in another was his "office," separated from the main room by a sheet-rock partition. In it were a desk, a chair, a file cabinet and some odds and ends that made it difficult for Stella Ross to concentrate as she methodically studied Lance's correspondence, receipts and ledgers. An old brassiere was hanging over the back of the chair, and although she could not feel it there, she found it impossible to forget. In a jumble on the floor at one side of the cubbyhole were a Confederate Army officer's uniform, a dancer's spangled tights, several pairs of panties, two nineteenth-century glass-shaded lamps, a torn hunting jacket and a scuba diver's gear.

The sloppiness was annoying to someone dedicated to neatness, but Stella had turned her back on the junk and tried, with fair success, to shut out the sounds from the studio, where Lance was working with two female models. His purpose made no sense, and the poses he photographed were disgusting: the girls, both totally naked, embraced and kissed, sometimes caressed each other and occasionally played childish games.

At last, to her relief, she could hear Lance telling the girls he was done. As they dressed, both told him they wanted drinks, one of them demanding what she called a "Balutis special." Ordinarily, it appeared, Lance did not care how many people were eating or sleeping, drinking or fornicating in the house, but now he drew the line. Good-natured but firm, he told the girls he was busy, and suggested they return the following day, when he would have less on his mind.

They departed at last, with Lance seeing them to the downstairs door, and the silence that followed their mindless prattle was welcome. Stella worked steadily, and was only vaguely conscious, a half-hour later, of approaching footsteps.

"You really do your thing," Lance said, leaning against the door frame. "You've been at it all day."

"That's why I'm paid." Stella did not look up.

"You're the first accountant I've ever known who is pretty enough to model for me or star in one of my films."

"I'm a financial and labor projection analyst, not an accountant." She continued to go through the correspondence. "There's a difference."

"You don't approve of me," Lance said, "do you?"

"You make money from taking pornographic pictures. That much I've been finding out."

He laughed. "What I do is called art," he said lightly, his pride

140

making him unwilling to explain his sense of utter dedication to his work and the principles behind it.

"Like anybody else," Stella said, "I have a right to my opinions."

"I think you could stand a break. Here," he said, coming into the partitioned cubicle and placing a tall, frosted glass on the desk.

She saw he was holding another, for himself, and her suspicion showed in her eyes.

"Muriel was jabbering so much about the Balutis special I thought you and I deserved these."

"What's in it?" Stella demanded.

"The right mixture to get rid of inhibitions."

"I live just fine with my inhibitions, so make mine plain ice water instead."

Lance grinned at her as he leaned against the partition, sipping his drink. "I've never met a bird like you."

"That's the first time I've ever been called a bird." She didn't mean to sound prim, and was amused at herself.

"Stay in the groove, and you'll start to live."

"I have no complaints."

"That's the nutty part of it. I don't believe you do, and it bugs me. How a chick like you can spend her life adding up figures is crazy. You could do a lot better in other kinds of figures."

Stella resisted the temptation to pull down her short skirt. She paused for just a moment. "Is there really a market for the kind of still photography you were doing today?"

"It isn't pornography, damn it! And—you've seen the books, sweetie!"

"I know, but it's so hard to believe. Who'd want a big, blurred photograph of two girls—well, doing things to each other—in his house?"

"The demand is so great I can't keep up with it. My films

141

and paintings keep me so busy I don't have much time for this kind of work, but I could spend all my time at it, and still not fill all the orders."

"At three hundred dollars a picture."

"You've seen the bills, and the bank deposit slips."

"It's incredible. And some of the models you don't even pay."

"Those kids this afternoon were doing it for kicks—and a Balutis special. Try the drink, why don't you? It doesn't have Mickey drops in it, and I'll give you a sworn statement I'm not a white slaver."

Rather than appear gauche or frightened, Stella took a small sip. "It doesn't taste like it has any liquor in it at all."

"That's why it's dangerous. One doesn't do much except whet your appetite, and it's the second one that hits you across the back of the neck."

"I don't drink much, so you can have the rest of mine."

Lance shook his head. "Unique, by God. She doesn't drink, she smokes in moderation and she does arithmetic for a living. How do you get your fun out of life?"

"None of your goddam business." Stella suddenly became vehement.

He was so startled that his smile faded, and he gaped at her for a moment. "I should have pegged your type right off."

"Wht's my type?"

"A tough Lithuanian broad. Just exactly like one of my sisters—and a half-dozen other girls I knew back in Indiana when I was a boy. You spit nails, you wouldn't admit to a sentimental feeling if you were shot for it, and you'd just as soon put a knee into the groin of a guy you didn't like. But if you secretly went for him, that would be different."

"Don't get any ideas. You'd get the knee."

"What's wrong with me?" Lance wanted to know.

Stella shrugged. "I analyze finances, not people. I've seen the way some of your girls fall all over you, so be satisfied with what you've got."

142

"You're different."

"Sure. I'm the one who doesn't want you. So that makes you want to chase me. Save your shoe leather."

"You don't know what you're missing until you sample it."

"I'll live in ignorance for the rest of my life, thanks. I've got to admit you have nerve, though. You know Max Berman's investment in your enterprises depends on my report to him, but you're still willing to risk antagonizing me by making passes."

"Very mild passes," Lance countered. "Just strong enough to be flattering—if you want to turn them down—"

"Which I'm doing."

"—but not so crude that you'll flip your wig and tell Maxie to spend his money elsewhere."

"You stay one jump ahead, don't you?"

"That's my system. What's your way?"

"I don't have one," Stella said. "Now, suppose you let me finish, so I can get out of here."

"I was hoping I could take you to dinner."

"We discussed all I need to know for my report at dinner the last two nights, thanks. I'll be done here in another hour, if I'm lucky, and aside from a few more talks with film distributors and theater owners tomorrow, I'll be all set."

"Doesn't anybody or anything rattle you?" Lance asked.

"Lots of things and all kinds of people. But not a boy who reminds me of the fresh kid in my old, old neighborhood who went on the make for me just because I was three years older, no other reason."

"If you'd looked in a mirror, you'd have found he had plenty of reasons."

"I wasn't blind," Stella said, "and neither were the fellows I dated. Nice, older boys who'd go to eleven o'clock Mass with me."

"Do you go to Mass now?"

"Sure. Don't you?"

Lance finished his own drink and reached for her glass.

"Missionaries," he said, "are having a rough time everywhere, including northwest Brazil."

"It isn't because I won't give you what you want that you're after me," Stella said abruptly. "At least, that isn't the main reason. You think I'd have to give you a good rating if you got me into bed. Isn't that it?"

"When the Lafferty kid told me you made all the final decisions for her father and Berman," Lance said, "I thought she was trying to make you sound like somebody important so I'd agree to leave Bobbie's party and go over to your place with her. But she meant it!"

"Janet and I have been very close ever since she was a little girl, so her perspective may be a bit off. I've never tried to measure my influence at the company."

"But you have plenty."

Stella borrowed a gesture from Max and shrugged. "Mr. Lafferty and Mr. Berman have been known to listen to me. Sometimes."

Lance decided to gamble. "By now you must know what you intend to say about me."

She saw her advantage and grasped it. "I never make up my mind until I've broken down every figure and weighed it."

"Maybe you've made a basic choice, and will just fill in the details."

"Maybe." Stella was bitchy enough to enjoy his uncertainty. "Your books are in order, and your correspondence with film distributors and theater owners indicates they'll take your product when you expand it. You have a steady market for your paintings and still photos, too, so—unless there are holes I haven't seen—I'll have to tell Mr. Berman you're okay, a fair enough risk. But I'll also have to tell him I've never seen anyone so anxious for the green light."

"You've never dealt with partners and backers who have artistic pretensions. I can get more than I'll ever need from fifty to a hundred people, but I'd regret it. Maxie is the perfect angel. He wouldn't try to censor me, and he wouldn't climb on my back."

"Don't be too sure of that." Stella issued the challenge calmly, making it sound like casual conversation. "He has a reputation to maintain, don't forget."

"All he has to do to keep up his reputation is build sky-scrapers and apartment houses that will last. Nobody who does business with him is going to know or care that he's betting on the future of that depraved destroyer of middle-class values, Lance Balutis. Why should you care about anything except the plain dollars and cents of the matter?"

The question, Stella thought unhappily, was valid. And she couldn't answer it.

Max studied the report with care, memorizing every pertinent fact, before he went downstairs to Stella's office. She was attending a staff meeting, he was told, and he left a note on her desk asking her to telephone him when she was free. Forty-five minutes later his secretary buzzed him to say she was outside in the reception room, and he admitted her at once.

Stella stood for a moment, stared at the huge painting which she recognized as Lance's work, but made no comment as she took the chair at one side of Max's desk.

He handed her an envelope. "I didn't want to put your fee through the payroll department. They've done enough talking about you and me around here."

"I enjoyed the assignment and I really don't want this, Max." She put the envelope on the desk.

"Would you like it better if I bought you a piece of jewelry?"

She picked up the envelope. "Have you read the report I submitted to you?"

"From end to end," Max said brusquely. "I knew you'd master the movie business."

"Hardly."

"It doesn't matter. Now I understand what Balutis is doing. I'm amazed there should be a market for that *dreck,* but there is."

"You saw what the commercial film people told me? I quoted them word for word. They expect to fill the theaters with his movies."

"Your report says I can expect a healthy profit. So I ask myself does it matter if I think they're insane? And I'm not sure of the answer. One thing bothers me though, in your report."

A great many things were bothering Stella, but she remained silent.

"In your regular reports to Paul and me, you always end with a section on recommendations. Sometimes we do what you suggest, once in a while we pay no attention. In this report you seemed to be leading up to a recommendation that I go ahead and invest with Balutis, but then you stopped short. No recommendations one way or the other."

"I know."

"So it was deliberate?"

"Not exactly. I—well, I didn't quite know how to express some reservations that have nothing to do with a professional analysis and projection."

"Don't write them. Tell them to me," Max said. "I'm listening."

Stella folded the envelope containing the check he had given her.

"Financially," she said, "you'll be taking very little risk with Balutis."

"That's what you were saying on every page. Except that you didn't sum it all up in a recommendation."

"I'm not an art critic, Max, so I can't tell you whether that monstrous thing on the wall there is any good or not. I don't have much of an education, so maybe that's why I don't care for it."

"I'll tell you something funny," Max said. "I surprise myself. I'm beginning to like it. And I don't have any college degrees, either."

"It's good enough, for purposes of a financial analysis, that there's a market screaming for work like that from Lance. Read what I've put into the report from the art dealers. They fight to get his paintings. The same is true of his still photos, and —most of all—his movies. He's hot these days, and it looks as though he'll be hot for quite a long time. As nearly as I could learn, underground movies as such are going to be big box-office for years to come, too. They're just starting to tap the commercial market."

"What else do I need to know?"

"Nothing, really." Stella bit her lower lip and stared at a spot over his head.

"But there is something."

"It's a personal, female reaction, that's all."

"If you've got one of your hunches," Max said, "I want to know it."

"No, not a hunch. A feeling. Max, I've seen two of Lance's films, and they turned my stomach. I don't think I'm a prude—"

"I can sign an affidavit that you're not."

"Maybe I am, though. In both of the films I saw, everybody was running around naked most of the time. There was some love-making—boys making love to girls, girls making love to boys—and I think, but I couldn't swear to it—people of the same sex making love to each other. Either the action was very mixed up and muddy, or I'm more stupid than I've believed. But sometimes I honestly couldn't tell what was happening."

"You're not stupid." Max nodded. "My one experience was when I saw Balutis making the movie on the skeleton of the new building uptown. I'm willing to take an oath he and his cast didn't know what they were doing, so how could an audience know?"

"Mostly," Stella said, "they just sit around without any clothes on and talk about sex. I'm not sure what they're talking about, either, and it isn't because they use big words. Sometimes they repeat themselves, like little children, and say things that don't have any meaning. And sometimes they mumble, so you can't even hear them."

"And this is what people want, and what theater owners are eager to show? You say so in the report."

"That's right, but—"

"Then what's the worry?"

"Let me finish. The still photos Lance takes and sells—very arty things that are often very fuzzy, and done on a thick paper that looks like it has pebbles in it—are more explicit than his movies. If you study one of them for a while, you can see, sort of, that two naked people are pawing each other. He seems to specialize in using two girls for that sort of photography. And he said to me—very openly, without any apologies—that there isn't as much of a demand for photos of men with men."

"Are you trying to tell me you think he'll be arrested? Say what you mean!"

"Am I the mayor or the police commissioner or something?" Stella asked. "What do I know about arresting people? I'm sure Lance is too smart to break the laws—"

"He likes it, having society friends," Max said. "And he does too well to want to hurt himself by making dirty movies for stag parties."

"This I wouldn't know, and I don't care. All I do know is that *I* think his movies and photos are disgraceful! You've always been in a clean business, Max—"

"How many throats have Paul and I had to cut in the last twenty years? How many sub-contractors have we had to push to the wall to protect ourselves? I'd hate to count. I don't think I could, Stell. Some of the rough things we've had to do, you don't even know about."

"But you've never broken the law! Sometimes you've bribed

148

inspectors so they don't hold you up forever, but you've never gone below official safety standards."

"We stay above them. And I don't like to call it a bribe when we help out a friend who happens to be an inspector. When one of them is a bastard he can make a contractor's life miserable, looking at our work under a magnifying glass, sometimes. So we make sure the inspectors assigned to us stay friendly. But Balutis doesn't even have to do that much in his kind of work, so I don't see the connection."

"There isn't any! You know I don't say things the right way when I get excited."

"Stop being excited, and maybe I can find out what you're driving at. In one breath you admit that it would be a good investment to put some money with Balutis, but I think you're also trying to tell me not to do it."

"I have no right to tell you what to do. But I wish you wouldn't. Everybody who knows Max Berman admires and respects him—"

"Who do I know? Hooligans like Paul and me, some of them rich, some of them poor. They're just people."

"You have a wonderful reputation, and I get sick when I think you could ruin it!"

It was astonishing how an overwrought woman could exaggerate. "Not one person I know," Max said, "would turn down a lunch invitation from me because I invested some money with Balutis."

"Let's say I'm the only one concerned, then. Nobody else. I don't want to lose my own regard for you, Max."

"A lot of good that regard does me," he said bitterly.

Disturbed by her own guilts, she misinterpreted him. "I know it doesn't make sense for a woman who spent eleven years as a man's mistress to preach morality like a priest. You could keep putting your money into bonds, the way you've always done. You don't have to help Lance Balutis spread his filth."

Only one portion of her statement was important to Max. "In eleven years, Stell, I never thought of you as my mistress. You were always my girl." He felt as deeply injured as he looked. "Somebody I loved and expected to marry."

Tears came to Stella's eyes. "It's my own fault for bringing it up, but that's something I just can't talk about." She rose and fled from his office before she began to weep.

Max started to follow her, changed his mind and slumped in his chair. Why the mere mention of their previous relationship should upset Stella so badly was beyond his comprehension. For the sake of his own stability, his own peace of mind, he had made a great effort to stop thinking about something that made no sense to him, and he could not afford the self-indulgence now.

But their personal problem had no connection with his going into this deal. He picked up her report, looked through it again and then corroborated her findings with those of the independent audit and his lawyer's investigation. He found Balutis' work boring, not smutty, but that was irrelevant. There was no reason to let his own reaction prevent him from putting money into something that promised him amusement and relief from his financial worries as well as a profit that not even a wealthy man wanted to refuse.

Max felt out of place in the studio, as though he were there under false pretenses, and moved restlessly around the large room while he waited for Balutis to finish primping before a mirror. "If I start getting a return on this fifty thousand as soon as you tell me—or even if it takes twice as long—I'll follow it with another fifty thousand immediately. That's a promise."

Lance busied himself trying to work a large, nineteenth-century cravat of silk into a satisfactory shape beneath a high, standing collar. Grinning slightly as he continued to inspect his handiwork in the mirror on the wall in the open corner of the studio that his models used for dressing-room purposes, he asked, "Suppose you got your first payment tomorrow, and a substantial payment at that. Would you be satisfied?"

"I'd say it was a miracle." Max stopped pacing for a moment. "And I don't believe in them."

"You'll see. I was a little disappointed when you put up only half of what I need, and I want to prove to you how fast you'll be paid back, with a return on investment that'll stagger you. That's why I asked you to come with me today."

"If you can make money in big chunks at a time," Max said, "I don't understand why you need outside financing."

"A lot of people have asked film producers and artists that same question." Lance inserted a mammoth diamond stickpin in the cravat, affixed it in the back of the material and inspected himself critically. "We seldom use more than a limited amount of our own money for two reasons."

"One is easy to understand after I saw that Italian sports car you've bought. It must have cost you ten thousand."

"A little over seventeen." Lance smoothed his slim, cuffless trousers and slipped into a double-breasted jacket of cream-colored velvet that fell almost to his knees. Nipped tightly at the waist, with wide lapels, it had exceptionally long side vents and, combined with the cravat and trousers, gave him an appearance similar to that of dandies during the early-nineteenth century Regency of George IV.

"Anyone in my position has to spend money in order to make it," he continued, starting to work on his hair with a comb and woman's "teasing" brush. "This house cost me a fortune, and it's costing me still more to redecorate it. I've got to be seen regularly in the best restaurants and travel to the best resorts. They'd bleed anybody."

"Not that it's any of my business," Max said, "but you seem to be running a hotel here, too. That isn't cheap."

"It's true that friends drop in," Lance murmured casually,

trying to arrange a wave of hair to his satisfaction. "I can't turn them away."

"I would!"

"You and I need different kinds of stimulation to do our best work."

It was impossible to argue the point, but Max couldn't imagine how anyone would be inspired by the limpid young men and odd-looking girls who flowed in and out of the house. "Don't you sock away some of your earnings?" he asked, changing the emphasis.

"Of course, whenever I can. I might earn a small fortune one year, and then go penniless the next, although I don't expect that to happen for a long time. But if it should, I'll need a cushion to tide me over."

Lance inserted a long, brightly colored piece of gauzelike material into his breast pocket in lieu of a handkerchief, and began to fuss with it. "The most important reason I don't put my own money into my films—the reason so few of us do—is that my anxiety would stifle my creativity. When an artist becomes tense, he grows too rigid, and his work is affected."

"So on other people's money," Max said with a dry laugh, "you can stay loose."

"Precisely!" Lance's hearty agreement was unabashed. "I think I'm ready, if you are."

Max knew it would be unpleasant to observe that he had been waiting for more than an hour. An artist, he was discovering, had as little sense of time as a woman.

Lance turned to him, preening. "How do you like the effect?"

No one else Max knew would have been seen either in public or in private wearing such gaudily outlandish attire. But any response less than tactful would be an insult, and Max, unaccustomed to diplomacy, sought the right words. "It's very different," he managed at last. "I never saw anybody dress like that."

"You will." As a final touch, Lance daubed himself with a

strong cologne. "I'm a trend-setter, you know. I've got to be." He started toward the door.

"Wait a second." Max realized he was wearing old, paint-spattered sneakers, and pointed at them. "Your shoes."

"What about them?"

"They don't exactly go with all that fancy stuff," Max said uncertainly.

"When I wear them," Lance replied loftily, "they do."

A speechless Max accompanied him down the stairs.

On the second-floor landing they could see that a bathroom door was open, and a young woman who had just emerged from the tub was standing naked on the mat, drying herself. She waved, showing no embarrassment, and Lance called, "Don't forget to dry behind your ears."

At moments such as this Max became uneasy, wondering if he had been wrong to invest in the enterprises of someone who gave every surface appearance, at least, of being a madman.

They emerged onto the street, and Lance, unlocking the door of his new sports car, climbed behind the wheel and pushed the button that electrically lowered the roof. Then, after donning a pair of heavy, tinted goggles, he astonished the older man by taking a long chiffon scarf from the glove compartment and carefully wrapping it around his head to hold his hair in place. Max could only hope he wouldn't be seen by anyone he knew as they drove uptown from the East Village.

Lance chuckled gleefully whenever the car pulled away from others at intersections, and, exhibiting no restraint, wove in and out of traffic so recklessly that his passenger closed his eyes. "If I couldn't have some fun, I wouldn't own a car, Max."

"Not many people get killed in city traffic, but I don't want to be the exception, okay? Maybe you don't care about smashing up a new car, but at my age bones don't mend overnight."

Lance swerved past a truck, his tires screeching, and darted between two taxis. Triumphantly cutting out the vehicle on his left, he paid no attention to the indignant shouts of the driver, and squeezed past a stoplight just as it was changing to red. "Don't tell anyone," he said, laughing, "but I'm a bit on edge about this afternoon's fun festival. Driving helps me to relax."

"If I drove like you, I'd be flat on my back with nervous prostration. As it is, I'm an innocent bystander who'll probably have an arm and a leg in casts for months."

"Max, you slay me. You climb a few miles into the sky on those new buildings of yours, and then you swing like a monkey from the girders."

"I know what I'm doing on the skeleton of a building. And I never take unnecessary risks."

Rather than brake the car, Lance went through gymnastics at the wheel to avoid hitting a woman who was climbing out of a taxi. "But nobody makes you climb around up there. You've got it made, and could spend all your time behind your desk."

"There are some who do. I happen to think it's better for business if I actually see for myself what the men on the job are doing."

"We operate on the same principle. What you'll see this afternoon will look simple, but it's harder than any other work I've ever done, and I worked in an oil refinery as an unskilled laborer when I was a kid, and lied about my age. It'll look so easy you won't even know I'm working, but without these emotional calisthenics, I'd collapse."

They had reached Fifty-seventh Street, and after a final, wild burst of speed, Lance pulled to a halt in front of a long canopy bearing the inscription in modest lettering, *Galleries of Benjamin Harrison Henry.*

"Harry!" Lance called sharply to the dour-faced uniformed doorman, who was engrossed in a conversation with a miniskirted girl in her teens. "Harry Allen!"

The doorman took his time glancing in the direction of the shout, then came running.

"Do something about my car, and if there's as much as one

scratch on it, I'll castrate you myself, with the dullest-edged blade on a Cub Scout knife."

Max watched as Lance removed the scarf, substituted rimless sunglasses for the goggles and started toward the entrance, like an actor moving onstage from the wings.

The only items on display behind the gallery's plateglass window were two rather ordinary Louis XIV chairs, done in petitpoint, a brass-topped piecrust table of indifferent design and a dusty tapestry that could have been either French or Walloon. But the Henry Galleries had no need to display its wares, and paid little attention to the unknown customer who wandered in off the street. The clientele, assiduously cultivated for more than three decades, needed no obvious enticements to recognize the marvels of art, furniture and decor discreetly scattered about its four spacious floors.

Standing inside the gilt-handled doors was a young-old man in frock coat and striped trousers, ascot and pearl gray waistcoat, who beamed mechanically until he recognized Lance. "Ah, Mr. Balutis! We've drawn an extraordinary crowd for this time of year. Good luck!"

Max, only a pace behind Lance, was totally ignored.

Benjamin Harrison Henry, quiety elegant in tailored worsted, with a giant carnation in his buttonhole, came around the edge of a circular marble fountain in which exquisite alabaster nymphs cavorted beneath a spray of perfumed water. "Lance, my dear!" he said effusively. "That gorgeous suit will turn everyone positively purple!"

Lance tolerated an embrace. "How is it going?"

"My commission on what we've already sold will buy me the summer house I've been renting for the past five years. You have a standing invitation." He turned to Max, beaming and extending both hands. "Mr. Berman, how kind of you to drop in."

Max, who had not exchanged more than a few words with him, was surprised that Henry remembered him.

155

"Make yourself at home, Mr. Berman, and feel free to wander anywhere—"

"Cool it, Ben," Lance said softly. "He came with me. Go back to the party while we inhale the situation."

Henry's mask slipped for an instant, but he was smiling again, as he hurried away.

Beyond the far side of the fountain stood three long tables spread with double damask cloths, each with a pretty and attractively attired young lady in charge. The girls looked vaguely familiar to Max, and he realized he had seen them at Lance's studio, where their grooming and dress had been less meticulous. One presided over a gleaming silver coffee service, another ladled punch from a huge crystal bowl into delicate crystal cups, while the third offered cocktails or highballs, each held in an individual ice container to keep it chilled, while a waiter hovered nearby, ready to replenish the supply from an unseen bar. Other girls, Max noted, were wandering through the crush of people beyond the tables, bearing platters of hot and cold hors d'oeuvres. The atmosphere that had been created was that of a gathering in a private home.

"Try the champagne, Max," Lance said. "I won't let Ben buy any but the best vintages for one of my showings. Lizzie Lou," he added to the girl, "I'll need two for myself." He gulped the contents of one and was just starting his second when he was recognized, surrounded and hauled away.

Max stood alone and uncertain, a glass of champagne in his hand. He would have preferred bourbon, but knew of no graceful way to rid himself of the long-stemmed glass. So, still holding it, he made his way past Lance and his admirers.

In all, approximately twenty Balutis paintings, photographs and collages were being exhibited, each occupying its own place of honor in a section separated from the others by sandalwood partitioning. Some stood on easels, others were held by invisible wires and a few, framed, were shown on sandalwood walls. Without exception they were superbly lighted, and Max, in spite of his ignorance, admired the skill of those who had arranged the lighting.

The rear of the cavernous first floor was devoted to Lance's pebble-grained photographs, some of them only slightly larger than standard portraits, while others were larger than life. For reasons Max could not fathom, they were shown in groups of threes, fours and fives. Whatever the purpose, they, too, enjoyed all the benefits of expert mounting and lighting, and however grating Benjamin Harrison Henry's personality might be, Max had to concede that the man knew his business.

Except several crisp, black and white studies of a girl's face shrouded with long hair, and a few others of someone with short, curly hair who could have been either a male or a female, the photographs were blurred and indistinct. Remembering what Stella had told him, Max paused to study one group, and after examining the largest for some minutes, finally made out two nude girls fondling one another's breasts.

No one else found the subject matter objectionable, however. People chatted light-heartedly and loudly while standing in clumps, but Max saw that when they moved into a partitioned section to examine a painting, collage or set of photographs, they became almost reverently silent. And even when moved to discuss some feature of a work, they muttered in low tones reminiscent of strained conversations in houses of worship.

Max recognized some of the guests at the showing from the cocktail party he had attended, but there was one sharp difference between the two crowds. Everyone here was exceptionally well groomed, and although some costumes were bizarre, all were expensive. And none of the young people looked like derelicts who had wandered in off the streets.

This was a self-assured, moneyed crowd, assembled for the purpose of seeing and, hopefully, buying. Most of the men were in orthodox business attire, their eyes hard, their faces showing the strain of the driving lives they led. Although pampered by their barbers and tailors, haberdashers and shoemakers, they were weighed down by too many responsibilities, carrying too many business plans and counterplans in their heads to relax with ease or grace. Some remained poised and tightly coiled, their self-control unyielding, while a few, after several drinks, sagged perceptibly, their faces deflating like the rubber of a punctured balloon.

The women, in the main, were at least ten years younger than their partners, and most, Max guessed, were the second or third wives of their wealthy husbands. Even the homeliest had been made attractive by outrageously expensive dressmakers, cosmeticians and hairdressers, and they spent far more time studying each other than they did the works of art on exhibit.

The showing, it seemed, gave them the opportunity to parade the very latest styles, which wouldn't filter down to the level of ordinary women, who bought modestly, for several months, by which time the leaders would be wearing something new. Each was trying to express her individuality, yet was fitting herself into a pattern that made her indistinguishable from her sisters. Skirts and hair were either atrociously short or absurdly long; necklines were revealingly low or Victorian and pants were everywhere.

Max was conscious of the gulf between himself and these people, but couldn't be bothered trying to define it. He had no desire to become a semi-accepted intimate of this new society; his standards were his own, as was his way of life, and he had no desire to change or be changed. In fact, his one strong feeling as he watched group after group inspect the paintings, collages and photographs was contempt. He was sure that they shared his bewilderment, his inability to understand the work that Lance Balutis was doing, but they lacked the intellectual honesty to admit the truth. So, in the long run, he would be the winner and they the losers. He, as an investor in Balutis' enterprises, would show a profit, while they would be buying art works that, he believed, time would prove to be garbage when fads again changed.

"Warm champagne not only tastes awful, it's bad for the disposition."

Max turned to see Bobbie Wayne standing beside him, offering him a frosted glass and taking his untouched, warm glass from his hand. She looked so unlike the abandoned creature who had passed out during their love-making that he scarcely recognized her. Her linen suit of pale yellow was conservative, unadorned and, except for the very short skirt that had become commonplace, totally lacking in spectacular effect. She wore no jewelry.

"Thank you. How about you?"

"I'm on the wagon," Bobbie said, her manner cool; detached. "I haven't had anything, not even beer, since a night I hope you've forgotten."

Max didn't want to pursue the subject, and sipped from the fresh glass. "You look well."

"I've been playing a lot of tennis. Have you seen the star exhibit of the show?"

"I'm not sure."

"If you've already seen it, another look is worth the time. And if you haven't, it's something you wouldn't want to miss." She took his free hand and led him to a partitioned section where a number of people were scrutinizing a canvas that was part-painting, part-collage.

Max hadn't seen it in his wanderings, and was as startled as everyone else. The background, done in oils with minute, exacting care, was that of a lush jungle, and he saw trees, vines, bushes and hints of brightly-colored flowers. In the foreground, Balutis had pasted two large, upright tufts of dried grass, with each strand painted a different color. Nestling in the tuft on the left side was a white egg, and in that on the right side was a golf ball.

"Lance calls it 'Birth and Rebirth,' " Bobbie said.

"What is it supposed to mean?"

She thought about the question. "I'm not sure, but I imagine he'd tell you to interpret it as you please, either within the realm of the super-real or the ordinary."

Max was curious. "What's the price?"

"I think Lance and Ben Henry decided to ask ten or twelve thousand," Bobbie said casually. "Something like that."

He found her matter-of-factness as astonishing as the price itself. "Incredible."

"It was sold about forty-five minutes ago," she told him, lowering her voice.

"Maybe," he replied with forced humor, "I'm in the wrong business."

"Not any more. The smartest thing you ever did was to start financing Lance."

Apparently she knew everything about Balutis' business affairs, which seemed to confirm his hunch that she was basically his mistress, with an understanding of some sort that both were free to play around on the side.

"You're wrong," Bobbie said.

"About what?"

"This really isn't the place to talk about it."

"I've got to leave," Max said.

"I'm going, too." She had no intention of being dismissed, and took his arm. "We don't have to say good-bye to anyone. Lance and Ben are too busy frying their own fish to care what we do."

Max let her accompany him to the door. When they reached the street he saw that the crowds were thinning. The afternoon had been warm, but the air was becoming a little cooler now, and he decided to get the taste of the cocktail party out of his system. "I'm walking," he said to Bobbie.

"Do you mind if I come with you?"

The doorman approached, grinning at the girl. "Taxi, Miss Wayne?"

"No, thanks, Harry. We're walking." As he retreated she

laughed and said to Max, "A character. He digs anything in skirts, provided they're short enough."

"You know him, huh?"

"I know all kinds of people, and I'd like to explain a little. Which way are we heading?"

He hesitated, so she knew he had no particular destination in mind.

"Let's go over to the East River and watch the boats. All right, Max? I can take barges or leave them alone, but I've been mad about tugs all my life."

They started eastward on Fifty-seventh Street. He had not been agile enough to disentangle himself, so what might have been a pleasant, solitary stroll would be complicated by the presence of an unorthodox young woman whose company he neither sought nor wanted.

"You disapprove of me," Bobbie said. "I expect people like my parents to dig me wrong, but I hoped you'd understand."

"Does it matter what I think?"

"Yes."

It was dangerous to ask why, so he fell silent.

"I'm not a kook, Max. Honestly. You probably don't believe me, but I have my standards and ideals." Bobbie's grip on his arm became firmer. "I refuse to be a hyprocrite, that's all. Some people make a thing about sex, for instance, but I refuse. When I want to sleep with someone, I do."

"Why tell me?" His irritation was rising to the surface.

"Because you and I would have slept together if I hadn't been bombed that night. And our relationship would have been very different today."

"Maybe, maybe not."

She surprised him by laughing. "True, and I agree. That's one of the things I like about you, Max. You say what you think, and to hell with the consequences."

He halted for a stoplight.

"I'll bet you believe Lance keeps me."

"It didn't cross my mind one way or the other."

"Maxie, you lie in your teeth. And after I just pinned a medal on you for candor!"

"All right, so he keeps you. What of it?"

"But he doesn't! Oh, we go to bed together when we're in the mood, but that hasn't anything to do with our friendship. Lance and I are very close. But skip the bed bit. Most of the people I take on for a roll don't mean a damn thing to me. I do it with them for kicks. And," she added casually, "not just men, either."

Max realized she was watching him, probably hoping to shock him. But he had no interest whatever in her sex life, and shrugged.

"With you, it wouldn't be for kicks."

"Forget it!"

"I'm serious, Max. It would mean something."

He found it ludicrous and denigrating that a middle-aged man should be propositioned in broad daylight on a principal midtown thoroughfare by a girl who couldn't be more than half his age. An exceptionally attractive girl at that, someone who'd have class if she cared enough. What made the situation so absurd was his strong desire to break free and run off down the street alone.

"Why, all of a sudden," he demanded harshly, "would it mean something with me?"

"My God, you're blind!" Bobbie became savagely intense. "I'm no damn good on my own. I'm a hedonist, and I know it. I'm undisciplined, and I know it. I enjoy wallowing in gutters sometimes, and I know that, too."

Max glanced at her, and saw she believed what she was saying.

"I need a man who'll make me behave, Max. I need a man strong enough to set rules and enforce them, a guy who'll slap my face and wouldn't hesitate to kick my ass, either."

162

"You're asking for a policeman."

"I want you, Max."

"I'm too old and too busy," he said bluntly. "And I've been a bachelor too long."

Bobbie misunderstood him. "God, I'm not suggesting marriage! I just want us to live together!"

A couple walking in the opposite direction heard her and stared at them.

Max fought his embarrassment. "I couldn't take seven nights a week with you," he said. "You like parties, going out until all hours every night, but I'm tired when I come home. I take off my shoes, sometimes I watch a little television. I even take naps in my chair. I can't see you living that kind of life."

"You could make me do it."

"Maybe for a week. But the novelty would wear off." He wanted Stella, not this wild young creature, and if she didn't drop the subject he'd be forced to become rude.

"It wouldn't have to be seven nights a week," Bobbie said. "If you were tired, you could stay home, and I'd go my own way that night. So why couldn't it work out?"

"Because I demand fidelity, the same kind I give. And you couldn't be faithful to anybody."

Bobbie did not contradict him, but walked in silence for the better part of a block. "You need me, too," she said at last.

Max was more amused than startled. "I do?"

"You call your broker when you want to buy some stocks—"

"I don't play the market."

"—and he gets them for you." She ignored the interruption. "You send him a check, and that's the end of it. Very neat. But you've just made a different kind of investment. You've bought a piece of Lance Balutis, the most volatile, fashionable material there is. You need somebody to guide you, and I'm not fooling. You're so straight, Max. You're the straightest straight man I've ever known. You have no idea what he can do to you or how your life can be changed!"

163

"I'll take my chances," Max said.

Older members of the Peter Minuit, one of New York's most prestige-laden gentlemen's clubs, sometimes complained about the site of the club building in the East Fifties. Things hadn't been the same, they said, since the club had moved from its original downtown headquarters. The fact of the matter was that few except the oldest had known the earlier location, since the Minuit had been at its present site, in a handsome reconverted double brownstone, for more than a half-century. But the complaints were symptomatic of the Minuit's unalterable conservative spirit. Younger members sometimes suggested, in an ill-received mood of helpful criticism, that the ancient shield used as an emblem should be replaced by a coin showing the Roman god Janus, both of whose faces should be turned toward the past.

The carpet in the entrance hall was worn, and so was the elderly attendant who took Max Berman's hat and coat, murmuring, "Mr. Christianson is waiting for you in the library, sir. On the second floor."

Max remembered its location from his previous visits, and slowly climbed the carpeted, marble stairs. The silence in this central well was shattering, and Max was tempted to smile. This establishment was the ultimate holy of holies for the white, Anglo-Saxon Protestant of means, influence and family background. Those who gathered at lunch to eat badly cooked, poorly served food represented, in their own persons, billions of dollars and a stranglehold on a number of major American industries. Four Secretaries of State had been members in the present century.

The recently refurbished cocktail lounge, paneled and softly lighted, was off to the left, and the voices of several women floated out to the landing. Their presence seemed strange, Max thought, and many of the members heartily agreed with him. But the wives and daughters had won their victory after decades of effort, and their small corner was tangible proof of their victory. The atmosphere, they soon discovered, was deadly dull, but having achieved their triumph they had no intention of throwing it away, and three or four ladies showed up each evening to await their husbands in the lounge.

The library, off to the right, was a rabbit warren of connecting rooms, all book-lined. A lack of adequate space for drinking in the third-floor bar, which adjoined the main dining room, had forced the installation of tables and chairs in the library itself. But the conviviality of the drinkers was so decorous that a member could read a book, the *Wall Street Journal* or the London *Economist* without fear of disturbance.

Quietly dressed gentlemen were sitting at three or four tables, chatting in low tones, and none looked up when Max walked in. Since their own parties were already complete, they had no curiosity about anyone else who wandered in.

Howard Christianson arose from a table in the far corner of the largest room, and waved, his smile bloodless.

Max went to him, trying to curb a feeling of aggressiveness.

"This is perfect timing," Christianson said as they shook hands. "I haven't even ordered yet."

"Paul asked me to extend his apologies," Max said. "His wife is ill, so he had to dash home."

"Nothing serious, I hope."

"No, Margaret's health is rather delicate, that's all. But I can speak for Paul as well as myself."

The banker made no reply, and summoned an elderly, white-coated waiter. "What will you drink, Max?"

"A bourbon and water, please. Easy on the bourbon, lots of water."

Christianson repeated the order, requested a sherry on the rocks for himself and then turned back to his guest. "I felt we could talk more informally here than at your office or mine."

Max had expected to endure unimportant chatter for at least a quarter of an hour, and was heartened by the prospect of getting down to business.

"The atmosphere is relaxing," the banker continued.

Max peered at him, and saw he was serious. Unable to think of an adequate reply, he merely nodded.

"You know, of course, why I called you this afternoon."

"I can guess," Max said. "You had a phone call from Foster in London."

"I've had many calls—and cables—from him in recent days. Poor Foster has been very busy playing detective."

"I'll gladly fill in any details he may have missed," Max said.

"Oh, we have the complete picture now. North Atlantic has its friends in many places."

"Including Boston."

The banker allowed himself a trace of a smile.

"What would you like to know about the deal, Howard?" Max felt self-confident, in complete control of himself and the situation.

Their drinks came, and the banker busied himself signing for them. Then, after raising his glass in a silent toast, he said calmly, "Only your motives."

"You know them already." Max sipped his drink, found it too strong and added water from a carafe. "You wouldn't support our London purchase, so we got the loan elsewhere."

Christianson's eyes looked bleak behind his glasses. "Those are the basic facts of the situation."

"You've just heard our motives. After all these years of working with us, Howard, you certainly know that when Paul and I go after something, we don't let temporary obstacles stand in our way. But there are no hard feelings on our part, and Paul and I both hope that you and Mrs. Christianson will fly over with us for the party we're giving when we take over the property."

The banker murmured his appreciation of the invitation in a tone that made it clear he would find himself otherwise occupied when the time came.

"That's all there is to it," Max said blithely. "Once Dave Franklin gets the place fixed up the way we want it, we'll gladly

166

entertain bids for it. From anybody, including—especially, I should say—clients of North Atlantic."

"Very generous." Christianson looked at him over the rim of his glass. "Max, I know you want me to be candid, as we've always been with each other through the years."

"Naturally."

"I've never before known you to be less than truthful with me, and let me finish before you lose your temper. I thought we had agreed that L & B would do nothing about the London property until we made our joint review of your financial situation."

"Not so," Max said. "We gladly agreed to hold the review meetings with you, which is what we're doing. But we entered into no agreement that would tie our hands or hamper our actions in any way. We reserve the right of any company to conduct our operations in a manner that best suits our interests."

Christianson sat back in his chair, removed his steel-rimmed glasses and polished them vigorously. "I can't dispute the point with you, since we have nothing on paper. But it was my understanding that you'd freeze the *status quo* until we completed the analysis. At the very least, North Atlantic assumed—"

"What you assumed," Max interjected, "was that we wouldn't be able to move. Because you weren't advancing us any funds for new real estate purchases. You jumped to your own conclusions. But you ought to know me well enough by now, Howard, to realize that I wouldn't agree to cripple my own company."

"In North Atlantic's opinion," the banker replied frostily, "the acquisition of new properties is crippling."

"Differences in opinion is what makes the stock market fluctuate," Max said.

Christianson laced his fingers. "The purchase of the London property overextends L & B financially. That's the North Atlantic opinion."

"How can you be so positive when we're just getting the overall review under way?"

"This situation goes beyond anything we'll cover in the long-range study," the banker replied. "You've put yourselves in an exposed position, and by doing it you've also jeopardized us."

"Believe what you want," Max said with a shrug.

"We must do what we think necessary to protect our own loans and investments."

"Sure." Max was tired of fencing, and cut to the heart of the problem. "You think the London hotel is a poor investment, we think it's good. We're convinced it will pay off."

"When?"

"Right now we're projecting two years, which gives us plenty of time for our redecorating program, followed by a heavy public relations and advertising campaign. I'll have Dave Franklin send you the details and schedules."

"That won't be necessary. From North Atlantic's standpoint, two years is far too long a time."

"We can squeeze, Howard. But I'm not prepared to give you a timetable you can hold me to. First I'd want to find out what Dave and some of his people think is feasible."

The banker made no reply.

"How much time will you give us?" Max asked. "Eighteen months? Twelve, which is impossible?"

"Since North Atlantic disapproves the purchase, it would be wrong of us to make any such estimate. We can't associate ourselves with the investment in any way, as we'd be condoning your action, at least indirectly."

There was a long, heavy silence.

"Will you have another drink?" Christianson asked politely.

"No. Thank you."

Max took his leave quickly after that. Retrieving his hat and coat, he hurried out to his waiting car. He picked up the car telephone and dialed his partner's private home number. Apparently Lafferty was waiting for the call. He answered on the first ring.

"I just left him," Max said. "And in a word, it won't be long before lightning strikes the outhouse."

The Lion's Den had an atmosphere of discreet opulence, and, in the bar, several impudent Lance Balutis charcoal drawings which added a deft touch. The lighting was dim, the carpeting very thick and the menu featured rich, second-rate French dishes served by obsequious waiters whose flair exceeded their efficiency. On the surface nothing distinguished the Den from thirty or forty other New York restaurants of similar caliber, but the velvet ropes were in place noon and night, barring ordinary citizens from its tables, and only the Beautiful People were allowed to pay its outrageous prices for the privilege of drinking and eating in the crowded, noisy room.

Since all three of the establishment's proprietors were themselves Beautiful People, guests were sure of finding their own there, particularly as one or another of the three was always in attendance.

Max Berman, following Lance Balutis to a banquette at the far side of the room, felt uncomfortable, out of place and outdated, and it didn't help to tell himself he could buy and sell most of these Beautiful People. Maybe he should have listened to Stella's lectures in the years they had been together, and found himself a new tailor. Not that he'd be caught dead in the styles he saw on the men around him.

On second thought, their consciousness of their appearance was ridiculous, and he swore he didn't give a damn that his suit was slightly rumpled, his necktie ordinary or his shoes in need of a shine. Nobody Balutis knew, he had decided some months earlier, ever went to a barber; the Beautiful People, or the jet set, or whatever the hell they called themselves, all went to hair stylists, and he'd be damned if he'd ever descend to their level. In his world there was nothing wrong with a head of closely cropped hair.

Deliberately remaining several paces behind his companion so he wouldn't be forced to undergo the indignities of enduring introductions to people who, it seemed, automatically treated him condescendingly, he halted when Balutis bent to kiss the cheek of a handsome woman of about forty. They chatted for a moment, and then Balutis turned to the adjoining table for an even more animated word with a ruggedly built young man who was heavily tanned. Not until they finished their conversation, both speaking in low tones, and the artist finally went to the banquette, did Max start forward again and join him.

"Henry is a real doll," Lance said, idly fingering the heavy gold chain that looped around the collar of his turtlenecked silk shirt and fell in gleaming strands across his chest.

Max, settling himself on the narrow banquette, grunted and paid no attention. Everyone Balutis knew was a real doll.

"She said she'd get the new federal appropriation for experimental films, and she came through, as she always does."

Something clicked in Max's mind. "That's Henrietta Walker? The senator's wife?"

"In person." Lance smiled indulgently. This was the first time Berman appeared awed by a celebrity.

"What's she doing here?"

The smile faded. "Well, the food is edible, and the people who come here take Wasserman tests before they're allowed in, so the place is safe."

Max was too surprised to heed the sarcasm. "I didn't know Mrs. Walker was part of your crowd."

"She's a friend who takes a great interest in all the arts, if that's what you mean."

Watching the regal woman exchanging effusive greetings with an inadequately clad girl who, in the opinion of a mature man, looked like a whore, Max shook his head. "Just the other day I read that her husband is either going into the Cabinet or will be made an ambassador."

"Is that bad?"

"I thought she'd travel in a different set, that's all."

"You'd be surprised how many of us have spent weekends at Newport or have been invited to the White House for dinner. And we never use the servants' entrance."

Max glowered, but a wine steward appeared at the table before he could reply.

Lance asked for a drink called a red radish, and, not consulting his companion, ordered him a bourbon on the rocks.

"Look, Lance," Max said, "you know I don't drink at lunch."

Lance waved the waiter away. "This is one day you'll want at least one and maybe two or three." He waved to the tanned young man, who was leaving. "Kevin has promised to do a film for me. Isn't that exciting?"

Max decided it would be easier to leave his liquor untouched than to make an issue of the matter. "Who is Kevin?"

"You honestly don't recognize him?"

"He looks like a queer."

"His sex life is his own business. He happens to be the world's best amateur tennis player, and he's just signed a pro contract that's fabulous."

"I don't read the sports pages very often. If he's going to make so much money, why is he going to act in a movie for you?"

"You're adorable, Max," Lance drawled, "but I sometimes wonder whether you live on this planet. Everyone is beating down doors to get in front of a camera. Acting, or at least playing yourself, is in."

Unable to understand the sudden enthusiasm for new fads that caused Balutis' friends to behave like sheep, Max shrugged. Sometimes their antics fascinated him, but today, when he was regretting having broken his rule to accept an invitation to a long and boring social lunch, they irritated him.

A man with tinted glasses approached the table, and Lance leaped to his feet. As they embraced Max caught the scent of a strong cologne, saw that the newcomer was wearing an Edwardian suit of exaggerated cut, and wrote him off as another of the innumerable homosexuals who, he had learned, frequented the world of art and films.

Lance introduced him as someone named Gaines, and, inviting him to join them for a drink, plunged into a discussion of movie-making techniques. Max, sipping water instead of the bourbon the wine steward had placed at his elbow, half-listened to the pair discussing people called Lelouch, Godard and Buñuel, who meant nothing to him.

Suddenly Gaines turned to him. "Mr. Berman," he said, "I know exactly how you feel. But stick with Lance for another year, and you'll start talking the way I do. There's nobody in the business hotter." He grinned. "You'll even dress the way I do."

"God forbid." Max didn't intend to be rude, but the words slipped out before he could stop himself.

"That's what my wife said. And even my kids thought a man

of my age shouldn't try to be mod. But when the money started rolling in, it made a difference."

It was possible, Max thought uncertainly, that his first impression had been mistaken, and that the man wasn't a homosexual after all.

Sardonic humor showed in the eyes behind the tinted glasses. "I started the way you did, Mr. Berman. I invested a few bucks. The thing is, you can afford it and I couldn't, but I took the gamble anyway. And it paid off."

Max continued to regard him warily.

Gaines was sympathetic. "When I was in the rag trade, my name was Ginsberg."

It hadn't occurred to Max that the elegant figure lounging in the chair opposite him was a graduate of the Seventh Avenue garment business, and he laughed. "Now you're in movies?"

"I own a chain of six art theaters, and soon it'll be an even dozen. I wonder if you realize you've moved into one of the fastest-growing lines in the world." Gaines took a large swallow of his drink, an Italian vermouth on ice, and leaned forward, elbows on the table. "It goes like this. Hollywood died, and all the good films came from abroad. Then the underground started here, and suddenly everybody was making films, even kids in school, on a budget of nothing. You should see some of those efforts of a few years ago. They're classics."

"I've seen some of Lance's work, and a few others," Max replied. "But they all go over my head."

"You'll learn. And if you don't, at least you'll appreciate. Like everyone else."

"Don't bet on it." Max was becoming interested in the discussion, but glanced at his watch; he couldn't spend all day at the Den when a crowded afternoon schedule awaited him.

"The smallest of my theaters has a capacity of six hundred," Gaines said, "and the biggest holds eight hundred. Today's movie house isn't an amphitheater. But from the minute we open every afternoon, they're crowded. Not with our generation, but with young people, kids in their twenties, some in their thirties, a few in the late teens. When you show adult films, you have to be careful children don't get in."

"From what I've seen," Max said, not glancing at Balutis, "that's a good thing."

"Look, I'm a family man myself." Gaines tapped a forefinger on the table. "My whole point is that today's films have become commercial. There is no such thing as the underground any more. Director-producers like Lance are in tune with their audiences. They give the public what it demands. And fellows like me cash in, too. This suit cost me three hundred dollars, I eat in places like the Den, and every winter my wife and I go off for a six-week vacation. How many people do you know who can afford this kind of luxury?"

"Not many," Max said. "You own your own theaters?"

"Originally they were all leased, but I'm gradually buying the buildings. The secret of how to make it big, except it isn't a secret any more, is that I deal direct—with producers like Lance. So does everybody else who hits it. We've eliminated the distributor. We hold down theater payrolls. We've even put in self-service coffee machines in the lounges. We pay healthy percentages of the gross to the producers—sometimes too big—"

Lance laughed derisively.

"—but we can still show a sound profit," Gaines continued, paying no attention to the interruption. "My smallest house brings me a net of two hundred a week—that's on an average week. And my biggest shows six hundred. Add it all up, and I'm in clover, without much risk."

"Except," Max said, "if the craze for these new movies that make no sense suddenly dies out. Then what do you do?"

"In the first place, I'm convinced it won't die out. It will snowball for the next ten to twenty years. Film is the only medium that reflects—authentically—the intellectual, sexual and emotional approaches of people who won't buy the old clichés."

174

Max resisted the temptation to ask what made him an expert on the subject. "You wouldn't be the first to make a mistake," he said.

Gaine's eyes looked hard behind the circles of tinted glass. "I'm betting my future and my kids' future that I'm right. But suppose I'm wrong. I don't have to tell you anything about the value of real estate in this town. I'll still be able to sell my properties for one hell of a lot more than I paid for them." Suddenly he jumped to his feet. "I see my lunch date, so you'll have to excuse me."

Max watched him as he hurried across the room to embrace a young brunette wearing a dress with a plunging neckline.

"Charlotte will clip him," Lance said. "She needs the money ever since her boutique folded and her ex-husband fell behind in his payments. And if she doesn't get to Gaines, someone else will. The word is out that tail is his weakness. You're lucky you don't have a soft spot, Max. This crowd would find it."

"I'll admit to one. When I don't eat, my insides feel they're going to cave in."

Lance summoned their waiter, and carefully went through the ritual of inquiring about the preparation of several dishes featured in red ink on the handwritten menu. Max ordered a simple mushroom omelet and salad and refused the house specialties. The waiter's lofty smile was eloquent.

Lance glowered at his retreating back.

"In places like this," Max said, "waiters are usually bigger snobs than the customers."

"I wish I were as tolerant of them as you are."

"If a fellow like me doesn't learn tolerance early in life," Max replied with a weary smile, "he can drive himself crazy. You said you had something important to discuss."

"Do I!" Lance took a small square of paper from his pocket and consulted it. "By now," he said, "you've invested eighty-five thousand in my enterprises."

"Correct. To the penny."

"And up until today, you've had a return of forty thousand, which isn't bad in less than a year."

"I'm not complaining."

Lance reached into the inner pocket of his velvet jacket and drew out a certified check. "Here's another twenty thousand, Max, and if *The Bohemian Boys* keeps playing to sellout crowds, you'll have your final twenty-five thousand in another few weeks."

"To be honest with you, I didn't really expect to break even so soon."

"By a year from now, you'll have doubled your investment."

"That's better than I can do in my own business."

"I'm glad to hear you say it, because a real opportunity has come my way, and I'd like to let you in on it."

Max was interested, but simultaneously became cautious.

"You heard what Larry Gaines was saying a few minutes ago about the craving of the public for films."

What Max had suspected became apparent; Gaines's little chat extolling the business of movie-making hadn't been a coincidence.

"You don't know him, of course, so I wouldn't dream of asking you to take his word, even though you could look up his credentials. I won't even suggest that you study the box-office figures in *Variety*. They can be padded. So let me get that lovely Ross girl from your office together with the accountants who have been making an independent audit—"

"You give me twenty thousand with one hand, and you want to take back a bigger chunk with the other. How much?"

"I'd like to explain the project to you first." Lance drained his glass.

"I'm listening."

"No one in this country has done a big-budget film for the art houses, the way Godard and a few others in Europe have done. We're still geared to the underground level of penny-pinching,

176

but we're wrong, and I'll tell you why. In the old days, when Hollywood splurged on its star-name spectaculars, a producer was satisfied if he broke even on the domestic market. The foreign market was his gravy, and a rich gravy it was. The foreign theaters are still in business, and a fortune—a solid gold fortune—can be made in them on a Lance Balutis super-production. Done with all the trimmings."

"I'm not denying it," Max said. "I'd have to see a complete financial breakdown and projection, though, before I could accept your optimism."

"You'll have a preliminary analysis on your desk by tomorrow morning, and I'll gladly provide any other data Stella Ross may want to see."

"Leave Stella out of this."

"Of course, Max."

"Hollywood has always gone to the banks for financing. Why can't you?"

"I've come up from the underground, that's why, and I haven't yet developed the international status of a Fellini or a Bergman."

"You still haven't told me how much you want."

Lance took a deep drag on his cigarette before snuffing it out. "I'm working on a tentative budget of a million."

"I invest that kind of money only in a business I know."

"I wouldn't expect any one investor to put up the whole amount. But you and I have done well together, Max, and I'd like to give you the chance to clean up with me. I've thought of putting you down for three hundred thousand. How does that strike you?"

"Right in the gut."

"And I certainly wouldn't ask you to gamble blindly. I'm prepared to offer you collateral. You'll have security as good as cash in the bank."

Their food arrived, and Max remained silent until the waiter moved away. "I've never yet heard of collateral as good as cash. Don't keep me in suspense."

"You can hold three hundred thousand dollars' worth of my paintings and photographs. Go to any art dealer you want, and I accept any fair appraisal. And if you don't get back your investment within twenty months, you'll be free to dispose of the paintings. By then they'll be worth at least twenty-five to thirty percent more."

On the surface, at least, the offer seemed good, and Max thought about it as he ate his omelet. "If you have an inventory of paintings and photographs worth three hundred thousand," he said at last, "I don't see why you need me. Unload them on a dealer, or let somebody sell them for you, and you'll have the cash for your own financing."

"I've played with the idea, but it isn't sound." Lance sipped the white wine he had ordered with his poached Dover sole. "In the long run I'd be losing money. As I told you, and as any reputable dealer in town will confirm, three hundred thousand dollars' worth of Balutis originals will be worth almost four hundred thousand in another eighteen to twenty-four months."

Once Max would have scoffed, but he had learned there was a steady, active demand for almost anything Balutis filmed and painted.

"I can't promise you a quick buck," Lance said, "but your long-range return will be great. Within five years your three hundred thousand should triple itself."

Max chewed on a piece of his roll. "Suppose the picture is a flop."

"I have confidence in my talent," Lance said, stiffening. "And my record speaks for itself."

"Until now you've been making movies that cost almost nothing. There's a difference between the loose change in your pocket and one million dollars."

"I'm very well aware of it, which is why I plan to do a big

film on a controversial theme. Of course, if you'd rather stay out, just say so."

"I'm trying to look at this from every angle, that's all." Max wasn't quite sure how he had been put on the defensive.

Lance smiled. "All I can say is that your initial investment is guaranteed. The worst that could happen is you'd get your money back in twenty months, with nothing more to show for it."

"Oh, I don't belittle the earning power of your work," Max said. "Let me examine everything you can send me. Obviously you don't expect an overnight decision."

"Take all the time you want. Within a few days I hope to have a synopsis of the idea on paper, too. A friend of mine who does poetry and short stories is putting the outline together."

"I'll read it, but it won't mean much to me." Max finished his omelet. "When do you need an answer?"

"Would two weeks be too soon?"

"Not if you get me all the figures." Max looked at his watch. "I don't have time for coffee, Lance. I'm due at my office in five minutes." Conscious of flickering glances, followed by blank stares, Max made his way through the room and retrieved his hat and coat from the checkroom girl.

The day was bitterly cold, but he felt a need for air. He decided to walk back to his office, even though he was pressed for time. Traffic was so heavy he could do the ten blocks on foot more rapidly than by taxi, even if it were possible to hail one.

To his astonishment, Stella was sitting behind the closed door of his private office when he arrived.

"Your meeting has been postponed," she said. "Paul has gone home."

"Is somebody sick?" Max forgot to remove his overcoat.

"Not exactly, but Margaret is terribly upset, and Paul asked me to tell you about it. That's the only reason I've come up here to wait for you."

"What happened to upset Margaret?"

"Janet has left home. Against her parents' wishes. Paul was pretty disturbed himself, and didn't explain too well, but I gather there's been a family debate going on for weeks."

"You mean she ran away—or eloped with some boy?"

"No, that's what I thought. The crazy kid said she couldn't work at home, and she wanted her own apartment so she'd have freedom to paint. Maybe there's something to what Janet claims. Paul has always been able to reason with her, but she wouldn't even listen to him."

Max unbuttoned his coat. "Look, this was bound to happen some day. The Lafferty family has always been very close, but Janet isn't a child any more. She's of age, and she isn't the first or the last to want a life of her own."

"Margaret and Paul wouldn't have minded so much if this had been an ordinary move. Oh, it would have been a wrench, but they're not the kind of parents to try to tie their children down. What bothers them is that she's taken up with people they don't like. She's been seeing quite a bit of Lance Balutis and that Wayne girl—"

"I didn't know that. Balutis hasn't even mentioned her name to me."

"Janet has moved in with some friend of Bobbie Wayne's."

"Who?"

"I don't know her name. I'm not even sure Paul knows it. All Janet told them before she left was the address and telephone number of the apartment." Stella handed him a slip of paper.

He studied it and shrugged. "This is way the hell downtown."

"The East Village. Off St. Mark's Place."

"I don't like this, either."

"Don't start sounding like Paul. I'm sure that ninety-five percent of the people who live in that neighborhood are decent and respectable—"

"Yeah sure. But Balutis and his crowd make up a good part of the other five percent." Max took a cigarette from a box on his desk and savagely struck a match. "And I'm not sure Janet can really handle herself with them."

"She's been brought up by a family that taught her right from wrong. Don't you start to panic, Max."

He ground out the cigarette in an ashtray, walked to the windows and turned back. "That whole movie bunch is rotten. They don't even understand what it means to have morals, and the way everybody sleeps with everybody else—" He broke off. "Janet is a good girl, but she can be around those people just so long, and before you know it she'll be a kook, like all the others. My God, this is my fault."

"Don't be foolish, Max. You said yourself that Janet is of age."

"If it hadn't been for me, she wouldn't have met those people. When I think of the way Balutis latched on to her at that party last year."

"I happen to know that Janet doesn't care in the least for him. His work may fascinate her, but his personality repels her."

"All the same," Max replied stubbornly, "he's the *macher* of that set. He's the important one, and all the others buzz around him. Well, I know how to handle this. Balutis happens to want something from me, and I'll tell him—today—that he won't get it unless he sends Janet back home."

"A girl of her age and temperament can't be handled like a sub-contractor you put pressure on." She ran a hand through her short hair. "What will you do?"

"I'll go down to her apartment myself and I'll talk to her. The afternoon schedule is loused up anyway, with Paul not here. I think I might as well go right now."

"I'm coming with you." She made a flat statement rather than a request.

"Okay. Get your coat." He was pleased.

"I'll meet you at the elevator," Stella said.

They were silent during the taxi ride to the East Village, the section east of Fifth Avenue that had, in recent years, replaced the increasingly middle-class-oriented Greenwich Village itself as the headquarters of young rebels and the artistically inclined. Snow and ice on the sidewalks and on garbage cans sitting outside buildings had turned the grimy color of the city, and Max, hunched in a corner of the taxi, brooded silently.

Stella knew he was working up to the point where he might lose his temper, but past experience had taught her that it would do no good to reason with him. "I guess this is the place," she said as the taxi pulled to a halt before an old brownstone building with worn, rubbish-strewn steps.

Max paid the driver and followed Stella inside. She was looking at a card, printed in violet ink, that had been inserted in a slot above the mailbox and read, *Browning—Lafferty*.

"Does the name Browning mean anything to you?" she asked.

"All I know for sure," he said, forcing a grin, "is that this isn't the one who wrote a poem about a rabbi."

Stella looked at him blankly.

This was not the moment to explain his feeble joke. "To me, all of Balutis' friends look alike. They don't have names. Ring the bell."

After a brief wait the buzzer that released the lock on the inner door sounded, and they pushed it open. Stella led the way up three flights of narrow stairs in reasonably good repair. But the walls were badly in need of paint and the plaster ceiling was cracked. Odors of stale cooking grease, onions and fish assailed their nostrils, and Stella turned for an instant to exchange a glance with Max.

The entrance to one of the two apartments on the third floor was open a crack, secured by a chain, and Stella gave Max no chance to speak. "Janet? We've come to see Janet Lafferty."

"She isn't here." The voice of a girl drifted through the crack, and they could catch a glimpse of a young, suspicious face.

"Do you know when she'll be back?" Stella was calm and reassuring. "We're old friends, not her parents."

"Give me your phone number, and if she wants, she'll call you."

182

Stella silenced Max with a gesture, and hid her own disappointment. "Well, all right, if we can't reach her now. Tell her that Stella Ross and Max Berman dropped in."

The chain rattled, and the door flew open. "Maxie!" the girl with long hair cried.

Max felt as though someone had struck him in the stomach when he recognized Muriel, the rump-obsessed girl he had found making love with Balutis in his Connecticut house. "I never knew your last name," he said, embarrassed and doubly annoyed with Janet because of her lack of judgment. "Miss Ross, let me present Miss Muriel Browning, who appears to be Janet's roommate."

Stella, who was scrutinizing the young woman, nodded with as much grace as she could muster.

"I'm not dressed for company, but come in anyway." Muriel indicated her flimsy minishift, wiggled her toes and, consciously or otherwise, revealed the sole of a very dirty, bare foot. "Where have you been hiding lately, Max?"

"I go to my office every day, and I spend my nights at home." He made an effort to conceal his dislike for the girl. "So Janet has moved in here with you." He looked around the room at several inexpensive, low-slung canvas chairs on wooden frames, the only furniture worthy of the name. Cushions of all sizes, shapes and colors, in every conceivable covering from terrycloth to silk, were piled everywhere, against walls and in corners, with a scattering of them in the center of the room.

"It took Jan to get you here, didn't it?" Muriel giggled. "Have some cushions. You, too, Miss Ross," she added a trifle primly, like a schoolgirl suddenly remembering her manners.

Both of the visitors preferred to remain standing, and Stella, sensing Max's ill-concealed antagonism toward the girl, swiftly took charge. "Do you know where we can find Janet?"

"You aren't going to drag her back home?"

"Nobody could do that, not even her father and mother," Max

said, his voice becoming strident. "We aren't detectives, Muriel, and we aren't going to kidnap her!"

"Don't lose your cool, Maxie." The girl seemed to enjoy his anger, but was aware, too, of Stella's unwavering gaze. "Okay, I guess you can't put the squeeze on her. She's just gone around the corner to get some paints and canvases. At a store called Modern Supplies."

"Why don't we go there and find her, then?" Stella edged toward the door.

"Well," Muriel said, "she could come back here either one of two ways. I'll tell you what. Why don't you go, and Max can wait here. If you miss her, you can come back."

Max's expression made it obvious he didn't want to be left alone with the girl.

Nevertheless Stella hesitated before rejecting the idea. If she found Janet, she would be able to speak a few words with her alone, before Max started to roar. And she couldn't reject the possibility that Muriel, who patently wanted to be rid of her, might confide in Max if she spent a few minutes alone with him.

"All of us are busy," Stella said brightly, "so your suggestion sounds good. We'll save time for everyone."

Max scowled at her.

"Which way do I go, Miss Browning?"

"Turn left at the corner, and then left again. You can't miss the place. And we'll be right here, waiting."

Stella refused to meet Max's angry eyes as she went to the door. "I won't be long."

The moment the door closed, Muriel secured the chain.

"Was it your idea to have Janet move in here?" Max asked her.

"Oh, the whole thing just sort of grew. Jan is real groovy, and she can do her thing here. I hate being alone, so it works out for everybody. Anything else you want to know?"

Max decided he would save the rest of his questions for Janet, and shook his head.

184

"Why don't you like me, Maxie?" Muriel asked plaintively, edging closer to him.

"Who says I don't?" Unless it proved necessary, he didn't want to antagonize her.

"You turn me on, but it doesn't work the other way around, and I don't dig it. I've never yet met anybody who doesn't go for my bottom." She turned, bent over and wiggled her rear provocatively.

"If you were my daughter," Max said, trying to speak gently, "I'll tell you what I'd do to your bottom. I'd spank it so hard you couldn't sit down for a week."

"You don't have to be my father for that!" The girl turned, and leaping at him unexpectedly, caused him to lose his balance.

They tumbled together onto a deep pile of cushions, and Max tried to raise himself to a sitting position.

But Muriel, her arms tightly clasped around his neck, struggled playfully. "Go on, spank me," she murmured. "I've got a surprise for you." An artful wriggle caused her tiny skirt to ride higher, revealing her plump, bare buttocks.

Her abandon outraged Max. Jerking himself upright, he caught her by the waist and stood her on her feet with such force that she was jarred for a moment.

There were tears in her eyes as he stood, brushing off his overcoat and tugging at his sleeves.

"What kind of an alley cat are you?" he demanded. "If you act like this all the time, you must get raped fifty times a day."

"It's none of your business what I do." She sounded more than ever like a sulky child.

Max watched her as she tugged ineffectually at her short skirt, which, even when restored to its full length, rode near the tops of her thighs. "I'm damned if I know what your generation is trying to prove," he said, "but you're not proving it."

"Even if we drew you pictures, you wouldn't understand!"

"That's fine with me, and I also don't care if you want to be a lousy little tramp. But I won't stand for Janet Lafferty being pulled down to your level."

Muriel returned his stare, then laughed scornfully. "Jan is with it, Maxie! Do you think she'll let you pull her coat?"

Her slang was beyond his comprehension.

The girl enjoyed her little triumph. "You really are out of the Dark Ages. Jan won't listen to anything you say to her."

"We'll see about that."

"We sure will." Muriel's grim tone matched his, and she looked old, debauched.

Max felt slightly ill. His associations would be the ruin of Janet Lafferty, and he was determined to take her home, no matter what she wanted.

A key was inserted in the door, and Muriel quickly removed the chain.

Janet entered the apartment, followed by a tight-lipped Stella, who shook her head bleakly.

Max felt frustrated by the appearance of his partner's daughter. Her short dress, wild-patterned stockings and knee-high boots were her generation's uniform, but Janet was obviously making a point, and her skirt was shorter and tighter than the demands of basic modesty tolerated. Max found it difficult to curb the urge to drag her into the bathroom, assuming the apartment was equipped with one, and scrub her face with soap and water.

Janet dropped a string-bag filled with tubes of paint onto a chair, and propped several canvases against the wall. "Hi," she said, her manner almost too casual. "I was expecting a fire-alarm visit from Mother and Daddy, but it didn't occur to me they'd send you and Stella."

"Your parents," Max said, the strain of speaking calmly thickening his voice, "don't know we're here."

"I told her," Stella said, "that they'd probably disapprove."

"That makes it unanimous," Janet said.

Muriel laughed shrilly.

186

Max blocked out the sound. "I've known and loved you since the day you were born," he said, "which is why I'm butting in. And also which is why you can hurt me very easily with sarcasm. So, if it gives you pleasure, go ahead."

Janet was shaken by his manner as well as his words. "All I want," she said, tears in her voice, "is the chance to live my life the way I think is best for my future."

"All we care about is your future." Max looked at Stella, wanting support.

"It's no use," she said. "Janet has made up her mind."

"She's entitled to that," he replied gravely, "provided she realizes that the kind of freedom she thinks she's gaining means running risks. I'm not a priest or a rabbi, so I won't deliver sermons." It was irritating to see Muriel standing to one side and a little behind him, silently mimicking his gestures, and he tried to block her from sight. "But your new friends could teach you bad habits. I know how you were brought up, and I know the values that were always important to you."

Janet dropped onto a pile of cushions, her skirt riding almost as high as Muriel's. "Look," she said, directing her remark exclusively to Max, apparently hoping to convince him of her earnestness. "Nobody can force me to do anything against my will," Janet declared, "just as nobody can stop me from doing what I want."

Muriel lost patience. "Why do you bother explaining all this crap, Jan? To him—of all people! The old queer!"

They all looked at her, and Janet seemed as puzzled as her elders.

"You wouldn't believe me at first," Muriel went on, "when I told you Lance is AC/DC. It took you a while to learn he's just as happy to make out with fellows as with girls. All right, use your brains. Why should Maxie, the peerless leader, become Lance's moneybags? Because they're lovers, natch. That's why it's a real gasser to hear pompous morality being preached by a fag!"

187

Even though Max realized the girl was making a foolish, vindictive effort to discredit him, he felt a surge of unreasoning, righteous anger.

"Why don't you get out?" Muriel was still vicious. "It doesn't bother me when a boy goes for another boy, but when somebody of your age is that way, it's disgusting."

Janet suddenly interrupted her friend's diatribe. "I was hoping you'd understand, Uncle Max. I was hoping you wouldn't be as narrow as Mother and Daddy."

"What is there to understand? Your family isn't good enough for you any more."

The girl did not hear him. "I might have known. It isn't just you and my parents, or even your whole generation. There's a special breed of you that lives on the upper East Side. You're the world's chosen people—the *real* chosen people. You come from all kinds of different backgrounds, you have all different religions, but you're united by two things. Money. And power."

"Money," Max said, "hasn't hurt you any. And your father's power has given you advantages that not many girls your age can claim. Be glad you've been so fortunate."

Janet ignored the interruption. "You isolate yourselves. You seal yourselves off from the world. Stella knows what I mean, even if you don't. Isn't that true?"

Stella looked uncomfortable, but had no chance to answer.

"I've thought about it for years. You seal yourselves off physically. Off you go to your offices, and to the theatre and restaurants. Yes, and on trips to Europe and places. But you come right back to that Upper East Side womb. Your expensive co-op apartments. Your Golden Ghetto."

"That's foolish," Max said.

"Is it?" Janet's anger was quiet but intense. "In every possible way you live in that Golden Ghetto. You really do, all of you. You insulate yourselves against new ideas, new trends, new thinking, new ways of life, new everything."

"Hooray!" Muriel applauded vigorously. "A touchdown for our team."

Max concentrated his full attention on Janet. "Are all these new things so wonderful?"

"Maybe. Maybe some of them are. Maybe some are terrible. Maybe they're all terrible."

He looked as confused as he felt.

"Why can't you see it, Uncle Max? We don't want to take your word that something is good or bad. We want to try it, and find out for ourselves."

"When somebody tells me poison ivy is bad," Max said, "I don't have to rub it on my skin. I'll take the word of the experts. When I hear a new drug is bad—"

"I don't take drugs," Janet cut in. "But that's a matter of personal choice. Maybe some day there will be a new drug that I want to try. What I really want is the right to make my own choice, to decide—strictly on my own—whether I want it or I don't. Living here, in a free world, I'm able to reach my own decisions. I couldn't do it if I were stifling in the Golden Ghetto."

"Every younger generation in history," Max said, "has thought the same thing."

Max, afraid he would further stiffen Janet's resistance if he started to speak, allowed himself to be led out of the apartment.

Muriel's high-pitched, triumphant giggle followed Stella and Max down the stairs.

When they reached the street they stood for a moment, and Stella raised the collar of her coat, shivering slightly, before taking Max's arm.

He remained silent as they started off down the street in search of a taxi, the biting wind stinging their faces. "That kid is bad news," he said at last. "She should be in a mental hospital. I guess you know she was trying to get even with me because I wouldn't play it her way. Imagine! Having to fight off rape by a girl who can't be more than twenty-two or -three. If she's that old. It makes me sick to think of Janet staying with her."

They reached the corner, and, when they halted, Stella stamped her feet to keep them warm.

"You want to stop for coffee?"

"After we get back uptown. I'm sure there are clean coffee shops in this part of town, but the atmosphere depresses me."

Max hailed a taxi. They sat in the cab quietly, thawing for several minutes before Stella spoke. "I think it will be better if we don't say anything to Paul and Margaret about this afternoon."

"They should know," Max said.

"What good will it do?"

"Do you think it will help to keep the truth from them?" Max shook his head. "They should know that Janet's in bad company."

"Whatever you say." Stella was troubled, but gave in.

"If she hadn't moved in with that Muriel, it might not be so bad. She's the one I caught in my house with Balutis. You remember."

"Very clearly."

"For what she said, I should have clobbered her."

"For calling you a fag? You needn't ever worry about that, Max."

"I'm glad your memory is good. Sometimes I've wondered."

Stella's attitude toward him became warmer, possibly because of Muriel's nasty attack. Whatever the reason, he wanted to savor the improvement in their relationship. He looked forward to sitting down with her over a cup of coffee.

The attractive woman, wearing a formal evening gown in midmorning, sat unblinkingly beneath the battery of high-powered lights in Lance Balutis' studio. Not moving, she held herself regally erect, looking straight ahead, but unable to see the artist at work on a canvas beyond the circle of lights.

"I'll cut the sitting short," Lance muttered, "but give me a minute or two, Max. I can't be obvious in the way I push Sandy around."

Max curbed his impatience as best he could and stared at Sandra Tilstrom, wondering what it was that made a woman one of the most renowned of the Beautiful People. Her photo appeared frequently in the newspapers, and of all the women Stella had mentioned when she had chattered about the names in the gossip columns, no one had been in print more often than the glamorous Sandra. Or was she glamorous?

Her face was attractive enough, but she lacked real beauty and the mark of intelligence that gave someone of her age character. The portrait Lance was painting resembled a child's drawing, in Max's opinion, and, he thought, no woman endowed with brains would spend her money on such rubbish. What created a celebrity in the international café society crowd was not only mysterious but irritating, he concluded.

Lance snapped off the lights. "That's it for today, Sandy angel," he called.

The woman relaxed and reached into a handbag on the floor beside her thronelike chair for a cigarette and lighter. "I was set for a long sitting, darling," she complained.

"Your expression was perfect for a half-hour," Lance told her, "but then you began to stiffen. We can't recapture it until next time, so it's best to leave well enough alone. Sandy, dear, you've met Max Berman."

Sandra nodded vaguely. "I wasn't conscious of freezing," she said, directing her full attention to Lance. "They told me the same thing when I did a bit of modeling, but that was ages ago, and you'd think that by now I'd have outgrown my self-consciousness.

"Sensitive people always stiffen, no matter how much experience they've had."

"Really, darling? That's a comfort." She tried to look at the painting.

Lance moved in front of the canvas, blocking her view. "Why don't you go and change," he said.

Sandra's laugh was conspiratorial. "This is what I wore to come down, and I'll wear it home. We live in the stuffiest block in town, and I'm just praying that some of my neighbors will see me getting out of a taxi a little before noon—in an evening dress. They'll be sure that everything they've been saying about me for years is true!"

Lance joined in the laugh, sounding as though he shared her idea of a joke.

After seeing her to the door, he said, "What a silly bitch."

"I thought she was a great big celebrity."

Lance missed his irony. "Only because she spends a mint on clothes, and the press agents for the dressmakers give her a ride in print."

"Are you holding her up to ridicule," Max asked, "in the portrait you're doing?"

"I'm painting her as I see her," Lance replied with care, "which is the artist's privilege. I didn't want to do her bloody portrait, but her husband offered me too much to turn down—and my only stipulation was that I do what I saw fit. I'm trying out a new technique to bring out the super-real, so it isn't wasted effort."

"Sometimes," Max said, "I think you try to tear the whole human race apart."

"I'd put it another way. I'd say we tear ourselves apart, but that isn't what I'm trying to prove. Everyone who is mature outgrows the conventional, and I'm fascinated by perspective. For example, these photographs—"

"I've been looking at them," Max said dryly, "and I haven't come here in the middle of a business day to talk about pictures that look like they weren't even made with a camera."

"That's precisely how they're intended to look." Lance smiled. "Shall we go into my office?"

"I didn't come here to discuss our business arrangement."

Lance concealed his disappointment.

"I have something more important on my mind. Janet Lafferty, my partner's daughter, has taken an apartment with your little tramp friend, Muriel."

"I hope you aren't blaming me," Lance said. "I knew nothing about the move until it was a *fait accompli*. I'm sure the girls realized I'd disapprove."

"Why would you?"

"For the very reason that you've come here. I wouldn't want it upsetting my relationship with you, a mutually profitable relationship, Max. I heard about the whole thing indirectly, through Bobbie Wayne. She's become something of Muriel's mother confessor lately. I haven't even seen Muriel in more than a month."

"Janet's parents are sick over this. I don't care how she's persuaded to go home, but that's where she should be."

Lance shook his head. "She won't go until she learns she has no future as an artist. I've seen too many girls like her, and they're all the same. They're earnest and sweet and good, and they have more ideals than talent. Janet won't make the grade, take my word for it."

Max tried to interrupt.

"Hear me out. These days it isn't enough to be a fair sculptor or painter or whatever. The competition is too great. The artist who really gets somewhere must have a flair, a sense of personal showmanship. And that's nothing new, really. Leonardo da Vinci pranced around Milan in a fur cape dyed to look like Joseph's coat of many colors. It was fabulous. Rembrandt was nothing until he rode through the streets of Leyden in a Roman chariot, and then there was a sudden demand in Amsterdam for his work. Van Gogh—"

"Spare me the history of crazy artists. Janet Lafferty should go home before she gets into some nasty trouble." When Max scowled, his face became menacingly ugly.

Lance took a single, backward step. "If I could, I'd lock her

193

into a chastity belt—for your sake. But I can't. And it isn't necessary. She won't give away anything until she's married. She positively reeks of virginity."

"She won't for very long, living with Muriel."

"Janet will get her kicks second-hand," Lance said earnestly. "Muriel's affairs will be a substitute for her own, and she'll convince herself she's living a great, free life—without the sweat."

"Until she makes a mistake."

"I've already done what I can to help prevent mistakes."

"Like what?" Max was unyielding.

"I've asked Bobbie to keep an eye on her—"

"My God! What kind of craziness is that, to tell a whore to protect an innocent kid?"

"Max, you're great when it comes to putting up new buildings, but you don't dig people under thirty. This is a new generation."

"All generations are the same."

"I could argue the point with you, but I won't. Look, Max, do you think I'm crazy?"

Studying him, Max saw the shrewd son of Lithuanian immigrants who had clawed his way to success, and, in spite of his anger, felt a measure of kinship with him. "I've never known you to miss a bet."

"Okay, my friend. Do you think I'd willingly destroy what you and I have worked out together? Especially right now, when I've just come to you for a really big chunk of money? Give me credit for some sense, Max. I wouldn't have told Bobbie to keep watch over your precious Janet Lafferty if I thought it was going to boomerang!"

Either Balutis was being too clever for his own and everyone else's good, or he had a valid point, and Max forced himself to listen.

"Is Bobbie corrupt? Sure. Is she dissolute? All the way. But she has two things going for her. She's loyal to her friends, and I've been closer to her than anybody. For years. I still am. She'll do as I've asked—for my sake."

"What's the other good thing about her?"

"She hasn't completely lost her Main Line background. When she's with her friends, she lets loose. But her own conscience wouldn't let her debauch a child, and that's what Janet is! Take my word, Bobbie is the best guardian that kid could have right now, one hell of a lot better than a policeman. Or the priest at her family's church! Just try dragging the Lafferty kid back to her family yourself, if you think that's possible."

"I've tried," Max said dryly.

"If she can stomach Muriel for six months, it'll be a miracle. Her work won't sell and I predict that she'll run home to Mama and Papa long before six months have passed. Then she can marry some nice boy from Holy Cross, and everybody will be happy."

"Holy Cross turns out some fine young men!"

"If I didn't know you, Max, I wouldn't believe your kind existed any more. You're an original!"

Paul Lafferty walked into his partner's office and dropped a sheet of paper on his desk. "If I were a clerk in the loan department of North Atlantic," he said, "I'd call this just another bank notice. But I'm not, and I call it a great deal more. In fact, I wouldn't be going too far if I called it the handwriting on the wall."

Max snatched the document, which carried the letterhead of the North Atlantic Bank and Trust Company, and absorbed it in a glance. "The bastards," he said. "They've started."

"They aren't hanging us quite yet."

"No, just dropping a noose around our necks."

"When did this arrive?" Max continued to scowl at the paper.

"Just now, in the mail."

"No phone call? No personal letter expressing the deep regrets of Howard Christianson?"

"Just the notice, nothing else. Right out of the blue."

"We knew it wouldn't be long before they started calling in their loans to us," Max said.

"Slow strangulation, I say. They could have shoved us to the wall with one big push. Instead they've decided to make us sweat by inching us toward the brink."

"The trouble is," Max said, "that we don't know when they'll press the buzzer again. Will they give us six months before they put the slug on us again, or will they recall the next loan tomorrow? There's no way of guessing."

"They won't wait six months. Or even two. When bankers gain the upper hand, they hold onto it. You don't suppose this is an ordinary bank-loan recall, Max?"

"All the evidence points the other way. No friendly little chat with Christianson. He's not providing us with a cushion, and he's giving us no explanation of a situation that normally would require one. This recall comes on the smallest loan we have outstanding at North Atlantic—when we owe them millions. So there's got to be some reason they're dunning us for a lousy seven hundred and thirty thousand. Hell, Christianson knows we can go into cash reserves for a loan of this size, and not feel the pinch. He'll expect us to call him now, so he can enjoy a little double-talk. You know, Paul, a surgeon finds a useful outlet for his sadism, and all mankind benefits. But when a banker is sadistic, he means it, and there's no escape."

"What do they want?" Paul asked bitterly.

"Our hotels, our office buildings, everything we own that isn't nailed down. All at the bargain prices that accompany a bankruptcy foreclosure."

"We'd better arrange a meeting with Christianson so we can make our peace with him," Paul said.

Max held up a brawny hand. "It's too late for that. If North Atlantic has made up its mind to squeeze us dry, a meeting wouldn't do the least good, not if we got down on our knees and crawled to them. But you're assuming we're down, Paul."

"If they recall all their loans to us, we can't survive. You know it, I know it—and Christianson knows it."

"True, but they may not be prepared to go that far. Knocking off a company the size of L & B causes all sorts of waves in the financial community. Other people get jittery. They become afraid to borrow for their own deals. Maybe the bank itself becomes shaky. This could be no more than a gigantic bluff on the part of North Atlantic."

Paul was silent for a moment. "What makes you think it might be no more than a bluff?"

"The odd way they've gone about calling in this loan. The formal notice doesn't commit them to anything beyond this one transaction. They aren't forced to give us any specific warnings about dreadful things to come. This is it, and they leave the rest to our imagination."

"I wouldn't have imagined they could be that subtle."

"For the present," Max said, "we refuse to admit to them we know there *is* a war. A bluff can work two ways. So we don't make any economy moves. If we sold a hotel or cut the payroll or called a temporary halt to construction somewhere, the bank would know it in a matter of hours. They'd also know we were frightened, and they'd attack all the harder."

"We stand pat?"

"That's what I want to do," Max said.

"All right. I'm with you." Paul inhaled deeply. "But it's going to take a lot of guts."

"Sure, because this is no game for punks. Look at all the marbles at stake."

The weekends were the worst. Max had heard widowers say it, and men who were divorced. In the months he had been alone, he had discovered they were right, and it was no use telling himself it was his own fault he was lonely. He was willing to grant that a man could make a social life for himself more easily than could a woman, but a man who was settled in his ways and tired after a week of work sometimes found the effort too great.

Looking around the living room of an apartment far too large for a bachelor who lived alone, he laughed wryly. It was a temptation to feel sorry for himself, but he tried to resist the urge.

If he chose, he could make a date with a woman for dinner and the evening, find some male friends with whom he could spend a few hours or even go out alone. There were hundreds of restaurants that would be delighted to accept his money, a score of plays—on Broadway and off—that he wouldn't mind seeing, concerts to hear, movies that might give him a few hours of entertainment. Instead, he was sitting here alone after finding reasons to spend the better part of the day at the office, and it was far too simple to claim that he felt lethargic because he was mentally and physically worn down.

Were he and Stella still together, they'd be going somewhere tonight, possibly with another couple or two, and tomorrow they'd be either visiting or entertaining friends, but he wouldn't think of being tired. On the contrary, he'd be rested and ready for a new week of work by the time Monday morning came.

The problem, as he well knew, was that the world of the mature was made for couples. Someone of his age had no desire to spend a Saturday or Sunday night at one of the countless single bars that could be found from the Sixties through the Eighties on the East Side. The mere thought of bar-hopping, hoping he might pick up a girl, made him feel foolish.

Max realized his situation wasn't unique. New York was filled with respectable, middle-aged men who were alone, thousands of them sitting in their comfortable apartments, wondering how to kill time until Monday morning. Pulling down his necktie and opening the top button of his shirt, he yawned and sprawled in his chair. He could get a woman to satisfy his sexual needs without any trouble, but it was far more difficult to buy companionship. And one's married friends, no matter how good their intentions, no matter how often they included one in their plans, built their basic social lives with other couples. The single or divorced man, or the widower, was still an outsider.

The doorbell rang, and he muttered as he hauled himself to his feet. He was expecting no one, and found he resented the unexpected intrusion. One of the most insidiously dangerous habits formed by someone living alone was that of guarding his privacy as though it were a precious commodity.

"Janet!" Max was surprised and pleased to see the girl standing on his threshold.

"I hope I'm not disturbing you, Uncle Max." Janet Lafferty's smile was uncertain. "I came to see Mother and Daddy, so I thought I'd drop in on you, too, and—"

"Since when does a visit to me need explanations?" Max waved her into the apartment.

She walked in slowly, shedding her short, lined leather coat.

"Sit down," Max said, "and let me get you something to drink."

Janet smiled. "Are you offering me liquor?"

"If you'd like it. What I had in mind though was iced coffee."

"Too cold for that. I'll take it hot."

She went with him to the kitchen, and, unbidden, took two cups from a cupboard.

"You came just now from seeing your parents, you said?"

"Yes, and it was a mistake." Janet's air of nonchalant self-confidence evaporated, and she became bitter. "They started jumping all over me the minute I walked in the door. Both of them let me have it as though I were twelve years old."

"Jan, they're your parents!" Max sounded more reproving than he meant to. "They've missed you, and they worry about you."

"Don't you start, Uncle Max!"

"All right." He held up a hand. "Not another word. We'll take our coffee into the living room, and you'll tell me about your new life."

199

"Okay." Janet led the way. Max's attitude relaxed her and she dropped her defenses. "Well, let's see. I haven't sold any of my paintings yet, but I have faith in them, even if no one else does."

"I've always enjoyed what you paint, and I'm willing to prove it with cash."

"Thanks, Uncle Max, but I can't accept a—a disguised present from you. No. I'm being criticized because my work is supposedly old-fashioned—"

"Who criticizes you? Balutis?"

His possessive ferocity made Janet smile. "Lance is very sweet to me. And he's been careful not to knock my work too hard. It's just—well, everybody says I'm not with it. But I'll find a niche for my work sooner or later."

"Sure you will," Max said. "Your father and I taught ourselves building. You'll learn in your own way how to be a successful artist. You look well, Jan."

"You don't sound convinced of that, Uncle Max."

"I admit I have to get used to your clothes. And your hair, and—"

Her whoop of laughter, which filled the room, cut him off. "It's amazing how much you and Daddy are alike in some ways. He said my skirt is too short, but it isn't new—I've had it for a year. My hair style isn't changed, and it couldn't have grown more than a half-inch since the last time we saw each other. But —you really do trust me, don't you, Uncle Max?"

"Why shouldn't I?"

The confidence of someone she was using as a parent-substitute made the girl ecstatic. "I think you're great!" She couldn't help glancing around the room again. "When you and Stella came downtown to see me, I thought—I mean, I wish—"

"I wish it, too," he said heavily, interrupting. "But when wishes don't get you anywhere, you try to stop. More coffee, Jan? Are you hungry?"

"Aren't you going out? I mean, it's Saturday—"

"To a middle-aged bachelor like me, a Saturday is the same as any other day. Let's see what we can find in the kitchen. Now," he said, opening the refrigerator. "Hanging up over there is some of that hard Hungarian salami you always liked. Except that you'll have to hold your breath whenever your date gets near you tonight."

"I don't have a date this evening."

He looked at her in surprise. "How come?"

"I could ask you the same question, Uncle Max."

"In the first place, I'm more than twice your age. And, in the second place, I didn't feel like going out."

"Even in my state of advanced adolescence, a girl doesn't always feel like going out with the people who've asked her. But I'm not ready to enter a nunnery, Uncle Max. I've had several dates this week."

"Let's go out to dinner. Let's treat ourselves to something really good."

"Oh, you don't have to do that, Uncle Max!"

"A girl's godfather," he said with mock severity, "is entitled to certain privileges. Where do you want to go?"

Janet looked at him. "You eat most of your meals in restaurants. You must be sick of them. Why don't you let me cook something right here, Uncle Max?" She gently pushed him aside and began to look through the freezer and refrigerator.

"No, a pretty, young girl like you should be having a good time some place—"

"I'd love doing it! Please, Uncle Max. Mother taught me to cook when I was little—"

"She tells me what I remember better than she does. I ate your first fudge when you were six. The first cookies you baked, too."

"Then my lurid past is of some use, isn't it? Oh, look—some Cornish hens in the freezer."

"I forgot they were there. When I'm here by myself," Max

added lamely, "I don't do much that's fancy. Usually I'm satisfied with a sandwich or eggs or something."

"Do you have any walnuts I could use in the dressing? I adore a walnut dressing. Or oysters."

"It so happens there are some cartons of frozen oysters on one of the freezer shelves. Don't ask me how they got there." He began to search for them.

Meanwhile Janet was looking through the drygoods storage cabinet. "Here are two jars of walnuts. I knew Stella always kept a supply on hand."

Max shrugged. Since he rarely took anything from the cabinet, he had almost no idea what might be stored there.

"We could be very wicked," Janet said with a giggle, "and eat a stuffing that has both walnuts and oysters in it. Lovely!"

"If you're the cook, you decide. Now, what can I do except stand here?"

"Do you have any lettuce and tomatoes for a salad, Uncle Max? And potatoes?"

He went to a far cabinet and triumphantly produced a bag of potatoes. "You see? I do keep some things in stock! But I won't allow you to do this alone, Jan. Put me to work."

"If you insist, Uncle Max, clean two potatoes, but don't put them into the oven to bake yet. It'll take the hens some time to thaw, and we'll have to give them a head start."

Max removed his coat, threw it onto a chair and started scrubbing potatoes at the sink.

Meanwhile Janet was chopping walnuts. She felt completely at home. "We could have a vegetable, too."

Max was aware of her relaxation, and was delighted. "Except that I don't have any fresh or frozen. I've got first courses though. There are some jars of marinated herring in the refrigerator. And I have all kinds of canned soup."

"You know something, Uncle Max?"

"What?"

"I'm enjoying this more than most of my dates. I really am."

202

The sky was leaden, snow flurries swirled past the windows of Paul Lafferty's office, and the single lamp that was lighted cast long shadows across the room. But Paul, sitting alone, stared with unseeing eyes at the papers spread out before him, occasionally raising a tired hand to rub his gaunt face.

Max opened the door between their offices and came in. "I wanted to take that call privately," he said, "and it was longer than I thought. I'll tell you about it, and then you should go home."

"We've been so busy all day that we've had no chance to talk about my meeting at the bank. It's important."

"It's more important that you eat a good dinner and get some sleep," Max said.

His partner merely glanced at him.

"That call just now was from Balutis. He gave me another report on Janet."

Paul sat upright, and color slowly appeared in his cheeks.

"She went to a party last night. In a townhouse over in the East Sixties."

"That sounds like—the sort of life she used to lead."

"It wasn't," Max said. "The couple who gave it are named Bowman, and there's a big spread on them in the new issue of one of the fashion magazines. Balutis thinks it's very funny because they're really famous for giving dirty parties. He has a warped sense of humor."

"The only way I can live with this," Paul said, "is to try forgetting it as best I can."

"The biggest problem of our lives is on the fire," Max said. "Let's talk about that."

"It makes me slightly ill just to think about it."

"All right, all right. Go ahead, panic. That'll save the business, I suppose. Can I see that new loan-recall notice again?"

Paul grimaced and handed him a document.

"Three million, nine hundred and forty-two thousand. To be repaid by next Thursday." Max took a cigar from its case,

203

clipped off the end and put it in his mouth. Then, lighting it, he resisted the temptation to burn up the bank notice. "We can do it," he said. "We'll have to dip a little into the floating reserve, but that's why we set it up in the first place."

"Okay, we send them the check Thursday. Then what? Climb into a bomb shelter and wait until the next recall notice comes?"

"We know there will be another. Soon. And that it'll probably be bigger than this one. Christianson's campaign is beginning to take shape, and we can start to predict his moves."

"A great comfort *that* is."

"No, but it can be a help," Max said. "We'll have to get ready for it."

"I propose that we call in our board of directors. Granted that you and I have the only major stakes, the others are still involved, and they deserve—"

"That's premature, Paul. I'm afraid we'll come to it, but Christianson will get calls from just about every director, and I don't want him to think we're that far gone yet. Because we're not."

"The alternative," Paul said slowly, "is to sell some of our property packages."

"Soon, probably," Max replied grimly. "But not this soon."

"You'll scream at this, but there's nothing left except the hotels."

"They'll be the last."

"The London property should be the first."

"We aren't far enough along in redecorating. I'd unload it without any feelings of sentiment, God knows, but we won't get enough for it to make it worth our while. In fact, we'll probably take a beating, and that's something we can't afford right now."

"There aren't any other options," Paul said. "I've just run through all of them."

"You missed one," Max replied. "We dip into our personal wallets and strongboxes."

Paul stared at him. "You aren't serious."

204

"Either we believe in our future as a company or we ought to get out right now."

"But to wipe ourselves out—"

"I didn't suggest we go that far, Paul. Although what I have in mind won't be particularly comfortable. Suppose we brace ourselves for a loan recall of about five million. What I propose is that we each take two and a half million from our personal funds. Then, when Christianson's recall comes, we can pay it off quietly without disturbing any of the properties in the corporate structure."

"We stand to lose two and a half million each that way." Paul looked very tired.

"Maybe, maybe not. If North Atlantic calls off its campaign, we can recoup the two and a half million as quickly as we'll be releasing it. But if our strategy doesn't work, everything else will go, eventually. If we're forced into bankruptcy, we'll be picked clean."

"I don't like this, Max."

"Neither do I, but it's the only way I can see at the moment."

Max began to laugh. "Suppose, twenty-five years ago, that somebody had told you that for the rest of your days you'd own a grand apartment and a summer place in the country. That you'd eat well, dress expensively and travel anyplace you wanted. That your family would be taken care of for their lives. What would you have done with an offer like that?"

"I'd have accepted it. I still would."

"Well, that's the bare minimum of what you've got. So don't lose your perspective, boy, and don't get too discouraged."

Paul studied him. "What about you?"

"Oh, I have all those things, too. But I don't have a wife and kids, so I need a sense of power as a substitute. So you see, Paul, you should be sleeping nights, and I ought to be lying awake, stewing. Instead of it being the other way round."

Max slapped his partner on the back and went off to his own office.

For a quarter of an hour he tried to concentrate on the papers that had accumulated there. He couldn't keep his mind on routine work, however, finding that his talk with Paul had disturbed him more than he had been willing to admit. Leaving his office, he found himself heading down the stairs from the executive suite, and he realized he was walking toward Stella's office. It was unlikely that he would find her still at work. The office had closed for the day, and, because of the snow, most employees had left promptly. But lights were still burning in Stella's office, and when Max approached he could hear the hum of her electric calculating machine. She was sitting beside the machine, looking at an open ledger as her fingers moved up and down the console, and he felt his temples throb as he stared at her. "Excuse me," he said, tapping at the open door. "I hope the world won't come to an end if I interrupt you for a minute."

Stella raised her head at the sound of his voice, and she felt a pang of guilt when she saw how haggard he looked. "I could have come up to your office, Max."

"This isn't company business, exactly. What I mean is, I need some advice from a cost analyst who also knows something about my personal finances."

Stella assumed he was disturbed by the confidential news Paul Lafferty had passed on to her early in the afternoon. Max looked so forlorn she felt a deep sympathy for him, and told herself it was because of her that he was so lonely. Although it was more difficult, supposedly, for a woman to create a new life for herself than it was for a man when a romance ended, she was managing to keep busy. But Max, she was afraid, spent most of his evenings and weekends alone.

"I don't know if I can help," she said, "but I'll be glad to try."

"Everybody needs a drink at this time of day, and after that, people get hungry."

Aware of her hesitation, he became annoyed. "What I'm

suggesting is strictly a meal, nothing else. You wouldn't get contaminated having dinner with a person."

"I was just trying to remember my schedule," she lied.

"A busy woman needs a social secretary, I suppose."

"There's no need for us to quarrel, Max. Honestly."

"We could go anyplace you like."

She glanced at her red wool dress. "I'm not dressed for anyplace that's special."

"The way you look, every first-class restaurant in town would be proud to serve you!"

She touched her dress as she looked out of the window.

"In weather like this, it would be foolish to go home to change. We can go to Dave's. It's only two blocks away, so we can walk. And after dinner, I'll take you straight home. I'll even put up a bond to guarantee I won't ask to come in for a cup of coffee."

Stella's laugh indicated her surrender. "I've never known you to break a promise, Max. And since when have you started drinking coffee again at night?"

"I haven't," he said with a grin. "One swallow after dinner, and that's it for the night."

"Give me fifteen minutes," she said.

Returning to his own office, he paced ceaselessly, chain-smoking. He was afraid to let himself dwell on the possibility that Stella might be softening, and realized that, if he pushed too hard, she might draw back again. "Don't make mistakes," he said aloud.

Precisely thirty minutes after leaving her office he reappeared, and found her ready, although he could see she had been busy with her cosmetics in the interim. Their conversation was desultory as they rode down in the elevator and walked through the thickening snow to the nearby restaurant.

They had dined there frequently in the years they had lived together, and in the year and a half Max had been alone he

207

had found it convenient to drop in there for most of his evening meals. Dave, the proprietor, who acted as his own maitre d'hotel, was surprised to see the couple together, but he greeted Max and Stella as though he had last seen them the preceding evening.

"This weather gives you a real appetite," he said, leading them to what had been their favorite table at the rear of the room. "The oxtail soup is very warming. And I recommend the schnitzel. I had it myself a half hour ago, and not even my own mother made it better."

"You don't change, Dave," Stella said with a laugh, genuinely pleased to see him.

"A few more photos of ball players and horses on the walls, Miss Ross, and the wood shavings we use on the floor now are thicker. But you've changed—you get prettier all the time." Quickly, so he wouldn't be suspected of trying to become too familiar, he asked, "The usual to drink?"

Both nodded, and Dave went off, beckoning a waiter.

"He has a good memory," Stella said. "I haven't been here in months, but I'm sure I'll get a vodka gimlet."

"It's his business to remember." Max stopped himself before he could say that he, too, thought she had grown more attractive.

As always, liquor was of minor importance, and as soon as their drinks arrived they ordered dinner. They talked about Janet Lafferty at some length, and Stella expressed the conviction that she would emerge unharmed from her attempt to create an independent life for herself.

"All those years of training she had at home weren't wasted, I know," she said.

"So far she hasn't done anything stupid. But I'm not forgetting she's just a kid."

"I wonder if she's going regularly to Mass."

"That would help?"

"Oh, I know what you're thinking," Stella said. "It didn't stop me from getting involved with you."

"Don't tell me what goes on in my mind, please. What happened to you and me didn't occur to me in connection with Janet. And if it had, I wouldn't worry so much about Janet." Their soup arrived and Max took a spoonful of it. "You haven't found anybody you want to marry?" he asked bluntly.

"Oh, I've had several proposals, but I turned them down. You spoiled me, Max."

"I'll take that as a pat on the back."

"It was intended as a compliment. I must admit it, Max, sometimes I wonder if I did the smart thing when I left you."

Max reached across the table for her hand.

She instantly withdrew it. "Please don't!"

"You have a real talent for confusing me."

"I shouldn't have said anything at all. Forget that I did."

"Any time you want to come back, I'm waiting."

"I know."

"I've told myself a million times that I wouldn't say it to you. But the very first chance I get, out pop the words. I wonder what's wrong with me."

"Nothing! And if you don't stop being so nice to me, I'll disgrace myself by bawling."

"Dave doesn't charge extra when a customer wants to cry."

"I'm not going to hurt you—or myself—again, Max." Stella spoke firmly. "I shouldn't have opened up tonight, before I can see ahead clearly. It was wrong of me. It was because of the snow—and both of us being lonely—and worrying together about Janet. I can't explain properly."

"Who needs explanations? I've heard enough."

"Max, I beg you, don't jump to conclusions. I haven't decided what to do. I keep telling you."

If Stella were any other woman on earth, Max thought, he would ignore her protests, make love to her and sweep aside

209

her doubts. But she was Stella, proud of her independence, determined not to be influenced by anyone else, and although storming tactics might gain him a temporary advantage and even bed her for a night, she would withdraw even further when remorse and doubts assailed her again.

"We're been playing according to your rules for a long time," he said, "so we won't change now. Okay? And I don't know about you, but I don't like to eat cold veal." He began to cut his meat, and was surprised, when he took the first bite, to discover he was ravenously hungry.

Stella obediently ate her meal, but had no interest in food. "We've jabbered about all the wrong things," she said, toying with her salad, "but I still haven't heard whatever it was that you wanted to discuss with me."

"I was coming to that." No one was sitting near them in the half-empty restaurant, but Max lowered his voice. "Paul told you about the demand from North Atlantic today."

"Yes, and I'm sick about it."

"It'll get worse, much worse, before it gets any better. Howard Christianson is putting the screws on us, and a more efficient torturer you won't find in New York."

"Then make your peace with the bank, Max!"

"They've tasted blood. They wouldn't be satisfied with less than our whole hides."

"But it isn't reasonable—"

"Stell. With all due respect. Columns of figures you understand. The inner motives in a big-business tug-of-war no woman can grasp. All right?" Max quickly outlined the plan he had worked out with Paul.

"You're willing to sacrifice two and a half million of your own funds?"

"I'll still eat. Caviar and filet whenever I want it. Now, you know my finances. You still have an inventory of my investments, cash holdings—and so forth."

"Not an up-to-date list."

210

"It hasn't changed much since—anyway, it's roughly the same. A few thousand shares of this or that gone. A few thousand of something else I've picked up. I'll send an up-to-date list to your office in the morning. Go through the list and mark what you think I ought to sell to make up the two and a half million."

"I wish you wouldn't leave it up to me, Max."

"You know much more about these things than I do. That was proved a thousand times. Besides, I'm not necessarily going to take your word for it. I simply want your advice and guidance, that's all."

"I'll do what I can."

"A few minor personal holdings I won't include. Like the backing I've been giving to Lance Balutis."

"You ought to get out of his business, Max."

"It gives me a kick. I see a world I never knew. It does no harm to anyone. So why get out?" He spoke in short bursts, immediately defensive.

"The money you have tied up with him—"

"Peanuts. Now we're really talking about peanuts." Honesty compelled him to tell her, in detail, about Balutis' request for three hundred thousand to help finance his million-dollar film.

She stared at him. "That's more than peanuts."

"It isn't the kind of money we've been talking about."

"All the same, it's a healthy sum."

"If I go ahead with Balutis," Max said, "I'll have complete protection."

"How?"

"He'll give me paintings and art photographs, worth at least that much, to hold in my office safe as collateral. A guarantee of repayment within twenty months. And a three-to-one return in less time than I can make it anywhere else!" Max was so intent that he waved away the waiter, who approached the table with a dessert menu.

"You make it sound good," Stella said, "but I don't like it."

"That's because you don't like Balutis. Neither do I, but he amuses me. He also pays off, and in a business deal there's no room for personal feelings."

"You're asking for trouble."

"How, for instance?"

"Suppose the bottom drops out of the market for the paintings and the other trash you're holding. It could happen with a fad. Then you'll be left holding some worthless pieces of canvas with lacquered grass on them."

"No, Stell, I can't accept something that dubious."

"You asked my opinion—"

"And you gave it to me. When I remember how Paul and I nearly killed ourselves for that first million it would be a crime not to take advantage of this break."

"No," Stella said firmly. "You're forgetting to put first things first."

"I'm convinced Balutis' movie is a sound proposition. How can I lose?"

"Suppose you have to put up still more collateral at the bank?"

"That has nothing to do with financing Balutis!"

"Now," she said, "you're evading my question."

"You think I'm sticking my neck out, I think I know what I'm doing, so we disagree. Let's order some dessert."

"None for me," Stella said.

"If the worst happened," Max said, "and I went stone broke because things didn't work out the way I believe they will, what difference would it make? I'll have enough to eat, a roof over my head somewhere and enough clothes to keep me warm. If I fall flat on my face backing Lance Balutis, nobody will suffer for it."

Stella's lips tightened.

"From here," he said, "it looks like the snow is coming down harder, so let's drink our coffee and get out. Pretty soon we won't be able to get a taxi, and we should take advantage of what I can afford before I have to take subways."

212

"I won't let you do it," Stella said.

Among the coffeehouses between Lexington Avenue and the East River, the Coffee Scraper was unique. Located on the top floor of a small office building, it was sufficiently out of the way to avoid the trade of the casual passerby; also, it charged too much for its coffee to appeal to the secretaries and stenographers who worked in the building.

Starkly modern, with huge cushions of upholstered leather instead of chairs, and low tables reminiscent of the Near East, the Coffee Scraper won its gamble when Lionel Green and Elmer Bates adopted it as their mid-afternoon hangout. There they debated life, art and literature, and there, overnight, a huge crowd of enthusiasts in their twenties and thirties gathered.

The conversation of patrons provided the only entertainment. This suited the habitués, who were never at a loss for words, and Elmer Bates provided inspiration by reading excerpts from the new novel he was writing.

Janet Lafferty still felt a little out of place with the literary-philosophical crowd, but she enjoyed the Coffee Scraper's atmosphere, and made no objection when Bobbie Wayne, after a shopping expedition that had taken them to a dozen boutiques, suggested they stop in there.

Four or five young people surrounded Bates at a corner table. He had just finished conducting a discussion that had followed the reading of his daily excerpt, and he brightened when Bobbie and Janet lowered themselves to the cushions on the floor.

"Visitors from the world of the super-real," he said.

"Don't get catty," Bobbie said.

He was tired, in no mood for a game of verbal darts with Bobbie, and immediately transferred his attention to Janet. "How's Alice in Wonderland getting along?" he asked indolently.

"I find some people get curiouser and curiouser," Janet retorted.

213

The others laughed, and Bates flushed. "I hear Lance is doing another film in a few days," he said.

It was common knowledge that he and Balutis were not on speaking terms, at the moment, after an argument. "I suggest you ask him," Bobbie said.

"Are you going to be in this one?"

"No, he's using some new faces."

"Faces?" Bates raised an eyebrow, and his friends rewarded him with a laugh. Encouraged by the support of his audience, he turned back to Janet. "How about you?"

She had no interest in fencing with him. "Lance would like me to do it, but I haven't made up my mind."

"Afraid to go in front of the camera without any clothes on?"

"Leave her alone," Bobbie said.

Janet was stung. "Would you?"

"Lance and I made several films together," Bates replied. "You can see me—all of me—in them. Now, are you or aren't you doing this one for him?"

"I'm thinking about it," Janet said, and concealed her face behind her huge mug of coffee. That, she thought, was strictly untrue. She was avoiding any consideration of whether to do the film, because she found it so difficult to grapple with the issue.

She had learned enough about super-reality to understand what Lance and his disciples were trying to say and do. And to an extent she approved of the stand they took. But she was still torn. Her sense of modesty made her shrink from the idea of appearing naked before the camera. On the other hand, if she were sincere in her desire to express freedom, she would do it.

The dilemma gnawed at her, but she thrust it from her mind again. There was no need to make an immediate decision, and she was having fun. Not long ago she would have been awed by Elmer Bates, but now she could see through him, and even feel a little sorry for his pretensions. She was growing up, and the realization made her positively smug.

Raw vegetables were piled high on the kitchen counter, and Max took the roast from the freezer and placed it beside the other food. He had forgotten to take it out earlier, which meant it wouldn't thaw in time for Janet's arrival. For no apparent reason, except perhaps the association with the preparing of food, he thought briefly of his mother. The food he threw away after a Saturday evening with Janet would have filled his mother's tiny larder for a week during the pre-*Anschluss* days in Vienna, when he had been a boy. Her widow's pension had bought less each month, and although she had wanted a job to augment her small income, the rising tides of anti-Semitism across the border from Nazi Germany made potential employers reluctant to hire her. He would never forget those days. He thanked God his mother had died before Hitler's Brown Shirts had swept into Austria. She would have died in a concentration camp, and the same fate would have awaited him had he not left the country for the United States a few months before Austria had been incorporated into Greater Germany.

The doorbell rang. Trying to rid himself of his grim memories, he went to the door.

Bobbie Wayne, in high boots and a huge cape that matched her pale-blond hair, stood in the frame.

Max was too surprised to speak.

"Aren't you going to invite me in?" she asked.

He stood aside to let her sweep into the apartment.

Bobbie marched into the living room and looked around. "Gemütlich," she said, "on a grand scale. Maxie, you live up to my expectations. Everything in this place is strictly traditional. This room could have been furnished fifty years ago. Nothing modern, nothing hip, nothing with any pzazz."

"So don't live here."

She laughed as though he had said something witty. "Wasn't I clever to get past those guardians down in the lobby without announcing myself?"

"If that's your idea of clever."

"I was afraid you'd tell them not to let me up."

"Why would I do that?" Max demanded.

"Because you've been avoiding me for months."

"I've been busy, and I imagine you've been busy. Anyway, you and I don't travel in the same worlds, Bobbie."

"Has it ever occurred to you that you and I have a fatal attraction for each other, sweetie?"

"You don't have anything better to do," Max said, "so you decided to come up here and make some excitement for yourself."

"You're psychic. Are you going to offer me a drink?"

He wished she would leave before Janet arrived, and hesitated.

"Oh, I'm stone sober," Bobbie said, misinterpreting his reaction. "All I want is one drink, sweetie—and you."

"The drink," he told her bluntly, "you can have."

"That's why you get to me, Maxie. Most men I know would stand on their heads to own my lily-white body for an hour or two. But not you. You pretend you're indifferent to me."

"Let's not start all that crap again."

"Okay, sweetie. I'll settle for the drink."

He reluctantly headed toward his bar. Max remembered she drank vodka, and took a quart bottle of it from the liquor cabinet. At that moment the doorbell rang again, and he was sufficiently flustered to answer the summons still carrying the bottle.

Janet Lafferty immediately looked past Max when she realized he had another visitor, apparently afraid she might see one of her parents. If she was surprised to see Bobbie, she did not show it, and greeted her warmly.

"You get around, after all," Bobbie said. "If I'd known, I wouldn't have cut in on you, sweetie."

The idea was so preposterous that Janet laughed.

But Max was shocked. "Her parents are my closest friends, and I also happen to be her godfather."

"Even if you were her own father, that wouldn't stop you if you wanted to swing together. Except it would stop you, Maxie. You're so square you aren't for real. Who cares what you and Jan do? Why explain to anybody?"

He felt his temper rising.

"If you have any lime juice, make it a gimlet," Bobbie told him. "A big one."

"She's just bugging you, Uncle Max," Janet said.

He went to the bar, still seething, and after mixing Bobbie's drink, opened a bottle of celery tonic.

"Lance should be making a film of this." Bobbie shook her head as she examined the label on the tonic bottle.

"Don't you know anybody who has a soft drink sometimes?" Max demanded.

"You're unbelievable." Bobbie took her gimlet from the bar

and toasted him. "Here's to bullshit. Next time it's thrown at you, may it smell like roses."

"To you," Max said, "being vulgar is being a woman of the world. To me it isn't attractive. And if that makes me old-fashioned, I'm glad I am."

"It isn't just that you're a prude!" Bobbie retorted. "It's everything. Watch this, Jan. Maxie, do you dare me to take off this cape?"

"You missed your vocation," Max said. "You should have been a stripper in a night club."

Bobbie struck a dramatic pose, opened two fastenings and threw her cape aside. "Disappointed, sweetie?" she asked mockingly.

"Very funny," Max said.

"I really do believe you expected me to be naked under the cape."

"You shouldn't tease him, Bobbie," Janet said.

"Why in hell shouldn't I? He's living in yesterday, and he's trying to drag you back there with him! He won't even recognize the problems that he and all the rest like him are handing on to our generation."

"You think honor and virtue have no place in the world you're inheriting?" Max asked. "You sneer at honesty and decency—"

"Because they're just words. Were you honest and decent making your pile, Maxie? Didn't you cheat somebody, just once? Didn't you stamp on a lot of people climbing up to the top?"

"In business it's necessary—"

"My father and my uncles spout the same line of crap, and I won't accept it!" Bobbie went to the bar and began to mix herself another drink. "The politicians say they've got to play rough in their field, but everybody else should be virtuous. Doctors and lawyers act sneaky behind those big screens called ethics. And clergymen are the worst of all—"

218

"People try to live up to their ideals," Max insisted. "Most people, that is. And just because they fail, sometimes, doesn't mean they should stop trying. It's the trying that counts, that makes the difference between human beings and animals."

"Maxie, you're a hypocrite! Do you try to help the black man?"

"As a member of a minority group myself, I have a great deal of sympathy—"

"They'd rather do without your brand of sympathy! How many cute gimmicks have you invented to keep somebody with black skin out of the fancy new apartment houses you build? How many of them are living in this place, for instance?"

"That isn't fair, Bobbie," Janet interjected. "You're trying to make something complex sound very simple."

"Can you convince a black man who lives in a slum tenement that it isn't very goddam simple, sweetie? Give him a solid roof over his head or he'll either tear down yours or take it away from you!"

"You think that's right, I suppose." Max tried to sound calm and reasonable.

"Why not? Don't the strong always get the goods by kicking the asses of the weak?"

"You sound like a Communist," Max said.

"They're as square as you are. They have rules, just like you have rules, but my generation doesn't believe in rules."

"That isn't quite true," Janet said mildly. "There are more of us who accept conventions than reject them."

"I'm not talking about your kind." Bobbie's anger was unfeigned. "We're forced to fight in wars that don't prove anything. We live under the threat of an atom bomb we didn't invent. The whole Establishment—and the Communist hierarchy in the Red countries is as much a part of it as the Mercedes and Cadillac crowd in other places—sets up the rules of the success game. Their kind of success in their kind of game. Even the old farts who educate us and who lead us in mumbo-jumbo prayers are members of the conspiracy when they ought to be the front ranks of the rebels who are tossing paving blocks."

"Every generation thinks the world should be made over," Max said. "It's the privilege of being young. Or the penalty, maybe. When you get older, you'll see things in a different way."

"Not us, Maxie! Black power, white power, student power, those aren't just empty words. My God, you don't even understand the freedoms Lance Balutis is expressing in the paintings you back, and the films!"

"In the construction business," Max said, "we know it's easier to tear down an old building than to put up a new one. When you young people stop demolishing and start building, we'll respect you. We might even listen to you."

"This will gross you out, but we don't care whether you listen." Bobbie finished her drink and threw her cape over her shoulders. "We're shoving you out of the driver's seat, and if you want to ride with us, you'll have to go to the back of the bus." She bent down, smiling, to pinch Janet's cheek. "There's still hope for you, sweetie. That's why we're holding a reserved seat for you. But not you, Maxie. You'll be lucky if we let you become a strap-hanger. Don't bother to show me out. I'm good at finding my own way."

Max started toward the door, too.

But Bobbie laughed, broke into a run and timed her exit so that she slammed the door behind her just as Max reached it.

"A wild one," he said.

"She doesn't mean all that," Janet said. "Part of her thing is shocking people." She rubbed her cheek.

"She's an expert at it. Maybe she doesn't mean it. All I know is that she lights a lot of fires. And somebody who does that should take out plenty of insurance. We'd better start fixing our dinner."

They headed toward the kitchen.

220

The camera kept clicking. The process was repeated endlessly, but Lance was tireless, pausing only to change cameras when the film in one had been exhausted. Slowly, patiently, he circled the table, photographing the stalks of dry wheat protruding from an empty, unwashed milk bottle, and he was so absorbed in his work that he failed to hear the door open behind him.

"I knew," Bobbie Wayne said from the entrance, "that when you stopped getting a charge from grass you'd switch to snow."

Lance continued to photograph the stalks of wheat, operating the light with an ingeniously devised foot pedal that was his own invention. "Close the door," he called. "Light is seeping in from the corridor."

"Don't we take ourselves seriously," Bobbie drawled.

"Do as I say or clear out," Lance snapped, climbing to the top of a stepladder to shoot the wheat from above.

"If Matthew Brady could see you now, he'd whirl in his grave like a gyroscope." Bobbie giggled loudly at her own humor.

"It wasn't an accident that Brady's pictures of those Civil War generals turned out the way they did. He was a pro, so he experimented. I'll lay you five to one on it, and I don't know a damn thing about his life."

"You can lay me anytime."

Lance descended the ladder one step at a time, still taking pictures from different angles. "Do you ever think of anything else, Bobbie?"

"If you don't want me, you've found yourself a new boy. Who is it this time? Let me guess. That Scandinavian fluff from the U.N. who was cruising you at Millie's on Tuesday night or—"

"Knock it off."

Bobbie made her way to the door and snapped on the light switch that stood beside it. "All work and no play makes Lance an even more vicious son of a bitch than the Lord created him."

He started to reply, then stared at her from the ladder. She had discarded her coat, and looked spectacular in a backless, halter-necked dress of thin, black silk with a neckline that

221

plunged almost to her waist. "Wear that in the streets," he said, "and you'll be arrested for indecent exposure."

"Lover," she said, striking an exaggeratedly alluring pose, "even you'll have to admit that I have a higher voltage than your little Scandinavian fag." She became incensed when he feigned a yawn, and glared at him. "Screw you."

"See? She can think of only one thing."

"Flattery will get you nowhere." Bobbie went to a supply cabinet, found a bottle of vodka and some paper cups, and poured herself a drink.

"Where have you been?" Lance continued to observe her from the ladder, obviously intending to resume work.

"You know I've been around too much to give you the story of my life in a paragraph." She shuddered as she took the first sip. "Armand Beech threw a party after his showing tonight."

"Since when do you go to dress designers' parties?"

"Since they started making outfits like this one for me, for free. All I had to do tonight was sit in the front row." Bobbie laughed. "And look inconspicuous."

"You've arrived as a celebrity."

"Crap. I've got the figure to wear a dress like this. And the guts. Most of the old hags buying from Armand at eight hundred dollars a clip have never seen one of my films—"

"*Yours?*"

"Let's not be technical, sweetie. They wouldn't know me from their husbands' newest mistresses. They don't even read the columns. But Armand obviously believes that when they see somebody like me in one of his outfits, they'll want the same. Modified, of course. Changed so much it couldn't be recognized. But I really can't complain. I got one sizzler of a dress in return for sitting in his perfumed showroom for an hour and a half and spending another hour or so drinking his perfumed drinks."

"You're stoned."

"Not yet, I'm not. But I'm working on it."

222

"Pass out somewhere else, Bobbie. I'm busy as hell tonight. Turn off the light on the way out."

She removed a pile of newspaper clippings and a camera from a dusty canvas director's chair and sat, legs extended, resting their weight on the heels of her silver kidskin shoes. "I've never known you to turn down a little nooky."

"Tonight's the night."

"My God, you mean it."

"You get the message, Bobbie."

She took a cigarette from a pack in her handbag, and, lighting it, let it dangle from a corner of her mouth. "Maybe you've sworn off girls, sweetie, but I'm special, remember? You and I invented fifty new ways of doing it."

"All by ourselves, too." Lance was impatient, but tried not to lose his temper. "If I weren't working against a deadline, there's nothing I'd like more."

"I could have had any man in that showroom tonight. A half-dozen Seventh Avenue moguls. Two actors, not counting the queers. Brian Westfall—"

"Never head of him."

"He used to be in the State Department, and he plays polo. He's married to that Social Register bitch with the big tits."

"Oh, that Westfall. You aren't missing much. He's muscle-bound."

"I intend to find out for myself, sweetie. You know I never accept hearsay evidence. But tonight I just wanted you. I knew that of all the people in this town, you'd appreciate me most in this dress. But I guess I'm losing my pzazz." She crossed her legs and hitched her skirt higher on her thighs, "Do you really prefer those dead weeds in an old milk bottle to me?"

"I told you on the phone yesterday," Lance said, his voice becoming grating, "that I have a meeting with some potential backers on Friday morning. They want to see some special-effects still shots, and I'm beating my tail off to take in the kind of shots that will impress them."

"You told me you were getting support from Max Berman and that old Flynn woman from Long Island. Get me the bottle, sweetie. I'm feeling lazy."

"You don't remember anything. Sure, Max is in the bag and so is Amanda Flynn. But I still need four hundred and fifty thousand—"

"Take me with you, and I'll strip for the boys."

"Bobbie, this is serious."

"Your publicity has gone to your head, sweetie. It wasn't so long ago that you'd empty a camera in ten minutes, do some offbeat developing and let them drool over your photography."

Lance grew pale. He descended the ladder slowly, pausing on each step as a torrent of words poured out. "What in God's holy name do you know about my work? Nothing. You mooch around in front of my camera, and you think it's all play. Do you know how many hundreds of hours I spend experimenting, trying new stuff, working on lighting and angles and things you never heard of? Do you know how much sweat I put into making my work significant?"

Bobbie gaped at him.

"You think you've become somebody because you're suddenly so glamorous and sexy? I've got news for you. You're famous because I recognized the abandoned streak in you and brought it out with my camera. All you've had to do is be yourself, while I've—"

"What's got into you?" Bobbie sat upright.

"I'm tired of being patronized by a bitch who has never done a day's work in her life. You think it's a game to keep after me until I flip—and drag you off to bed. What fun. Nothing but fun!"

"I've seen your artistic temperament in high gear, but you've gone and invented a new gear. Wow!"

"I've been working since seven o'clock this morning, and I worked eighteen hours yesterday!" Lance shouted, rubbing the stubble on his chin. "I've been breaking my can ever since I was a kid. If I hadn't, I'd be trundling drums of oil around a freight yard in Whiting, Indiana, like my father did—until it killed him."

Bobbie recovered her poise. "How long since you've had something to eat?"

"I had a sandwich sent in a couple of hours ago."

"Then it isn't food you need." She rose swiftly, went to the cabinet, and, after pouring herself another drink, found a cup for him.

"How do I persuade you that I've got to keep bearing down between now and that meeting Friday?"

"You're so tense you'll psych out before then if you don't get relief, Lance. What you need is a stiff drink. And me."

Suddenly he laughed. "I might as well have been talking to myself. Finish your drink, and then go away." Making some rapid adjustments on the camera hanging from his neck, he began to take shot after shot of her.

"Even when I'm looped," she said, "I'm consistent."

"I wanted to catch your expression. If I got it, with the wheat looming up behind your shoulder, I'll have some useful additions to my portfolio."

"You've changed."

"No, you never knew me."

"I wonder why I ever thought you were out for kicks," Bobbie said. "Sweetie, you're as earnest a little grubber as my cousins who work in their father's Philadelphia bank, and there's nothing stuffier."

"Once I've lined up all the money for my film," Lance said grimly, "I'm going to take a breather before I start working on it. And then I'll show you who's stuffy. It won't be the first time you've had enough and begged me to stop."

"Any time, sweetie. But I'm not going to wear the veil while I'm waiting for you." She drained her cup, then reached for the one she poured for him. "I need some excitement tonight. I'm in the mood. I want to be where it's happening."

225

"I'm sure you know enough men who'll oblige."

"If I'd been looking for an ordinary lay, I could have had it hours ago. I don't have to draw you pictures, sweetie. You always like it kinky."

He picked up her coat from the floor and draped it around her shoulders. "You know the way out."

Staggering slightly, Bobbie wandered to the dressing cubicle at the far side of the studio to freshen her make-up before the mirror there. "You don't mind if I use your phone, do you? I think I'll see if Jan and Muriel are at home."

Lance crossed the studio in long, quick strides, and stood in the dressing room entrance, his eyes darkening.

"It will probably take some doing to bring Jan around, but before the night is over the three of us can kick up a good, thick dust storm. Besides, Jan needs to get with it."

"Stay away from Janet Lafferty!" The last vestiges of the amused, tolerant artist had vanished.

"You're full of surprises, sweetie. She's working on a film with you, isn't she? Not the big one, but one of your usual."

"Whether she does or doesn't work with me has nothing to do with her personal morals. And you know it. She's just a kid."

"I've never had a virgin, and you're always bragging about how great it is. Why should you have all the fun?"

"The world is lousy with virgins. Find yourself another one."

"Tonight? Just like that?"

"Hook up with Muriel tonight, if it's a girl you want. She's a handful for anybody. But do it at your place, and keep your distance from the Lafferty kid!"

"Why the big-brother act? Or are you trying to make out there yourself? I wouldn't be competition for you—or would I?" Bobbie reached for the telephone and started to dial.

Lance snatched the instrument from her, slammed it back into its cradle and lifted her to her feet. "I mean what I'm telling you. And you know I can play rough. Keep your pretty little mitts off Janet Lafferty."

226

She tried to wrench free, but could not.

"And don't try the old excuse that you were drunk and didn't remember. That girl is a direct pipeline to my bankroll!"

"Now I begin to see," Bobbie said.

"One dyke party would send her screaming to her parents and her priest. And Max would land on my head. I won't let you or anyone else spoil my chance of doing my big film."

"You've made your point, Lance. Now let me go."

He began to shake her, with slow deliberation at first, then with increasing vehemence. "I know you, Bobbie, and I won't stand for any of your cutie tricks. Don't forget it."

The girl gasped for breath.

Lance released her so suddenly that she fell against the partition separating the dressing cubicle from the rest of the studio. "You can be a prime shit when you want to."

"I'll be worse than that."

Rubbing her arms, Bobbie began to weep as she picked her coat off the floor. "It will be a cold day before I come around here again. The hinges of hell will have to freeze."

He was totally unimpressed by the threat. "You'll be back because I have a juicy part for you in the film. And without me you're just another post-deb who drinks too much."

"I could kill you, Lance, I really could."

"Some day," he said, "we'll destroy each other and have a ball. How does that sound?" Gently, but without subtlety he edged her toward the door, one arm around her shoulders.

"Screw you."

"It's a date, after my portfolio has done its job with the new backers. Oh, one more word of advice, Bobbie—"

"I've had enough for one night, even from a genius. Your work is so brilliant, but you just don't know how to get along with people. You hammer and pound until everybody who really knows you wants to slit your throat!"

Lance was unperturbed. "You've smudged your mascara. Fix it up after you get home, or whoever it is you'll get together with tonight is going to think your eyes are too small." Paying no attention to her continuing objections, he pushed her into the corridor, closing the studio door behind her.

Then, for a few moments, he suffered doubts. Uncertain whether he should have escorted her to the street, he walked to the window, lighted a cigarette and waited until he saw her appear below. She lurched away in search of a taxi, and Lance, smiling to himself, made his way back to his stepladder. Soon he was immersed in his all-consuming work, and Bobbie, like the rest of the world, was completely forgotten.

"You're the very first to see it," Sandra Tilstrom said. "Come along."

Janet Lafferty, trailed by Lionel Green, followed the hostess through the lush tropical garden set in the middle of her upstairs den, and, after climbing the steps at the far end, moved on into the bathroom. This chamber, Janet thought, was as large as her own apartment.

Fully carpeted, with a huge sunken bath, it not only looked like a bathroom-fixtures advertiser's paradise, but, as she had recently learned from Bobbie, actually had been copied intact from a magazine advertisement. There were lush plants here, too, and three paintings were hanging on the walls, one of them by Lance. The sheer luxury of the room was overwhelming.

"Fantastic," Lionel Green said, with no hint of mockery in his tone. "What do you *do* here, Sandy?"

Sandra giggled.

Janet felt compelled to say something. "It's just gorgeous," she lied.

Sandra went to the far end of the chamber and beckoned. "Here's the new pièce de résistance, children."

They approached a bidet, and stared at it curiously. It had been carved from a single block of marble, and its gleaming faucets were gold-colored. In short, it was the most luxurious and ludicrous bidet that Janet had ever seen.

"I commissioned it in Florence," Sandra said, "and I actually have an affidavit assuring me the marble comes from the same quarry that Benvenuto Cellini used. Of course, the only marble still there for the past hundred years or so is this coarse stuff, but it produces just the effect I wanted to create."

"I'm impressed," Lionel Green murmured.

"I had fourteen-karat gold flashed onto the fixtures in Munich," Sandra told them. "There's a gold worker there who is said to be far superior to anyone in Italy, and I think he really did a superb job."

"I've never seen anything like it," Janet said truthfully, and could not resist asking, "Is there some—special reason—you had it made, Sandy?"

The question seemed so superfluous that Sandra looked surprised. "I like being surrounded by nice things."

"Let me christen it," Lionel Green said.

The mood of the hostess changed at once, and she became animated.

"Nothing spectacular," the poet warned. "Do you have a glass I could use?"

Sandra opened a cabinet and handed him a thin-stemmed goblet of hand-blown Venetian glassware.

Green held it up to the light and then twirled it slowly, enjoying the rainbow hues that appeared. "Lovely," he murmured.

Sandra watched him in fascination.

Janet hoped he wouldn't do something revolting.

Green turned on the cold-water tap, tested the water with a manicured fingernail and then filled the glass, which he rested on the side of the bidet. Then, with great solemnity, he took a gold enameled pillbox from the inner pocket of the loose Bulgarian peasant's jacket he was wearing, and extracted a red pellet. After a moment's study he took another pill, too, this one

229

yellow. Bowing first to Sandra, then to Janet, he popped the pills into his mouth and washed them down with the water.

"Thank you so much," he said politely.

"Is that all there is to the christening?" Sandra was disappointed.

"For me, it's just the beginning." Using the bidet as a lounge chair, Green tried to make himself comfortable. "Join me, birds?" He proferred the pill box.

"What are they?" Janet tried not to sound stiff or hostile.

"The magnificence of this chamber will soon double and redouble."

She had no intention of experimenting with psychedelic drugs. "Thanks all the same, Lionel, but that isn't my hang-up."

"More's the pity, dear."

Sandra was torn. "What do those pills do to you?"

"Intensify your perceptions and illuminate your soul."

"How long—do you feel that way?"

"It depends," Green explained patiently, as he would have to a child, "on how many you take. But the most intense part of the trip should wear off in a couple of hours. And you'll still be high for about four hours after that."

Still Sandra hesitated. "Why not?" she asked at last, talking more to herself than to the others. "Marty won't be home until late tonight." She accepted a red pill and downed it.

Janet had seen enough people under the influence of psychedelic drugs to know what would happen. In about forty minutes to an hour their eyes would become wide and somewhat glazed. Then each would begin a separate trip, slipping completely into his imagined world. They might silently stare at something, the gold faucet perhaps, for a very long time, completely absorbed and unconscious of anything else—then suddenly proclaim that the whole secret of the universe had been revealed. If either of them had a bad trip, however, and became terrified by paranoid hallucinations, the room would become a living chamber of horrors. In either case, Janet didn't want to be there.

"I'm afraid I can't stay," Janet said politely.

Sandra's smile was vague. "You can show yourself out, can't you, dear? I don't want to miss one second of sharing this fun with Lionel."

A large bowl of steaming beef Stroganoff sat in the center of the private dining room in the L & B executive suite, but neither Max nor Paul had any appetite. The former picked at an occasional morsel and ate it without tasting it; the latter broke a roll, forgot it and stared out of the window.

"I guess this is it, Max," he said at last.

"The hell it is. We can't quit now."

"We don't have another twenty million in liquid assets. This time Christianson has thrown the book at us. The debtors' book."

"We'll manage." Max spoke through clenched teeth.

"By starting to sell properties, maybe."

"I refuse. The bank will bounce back at us that much faster with still another demand. And once the word gets out that we're really in trouble, potential buyers will hold out for real bargains. That way everything we own will go. For a fraction of what it's worth. I say we continue to hang on."

"Where do we get the twenty million?"

"We start with our personal reserves, and each of us sells some of his L & B stock. We can scrape up another five million or more that way."

"Now I refuse," Paul said. "We'd be wiping ourselves out, and we'd have no personal cushions left. Damn it, Max, suppose the breaks keep going against us. I don't want to start again at rock bottom."

Max scowled, but was forced to agree. "Fair enough," he said at last. "But I'm still fighting."

"With what weapons?"

"Hell, Paul, we've got plenty. Don't forget that every time we pay off one of these loans, we own that property outright. North

Atlantic can't touch it. Combine those properties with the construction end of the business, and you'll see we're hanging on to a very respectable nucleus."

"But not big enough to save the real-estate empire. I shudder when I think of how much North Atlantic can take away from us."

"It won't be pretty. But we can save more. A great deal more, until maybe Christianson becomes discouraged and leaves us alone."

"How do we save more of the real estate? By unloading the hotels?"

"No! I'm proud of the hotel chain."

"I realize it's a symbol. I share your pride, although I don't feel as strongly as you do. But there's at least a chance we'd get enough capital to carry us over the hump. I think we ought to put out feelers to Hilton. And Sheraton."

"We aren't that desperate," Max said firmly.

"Any way to avoid it that you know?"

"There's always a way. You're goddam right there is." Max reached for the nearest phone. "Send Miss Ross up here with her confidential directors' file."

"What's on your mind?" Paul asked.

"An obvious step that we've been avoiding, but can't avoid any more. Wait until Stella gets here, and I'll spring it on both of you at the same time."

Neither spoke again. Max restlessly roamed around the dining room, picking up ashtrays and absently putting them down again. Paul remained at the table, drumming with his fingers.

A knock sounded at the door, and Stella, not waiting for a reply, came into the room. A single glance at the food in the casserole told her they had eaten virtually nothing, and their taut faces confirmed the atmosphere of crisis.

"Here's the directors' file," she said simply, and placed it on the table.

232

Max waved her to a chair, his gesture more peremptory than he realized.

Paul, speaking quickly, brought her up to date on the financial situation.

"Now," Max said, "it seems to me the time has come to turn to our directors for personal help. Between the half-dozen of them, they're worth more millions than we can count."

Paul reached for the file and leafed through it. "This is impressive, I must say. I can't estimate the extent to which they'd be willing to bail us out, but they could give us a big boost."

"One of the principal reasons we've stayed away from them," Max said, "is because we've wanted to keep this crisis quiet as long as possible. Well, I think we can still avoid publicity."

Paul shook his head. "I doubt it. Once their own senior executives know, stories will start shooting up and down Wall Street."

"Listen," Max said, "then criticize. We invite them up to my place in Connecticut for a weekend. A social weekend—"

"With their wives?" Stella interjected.

"Not that social," Max said. "Wives need time and attention. But Paul and I need lots and lots of time to present the situation to them in the right way. In a nice, relaxed atmosphere."

"That won't be easy to achieve," she said.

"In this world," he snapped, "nothing that's worth doing is easy."

"They'll know it isn't a social weekend if you don't include their wives," Stella insisted.

"Okay, okay." Max sighed. "They're not idiots, so they'll know. Nobody will be at all surprised when Paul and I talk business. After all, what else do we have in common with those guys? Nothing, that's what. But we don't spell it out ahead of time, that's all. We're a little bit subtle about it."

"I don't see why it shouldn't work," Paul said.

Both men turned to Stella, and Max challenged her. "You don't like the idea."

"I didn't say that."

Max was exasperated. "We're doing you the courtesy," he said, "of waiting to hear the results of your very deep thinking."

Stella ignored the sarcasm. "Okay, okay. Let's do it."

"If Lance had given me a little more notice, even an hour or two, I'd have had time to buy a new dress." Janet, clad in a bra and half-slip, searched frantically through the clothes hanging in her closet.

Muriel watched her in languid amusement from her own rumpled bed. "What good would that have done? You don't have any more charge accounts."

"I've never been to a big-name fashion designer's opening show. With a buffet lunch, Lance said. What's it like?"

"Posh. And swish. The Beautiful People will be there in full force. Including the women who'll spend money on the collection, and all the limp-wrist boys who come out of the woodwork for openings of every kind. Theatrical first nights. Art shows. Concerts. Chamber music recitals. Anything at all."

"How's this?" Janet held up a black wool dress.

"Awful. They'll think you're a salesgirl taking orders."

Janet resumed her search.

"You said it's Anabel's show?"

"Yes. She's horribly expensive."

"Half the clothes she'll bring out will belong in the utter end of space. Really freaky stuff. The rest will be as conservative as that muck you always wear, except for a little slit here or a dip there. Most of her clients are middle-aged frumps who want to think they're daring."

"You're no help at all, Muriel!"

"They'll serve champagne, of course. You can get stoned in no time at all."

"You know I won't. Help me decide."

234

"Why don't you borrow my sleeveless safari print?" Muriel asked.

Janet shook her head. "It's a summer dress!"

"All the more reason to wear it. Everybody in the place will gape at you."

Janet's sigh was compounded of exasperation and amusement.

Muriel hauled herself out of bed, and, not bothering to throw a robe over her flimsy nightwear, padded in bare feet to her own closet. "Here," she said, taking the dress from a hanger and flinging it to the other girl. "Try it."

Janet hesitated. "That's the dress I gave you because it was too small for me, and you've taken it in, as well. It's short on you, and I'm taller—"

"For God's sake, you won't lose your virtue just seeing how it looks."

Dubious but browbeaten, Janet pulled the dress over her head and zipped it up. "It's *really* short," she said, looking at herself in the mirror set into the back of the bathroom door.

"You have the legs for it," Muriel told her complacently.

"And it's so tight around the fanny!"

"Everything I own is that way."

"Well, as you always say, it's your trademark, Muriel. But I'm afraid the seams will burst when I sit down."

"They haven't on me, and they won't on you. The trick is not to let anyone think it's accidental. When somebody looks at you, wiggle."

"I couldn't." Janet removed the dress, returned it to its hanger and went back to her own closet. "You can get away with it, but I don't have the nerve."

"You will. Stick around for another six months."

"If I don't go broke. This will have to do." Janet took a red wool dress from the closet and put it on.

"Just right for an alumnae tea at the Plaza," Muriel said in disgust.

Accustomed to such comments, Janet made no reply as she went to the dressing table they shared, and, sitting, pawed through a jumble of cosmetics.

"Pile it on, Jan. The people out front wear more make-up than the models."

"Where's my eye shadow?"

"Oh, I used it up the other night. Didn't I tell you?"

"No, and there isn't another. I don't mind when you use my things, but the least you can do is tell me when something is gone. This happens all the time."

Muriel yawned. "You don't have to get snotty about it."

Janet tried to speak politely as she made up her face. "When girls are living together, they owe each other certain basic courtesies, that's all."

Muriel propped herself on an elbow. "One reason I couldn't stand living with my parents was the goddam lectures all the time, and I don't have to take all these prissy speeches from you. You don't like my friends. You're always criticizing the way I look. You make a scene every time I want the apartment alone for a night—"

"Only because I have nowhere else to go."

"Go shack up with somebody and come home the next day! If I'm willing to do it for you, why can't you—"

"You know I don't sleep around," Janet said.

"That's tough for you, then. But I don't see why I should be penalized for your hang-up. I can't have anybody here for the night any more!" Muriel was working herself into a fury. "If I'd known you were a—a nun who belongs in a convent, I wouldn't have asked you to share this place with me. And I wish to God you'd get out!"

Janet, applying mascara to her lashes, did not turn. "I'll gladly leave today, in fact I'll be delighted, if you'll give me your share of the rent so I'll have enough for another apartment. I've paid the whole amount for four months, and you've borrowed two hundred and twenty-three dollars from me besides."

"You know I won't have any cash until I get the dividend payments on those bonds my grandmother left me. I've told you and told you! It'll be another two months."

"Then," Janet said, finishing her eyes and selecting a lipstick, "we'll have to put up with each other for another two months. I don't see any choice."

"I'm so sick of you," Muriel said venomously, "that I could puke."

Goaded beyond endurance, Janet twisted around in her chair. "I'm not exactly fond of you, either! I don't mind telling you that when you get bitchy, it would be a pleasure to slit your throat!"

"You wouldn't have the guts, chick."

Janet turned back to the mirror and steadied her trembling hand as she applied lipstick, blotted her mouth with a tissue and then put on a second coating.

Muriel was silent for a few moments. "Even the people you go out with are ghastlies. Lance Balutis."

"There's nothing wrong with Lance. He's being very sweet to me."

"Only because he wants to make it with you."

"Oh, shut up. He tried when I first saw him, a long time ago, but now he never makes a pass. So don't judge people by the way they treat you, Muriel. You ask for rape." Janet, satisfied that she scored, brushed her hair vigorously.

"If he leaves you alone, there's only one explanation. He's gotten so gay that he isn't interested in girls any more."

"He doesn't come around here since you made such a fuss about it. I'm even picking him up at his studio now instead of letting him drop by for me. And that's more than I can say for those dropouts from a pigsty who hang around you!" Janet went to her closet for a pair of high-heeled boots and began to pull them on.

Muriel, eyes narrowed, cursed her fluently, using four-letter words separately and in combination.

Janet snatched up her coat and handbag, and beat a retreat. Never had she despised anyone so much, she thought. She slammed the front door behind her.

Muriel felt she had won the encounter, and laughed softly. Lighting a cigarette, she wandered to the pullman kitchen, found some coffee Janet had made still warm in the pot, and absently rinsed out a dirty cup. Then, meandering back to the bedroom as she sipped the coffee, she lighted a fresh cigarette from the stub of the old, and, after a glance at the battered electric alarm clock on the table between the beds, she reached lazily for the telephone and dialed a number.

"Hello." The feminine voice at the other end of the line sounded husky.

"Hi, Bobbie. Muriel."

"Well, this is ESP in operation," Bobbie Wayne said. "I was just thinking about you."

"Me, too." Muriel sprawled on her bed, wriggled and laughed. "What were you thinking?"

"Very wicked thoughts."

"So was I. I was remembering the other night."

"That's what I meant, sweetie." Bobbie's voice dropped a half-octave. "Some things are a little fuzzy—I mean, we did kill a fifth of vodka, on top of everything I'd had earlier. But some of it I couldn't forget, even if I'd been stoned out of my mind."

"It was just great." Muriel became a trifle breathless. "It makes me mad when I think of all the time I've wasted with men."

"Oh, you need them, too." There was a pause, and Bobbie chuckled. "To put other things in perspective."

"I guess. But," Muriel added deliberately, "I'm very greedy, Bobbie."

"That won't be a problem."

"What are you doing right now?"

"Putting on my face for a lunch date."

"Oh."

"I could cancel it, of course."

"Why don't you?"

"Okay, come on over."

"I'm not even dressed."

"Throw on anything," Bobbie said. "You won't be wearing it for long."

"I'm on my bed." Muriel's hand ran up and down her body in a lingering self-caress. "I'm in my black chiffon nightie. You'd flip over it, and I wouldn't even bother to change, if you could come over here instead."

There was a moment's silence, then Bobbie said briskly, "That won't work. You have a roommate who doesn't understand about big girls and what they do."

"Oh, Snow White has gone out."

"When will she be coming back?"

"Not for hours. She's meeting your little chum, Lance, for a fashion show and lunch at Anabel's."

"What a little bastard he is." Bobbie's voice became savage. "How he lies!"

"About what?"

"He swore to me that Janet doesn't mean a thing to him."

"That's what she thinks, too. But what do we care?"

"Not. A. Thing."

Muriel could feel the other girl's anger. "It won't take very long to make you forget both of them."

Bobbie's sudden laugh was explosive. "You'd better believe it, sweetie!"

"How soon can you be here?"

"Just keep your panties on for fifteen minutes, and leave the rest to me." Bobbie rang off.

Muriel continued to hold the telephone until the buzzing sound startled her. Replacing the instrument in its cradle she sighed, wriggled and closed her eyes. Every moment of waiting was an agony, but a quarter of an hour would pass quickly.

Lance, in a multi-colored, embroidered tunic, with a sash of scarlet silk encircling his waist, was more resplendent than most of the women who were crowded into Anabel's salon. And Janet, close beside him on a slightly rickety, gilded chair, was embarrassed by the attention that everyone in the room paid him, but there was so much to see that her self-consciousness gradually faded.

Only an arm's length away, her often photographed legs jutting into the narrow center aisle from her second-row seat, was one of the world's most celebrated women, the Countess of Trent. Brazilian born and educated in New Orleans, married at one time or another to a Swedish businessman, an American manufacturer and a Portuguese novelist, the countess had surprised her friends and the international press by settling down with the former British cabinet minister who had been forced to resign his seat in the House of Commons seventy-two hours before their wedding. Now, five years later, she was still the epitome of chic glamour, a permanent fixture on the lists of the best-dressed, and responsible—with her husband—for the surge in popularity of Sicily, Dahomey and the Caribbean island of Huanta, where they maintained homes.

Lounging beside her, a gem-encrusted gold chain looped around his neck and disappearing beneath the waves of his long hair, was a former Bulgarian Olympic swimming champion who, as the tabloid newspapers declared with transparent delicacy, was "the countess' frequent companion when the Earl of Trent was otherwise occupied." The swimmer, whose defection from his homeland had caused a stir throughout the Communist world, made no attempt to conceal his boredom and paid no attention to the fashion show. Failing in his attempt to flirt with Janet, he was busily exchanging glances with a young blond reporter for a Midwest chain of newspapers.

In the front row, a few seats to the right, were the greying heir to a flour fortune and his fifth wife, a nineteen-year-old red-head he had found working in a Denver hotel flower shop when his private jet plane had been grounded by a snowstorm in that city. They whispered incessantly, the bride making sweeping gestures with her left hand so everyone in the salon would notice her seventeen-karat diamond ring, her husband busily scribbling the numbers of the Anabel gowns they would buy for her already vast trousseau.

Janet could not help thinking of a comment she had read recently in a gossip column: "A recent bridegroom who has traveled the same route much more than once is ladling goodies to his redheaded frau by the baker's dozen. He's spending dough faster than his family's mills can turn out flour."

Perhaps the most intent guest in the salon, who took in every detail of the fashion show, every nuance in the audience, was the renowned Prince Severin Konarski, who smoked perfumed Turkish cigarettes in an Indonesian holder of carved ivory. The tall, arrogant prince was always involved in controversies, not the least of them with the aristocratic Konarski family, who claimed he was not a member of the old Polish nobility and had stolen their name. He blithely ignored their charges, as he did all unpleasantness, and was eagerly sought as an escort by widows, divorcees and married women whose husbands had neither the time nor the inclination to attend charity balls, art exhibits and theatrical openings.

Prince Konarski was attending the Anabel show in a professional capacity, and although he had bestowed broad smiles and deep bows on his favorite ladies, they knew from experience that he was mentally photographing every dress, suit and evening gown in the show. His own living, which was said to run well into six figures per year, depended on it. It was probable that every woman of means present, as well as many who could not afford it, wore Konarski lingerie, wisps of silk and lace that magically improved a figure while at the same time making even the most unimaginative Puritan feel naughty.

Janet, who had splurged on a tiny, extravagantly expensive Konarski uplift bra that actually made no improvement in her youthful figure, surreptitiously watched the prince as he stroked his neat mustache. His concentration, she thought, disproved the charge made by his former wife, an actress, that anonymous designers were responsible for the products put out under his name, and that he knew nothing about lingerie except the art of divesting a woman of her undergarments. Lance had said that Severin Konarski was a playboy because it was good for his business, but that he was as clever a designer as he was a self-publicist. A mere Don Juan wouldn't pay that much attention to the flat-chested, painfully thin models whose outlandish hair styles and bizarre make-up made them attractive only to the editors of fashion magazines whose demand for the unusual to fill their pages each month was insatiable.

Holding a seat of honor on the aisle in the first row was one of the most famous of New York's housewives, Madeline Milton, and Janet had to laugh at herself for not recognizing someone whose photograph appeared with clocklike regularity in newspapers and magazines. The mistake had been natural enough: for five years Mrs. Milton had worn her hair in wild, long disarray, a style—or, as her critics claimed, a lack of it—that had been copied by countless other women in the United States, Canada and Europe. Marvelous Madeline, as she was called by her admirers, had just cut her hair very short, completely altering her appearance, giving her something of a scalped look and, as her hairdresser and his colleagues hoped, starting a new trend.

Janet had to admit that Mrs. Milton, who was only a few years her senior, did have a good bone structure and photogenic eyes, but it was difficult to understand why she had become a celebrity. The wife of a wealthy dealer in scrap metal many years her senior, she had no genuine social standing and no discernible artistic, intellectual or managerial talents, yet her name had become known in every city and town on two continents. Rarely attended by her husband, she was escorted by theatrical stars, socialites and diplomats to important events, she was interviewed regularly on a variety of television programs, and her latest costumes invariably made news on the fashion pages.

Her devotion to high fashion, Lance had said, was the secret of her renown. She spent vast sums every year, judiciously patronizing the designers currently in favor, and a press agent discreetly hired by her husband saw to it that the depth of her neckline or height of her hemline was made known to the press.

It was impossible for Janet to judge whether Marvelous Madeline had any taste; her expression remained blank as model after model appeared. Only when her woman companion, later identified as her press agent, whispered to her or nudged her gently, did she mark the number of a dress or ensemble on the form that the management had thoughtfully provided for everyone present.

At the rear of the salon, quietly supervising the showing, and timing the length of each model's appearance according to the reaction of the audience, was Anabel herself, a tiny woman in her mid-fifties with hair dyed jet black and cut in a 1920's bob that never changed, no matter what the current vogue. She was dressed in lounging pajamas and sandals, with long diamond earrings that matched a bracelet and ring.

She ran her showing with the precision of a Marine drill sergeant and the sensitivity of an artist. Long experience had taught her to gauge the "feel" of an audience to a dress. Women sat upright when they saw something they liked, men uncrossed their legs, and a low murmur of conversation filled the mirrored salon. Then, while heads bent and the number of the outfit was jotted down, Anabel signaled to the model, who remained in the room for an additional fifteen seconds, just long enough to give the uncertain another look.

Anabel's private life was her own, and her background was a constant source of rumor. She was said to be Spanish, Greek, Italian, Portuguese, French, or part American Indian, depending on the source of any given story at any given time. Only a few of her close friends knew she was of Russian Jewish parentage, had grown up in the Bronx and had been happily married for many years to a pediatrician, now retired, who went on fishing vacations when she made her highly publicized semi-annual trips to Europe.

Recognizing incipient boredom instantly, Anabel speeded the showing, her models appearing in quick succession as they paraded in their last costumes. The show, as the *Times* reported the following morning, ended at precisely 1:00 P.M. Anabel was noted for her punctuality.

The guests crowded around the designer to kiss and congratulate her, white-coated waiters appeared with endless rows of chilled champagne, and the models, miraculously reappearing in the dresses that had made the greatest impact, mingled with the guests. Everyone, Janet decided after Lance presented her to Anabel, knew everyone else. Almost without exception the guests embraced one another, and everybody, it seemed, was called "Darling."

Only the Countess of Trent was accorded more respectful treatment. Graciously accepting a half-glass of champagne, she exchanged a few quiet words with Anabel. Then, her ex-swimmer looming behind her like a bodyguard, she allowed a few of the men to kiss her hand, and exchanged cordial but distant greetings with several of the women.

Lance shared none of his peers' inhibitions. Ignoring the scowls of the ex-swimmer, he smiled informally at the countess. "Lady Trent," he said with boyish sincerity, "you're looking wonderful."

Dark, thoughtful eyes studied him, flicked to Janet for purposes of identification and immediately dismissed her. "Young man, you've said the same thing the last three times I've seen you."

"This is the fourth time it's been true, ma'am."

"I suppose," the countess said, "you want a commission to paint my portrait."

"Not a commission, Lady Trent, and not right now. I'm going to be busy for the next few months, but if you're in town late in the spring, I'd be honored if you'd let me paint you—and present you with the portrait."

"Well." The countess was surprised by the unexpectedly generous offer, and thought about it for a moment, trying without success to find a trap. "We're sailing in late May," she said. "If you're free before then, call my secretary and we'll make an appointment." Refusing another glass of champagne, she made her way to Anabel for a farewell, the crowd parting as she approached.

Lance was quietly elated. "I pulled it off," he muttered to Janet. "She thinks I'll accept a payment after I've done the portrait, but I won't. Severin," he said turning quickly, "how are you? Miss Lafferty, let me present Prince Konarski."

Janet's hand was kissed for the first time in her life, and she felt gauche, not knowing whether to call Konarski "Prince" or "Your Highness."

He immediately made it clear that he had no interest in formalities. "I have been observing you, and I find you beautiful," he said, only a hint of the Continental in his British accent. "Are you a model, Miss Lafferty? Or an actress?"

Janet, slightly bewildered, shook her head. "An artist," she replied, feeling like an imposter because she had as yet earned nothing as a painter.

The Prince was undismayed, and grinned at her, then at Lance. "No matter." He clicked his heels, bowed and drifted away before she could reply.

Janet felt grateful for the champagne a waiter offered her.

Lance, meanwhile, was enveloped in an embrace by Madeline Milton.

Marvelous Madeline scarcely bothered to acknowledge an introduction to Janet. "Lance honey you'll never guess," she said breathlessly, running her words together. "I did a kinetic

245

short for Wilbur Ackey the other day and it was a blast just gorgeous. All I had to do was sit around in my new polka dot bikini while polka dot lights were flashing on me and he let me say anything I wanted I mean even when I told him I had to go to the bathroom. It was a howl really and Wilbur is giving me a print of the film. Would you like to see it?"

"Of course. I might have a real part for you in a very important film I'm going to shoot soon."

"How marvy! I mean Wilbur was right wasn't he when he said that doing a bit in his short would lead to bigger parts? I've always wanted to be an actress."

"It will be a challenge for you, Madeline."

"If you'll tell me something about the part I can start shopping for my costumes now or I could have one of the designers whip them up for me."

"That won't be necessary."

Something in Lance's tone caused Marvelous Madeline to pause. "How do you mean?"

"I'm going to cast you as a Greek statue who comes to life."

She giggled. "You mean I won't be wearing anything at all just like the people in your other films? Oh I hope I have the guts."

"You will," Lance told her. "The atmosphere on my sets is so contagious that everybody wants to get rid of clothes." He reached out toward a passing waiter for another glass of champagne.

Madeline raced off to tell all the guests within earshot that she was going to appear, unclad, playing a major role in a Lance Balutis film.

A room adjoining the main salon was opened, and the guests flocked to the buffet tables for an elaborate lunch. People jostled and elbowed one another in their efforts to reach the pâté, cold salmon and larded beef with wine gelatin. Desserts were conspicuously absent, however. Without exception the

Beautiful People were calorie watchers, men and women alike making their obeisance to the cult of youth by keeping themselves slender. Besides, even if Anabel had made allowances for human frailty, she would have been the last to serve dishes that would make her guests too heavy to wear the clothes she created.

Lance was in an expansive mood as he and Janet settled into the bucket seats of his new roadster. "Madeline Milton can't act," he said, "and when she's on camera no one else will be able to say a word."

"Then why use her in your film?" Janet wanted to know.

He chuckled. "Did you see her figure?"

The girl shook her head.

"She's built. And she loves to show off her body in the raw. She's one of those inhibited people who wouldn't dream of stripping in front of her sister, but she jumps at the chance to do it in front of a camera. She convinces herself it's art, you see, and I don't believe she realizes she's really doing it for kicks."

Janet's interest in Madeline Milton was slight. "I certainly wouldn't, and I'm still not sure I can do that film for you."

"Of course you can. And will."

"I'll just have to see how I feel. For one thing, my figure isn't good enough to let strangers stare at me when I'm not wearing any clothes."

It was impossible to refrain from goading her. "Prince Konarski doesn't agree."

"Oh, stop."

"You're wrong, Jan!"

"Well." In spite of herself, she felt pleased.

"As you'll find out fast enough if Konarski ever gets you in a room alone for as long as sixty seconds. He can separate a girl from her clothes faster than any man in town."

"I'll remember that, thank you, if I should ever meet him again. But I must say I'm surprised. He doesn't look the type."

Never had Lance met anyone so naïve. Most girls, even the inexperienced, would know instinctively that Konarski was a rape artist. But not Janet. She was of another world.

Stella, trim in a green dress, with freshly applied make-up on her face, stood in the apartment entrance and smiled at Max as he approached down the corridor. "You certainly got here in a hurry."

"I was calling from around the corner. I took a chance on your being home. On most week nights most people don't have dates." Removing his hat, Max was about to kiss her, when he halted awkwardly outside the door.

"Come in, please." She realized what had happened.

He paused in the little foyer and looked at the living room with which he once had been so familiar. "That's a new chair over by the window."

"You'll have to try it. I couldn't resist buying it. On sale of course. It's as comfortable as it looks. Give me your hat and coat." She took them from him and opened the door of the hall closet.

"I'll only be a few minutes," Max protested. "Just throw them someplace."

Stella placed the coat on a hanger and the hat on a shelf. "Come try the new chair."

He followed her into the living room, where he lowered himself into the easy chair as though a box of raw eggs rested on the seat. Then, finding it comfortable, he grunted and sat back.

"Could I get you a drink? Or a sandwich?"

He leaned forward again. "No, Stell, I don't want you to make a fuss. I told you on the telephone this isn't a social visit. I'm here on business."

"Even people who do business don't mind eating when they're hungry or drinking when they're thirsty."

248

He shook his head, smiling stiffly. "If you don't object, I'll smoke one of my cigars."

"Has Paul talked you out of giving your money to Balutis?" she asked hopefully.

Max paused in the act of lighting his cigar. "Nobody talks me out of anything once I've made up my mind," he said forcefully.

"This is no time to be squandering your money. I felt so sure that Paul could—"

"You forgot the kind of fellow I am." He puffed hard on the cigar. "This will end the subject once and for all. On Monday I'm meeting Balutis for lunch, and I'm giving him a certified check. Then we'll go back to his studio so I can pick up the paintings and photographs he's giving me for collateral, and the deal will be closed. You've always been smart, Stella, so this time be smart enough to save your breath. Anyhow, the real reason I wanted to see you is about opening the Connecticut house for our weekend meeting.

"Margaret is very capable. You'll be in good hands, with her in charge."

"That's the problem. She won't be."

Stella immediately sensed what was coming.

"You know how delicate Margaret's health has been these last few years."

Stella resisted the temptation to say that she believed most of Margaret's ailments were imaginary.

"Well, she just isn't up to this weekend. She's still grieving so hard over Janet that she's made herself sick again."

Max chewed nervously on his cigar. "Wilson of Intercontinental Steel is very fussy. He even likes his eggs at breakfast just so. And Fouchet of Franco-American Airways isn't much better."

"He's worse," Stella said. "I remember him well."

"Stell," Max continued, "there's nobody except you to take charge of this house for us. If you will. I wouldn't ask it if we could turn to somebody else, but I don't know who. You know the house, you know Paul and me, you're familiar with the crisis. Well? What do you think?"

"I suppose I could manage it," Stella said. "How many will there be in the party?"

"You and Paul and me. And the six directors, or maybe just five if Jerry Thornton can't get out of a date to inspect his Chicago and Milwaukee plants."

"The cook and the maids will be sleeping in?"

"Yes."

"I hope you realize," Stella said, "that with this many, it leaves you and me no choice. I'll have to use my old bedroom in the master suite."

"Is that so bad?"

"Do you have enough linen in the house?"

"I didn't think about linen."

She laughed. "I'll get some in the morning. And towels. I hate to think of what's happened to the towel supply. Now, what about food and liquor?"

"I'm going up in the morning to open the house, and make certain there's nothing wrong with the heat and water. I'm not sure what I have in the way of liquor, but I can call a package store for whatever we may need."

"When is Paul going up?"

"He's driving up with Wilson and Barton late in the afternoon. You could come with me. The hired help, too."
Do you want to ride with them?"

"That's too late. Maybe I'd better rent a car. I'd like to drive the cook up, so I can discuss menus with her. And the maids. It's one way of making sure they'll get there."

"I've got to buy the linens as soon as the department stores open. And on the way to the house I'd like to stop off at the markets. Once I get there I'll have so much to do that I don't know whether I'll have a chance to go out again."

Max made a quick decision. "Use my sedan, then, and I'll take

250

the train. It's a ten-minute taxi ride from the other end." He did not add that the thought of Stella driving his car pleased him. "I won't even go into the office in the morning, so I should reach the house by ten."

Stella was motionless, lost in thought. "I'll have to stop at the office for a few minutes, but I should join you at the house by one, at the latest."

"It's settled, then. Could I use your telephone to tell Paul you're going to help us?"

"You know where it is." She gestured toward the bedroom. "When you're finished, I'd like a word with Margaret. She must be feeling guilty because she can't go, and I'd like to reassure her that everything will be all right."

"When she hears you're in charge, she'll know." Max went off to the bedroom to use the telephone.

Stella came into the living room quietly for another load of empty highball glasses and filled ashtrays, which she piled on a tray. The directors had retired for the night, but her employers were still engrossed in conversation, and seemed unaware of her presence.

"Relax," Max said. "Barton is a reasonable fellow, and so are the others. They're beginning to understand our problems, and with luck they won't make more than the usual number of impossible demands on us."

"You're an optimist."

"Why not?" Max grinned. "We have the rest of the weekend to soften them up, and a flexible schedule that will give us plenty of time for hassles. Stell," he demanded, turning suddenly, "why don't you stop? You've done plenty for one night, and you have a cook and two maids to clean the place in the morning."

Stella continued to collect ashtrays and glasses. "I just want this room looking tidy if anyone comes downstairs early in the morning."

Max started to protest.

"You take care of your department," she said, "and I'll look after mine."

Paul was reminded of the past, and chuckled.

"Would you like another drink?" she asked him.

"I've had enough for one night, thanks, and tomorrow will be a long day." Paul began to gather sheafs of paper from the coffee table.

"What about you, Max?" She knew he had been drinking nothing stronger than ginger ale, which had always been his habit during long business conferences. "Maybe you'd like to relax with a nightcap."

Max glanced at his watch. "Why is it liquor makes some people sleepy, but after I've been tense, I just get more awake?"

She had been asked the same question on countless occasions, and her reply was automatic. "That's the way you are. Isn't there anything I can get you?"

"Yes, Stell. Do me a favor and get some sleep. You've been working for nearly twelve straight hours—"

"I've done no such thing!"

"—and everything has been perfect. It was a wonderful dinner—"

"It sure was," Paul interjected heartily.

"That was the cook's doing, not mine," Stella said.

"You think I never ate your dumplings?" Max demanded. "There's only one person who makes them like that."

Her flush denied her self-deprecatory gesture.

Paul looked at Stella, then at Max, and quickly rose to his feet. "You two can talk all you want about dumplings. I'm knocked out. What time is breakfast?"

"Whenever you come down." Stella picked up the tray and started toward the kitchen. "The last time you were here you liked coffee around seven, so I'll send a pot up to you then."

Paul thanked her, and stood beside his partner, who watched

her as she left the room. "It must be two years since Margaret and I were last here. What a memory that girl has."

"Yeah. For some things," Max said.

Paul wanted no explanation. Aware of the strains that both were suffering, he called a general good-night and mounted the hall stairs.

Max continued to stand for a few moments before gathering the liquor bottles and replacing them in the bar that stood at one side of the hearth. Conquering his desire to follow Stella into the kitchen, he removed the protective screen from the front of the hearth and jabbed with savage force at the last log still burning on the andirons. Showers of sparks scattered across the open face of the fireplace, and he jabbed at the log a second time with the brass-handled poker, then a third.

"That's a good way to burn down the house." Stella came up behind him.

He turned, still grasping the poker. "I don't like to leave too big a fire at bedtime."

"I know."

Max was unable to reply, and stood for a time, staring at the poker. "You cleaned all this brass today," he said at last.

She shrugged. "It hadn't been touched since last summer, and the maids had too many other things to do." She met his gaze briefly. "You're tired."

"I suppose."

"But you're satisfied with the start of your meetings?"

"First you excavate, then you build. Nobody could complain about the foundations we dug tonight." He paused.

She headed back toward the kitchen. "I want to wash out the ashtrays."

Max stood motionless until she disappeared. Then, rousing himself, he snapped off all the living room lights except the one near the hall, which Stella had always wanted him to leave lighted when she was in the kitchen. His buoyance vanishing, he climbed the stairs, his legs feeling heavy.

253

The door leading into Stella's room was open, and he couldn't resist peering inside. A maid had laid out her nightgown and robe, and he felt a sharp, twisting sensation inside him as he recognized a sleeping set he had given her. As nearly as he could recall, he had bought it for the last of her birthdays they had spent together. Recalling how she had looked in them, he continued down the corridor to his own bedroom.

Far too restless to think of sleep, he piled kindling and newspapers in the hearth, placed two logs over them and lighted a fire. The luxury of spending the night with a fire glowing across the room was one he had not allowed himself since he and Stella had separated. Why was he reverting to an old and treasured custom tonight? It occurred to him that, perhaps, he was hoping she would consent to spend the night with him as a prelude to a permanent reunion.

But it wasn't wise to count on anything when dealing with Stella, he cautioned himself. Shrugging, he stood erect and watched the flames rise, then gradually die down again.

"Max." Stella had appeared in the open doorway, a small tray in her hand.

He spun around.

"I brought you some warm milk. It should help you sleep."

"Thanks," he said, and grinned at her. Nothing had been further from his mind than a glass of milk.

"Take the tray." She remained on the threshold.

He did not move. "Would it be a crime if you came in for a minute?"

She hesitated, then advanced into the room and placed the tray on a table beside his easy chair.

He went to the door and closed it.

"Oh, Max," she said reproachfully.

He spread his hands. "That isn't what I was thinking. Suppose one of the directors is wandering around. I wouldn't want anybody to get the wrong idea."

"God forbid." She couldn't help laughing.

254

Max smiled sheepishly. "All right. I've had ideas. But I'm not the romantic type, and anyway, you know me too well. But you can't sue me for what goes on in my head."

"I wouldn't sue you for anything."

He took a step toward her.

"Drink your milk before it gets cold," Stella said.

"No, I—"

"Do you know what a mess milk makes in a saucepan? After all that work you can't just leave it."

"You drink it," he said.

"You forget what milk does to my figure."

"I forget nothing. Especially about you, and including your figure.

"Stella, I love you. I still want you. I need you."

She blinked rapidly, her mouth tightening as she fought against tears.

"All right, don't answer," Max said. "You don't have to. Even if I didn't know a little something about you, after all this time, I'd be blind not to see you're tired of staying apart. The same as I am. I realize how important your religion got to be for you after your mother died. But we're adults, Stell, and we're aren't getting any younger. Somehow we can work it out together."

"Max," she said at last in a choked voice, "not another word. If you have any real regard for me, you'll stop right now."

"Why? That's all I want to know. It doesn't make sense. You haven't found somebody else—"

"If it will make you happier," she interrupted savagely, "I'll admit I discovered I didn't even want anyone else. Now will you shut up?"

"No! Your Church is relaxing more rules all the time, but you—"

"This has nothing to do with the Church." Stella looked down at the carpet.

He stared at her, dumbfounded. "Now what?"

"I can't explain."

"Stell, for God's sake!"

"I know I'm being inconsistent." She spoke rapidly. "I know I sound crazy. Maybe I am. But you'll have to take my word for it!"

"So you have pride, and you won't want to admit you made a mistake. But we can't ruin the rest of our lives just because—"

"Why did you have to bring up everything this weekend, of all times?"

His confusion grew worse. "What does the weekend have to do with it?"

"Stop asking so many questions!" There was hysteria in Stella's voice. "I can't stand it!"

He raised his hands, half-reaching toward her, then wearily let his arms drop again.

"For the rest of the weekend," Stella said, her volume continuing to rise, "pretend to yourself I'm a housekeeper you hired to look after your guests. I—I'm feeling bad enough!"

Obviously she had no intention of telling him the cause of her upset, so Max forced himself not to press his inquiry. He could not remember seeing her so miserable.

"Don't look at me like that, either! It's too much!" She turned from the room and ran.

The roads were free of snow and the weather had turned a trifle warmer, so the Sunday-night traffic moving into New York City from Connecticut and Westchester County was fairly heavy. Max, telling himself he was foolish to hire a chauffeur whom he then gave too much time off, concentrated on his driving. The weekend had been a strain, and for once he was willing to admit he was tired.

Stella, riding beside him in the front seat, leaned back, her eyes closed, and although she had participated in none of the discussions with the industrialists on the L & B board, he knew she felt much as he did.

Unfortunately, they had been alone so little since the guests had gone in mid-afternoon that there had been no opportunity to fill her in on the details of the discussions. "Things went pretty well," he had told her briefly. "Paul and I didn't get everything we want, and there are strings attached to what we got, but I think we'll be able to weather the storm, and that's what counts."

She seemed content to wait until he had the chance to tell her a fuller story. Meanwhile she responded lethargically to his comments on the traffic, the current state of disrepair on Bruckner Boulevard, which led to the Triborough Bridge and the East Side Drive, and similar small talk.

Stella seemed depressed, and it wasn't difficult to figure out the reason. Early in the day their old friend and Connecticut neighbor, Fran Howley, had telephoned to invite Stella and Max for a drink and light supper before their return to Manhattan. He had accepted eagerly without consulting Stella, hoping the visit would be a potent enough reminder of old times to soften her approach to him.

But the date had not worked out as he had hoped. It did no good to look back over one's shoulder, he had often said, and now he had cause to believe it. Stella had become silent and withdrawn the moment they had arrived at the Howley house, and, as the evening had worn on, had crept even more into a shell.

Max had discovered that, he too, had been uncomfortable. The Howleys were a living reminder of happier days that, it appeared, had vanished for good, and his sorrow had worn him down.

The Howleys, sensing the reactions of their guests, had been ill at ease, and had tried to compensate for their embarrassment by becoming too boisterous, too insistently hospitable. In brief, the visit had been a bad mistake, and Max had actually felt a sense of relief when the time had come to leave, lock up his own house and start back to town.

The maids, riding in the back seat, inhibited conversation, so he did not progress beyond generalities. They asked to be dropped off at Lexington Avenue and 125th Street, and Max, joining Stella in thanking them again, complied with their request.

Then he turned south and headed toward midtown. "I want to tell you about the meeting."

Stella was leaning back against her seat again, eyes closed. "I want to hear," she said, but didn't sound as though she meant it.

He realized he was being overly sensitive. "Not in the car, though. We'll stop off. At the office."

"It's getting late, Max."

"It won't take long. Besides, there's one thing in particular I want to take up with you."

She opened her eyes to look at him, but he offered no explanation, so she turned away again. Perhaps she was wrong to refrain from asking him to drop up to her apartment for a visit, but tonight she was just too tired to cope.

Neither spoke again, and the car moved rapidly through midtown streets of darkened office buildings, restaurants and shops. Max drew to a halt after being stopped at only a few traffic lights.

They did not speak as the night watchman took them up in the express elevator to the executive floor. Max unlocked the door, and, after snapping on the reception room lights, waved Stella ahead of him.

"Some of these plants need watering," she said vaguely.

"Yeah. Carol—or somebody—always does it on Monday mornings."

"I could do it right now."

"You've done enough housekeeping for one weekend." He snapped on his own lights, then grimaced when he saw a stack of correspondence and the usual Friday reports from the heads of sub-corporations and major departments. "Tomorrow," he said, "is going to be a grand day. I'm glad we're going to have our chat tonight."

Stella, not bothering to remove her coat, sank into the nearest leather visitor's chair and kicked off her shoes.

Max started toward his desk, decided it would be too formal a gesture and stood near her, his hands clasped behind his back. "We're getting up to thirty million in financial support from the directors," he said.

"That's wonderful!"

"It could be worse," he admitted with a weary grin.

"What kind of time limit are they giving you?"

"Eighteen months for half the sum, twenty-four for the rest."

"Very generous."

"Uh-huh. They've come through handsomely. The worst North Atlantic can do to us now is chip away at the edges. They may force us to give up some of our properties, but the heart of the business will remain intact."

"Congratulations."

"That isn't the whole truth, of course. Between you and me. The bank still holds the upper hand, and if Christianson is really determined to put us out of business, he can do it. Also, our directors are businessmen, not philanthropists. Paul and I are guaranteeing them our personal interest in the hotel chain and several properties around town. We're each putting a million dollars in L & B common stock into escrow for them, and a million, two hundred thousand in L & B preferred. We'll be slightly strapped for a while. Enough to prevent us from buying any new properties, but that won't necessarily be a bad thing. So I'll have to impose on you tomorrow morning by asking you to come to the safety deposit vault with me."

"Why, Max?"

"When you and I started to go in opposite directions," he said, "we left some unfinished business. Remember? The L & B preferred stock is registered jointly. In both our names. And we've never done anything about changing it. Two million worth of preferred. You can sign over all but five hundred thousand to me, so allow about an hour for the whole thing, okay?"

Stella frowned, "I understood you to say that you're going to put a million, two hundred thousand of the preferred stock into escrow for the directors."

"You understand right."

"But you want me to release a million, five hundred thousand." Her frown deepened.

Max did not look at her. "I need the rest for another transaction."

Stella was silent for a moment, then exclaimed, "Lance Balutis!"

Max could not conceal his uneasiness. "I told you about it. I've agreed to become a major backer of the big film he intends to make."

There was a long silence and Stella stared off into space. Then, still not looking at him, she said quietly, "No."

"What's this?"

"I told you I thought it was insane of you to invest any more with him."

"Why shouldn't I?" Max retorted. "It's safe. I'll make money. And I have a little fun doing it. Would you deny me the only pleasure I get these days?"

"When your own funds are short, it's a mad extravagance to invest in an expensive art film. Leaving all other considerations aside, and there are plenty of them, Balutis has never proved himself on that level." Stella was speaking very rapidly now. "It's too great a risk, Max, and I won't let you take it."

"How do you mean, you won't let me?" He was beginning to shout. "We're talking about *my* money!"

"I'll release the preferred stock for the directors, but I won't sign one single certificate that would go to Balutis. I'm sorry, Max."

"You'll damn well do as I say. That stock belongs to me!"

260

"Rant and rave all you please. No." Color had drained from her face, but she would not retreat.

"This is a goddam outrage!" Max roared. "You shouldn't even have your name on any of that stock!"

"I'm more relieved than you'll ever know that I have some control over this ridiculous situation," Stella said. "You don't have enough sense to know what's good for you! You've been taken in by Lance Balutis—"

"I know him for what he is! A talented screwball! A dedicated artist who has a genius for making money. So you don't like his morals. So what? I don't like them, either. But I'm not living in his house, and he isn't moving into mine. Am I responsible for the morals of everybody I do business with? Do I have to submit their names to you for censorship and approval?"

"Save your breath, Max. I'll sign the certificates for the escrow fund. I'll sign them direct *to* the fund, so there can be no mistake, and no hanky-panky—"

"My God, you got your nerve!"

"It's too much," Stella said, "to predict that some day you'll thank me for what I'm doing."

"Thank you? Goddam it, I could break your neck." He clenched a fist, and, scarlet-faced, shook it under her nose.

"If it will give you joy to hit me," she said, "I can't stop you. You're stronger than I am."

His eyes bulged, and blood vessels stood out at his temples. But gradually Max regained control of himself. "I wish," he said bitterly, "that I had the guts."

"If it would give you relief and make you feel better," she murmured, "I wish it, too."

Again he flared. "Do you have to mock me?"

It would be useless, she knew, to even try to convince him that mockery was furthest from her mind.

Max stared at her dully. "When a Lithuanian peasant woman makes up her mind, nothing—not even a hurricane—could make her give ground. How can I persuade you—or beg you—to give me those funds for Balutis?"

Stella was too bone-weary to reply, and could only shake her head.

He regarded her bleakly. "That's the way it is?"

She nodded, then whispered, "And that's the way it's going to be."

"You couldn't mean it!" Lance ran a trembling hand through his long hair. "If you've got a sudden case of cold feet, tell me what's bothering you, and we'll work it out."

Max leaned heavily on his desk. "I don't have cold feet, and I mean every word. I was awake all night, wondering how to break this to you, and I knew I couldn't delay. That's why I came in early this morning, and called you the minute I got here."

"How in God's name can I make my film when you pull the rug out from under me?" There was a note of hysteria in Lance's voice.

"I know how you feel, but it isn't hopeless. I feel reasonably sure I'll be able to go ahead with the deal soon."

"How soon?"

"I wish I knew," Max replied honestly. He couldn't explain that he had decided to wait a short time, then try to convince Stella he had abandoned the idea of backing the movie. Eventually, after he recovered the securities from her, he would go ahead with his original plan.

"What am I supposed to do in the meantime? Play with myself?"

"I know this is tough for you—"

"Tough? I've raised the rest of the money, and I'm ready to go into production. But your copout kills me!"

"Maybe you could get a loan on some of your paintings and

photographs, and when I'm ready to invest, I can redeem them for you."

"Forget it! I could sell them, but I couldn't get anything close to what I need on a loan." Lance completely lost his self-control. "Berman, you're a lousy Jew welsher——"

Max reached out, caught him by the front of his fur-collared coat and lifted him off his feet with seemingly effortless ease. "I feel bad about this mess, nearly as bad as you do. But nobody calls me names, Balutis. I'm a Jew, and proud of it, so I don't like it when the word is used as a curse. And I'm no welsher. I don't want to hurt you, so mind your manners!"

Lance felt himself being released. His heels jolted on the floor, his legs buckled and he had to grasp wildly at Max to prevent himself from sprawling on the floor. The unexpected physical manhandling was an additional insult, the last straw. He raced from the office, his only consolation the knowledge that no members of the construction company's staff had yet reported for work. But it was small comfort to know that no one had witnessed his humiliation.

It was inconceivable to him that Max had not withdrawn purposely, and Lance realized, after his recent, intensive efforts, that he had exhausted his list of potential investors. He wanted to throw up.

Photographs were suspended from a wall board, most of them prints on a dull-finish paper, and the informal exhibit was illuminated by a floodlight. The photos were hanging in clusters of about a half-dozen to each group, but without exception were so indistinct that Janet Lafferty, unable to identify even the subjects, didn't know whether the arrangement was deliberate or accidental.

"I came over as fast as I could," she said. "I was intending to go apartment-hunting again, but I dropped everything when you said it was important." She took off her coat.

"Keep looking at the photo prints." Lance Balutis was busy with some equipment on the far side of the studio. "Study them carefully, and then I'll explain."

The girl studied the murky prints more carefully. They were large, but so blurred she could not make them out. In fact, she was uncertain whether she was looking at presentations of two people or four, whether they were posing or shot in action of some sort. She could not distinguish their features, much less determine what they were doing or how they were dressed.

"What are they, Lance?" she called.

"The start of some experimental work," he replied.

"That's what you said, but what? I mean, I can't figure them out."

"They're meant to be felt. What *do* you feel?"

"Confused, if you'd really like to know. All I can see are some pools of light and shadow."

"That's all you're meant to see. Most of them are triple and quadruple exposures but that's a technical matter. What do you *feel*?" He sauntered across the studio toward her.

Janet tried to reply honestly. "They give me a sense of intimacy, I think, and at the same time they make me feel lonely."

Lance felt a sudden lift. "That's good, damn good. I got across exactly what I wanted the viewer to feel, and you were sensitive enough to pick up my message." His reasons for summoning her to his studio became dominant again, and he smiled. "I'm right about you." He waved her to a stool.

Still mystified, she perched on the seat, hooking her heels in a rung.

"I've been telling you for a long time that you have talent—"

"You're the only one who thinks so, Lance. I still haven't sold a single painting."

"Of course not. You're too tense when you work, and your tension shows."

"Aren't you tense when you're creating? Every artist must be!"

264

"No. But I see plenty of tension in you. Are you thinking that people who saw the film might make fun of you?"

"I can't say I'm very proud of myself."

"You saw the rough screening yesterday with the rest of the cast—"

"Let's say I was there," Janet cut in, "but I didn't really see the film. I found it rather difficult to look at myself up there on the screen, naked."

"Are you afraid your audience might have erotic thoughts and desires?"

"I suppose."

"That happens anyway, regardless of whether you're dressed or nude."

"Oh, sure." She laughed. "I know that much."

"Next step. Did you think some clown would try to rape you, or something?"

"No," Janet said honestly, "I thought that's how I'd react, but I didn't. Everybody else was so natural and matter-of-fact that I wasn't in the least afraid of them."

"The first major step toward the expression of a conscious sense of super-reality. You're getting there."

"You see, too much modesty—prudishness—call it what you will—distorts the image. In fact, it can actually create a smutty or even obscene feeling where none is intended. Do you follow me?"

"Maybe. I want to personalize this." Janet was equally intense. "Are you trying to tell me that I came over as smutty in my film bit?"

He grinned and patted her shoulder. "That would be stretching the truth, unless someone was looking for smut. In the main, I'd say you looked awkward."

"This gets worse and worse." She would be teased, mercilessly, by everyone she knew, and the prospect made her miserable.

"You weren't as bad as all that," Lance said. "Look, why don't we shoot your scene over again, and I'll splice it into the film."

"Could we?"

"Of course. Why give you a false reputation as a simperer? On the other hand, I can't really direct your movements, you know. You'd still be responding to a false stimulus; in this instance, me."

"Then it's hopeless, Lance."

"Not at all. I suggest we use a method that's worked with a lot of others. Let me shoot some still pictures first, and as we go along I can give you an idea of what looks easy and what looks awkward. Then I'll make some quick prints for you, and when you study them yourself—or when you take one look at them, really—you'll fall right into the groove. It never fails."

"Why doesn't it?"

"Because every sensitive person has a natural affinity for the super-real, and needs only to be pointed in the right direction. That's my whole point about the basis of real art. Tear away the false, inhibiting restrictions of the hypocrites, the Puritans and the stupid, and the beauty of super-reality emerges."

"Okay," she said. "Let's try it. There's no point in doing something half-way."

"Help yourself to a dressing room."

Janet went off to one of the cubicles across the studio, and, dropping her coat and shoulder bag onto a chair, pulled her dress over her head, then removed her half-slip. Clad now only in her bra, panties, stockings and boots, she rubbed her bare arms, hesitating. Her parents and Uncle Max would flip out if they could see her now, but they couldn't understand. Lance was devoted to his work, and she had become convinced that it *was* important. Certainly she was safe enough here, and it would be ridiculous to behave like a prude.

She removed the rest of her clothing, hesitated very briefly and then returned to the studio.

Lance, intently snapping on floodlights and adjusting them, glanced at her impersonally. "Fine," he said. "I'll be with you in a second.

Janet involuntarily shivered.

"Sorry about that," he called. "Everybody complains about the cold here in the winter. Move under these lights and you'll be warmer."

She did as she was bidden, and found he was right.

"Are you concentrating on any one neighborhood in your apartment hunt?" he asked.

"No, not really." She knew he was making small talk to put her at ease, and was grateful for his thoughtfulness. "I'm anxious to get away from Muriel, of course, but I don't want to rush things."

"That's wise." He extinguished several lights, and only one was trained on her for the moment.

"I had the tourist feeling of Greenwich Village," she said. "If I can find a place that's half-way suitable, I prefer to stay on the East Side."

"I like this part of town, of course, but you can paint anywhere, and don't let anybody try to tell you otherwise." From a rack he took one of several cameras. "You were at home on the stool before. Let's start there."

Janet returned to her seat.

Lance pulled a switch, pressed several buttons and bathed her in dazzling light.

Janet could scarcely see him beyond the lights, which seemed to form a protective shell around her, and felt almost ashamed of her reluctance to pose.

"In the summer," he said, "it's ghastly under those lights."

"I can imagine."

Janet could see that, when Lance turned, he was holding his camera to his face, which made him even more impersonal and remote.

He continued to chat as he moved around at the edge of the light circle, taking picture after picture. At his casual suggestion, after a time, she stood and moved around within a limited area, and finally he called, "Take a break while I get another

267

camera. If you want to smoke, there are cigarettes and matches in the dressing room."

Janet hesitated before venturing from the lighted area in which she now felt separated, as an actor on a stage, and therefore safe. She had to summon her courage before she darted into the dressing room. Once there, she glanced at herself in a long mirror, and was surprised to see that perspiration covered her face and body; she hadn't even realized she was warm. But when she returned to the floodlit area she was conscious, this time, of the intense heat.

"Keep the cigarette, if you like," Lance called. "Do whatever makes you feel most comfortable."

She took a deep drag and slowly exhaled.

"Pretty ghastly under the lights, isn't it? Maybe I can make it a little better for you." Lance opened a window.

A blast of icy air swept across Janet. "That feels good," she said, flicking aside a long strand of hair, "but my blood may congeal. Let me know if I start turning blue."

"Pull on your boots, why don't you?" he called.

Janet blinked at him, but could not make out more than a blur beyond the lights.

"Let's go!" He sounded impatient.

Recently, just because it was so campy, Muriel had brought home a pile of girlie magazines, and their pages had been filled with nudes wearing boots. "This is a put-on, isn't it?" she asked uncertainly.

"Why should it be?" Lance's irritation increased.

"Well, it's so—cheap." She felt the urge to hide, but there was nowhere to go. "I mean, every little tramp model in town must pose that way."

"Sure. There's a universal demand for that kind of picture. But I'll explain all that to you later."

"I—I'd really feel self-conscious," Janet said.

"We don't have to make a Federal case out of this," he said

patiently, "but your feet are cold, and you're curling your toes. It doesn't make very good pictures."

"I see." She made no move.

"So get the boots, chick." He adjusted something on the camera lens.

Janet continued to envisage the girlie magazine photos, and for the first time felt a sense of shame.

Lance was irritated. "What's your hang-up?"

She was ashamed to tell him. "It's—nothing, really."

"Now is the time to get over it. The whole purpose of this session is to give you the sense of freedom that only the super-real can produce." He waited, and when she still did not move, he said, "Oh, for Christ's sake."

Janet flinched.

Lance, still holding his camera, quickly snapped a picture. It occurred to him that he had enjoyed her discomfort, and wanted more. Most of the girls he knew were fairly hard-shelled, so this was an unusual experience, a form of super-reality that he rarely encountered.

It might be rough on Janet, of course, but she'd soon get over it, and would, in fact, benefit.

Then, all at once, it occurred to him that she was Max Berman's protégée, and his mouth hardened. It wasn't fair to take out his frustrations on Janet, of course, but Berman had lied to him, and now his major film was postponed. Indefinitely.

Maybe, as Bobbie so often told him, he was a sadist at heart. But this was no time for self-analysis.

Lance deliberately raised his voice. "My time is too valuable for me to be wasting it! Do you think there's something special or sacred about your precious body?"

"Let's call off this whole thing." Janet was conscious only of her vulnerability, but was afraid to run toward the dressing room.

"Kid," he said, his voice ugly, "I'm giving you a choice. Climb into those boots, fast, or I'll beat your ass off. Now move!"

A chill numbed her as she realized he meant what he said, and she knew she had been unbelievably stupid to let herself be placed in this predicament. Panic-stricken, Janet raced toward the dressing room for her boots. Then, standing in the open studio, she leaned against the nearest wall to don them. Her fingers were trembling, and she found it difficult to gain a firm grip on the leather tops.

When she heard a repeated clicking sound she realized that Lance was already at work with the camera.

"Face me!" he roared. "Don't turn away!"

She obeyed.

Lance's arm stabbed into the circle of light. "Here's another cigarette."

"I—I don't feel like—"

"I don't give a good goddam what you feel like doing!"

She reached out for the cigarette.

A moment later the camera started clicking again.

The ordeal seemed endless.

"Even virgins know how to smile, don't they? That's better! Now look this way, and burn a little sex into the camera. Now you're cooperating!"

Janet loathed herself almost as much as she hated the man who was bullying her. The camera clicked interminably.

"That's the end of the film," Lance said at last, and laughed quietly, his play-acting finished. "That's also the end of today's session, and now I'll make some prints."

Janet was too miserable to feel relieved as she headed toward the dressing room. Wearily, trying to compose herself, she stood for several minutes, staring blankly into space. All at once the realization struck her that she was still vulnerable, and she reached for her panties and bra, which she had left on a chair. They were gone, as were her half-slip and stockings. Her dress and coat, which she had placed on hangers, were nowhere to be seen, either.

At first she thought she had left them elsewhere, but deep fear gripped her as she looked around the dresing room and could not find them. The possibility crossed her mind that she had become confused and had undressed in the other cell that had been installed for that purpose. It was located on the far side of the studio and was much smaller. It could be reached by going down a long, dank corridor that by-passed the studio itself. Trembling, Janet headed down it afraid that at any moment she and Lance would collide. When at last she got there and found the cubicle empty she thought she must surely be going out of her mind. Finally, she made her way back to the first dressing room, fighting tears and increasingly afraid of calling Lance, who, she was now convinced, was holding her clothes as ransom for her sexual surrender.

Finally, there was no choice. She stepped back into the floodlit studio and called his name.

There was no answer. Something ahead of Janet caused her to stop short, catching her breath.

Lance Balutis lay crumpled on the floor, dead, his glazed eyes fixed on the ceiling. Blood was oozing from a half-dozen jagged wounds in his back and neck, and there was a deep gash on one side of his face.

There was no one else in the studio, and Janet heard no sound but that of her own tremulous, shallow breathing. More conscious than ever of her nudity, she tried to shield her body with her arms and hands, then involuntarily began to scream, her cries becoming louder and more piercing in a mounting crescendo of terror.

A police photographer was taking pictures of the corpse, circling Lance's body in order to make his shots from every angle. Two detectives in plain clothes were dusting for fingerprints, and another, an artist, was drawing quick sketches showing the position of every piece of furniture.

Lieutenant William Wilson, directing the operation, was crisp.

271

"Be careful when you come to this," he told the men as he pointed to a narrow, razor-edge paint scraper on the floor a few feet from the body. "From the looks of things, this was the murder weapon."

Janet, wrapped in an old tweed jacket of Lance's, sat huddled in a far corner, weeping quietly.

Wilson sauntered toward her.

"My clothes," the girl muttered. "Please find them."

"If they were here, you'd have them," Wilson said, running a hand through his short-cropped, grey hair.

She wept helplessly.

"Don't touch the body until the coroner's people get here," the Lieutenant called. "Sergeant Brennan, don't let the press in until you and the deputy coroner are done. I don't want those elephants moving or upsetting anything."

Janet continued to whimper.

"Miss," Wilson told her, "you can wear my overcoat for now. There's a swarm of photographers outside, so you duck your head on the way to my car if you don't want publicity."

She made an attempt to speak clearly. "I didn't—"

"Nobody says you did. Yet. No charges have been lodged against you. We're going to headquarters, and we'll have a long talk about it there. If you want your lawyer there, we'll call him in for you. I'll explain your rights to you in the car."

Janet allowed herself to be drawn to her feet, and stood in a daze as he enveloped her in a long, dark overcoat.

"Even a kid like you," Wilson said, a trace of sympathy in his gruff voice, "ought to have known that you take risks when you're one of Balutis' girls."

It was useless to explain, Janet thought wearily, that she hadn't been one of Lance's girls.

Max unlocked the apartment door and ushered Janet into his living room. "Now you can relax," he said, helping her remove the new cloth coat her parents had bought for her while she had been held at police headquarters.

The girl wandered around the room, touching ashtrays and bric-a-brac.

"Sit down," Max said, watching her.

"The past two and a half days have felt like a year," Janet murmured.

"For all of us, but that's finished now." He was quiet but firm. "Wilson doesn't think you killed Balutis any more than your family does. Or Stella. Or me. That's why he let you go."

"It's because those clear fingerprints on that—that paint scraper weren't mine."

"The paint scraper was one reason. There were plenty of

others." Max refrained from mentioning that one of the more important reasons had been the voluntary physical examination she had undergone, which had revealed that she had not engaged in sexual intercourse with anyone. "Wilson understands character. He knows how to analyze people. That's his job, and he meant it when he told your father and me—and the lawyers—that he doesn't believe you were the killer."

"He doesn't want me to go away anywhere?"

"Of course not, for your own protection as well as their own. You're still on their list until they find out who did it." Max smiled sourly. "What a list. Muriel Browning. Bobbie Wayne. That fag actor, Gerry Jarvis. All those society people. They've been questioning everybody Balutis knew. Even me. And he ran around with so much *dreck* they could take months to investigate."

"I just wish the whole thing was over," Janet said, collapsing onto a sofa.

"For you, it's over."

"You don't know how grateful I am to you, Uncle Max—"

"So who wants gratitude? You insisted you couldn't go back to your parents—"

"I can't! I've embarrassed them enough, with all those headlines and pictures. And those hints about why I wasn't wearing anything except my boots."

"You were foolish, you paid for it, and that's the end of it. Nobody is going to lecture you, any more than we'd let you go back to the East Village apartment with Muriel."

"I wouldn't want to." Janet shivered and rubbed her arms. "Not just yet."

"Not ever, I hope." Max didn't allow himself to elaborate. "Look, it's like Stella says. When the chips are down, you can always tell class. Let the police worry about their business while you concentrate on Janet Lafferty, and pretty soon you'll be fine."

274

"L & B has surprised me, Max." Howard Christianson moved around his office with a watering can, pausing at each of the many small plants clustered on window ledges and shelves. "We've always known you and Paul had ingenuity, but you've surpassed yourselves in these past months. And your agility really has surprised us."

"If that's a compliment," Max replied, carefully clipping the end of a fresh cigar, "I'll accept it. We aren't getting much from North Atlantic these days, so we'll take anything, even back-handed compliments."

"We've hoped you wouldn't be bitter, but that would be too much to expect." The banker continued to busy himself with his plants.

"If Paul and I tried to take your business away from you, would you pin medals on us?"

"It wasn't North Atlantic's aim to drive you out of business. We simply wanted you to cut back. It's always a temptation in times of monetary inflation to expand. It's done in every business, every industry. But L & B was growing too fast."

"So I'll congratulate you," Max said. "You stunted our growth." His smile was sour.

"Your operation is rapidly approaching a sound level." The banker put away the watering can and returned to his desk.

Max twisted in his seat to face him. "What you mean," he said, "is that we've stretched our credit to the limit in every direction. So you think you've got us where you want us, finally."

"You're mistaken. The credit committee recommended that North Atlantic resume full, normal relations with L & B, under certain conditions. And I've been authorized to tell you the board has given its approval."

Max felt a limited measure of relief, but concealed it. "If I'm supposed to be impressed, Howard, I'm not." He took his time lighting the cigar. "What are your conditions?"

"Cut back your realty and holding operations to what we

believe to be healthy. Here are the credit committee's recommendations." Christianson handed his visitor a neatly bound folder. "You'll find a summary on the first page."

Max opened the folder, and, puffing on his cigar, read the summary slowly.

"Well?" Christianson's edge of anxiety revealed that the bank didn't want to lose a valuable client.

"They want no change in our construction program. That's good, because we wouldn't touch it. They want us to sell the new Holland Towers apartment complex and America Plaza. All three skyscrapers in the Plaza?"

"All of them."

"Mmm. I can't commit myself. Paul and I will have to think about it, and maybe go back to our own board."

"Fair enough. But you agree the point is negotiable?"

"At this meeting, I agree to nothing. We're exploring, that's all. But on the final recommendation," Max said, "the answer is no. We won't do it."

"You're referring to the hotels?"

"We won't dispose of them," Max said. "Keep tightening the screws, if you want. You can't hurt us much more than you've done already. But I won't give up the hotel chain until you force us into bankruptcy."

"You and I," Christianson said, "are merely holding a preliminary chat today. We won't negotiate until we sit down in a formal session, you and Paul, the lawyers—"

"Over my dead body you'll get those hotels. It's the only way you'll get them, Howard. And you're foolish if you try. Since we've improved them, property values have gone up in every neighborhood surrounding every one of the hotels. We happen to know that North Atlantic is a major property owner in some of those areas, so you have no kick. You've been making a healthy profit, and we ought to charge you a percentage as a fee."

Christianson smiled, but not in appreciation of the joke. "We'll hold the formal meeting whenever you and Paul are ready."

"We'll need a little time. That mess his daughter got involved in is making it hard for him to concentrate on business."

"North Atlantic is in no hurry."

"Yeah, I know. This week, next week, what does it matter? You can crack down on us whenever you feel like it."

The restaurant was small and unpretentious. Max was heartily tired of dining out, but Janet needed a change of scene after ten days of seeing the Balutis murder splashed in headlines. She was enjoying herself and was eating her filet with relish, so he was pleased he had made the effort. Even though there was no escape from the sensationalism of press speculation regarding her own possible role in the Balutis murder, the shadows under her eyes had vanished. Stella had been right when she said, "At Janet's age a juicy steak is better than a tranquilizer. Feed her, Max, and stop worrying."

Watching the girl consume steak, a baked potato and French-fried onions, Max smiled.

Suddenly Janet stiffened, her fork poised in midair. "That girl," she said, "is wearing my dress."

Max followed her glance and saw a young woman, perhaps a year or two older than Janet. She had blue-black hair, probably dyed, heavy eye make-up and a pair of shapely legs beneath a miniskirted dress of red wool. The high-necked, long-sleeved dress flared at the wrists, and featured a large, pointed collar. As nearly as Max could see, it looked like any dress a woman under forty might wear.

"What I mean," Janet continued with a faintly apologetic smile, "is that it's exactly like the dress I—lost—at Lance's studio."

"I'm sure the manufacturer made more than one," Max said.

"I suppose." Janet continued to smile. "I bought it at Bonwit's when I could still use Mother's charge accounts."

Max plunged his fork into his salad. "For a minute you had

me going," he said. "Fred makes a dressing that's supposed to be special, so try your lettuce." The girl in the red dress, he noted, had paused to speak briefly with Fred, the proprietor who acted as his own maitre d'.

Janet nodded, absently tasting her salad as she continued to gaze surreptitiously at the girl, who finished her conversation with Fred and moved on to the cloakroom, where she stood gossiping with the hat-check girl.

Suddenly Janet gasped and caught Max's arm in a tight grip.

He saw she was wildly excited.

"Look," she whispered. "That's my green coat she's putting on!"

The girl was donning a coat of green wool with fur collar and cuffs.

"Mother bought it for me my last year in school. It was short on me, and it's far too short for her. She's an inch or two taller than I am!" Her meal forgotten, Janet stood up.

"Wait," Max said.

She ignored his injunction. "The coat *and* the dress are too much of a coincidence! They're mine, and they were stolen from me—that night!"

Max took some money from his pocket and threw it onto the table, then hurried after Janet, who was making her way through the maze of closely placed tables. There was only a chance she might be right. The odds against seeing someone in the identical dress and coat she had worn to Balutis' studio were too great.

Janet, who had worn her new coat to the table, followed the girl out of the restaurant.

Max fished for his coat check, snatched it from the cloakroom attendant and slapped a coin into her hand as he dashed out into the cold, struggling into his overcoat.

The doorman, who was standing at the curb, looked at him expectantly.

But Janet pointed off to the left and took Max's arm. "She's walking, and she has a head start!" She set a rapid pace.

278

"We have to be careful," Max told her, wishing there had been time to telephone Lieutenant Wilson.

"She stopped at the corner." Janet slowed somewhat. "The traffic light is against her."

"We can't stop her and accuse her of wearing stolen clothes," Max said, trying to organize his thoughts.

"Oh, I agree. We've got to follow her and see where she's going." Janet, in spite of her extreme nervousness, appeared to be enjoying the chase.

Max, thoroughly uncomfortable in the bizarre situation, reflected that the young loved adventure for its own sake. But he had no time to dwell on the matter.

After a walk of a few blocks they saw the unknown girl pause to say a few words to the doorman guarding the entrance of a terraced, grey concrete and glass apartment building.

The man nodded and opened the door for her.

Max and Janet walked more rapidly, resisting the urge to break into a run.

The doorman halted them. "Who did you want to see?" he demanded, barring their path.

Max was startled by the unexpected question, and groped for an appropriate answer. By the time he told the man the whole story, the girl would be gone.

"Sorry," the doorman said, his tone polite but firm. "But we don't let anybody in here unless we know where you're going. That's our orders."

Bribing him with a five-dollar bill might cause complications, but there was nothing to lose. Max reached for his money, extracted the bill and held it out to the man.

"Sorry, mister. It would mean my job."

Janet was becoming frantic.

Max patted her shoulder. "It was a good idea, maybe, but I'm afraid we've got to forget it."

She started to argue as he turned away.

At that moment a taxi pulled to a halt at the curb, and a

blonde with short hair, wearing a voluminous silver fox cape, emerged. "Hi, Jan!" she said. "Maxie, you do get around."

"Hello, Bobbie." Max felt himself grow taut. If Bobbie Wayne, one of Balutis' closest associates, had business in the building, she might be able to lead them to the girl.

"Going to the party, friends?" Bobbie allowed her cape to fall open and stood revealed in a two-piece dress of purple silk with bare midriff.

"The doorman isn't the friendly type," Janet said, without committing herself.

"They're with me, Chuck," said Bobbie. The doorman bowed and opened the glass portal.

"The *flics*," Bobbie continued, "played spin-the-bottle with me all of one day and half the night. My God, they're stupid! I've been moping around for days, but tonight I just had to cut loose, and I'm glad you feel the same way. Lance would be the first one to laugh at the spectacle of people mourning for him."

If she had committed the murder, Janet thought, she was remarkably poised.

Max saw no sign of the girl in the lobby or the waiting elevator, which, apparently, had already gone up and returned automatically to the ground floor. Taking Janet's arm, he exerted a slight pressure, warning her to say nothing of their quixotic mission.

"I've often thought of calling you in this past week, Jan," Bobbie said as the elevator carried them up toward the higher floors. "I'd love to know what really happened to you at Lance's studio."

"Lieutenant Wilson told me not to discuss it with anybody. But I'll be glad to fill you in—after they catch the murderer and the case is closed."

"I can hardly wait. God, that Wilson is a square."

Max saw that Bobbie, in spite of her aplomb, had been suffering. Her face looked ravaged, and cosmetics could not hide the hollows beneath her eyes.

She became conscious of his scrutiny. "Maxie," she said, "I plan to get stoned tonight, and if you want a blast, join me. You and I are due for an old-fashioned reunion."

The elevator stopped and the door opened, making a reply unnecessary.

A servant in seventeenth-century livery took the guests' coats, but an even greater surprise was in store as Max and Janet stood uncertainly behind Bobbie Wayne in the spacious, print-lined foyer. A tall man wearing the elaborate costume of a seventeenth-century European nobleman bore down on them, appearing from the dim recesses of a cavernous living room. His costume was authentic in every detail from his high-crowned, shoulder-length wig, embroidered tailcoat with splashes of lace at his throat and neck, and satin knee breeches, to his gold-buckled pumps and white silk stockings. Diamond and ruby rings flashed on his fingers, and his left hand rested on the hilt of an ornamental dress sword that was worth a small fortune.

Prince Severin Konarski, the Polish nobleman-lingerie designer and manufacturer, embraced Bobbie and then turned to the pair behind her. "Miss Lafferty," he said, bending low to kiss the startled girl's hand, "you lend enchantment to the evening. And a fillip. Your fame precedes you."

Janet was too flustered to reply, much less introduce Max to their host.

Bobbie performed the honors before announcing she intended to get herself a drink, and then disappeared.

The prince was in command of the situation. "Mr. Berman, your servant, sir." He bowed before shaking Max's hand. "As you appear to be a member of my generation, you may want to help me perform the duties of a chaperon." He led them down several steps into the huge living room.

"Sure," Max said vaguely. "Glad to." As nearly as he could make out in the soft lighting, there were at least twenty to thirty people in the room, and he began to search, unobtrusively, for the girl in the red wool dress.

A second uniformed lackey appeared with a tray of chilled champagne glasses.

Max knew a pleasantry was required of him. "We had no idea this was a costume party."

Janet was looking around the room carefully.

"Your attire, sir, is far more formal than that of most members of the evening's company." Haughtily erect, Konarski was an aristocrat incarnate. "I myself am dressed as I always dress for these little gatherings. The Polish nobility enjoyed its first intellectual flowering in the seventeenth century, you know, which enabled it to drape its libertinism—which goes back hundreds of years earlier—in philosophical trappings. I'm reminded of the parallels in our present-day world, obviously."

A curved sofa, upholstered in velvet, sat empty in the middle of the room, and Konarski conducted them to it.

Max was relieved when he realized he could catch an unobstructed view of the lighted entrance foyer. The girl couldn't leave the apartment unnoticed.

"Join me on my throne," the prince said, "and help me observe the foibles of our times. My favorite sport. As a matter of fact, I liken myself to François de la Rochefoucauld."

Janet cast an agonized glance at Max.

We're stuck, he told her silently. Keep looking. Aloud he said, "I studied Rochefoucauld's *Maxims* at school. I had no choice."

"The finest aristocratic mind of the seventeenth century," the prince said enthusiastically. "He was a soldier, as I was. A man of action, as I hope I am. Even though I earn my living selling outrageously expensive lingerie to middle-aged women who want to pretend they're young."

Max caught a glimpse of red in the frame of a door leading to an adjoining room, and half-stood. But he saw a young woman in some filmy material, and sat abruptly.

Konarski was gazing at him curiously.

Max wrenched himself back to their host. "You were telling me how much you and Rochefoucauld are alike." His eyes were becoming accustomed to the dim lighting now, and he looked around the room with great care.

More people were gathered there than he had thought, perhaps forty in all, most of them in the costumes and pants suits that were the uniform of the young. A girl and boy, both somewhat younger than Janet, perched on the arm of the sofa, and although within reach, seemed unaware of Max's proximity. Both had shoulder-length, pale hair and wore matching turtlenecked shirts with huge Jerusalem crosses suspended from silver chains.

"The pill," Konarski said, conscious of Max's flicker of interest in the pair, "has robbed the sex act of its primary function. Since the male is no longer required to demonstrate his aggression—and, indeed, is given less and less chance to do so by the female—we find ourselves in a mono-sex society. Do you see the young man to the left of the fireplace? Handsome, don't you agree?"

Max, half-watching the foyer, glanced quickly at a man in his thirties who was wearing a semi-transparent voile shirt, with a lace jabot at the throat, and skin-tight trousers.

"He's gorgeous," Janet said.

"Do you hear of the voice of youth, Max?" Konarski asked. *He's* gorgeous! The male has resumed his natural peacock role after spending one hundred and fifty years in the shadow of the female." He regarded the man critically. "I object only to his trousers, which are vulgar. He'd show off his legs to far better advantage if he had the complete courage of his convictions and wore a miniskirt. That will come next."

A servant came up to them, but Max refused another glass of champagne.

"You want to make all men homosexuals?" he demanded.

"Certainly not!" Konarski was emphatic. "Scotsmen have worn kilts for hundreds of years because that type of dress doesn't inhibit them. And look at the short skirts of the ancient Greek men."

"Aha!" Max, enjoying the discussion in spite of his real aim,

283

was triumphant. "You prove my point. In ancient Greece men wore short skirts, and homosexuality prevailed."

"Surely not because of clothing," Konarski replied with a smile. "Today, every man is something of a transvestite, and so is every woman. Beware when you cling to old-fashioned precepts, my dear Max."

"Everything today is upside down," Max admitted.

"Like *Alice in Wonderland*," Janet said.

The prince nodded. "A literary product of Victorian England that wasn't included in my education. But I do know it was written for small girls by a clergyman who had his secret lusts. Today he'd be more inclined to bring his desires into the open, in which case he wouldn't write a work of enduring interest and stature. There you are, Max. I've given you ammunition for your counter-attack. To be successful in the arts one must be strongly inhibited, which may account for the abysmal decline in today's literature, music and art."

Max shrugged. "Architecture I know a little something about."

"Very well, architecture. Is it accidental that the functional buildings of Gropius' *Bauhaus* school have sprung up in every modern city on earth? Frankfurt, Tokyo, São Paulo—"

"Oh, they have clean lines," Max said. "But there are so many of them because they're relatively simple to put up."

Janet rose to her feet. "Excuse me. I feel like wandering around."

"Enjoy yourself, my dear," Konarski told her, waving.

She cast a significant glance at Max, then wandered off toward the dining room.

Max kept an eye on her.

"The young," Konarski said, "are interested only in themselves. Now, where were we? Ah, the *Bauhaus* buildings. They're ugly. I'm delighted that Chicago is breaking away, for the second time in a century. Chicago, my dear Max, which is regarded as a bourgeois cultural desert."

"Not by me! Chicago architects are doing the most exciting

designing in the world." For a few moments Max could almost forget the mission that had brought him to this apartment. "Maybe it was a good thing a few years ago when the old Garrick Theater there was torn down. The people who had tried to save it were so angry they made the city conscious of architecture again."

"Permit me," the prince said, "to quote for you the most famous of the Duc de la Rochefoucauld's maxims. 'Our virtues are most frequently but vices disguised.' I prefer to think of it in terms of our own age. One man's neglected wife is another's cherished mistress. I applaud the young, my dear Max, just as I applaud the Chicago architects. Candor is their god, so they bring everything into the open and conceal nothing."

"But modesty—"

"Only the inadequate are really modest. Are you a good builder?"

"Damn good."

"Hardly a modest assertion, yet I'm sure you think of yourself as a modest man."

Max grinned.

"You get my point."

"You don't give me a chance to miss it." Max saw Janet across the room, appearing from the direction of the dining room, and peered at her.

She shook her head, slowly, then vanished again.

A sense of failure enveloped him.

"I'm not worshiping the cult of youth, however," Konarski declared. "I hope you understand my position."

Max told himself that he and Janet couldn't leave until they made a thorough search for the girl and convinced themselves she wasn't there. So it was essential that he prolong his conversation with the prince. "I'm trying to understand. I've been trying to figure out this new generation for months."

"Let me illustrate," Konarski said. "I think it's healthy that a couple overcome by natural urges or curiosity will make no secret of using one of my bedrooms. They're saved the inconvenience and expense, as well as some possible embarrassment, of signing false names on a hotel or motel register. On the other hand, I deplore the decline in gracious living."

"What else do you expect of people who have thrown away the values of generations?" Lance Balutis had died, Max thought, because his kind had rejected the essential dignity that distinguished humans from animals.

"I give one of these little parties about once a month," the Prince said. "I know what to expect, even though I've never before seen half of my guests and don't know their names. Many of the young people ask for beer, but I refuse to compromise my own integrity and I serve only champagne. They won't eat my caviar and pâté. Which reminds me that I'm neglecting my duties as a host." He beckoned to a servant, spoke a few words to him and then resumed. "I'm a masochist, obviously. My pain becomes contempt when I see them turn up their noses at my grey Iranian caviar. But I'm not completely neurotic. I'm able to buy a pound or two of the superb golden Russian every year, and I serve it only to mature, appreciative guests—with taste buds."

"Giving caviar to people you know don't like it," Max said, increasingly convinced that Konarski was as erratically unpredictable as the young people he entertained, "is an expensive joke!"

"We live in an era of waste that justifies even the most dubious of Veblen's theories on conspicuous consumption. The barbarian hordes have not merely penetrated our gates, but have become the pacesetters and tastemakers. I surrender to them in most matters, and accept their codes in such trivial fields as ethics and morality. But I owe it to the unborn generations of the future to fight for the preservation of basic social values. If I can persuade enough of the young to develop a taste for champagne and caviar, civilization will not be swept away in a tidal wave of cola drinks and pizza."

286

The servant returned, and the prince took a plate from him, then handed it to Max with a flourish.

In partitioned sections were mounds of caviar, hardboiled egg whites and yolks, separated and shredded, chopped onions and wedges of lemon, crisp Melba toast and slices of miniature rye bread. Max emitted an involuntary sigh of pleasure.

"Like me," Konarski told him, "you are a relic of a bygone era."

"You flatter me. Maybe you were brought up on this stuff, but I ate sausages and pumpernickel when I was a boy in Vienna. I was over thirty the first time I tasted caviar, and I had to acquire the taste."

"Precisely. If you've developed an appreciation of the symbols of an advanced civilization, so can the young rebels."

"Severin, I'm an optimist, and I hope this new generation will adopt higher standards as it becomes responsible for the world."

"Impossible!

"Wait. Give me a chance to prove what I'm saying. Where was your home in Poland?"

"Our principal estates were near Bydgoszcz."

"Some distant cousins on my father's side lived in Bydgoszcz," Max said, "and it isn't a coincidence, because I had relatives in nearly every part of Poland. You didn't know my relatives, but it had to be they knew your family. The sport of the nobility was riding down Jews in pogroms."

"See here, I resent—"

"I make no accusations, and I'm not abusing your hospitality. My point is just the opposite. Somewhere along the line, you know, Konarskis killed Bermans. But here we are in America, you and I. You open your door to me, a Jew. I eat your caviar and drink your champagne. Do you wonder I'm an optimist? This, to me, is a more important symbol of civilization's future than the haircuts or food tastes of the young people."

Konarski regained his poise, and laughed. "You and I are eliminating the prejudices of several thousand years. A mere nothing. The younger generation is trying to achieve a real miracle. Parthenogenesis."

Max looked blank.

"I'm afraid I don't know the German word for it. Birth without male participation in the act of procreation."

"You're talking about a small group, the sons and daughters of people who have money and can afford eccentricities."

"I speak of an entire generation throughout the world," Konarski said. "It won't be long before you're hiring men with long hair for your building crews. There won't be anybody else, and on weekends they'll use perfume and wear jewelry. Ah, some dear friends have just arrived. Excuse me."

Max watched him as he went off to greet a newly arrived couple.

Janet was working her way through the crush when he reached the door, so he waited for her.

"No luck yet," she said.

"I thought I'd never get away, but I can help now. You go that way and I'll go this."

At least thirty people were gathered in the room, but, as Prince Konarski had said, the platters of pâté and bowls of iced caviar were being ignored. The guests were drinking champagne, however, because they were being offered nothing else.

Max's heart skipped a beat when he saw the girl from the restaurant. She was standing on the far side of the room, near the windows, with a group of three or four others. Aside from her distinctive hair and a willowy figure, her appearance was ordinary. And, Max thought, it would be difficult for him to describe her to Lieutenant Wilson. He debated whether to telephone Wilson at once, but decided to wait; by the time he found a phone in an empty room and could speak openly, she might be gone again.

The girl looked across the room at Max.

He was uncertain whether he saw a flicker of recognition in her eyes or whether she glanced through and past him. His palms were sweating and his forehead was damp as he made his way across the room.

The pounding of his temples was so loud it deafened him. But perhaps it wasn't far-fetched to think the girl knew she had been followed. Suppose it had been she who had killed Lance Balutis. She'd be apprehensive, and, if cornered, ready to put up a fight.

Maybe she carried a pistol in the leather bag hanging from her left shoulder. It wouldn't take more than an instant for her to reach into it and then put a bullet between the eyes of the man who was moving toward her. Max's pulse raced still harder.

It took him an eternity to cross the room.

No one in the group paid any attention to him. The girl did not look at him again. She, like the others, was listening to a monologue being delivered by a tall, broad-shouldered black man in a faded work shirt, a nail-studded belt, tight-fitting trousers that looked tailor-made and heavy boots. If he were the girl's accomplice, he could tear apart an inquisitive bystander with his hands.

Max halted beside the girl, his shoulder almost touching hers.

She seemed unaware of his proximity.

The black man was laughing at a story, his own grim humor, and his listeners joined in uncertainly.

"Who is this fellow?" Max asked the girl softly, in what he hoped sounded like a conversational tone.

She turned to him, her brown eyes bright but expressionless, and giggled inanely.

He wondered if she were drunk, but she held no glass.

"This is Harley Jones," said a young man who had heard the question.

Max had seen Jones's name in print on scores of occasions, and knew he was a dedicated black power advocate. Under ordinary circumstances Max would have been fascinated, but right now he could think only of the girl who was wearing Janet's stolen clothing.

289

Lowering his voice still more, he murmured to her, "I wouldn't have expected to find him here."

Again she giggled.

Max studied her surreptitiously, and realized her thoughts seemed far away.

"Some of you," Jones said, "may want to lynch me. I admit I'm a rabble-rouser. I'm proud of it. Remember that exaggeration is the key to the achievement of just goals in a polymorphous society. Theodor Herzl used the technique effectively in establishing the nucleus of his Zionist state, and publicly acknowledged his debt to Sam Adams in the American Revolution. I've studied Adams myself, and I'm pleased to be working in the tradition established by a Founding Father of the Republic."

"What are you driving at, Harley?" someone asked.

"The black moderate and the white liberal have been traveling in concentric circles, which isn't the shortest distance between two points. I'll grant you, privately, that the N.A.A.C.P. and the Urban League and all the rest paved the way, but they haven't been able to meet the need. When a man is dying of thirst, you don't feed him water with an eyedropper. The fundamental lesson history teaches us is that a people, any people, who want their rights must work for themselves. They can't sit back while others do the job for them."

Max wished he could concentrate on what Jones was saying. Instead he turned again to the girl in an attempt to strike up a conversation with her. "Could I get you a drink?"

She gave no indication that she heard him.

As nearly as Max could judge, she was relaxed and at ease, however.

"I won't insult your intelligence," Jones said, "by bringing up the old cliché about breaking eggs to make an omelet."

"Breaking eggs," a man said, "isn't the same as cracking heads or murdering senators and governors!"

290

"I sometimes speak metaphorically." Gentle amusement showed unexpectedly in Jones's eyes. "I've discovered that Charlie listens only when a club is brandished over his head. My people dig what I preach."

Max, watching the girl, lost the thread of Jones's argument. The girl, although physically present, was remote, wrapped in a cocoon of her own making. She displayed no symptoms of over-indulgence in alcohol, but her reactions to the people around her were anything but normal. If the entire group moved away, Max thought, she would continue to stand immobile, almost in a trance. Aside from vacuous laughter when directly addressed, she had shown no response to anything taking place around her, and his flesh crawled. She was obviously on drugs.

Suddenly, for no apparent reason, she giggled again, at length.

The observations of the black power advocate could not have been responsible for that.

"In Eire," Jones said, "the I.R.A. was a minority dedicated to violent means on behalf of a passive majority. But the black is in the minority in the United States, and that position won't be changed. So we must win concessions from the white majority. They won't give them to us willingly, so we've got to use other means. We must use fear as the weapon that will force them to give us our rights."

The girl's high-pitched laugh died away as unexpectedly as it had begun.

"Cooperate with us, Charlie," Jones said, "and grant us the equality you admit we're being denied. Refuse at your own risk. I'm not telling you what we'll do, Charlie, because I hate threats. I've been on the receiving end for too many generations. But I am telling you something. What we might do. You taught us the game of racial supremacy, and we've been students long enough. Now we're going to be the teachers."

Suddenly someone caught Max from behind, twisted his head

and kissed him. A tongue pushed itself between his closed lips, and a pair of surprisingly strong arms were wound around his neck.

He struggled to free himself.

"Maxie," Bobbie Wayne said, "I adore you."

As she caught hold of him again, Max saw that she was very drunk.

"I've waited a million years for you, Maxie. Let's go find a little privacy so we can screw."

"Later." He managed to grasp the hands that were pawing at him.

"What's wrong with now?" she demanded loudly.

Harley Jones, who had been interrupted, was startled.

Bobbie became aware of him. "Sweetie," she said, hurling herself at him, "you look like somebody who'll appreciate a little action."

Max turned away, and felt a sinking sensation in the pit of his stomach. The girl in the red dress was gone.

Only a few diners were lingering over coffee and cognac in the restaurant, and a single waiter stood sentry duty near the swinging doors that led to the kitchen. But Fred, leaning on his small reservation desk that stood between the bar and the main dining room, had spent too many years building up his establishment to say or do anything that would spoil its public image.

"Mr. Berman," he said, speaking so softly that his voice was barely audible, "you've been one of my regulars since the old days, but I'm not sure I can help you."

"All we want, Fred," Max said, "is the name of the girl who was talking to you earlier tonight. She went from here to a party, and we saw her there. But we lost track of her. And we have to talk to her."

Fred hesitated.

"I know the person you mean, Mr. Berman, but I've always made it a house rule not to reveal information about my employees."

"She works for you?" Max's voice grew very loud. "Fred, if you don't come clean with me, the police will have to get this information from you. That's all there is to it."

Fred scrutinized him. "Is she in a jam?"

"Right now you know as much as I do. I hope not." Max glanced at his watch. "How about it, Fred?"

"Her name is Ruth Anton. She's my assistant cashier."

"Janet, does the name mean anything to you?"

"No."

"For an assistant cashier in a restaurant," Max said, "she knows some fancy people."

"Her social life," Fred said, "is her own business. I don't know anything about it."

"I don't expect you to tell me her life story. Do you know where she lives?"

"Her address is in my files upstairs in the office. Do you want to come up with me?"

"Yes."

The office, which they reached by way of a narrow, winding flight of carpeted stairs, was a tiny two-room suite. In the outer room were file cabinets, adding machines, typewriter tables and the usual clutter of a business establishment.

Fred led the pair to his inner sanctum. The walls were filled with autographed photos of prominent clients, and sample menus were scattered on a table. The proprietor went to a drawer and leafed through a small, metal card file. "Here we are," he said, "Ruth Anton," and told them an address in the Chelsea area.

Max had done all he could unaided. He drew a deep breath. "I said I'd keep you out of this if I could, and I'll do my best, Fred. But now I've got to call police headquarters."

A squad car took Janet back to the apartment while Max, riding with Lieutenant Wilson, told the full story of everything that had happened that evening. "It's a long shot, I know," he said as he brought his account to an end.

"But worth following through." Wilson nodded.

"Do you have somebody talking to Konarski tonight?"

Wilson smiled, but did not reply.

"Sorry," Max said. "Let me offer you a cigar."

"Thanks. I'll smoke it later. Sure you haven't left out any details that could be important?"

"I wouldn't know what could be important, so I've left out nothing." Max peered out of the window. "This part of town is seedy and still running down. It'll be a few years before the new apartment houses that are starting to go up can turn the tide."

"Here we are, Lieutenant," the chauffeur called, pulling to a halt. "The brownstone with the iron railings, it looks like."

The building was old and somewhat in need of repair, similar to thousands in every part of New York.

"Wait for us, Larry," Wilson said.

"Yes, sir."

"You want me to come along?" Max asked, suddenly feeling out of place.

"I'll need you to identify the girl, Mr. Berman. A name isn't enough. I've got to connect it with a face."

Max grinned as he climbed out of the car. "I guess I wouldn't be a very good detective."

"Don't be too sure of that. You may have found the first real clue in this case." Wilson led the way into the entrance hall, which smelled of cabbage, and inspected a long, double row of names in slots adjacent to doorbells.

"They've got a lot of apartments here for a small building," Max said.

"It's probably a rooming house. Here we are. Anton." Wilson loosened the pistol in his shoulder holster, then rang a bell.

Max shifted uncomfortably as they waited.

Again the lieutenant rang, but there was no answer. "She isn't home, apparently, but I hate to waste the ride down here. We'll try the superintendent." He punched another button.

A two-way speaker clicked on, and a metallic, irritated feminine voice rasped, "What do you want?"

"Police," Wilson replied laconically.

A buzzer sounded, and Max followed the lieutenant into the building, but stayed behind during a brief conversation with the middle-aged woman who came to her door in a shabby man's bathrobe. Whatever Wilson said to her must have been convincing, for she went inside, returning with a large key-ring, and started up to the second floor.

"What we're doing is strictly illegal," Wilson said quietly to Max. "We have no right to go in without a search warrant, so you can forget this whole incident. People who run places like this do us favors sometimes, in the hope we'll scratch their backs when they run into trouble."

Max's discomfort increased.

The woman opened a door with a key, then stood aside. "If Miss Anton comes home while you're here," she said, "I didn't let you in."

"I've never set eyes on you." Before Wilson could snap on a light inside the door, the woman was scurrying down the stairs.

Max found himself in a small chamber that was a combination living and dining room. On one side were two easy chairs, with a coffee table between them, and on the opposite wall were a kitchen table and chairs, with a two-burner hot-plate protruding from a shelf. There were only a few feminine touches in the room: some artificial flowers sat in a delicate vase on the kitchen table, the curtains were frilly and the chairs were covered in a pretty chintz.

"She doesn't stay home much," Wilson said, surveying the room with a practiced eye, "and she doesn't spend much on it."

Max watched him as he moved methodically around the

room, picking up the hot-plate, looking into a cupboard where a few staple foodstuff boxes were jumbled, shaking out the two women's fashion magazines on the coffee table.

"This is about as personal as a transient hotel room. Let's see if there's anything more personal where she sleeps." He snapped on a light in a small inner room. Want to look at the rest of the place, Mr. Berman?"

"I think I'll wait here."

"Suit yourself." Wilson shrugged. "Make yourself at home, but not too much. I wouldn't advise you to smoke."

Max continued to stand for a few minutes, then moved to the nearer easy chair. The strains of the evening had taken their toll, and his legs ached. He sat, listening to Wilson rummaging in the inner chamber, and hoped they would leave before Ruth Anton came home. Never before had he felt like such an intruder.

Wilson was taking his time.

Max reached for a cigar, remembered the lieutenant's injunction and smiled wryly. Tired and increasingly restless, he found it impossible to sit still, and wished he hadn't had to accompany Wilson. He had done his duty, and that should have been the end of the matter.

As he shifted his weight he heard a faint, crinkling sound and absently reached down into the space between the cushion and the chair. Something was wedged there, and he tugged at it, drew it out and found he was holding a plain manila envelope about six inches long and four inches wide.

The envelope contained several sheets of heavy paper or cardboard, and Max drew them out, then caught his breath. He was staring at a photograph of Janet, naked except for her boots, with a burning cigarette dangling from her lips.

He reacted instantly, his instinct impelling him to protect Janet. Thrusting the photographs back into the envelope, he placed it in his inside jacket pocket.

Max well realized he was doing something wrong, that he

had discovered positive evidence linking Ruth Anton with the murder of Lance Balutis. He knew, as did every newspaper reader, that Janet had posed for Balutis in the nude immediately prior to the murder, even though the film he had used had been missing from his cameras by the time the police had arrived. That film had never been found, but now there were finished prints reposing in his own pocket.

For the immediate present, at least, Max could not force himself to give Lieutenant Wilson the photographs. Janet would be subjected to new, unsavory publicity, and he wanted to spare her and her parents additional pain and humiliation.

Wilson reappeared in the living room. "If she's a party girl, she sure doesn't have much of a wardrobe. I didn't run into anything worth spitting at, but I'll station somebody outside to wait until she comes home, and maybe she'll talk. Shall we get out of here?"

Max made a supreme effort to speak calmly. "I'm ready," he said, "to call it a night."

The lights had been extinguished in Janet's bedroom, and Max walked quietly down the corridor to his own. Closing and locking the door behind him, he drew the drapes, aware that he had not yet removed his hat and overcoat. Not bothering, however, he took the envelope from his pocket and spread the contents on his bed.

In all, there were five photographs, and Max stared at them for some moments before it occurred to him that four of the five showed Janet in the same pose. But there were differences: each picture in the sequence was a blurred enlargement of the one which preceded it, each increasingly emphasized the grainy quality of the printing. In the fourth photograph he could no longer distinguish Janet's features, and could see only the outlines of her nude body.

The fifth photograph was a grainy pattern of lights and

shadows, and Max doubted that anyone, no matter how long he studied it, would be able to identify the subject matter.

The sequence made no sense, but the person who had developed the photographs had not been playing a pointless game. What had been the purpose?

Max continued to study the photographs as he removed his hat and coat, throwing them onto the nearest chair. From what Janet had said, Balutis had taken many photographs of her, yet only one negative had been developed. Why?

Sitting on the edge of the bed, Max changed the sequence of the photographs, but the difference in their order told him nothing.

He realized he could not keep his discovery a secret for more than a very limited time. No matter how much the fresh publicity might hurt Janet, the photographs could well lead a trained professional like Lieutenant Wilson to the killer.

But he wouldn't tell Wilson yet. For a few hours he would do what he could, on his own, and would continue to shield Janet and her family.

It had been a long time since Stella had eaten in the private L & B dining room, but she still felt at home here, and with good reason, she thought. She had not only been responsible for the decoration and had bought every stick of furniture, but had selected the linen, silver and china. It was almost like coming home.

"Well," she said, "I guess today is the big day."

Max wondered what she meant. Certainly she had no way of knowing he might be on the verge of tracking down Lance Balutis' murderer. In fact, he had telephoned her because he had felt the urge to confide in her. But now, face to face, he was less certain that he wanted to mention the photographs he had discovered. Stella might try to persuade him to go straight to

Lieutenant Wilson, but he had some hunches and first wanted to do a little snooping on his own.

"You and Paul are meeting the North Atlantic committee in Howard Christianson's office this afternoon, aren't you? Or do I have the date wrong?" Stella asked.

Max could not admit to her that the urgency of his discovery had driven his own business from his mind. It was the first time he could recall that this had happened, and it was inconceivable that it could have happened today, of all days, when the ultimate fate of L & B would be decided.

"No, it's today," Max said. "We're accepting one of their recommendations without reservation, even though it's a big kick in the teeth. We'll sell the entire Holland Towers complex and all of America Plaza."

"I'm sorry." Stella ached for him.

There was no bravado in his shrug. "Most men who suffer a failure," he said, "should come out of it smelling as much of roses as Paul and I smell. According to the standards of most people we're still rich. Only our own standards make us punks again."

"You aren't a punk, Max, and you never were." Sudden tears came to Stella's eyes.

Max turned his car over to the doorman of the Benjamin Harrison Henry Galleries and stood on the sidewalk, looking at the art dealer's salon. At dawn he had remembered seeing some of Balutis' grainy-print photographs on exhibit there during the cocktail party that had opened the much-heralded one-man show.

Now, minutes after the gallery had opened for the day, he had come here on a hunch. With luck, he might be able to glean additional information.

Harrison came into the main salon in response to Max's request, dapper in a double-breasted cashmere suit.

"I'm Max Berman. Maybe you don't remember me. I was one of Lance Balutis' backers."

Henry's face came alive, and he pressed Max's outstretched hand between both of his own. "Of course! We met on several occasions. What a ghastly tragedy! I wept at the funeral, my eyes still haven't dried. Lance was such a darling!"

Max muttered inaudibly.

"We'll never meet another like him." Henry sighed. "And we won't see a talent like his again."

"That's why I'm here," Max said. "I've been wondering whether you have many of his works for sale these days."

The gallery owner's manner changed, and his eyes became lidded. "I'm sure you'll get more than your original investment back, through his estate, by the time all his paintings and photographs have sold."

"I've already made a profit," Max assured him.

Henry's stiffness eased. "You shall make more, and so shall I." He waved toward the rear of the main salon, then hurried to a wall switch and snapped on some lights. "Five portraits and three still-life studies. Worth their weight in solid gold!"

Max hastily scanned the paintings. "I'm glad for you, Mr. Henry, and for me, too. It's a shame this is the end of them."

"Oh, there are others. I'm trying to persuade the owners of several Balutis originals to sell to me."

"Good for you." Max concealed his hearty dislike of the man. "Do you happen to have any of his photographs left?"

"A few. Precious few. Let me show you." Henry led him to an alcove, and turned on additional lights. "Dear Lance used his camera like a brush. His technique was extraordinary."

Max glanced at several grainy, unidentifiable photographs, then broke into a sweat. A vastly enlarged print of the most blurred photograph of Janet was hanging on one wall.

Henry became aware of his scrutiny. "Remarkable, isn't it?"

Max nodded.

300

The gallery owner's sigh semed to hang in the air. "This is my latest Balutis photograph, and perhaps my last. His camera studies are much harder for me to buy than his paintings, which are scarce enough."

"You just got this one, you say?" Max tried to sound casual.

"A few days ago. Lance always brought me his own things, of course, on the usual split-commission basis, but I sometimes made outright purchases of his work from other people, usually friends of his to whom he'd given a painting or photo, and who found themselves in debt. Word got around, you can be sure—"

"I can imagine," Max said.

"—so they still drift in, now and again. How I'd love to get my hands on some more of his camera studies."

"You don't happen to know who sold you this one?" If necessary, Max was prepared to call in Lieutenant Wilson at once, but for Janet's sake he hoped he could follow the blurred print to its source unaided.

"It was someone I've never seen before." Henry frowned, then smoothed his eyebrows. "My secretary has all the information."

Max felt his temples throb. "I'd like to meet that person."

The gallery owner didn't think the request unusual. Long accustomed to dealing with eccentrics, he was able to take anything out of the ordinary in his stride. Excusing himself, he went to his office, returning a few moments later with a name and address written on a slip of paper.

"Karl Stornheim." Max read the name aloud, disappointed because it meant nothing to him.

"I don't know him either, but that isn't strange. Lance was such a dear there must have been hundreds and hundreds of people who were close to him. Once you met him, you couldn't help loving him."

"There was at least one person who didn't," Max replied

grimly, pocketing the slip of paper. "Somebody armed with a paint scraper."

The workmanship in the small-unit, high-rise apartment building was shoddy, Max told himself as he walked through the small lobby to the self-service elevator. The walls were thin, and he was willing to bet that the electrical, plumbing and heating sub-contractors had used inferior materials in order to save money.

Stepping into the elevator, he began to concentrate on the menacing business at hand. The photograph Karl Stornheim, whoever he was, sold to the Henry Galleries was a direct link to the murder of Lance Balutis. The picture of Janet had been taken only moments before Balutis' death, then removed from the camera after he had been killed, and subsequently developed. It seemed likely that either Ruth Anton or Stornheim was the murderer, and Max hoped he wasn't being foolish.

Common sense told him he should have called in Lieutenant Wilson and turned over the entire matter to him. But it was worth taking a risk in order to avoid once again involving Janet in the mess. A man who had spent all of his adult life in construction work was still in sufficiently robust physical condition to look after himself. Unless Stornheim was armed with a gun.

The elevator shuddered to a halt at the seventeenth floor, and Max made his way to the apartment at the end of the dimly lit corridor. The tension became unbearable as he pushed the buzzer and waited.

At last the door opened a crack.

"Mr. Stornheim?"

"Yes."

"My name is Berman. I'm a building contractor. I'd like to see you for a few minutes on a private matter." Max could feel the man inspecting him.

"I don't want to buy anything."

302

"This is personal. I'm not selling anything."

"Maybe you're not." The door opened.

Karl Stornheim, Max saw, was a man of about thirty, of medium height and slender build. He was wearing steel-rimmed spectacles.

"Come in. I wasn't expecting company."

Max walked into a one-room and kitchenette apartment, dominated by a rumpled bed at the far side of the chamber. He faced the younger man. "I've just come from the Benjamin Harrison Henry Galleries," he said. "I'm very much interested in a camera study you sold to Mr. Henry the other day."

"Who?" Stornheim's eyes were blank behind his glasses. "I'm afraid you've come to the wrong guy."

"Mr. Henry gave me your name and address himself." This wasn't going to be easy, and Max's tension increased.

"I still don't know what you're talking about."

"A photograph. Made by Lance Balutis."

"What would somebody like me be doing with a photograph?" Stornheim smiled politely and shook his head.

"Mr. Henry says he paid you one hundred and forty dollars for it."

"Not me."

"He offered you a split commission, and told you that you might get a little more if you waited until one of his patrons bought it, but you preferred the cash."

"I could use a hundred and forty in cash, any day."

Max wondered, fleetingly, whether the man was hinting that he would accept a bribe.

"But," Stornheim continued, his voice firm, "I don't know anything about photographs, and I've never been near a gallery in my life." He took a step toward the door, inviting his visitor to leave.

Max did not move. "How do you suppose Mr. Henry got your name and address?"

"How should I know? Mister, all this may be some kind of a gag!"

Before Max could reply he heard a key in the lock of the apartment door.

Stornheim heard it, too, and both men turned simultaneously.

Ruth Anton walked into the room.

Max saw she was still wearing Janet's green coat and red dress.

The girl looked through him, then smiled at Stornheim as though he were alone in the apartment.

"Where the hell have you been?" he demanded.

Ruth Anton giggled and wrapped her arms around his neck.

Stornheim tried to escape her embrace. "Mister," he said to Max, "I can't talk to you any more. You'll have to leave."

"I'll stay," Max said. "I've been looking for Miss Anton, too. So have the police."

The girl giggled again, wildly.

Color drained from Stornheim's face. "Shut up!" he ordered, and pushed her onto the unmade bed.

"Are you ready to talk?" Max watched him closely, ready to spring if the man reached for a weapon.

"I haven't done anything wrong!"

"Who says you have?"

"Neither has Ruth!" Stornheim sank into a chair, pulled off his glasses and covered his face with his hands.

Ruth Anton was looking at him, her face expressionless.

"Mister," Stornheim mumbled, "I swear to you we haven't broken any laws."

"I'm not here to arrest you."

The young man sucked in his breath, straightened and reached for his spectacles. "All right, what the hell. I did sell that camera study to Henry. I made it myself."

"*You* did?"

"I've been a photography nut for years, and I developed that print so it would look like a Balutis. Henry didn't know the dif-

304

ference, and neither will the person who buys it from him. Developing a tricky print is no crime."

"Where did you get the negative?"

Stornheim made no reply.

"What the police want to know," Max said, "is where Miss Anton got that dress and coat. They've been identified as the property of—somebody else."

The girl started to giggle again.

"Cut it," Stornheim told her, "or I'll have to belt you."

She spoke for the first time. "Karl, you promised me—"

"Later!" Stornheim turned back to Max. "If the police are going to find out everything, anyway, I might as well tell you. I got all the stuff from my boss. The dress and the coat and some other clothes to get rid of. And a couple of rolls of film to burn. I gave the clothes to Ruth. She wouldn't know where they came from, and she wouldn't care. I was curious about the film, so I developed it. I knew—anyway, I guessed—that it was Lance Balutis' work. So I got the idea of making a camera study print like his and picking up a little extra money. That's all there is to it, and all I can tell you."

"Except the name of your boss. Who is he?"

"She," Stornheim said. "I work as a chauffeur for Mrs. Martin Tilstrom. Sandra Tilstrom. Her husband is a produce wholesaler. Now will you leave us alone? Ruth is high on pot, as you ought to be able to see! I've got to get her straight so she can go to work at noon. She'll be fired for sure if she misses another day."

Max made no attempt to leave. "Where did Mrs. Tilstrom get the clothes and film?"

Stornheim winced. "How should I know?" His voice sounded ragged. "A guy like me who drives a car for a living doesn't ask his boss questions, and when she finds out I didn't obey her orders, even though she's asked me a half-dozen times if I destroyed all the stuff—"

"If I were you," Max said, moving toward the door, "I

wouldn't go very far from home today. I have an idea the police will want a few words with you."

Ruth Anton's high-pitched giggle followed him down the thin-walled corridor to the elevator.

Max, following the maid into the living room, noted the exquisite provincial French decor, and concluded that the Tilstroms had taste as well as money.

The maid fingered his business card. "I'll find out if Mrs. Tilstrom is free to see you, sir," she said, and left the room.

Max wandered around for a few moments, then stopped short when he saw a large painting over the mantel. Sandra Tilstrom's name had meant nothing to him, but he immediately recognized her portrait. Lance Balutis had been painting her one day, months ago, when Max had come to his studio, and Balutis had introduced them. Come to think of it, he had seen her around town, too, in restaurants and other places.

She was, as Max remembered her, an auburn-haired woman in her late thirties whose charms were just beginning to fade. It was difficult to imagine her as a cold-blooded killer.

"Well, Mr. Berman! You're looking at the monstrosity by the latter-day Rembrandt. What do you think of it? Don't tell me!"

Max turned as Sandra Tilstrom came into the room. Her red hair was tousled, her eye make-up was a little smudged, and she was dressed, somewhat incongruously for a matron of her age, in a miniskirted jumper of imitation fur. In her left hand was a glass half filled with what looked like straight Scotch.

"The ultimate masterpiece of a genius, isn't it?" She lurched as she joined him in front of the portrait. "Marty—my husband —loves the monstrosity. So do you, I suppose. Because you're a man. It takes a woman—or a half-man like Lance—to appreciate subtle humor."

306

The portrait resembled her, although it didn't do justice to her figure, and Max couldn't understand why she was so bitter. "Look at the lines in my face," Sandra Tilstrom said in disgust. "Every last one. Exaggerated. Along with a few dozen that haven't appeared yet. Look at my belly. Pregnant, see? A private joke. Lance knew I was frightened silly by the possibility of having a baby. And notice the bracelet on my right wrist. It doesn't go with the evening dress I wore when I posed for the portrait. It's an identification bracelet that *I* gave *him*. Inscribed. Which gave him the chance to blackmail me. The shit."

She was drunk, Max realized, but was still in sufficient command of herself to know what she was saying.

"I leer down at myself, Mr. Berman, and if you'll look closely at those lips you'll see it *is* a leer. Lance swore that was my expression in bed. But Marty makes such a scene that I can't take down the portrait and burn it, damn him. Damn men."

Max was surprised to find he felt sorry for her. "Mrs. Tilstrom," he said, avoiding the subject of the portrait, "I'm here for a reason. I've just seen a man who claims he works for you. His name is Stornheim—"

"Karl. Of course."

"He gave some stolen clothing to a girl, and says you told him to dispose of it. He developed a photograph from some film he says you told him to burn."

Sandra Tilstrom laughed savagely, then took a cigarette from a box with a mother-of-pearl lid. "Be a dear and give me a light. Thanks. Karl, the greedy pig. Mama always warned me not to trust a man, and Mama was right. You'd think that two years with Lance would have taught me a lesson. But I've always been slow. I flunked reading in fourth grade."

Max was stunned by her tacit admission of guilt. It seemed indecent for anyone to confess a murder so willingly.

"The Lafferty kid's father is your partner, isn't he, Mr. Berman? Oh, how I've been reading the newspapers. Tell her for me that I let him have it for both of us. My God, I've never felt so sorry for another woman in all my life. But if someone had told me, I wouldn't have believed I would. Or could." She took a long swallow from her glass of whisky.

Max discovered he was reluctant to ask, "You were there—when he was taking those pictures of Janet?"

"Behind the goddam drapes. Like a character in a French farce. Oh, it was my own fault for going to his house in the first place. I knew better." Sandra Tilstrom staggered as she crossed the room to a portable bar and refilled her glass. "But he swore he'd take me back. I wanted to believe him, so I did. Here's to me."

Max decided to wait until she lowered the glass.

She gave him no chance to speak. "I wanted to leave when the Lafferty girl showed up at his house. But he wouldn't hear of it. He held her off downstairs while he persuaded me to hide behind his photography drapes. Kept telling me what a huge jolt I'd get out of it. The bastard knew he could talk me into anything." She dropped her burning cigarette onto the rich Turkish rug.

Max started toward her to pick it up.

She ground it out beneath her shoe before he could reach it, then went to the box for another. "Lance could have given lessons to the Marquis de Sade. He got a double jolt—torturing her and driving me crazy at the same time. By God, he was so vicious to her. You never saw anything so cruel and depraved. And all through it, there I stood behind the goddam drapes, jealous and miserable—" She broke off and stood, weaving.

Max lit the cigarette for her.

"The paint scraper gave me the idea. When I found it on the floor. At first I thought I'd geld him. That's what he deserved. I still thought it when I went to the dressing room and took the kid's clothes."

"Why did you take them, Mrs. Tilstrom?"

"Why the hell do you suppose? So she couldn't get dressed —follow me! It was when I went after the bastard with the scraper that I lost control. The newspapers say I stabbed him half a dozen times, but I wouldn't know. Or care. I felt good for the first time in two years. Even though she was screaming when I ran down the stairs."

Max was speechless.

"I felt free. I still do." Sandra Tilstrom gazed up at her portrait. "I'm going to slice the monstrosity to shreds before I surrender. Marty won't really mind. Nobody gives a damn about me. Except me."

She paid no attention as Max went to the telephone and dialed Lieutenant Wilson's number.

Janet sat quietly on the sofa in the living room of Max's apartment as she listened to his recital, but finally she couldn't help breaking in. "I know how Mrs. Tilstrom felt, Uncle Max."

He was pacing up and down the room. "I hope you don't."

"What will happen to her?"

"The criminal lawyers her husband hired this afternoon are the best in the business. They won't get her off, but by the time they're finished, any judge in the state will give her a reduced sentence. There's just one thing. You're certain to be called as a witness. You'll have to live through that photograph-making scene again in the courtroom."

"I can take it," Janet said.

Looking at her, Max realized she could.

"For all I know, she saved me from rape, and I'm perfectly willing to say so."

"Well," Max said, "you're important to the trial, that's sure. Lieutenant Wilson had the other photographs developed after he took them from Stornheim this noon. Mrs. Tilstrom would have been smart if she'd destroyed them after taking them from Balutis' cameras."

"Why did she bother to take them?"

"In her formal confession this afternoon she said she was afraid she appeared in some of the photographs. That's why she took the negatives. They may have to use those photos at the trial, Janet, although he assured me they won't unless it becomes absolutely necessary."

Janet shrugged. "I know who my friends are."

Max changed the subject. "Wilson was annoyed at me, I can tell you! For taking the prints after I found them in Ruth Anton's apartment, and for barging around on my own today."

"You were taking a chance, Uncle Max."

"A bachelor of my age is entitled to take chances. So that's the story, Janet. You're in the clear, and tonight we'll go out to celebrate."

The girl shook her head. "Thanks, Uncle Max, but I can't. I'm moving."

He looked at her, startled.

"Oh, I'm not going back with Muriel, never fear. But I just can't be a little girl again with Mother and Daddy, either. After you called me today to say I'd been cleared, I went out and found a studio apartment where I can live and work. I'm going to make it on my own somehow."

"I'll give odds in your favor. But you still have to eat dinner—"

"Tonight," Janet said, smiling, "you have some odds and ends of your own business to look after."

He looked puzzled.

"Stella tells me you called her from Lieutenant Wilson's office with the news, too."

"Stella." There was deep resignation in his shrug.

"You take her at her word when she tells you something, Uncle Max. You shouldn't."

"For years," Max said, "ever since you were a little girl, we've had problems. You don't understand."

"No, Uncle Max. *You* don't. There are some women who aren't as independent as they claim. Sometimes they don't even realize it themselves."

"I wonder if you know how many times I've proposed to Stella, Janet."

"For a long time she had to be asked, so she could prove her independence by refusing. This time don't ask her, Uncle Max. *Tell* her. She'll marry you. I know she will."

For a long moment Max stood still, pondering. Then a broad smile creased his face. "That," he said, "is exactly what I'll do. You know something, Janet? That's *exactly* what I'll do!"

They walked, hand in hand, along the narrow asphalt path overlooking the East River in the Seventies, and, content with each other's company, neither spoke. A tugboat hooted in a deep basso, and they stopped to lean on the rail and watch it.

They walked again, passing a booted, miniskirted young mother pushing a baby carriage. "A few years ago," Stella said, "nobody would have believed that a girl who looked like that could be a mother."

"She's dressed for her time. You and I are a transition generation, Stella, and that's all there is to it. You know, it's funny, I don't regret anything that's happened these past few months except Balutis' death. I almost miss the son of a bitch."

"What you need," Stella said, "is something to occupy your evenings."

"I'm open to suggestions."

"You might marry me, Max. Will you?"

The day was no longer cold and raw, the sky no longer leaden, and Max tightened his grip on Stella's hand. "What I like best about our generation," he said, "is that we're so sensible. Most of all you, Stell."

Young people filled the studio-living room of the small apartment, and it was impossible to walk, turn or wave an arm without bumping into someone. Girls in miniskirts and pants, young men in beards and beads were everywhere. In the tiny bedroom the crush was even worse. Three couples, all deep in earnest conversation, perched on the edges of the bed, and another, sitting cross-legged, occupied its center. A girl and boy, in a casual embrace, filled the room's one chair, and were engaged in a heated discussion with two other young men on the significance of art as a reflection of life.

The noise was deafening. A stereo set blared endlessly, carrying the songs of a quartet, with guitar and drum, to the entire East Side neighborhood. Since everyone present was thoroughly familiar with both the singers and their number, it was unnecessary for anyone to listen. But the absence of that quartet and their song would have created a void.

People talked simultaneously, but it hardly mattered. Friends had come together, and the proximity—in this case the close proximity—of everybody one knew and liked was all that was important.

Janet Lafferty, dark-brown hair streaming down her back, appeared in the bedroom entrance and fought her way into the chamber. "Food!" she shouted, trying to make herself heard above the hubbub. "I've got cold cuts and spaghetti in the kitchen for anybody who wants them."

Only a few heeded the invitation and made their way out of the room.

Elmer Bates saw Janet, and breaking away from a group to whom he was explaining the kinship of politics and literature, went to her. He threw an arm around her shoulders, and said something to her.

The din was so loud that she couldn't hear a word, and indicated as much in pantomime.

Bates tried again, with no success, and then, laughing, dragged her off to the bathroom, the apartment's one sanctuary of relative quiet.

"Anyway, all I wanted to tell you is that this housewarming is it. Out of sight. It's quite wonderful."

Janet beamed at him. "I'm so glad. You know, I'm having such fun I've almost forgotten that I'm the hostess."

Bates returned her smile, then sobered. "You're really together now, aren't you, baby? You aren't up-tight any more."

"No. I'm—just fine, Elmer." A shadow crossed her face for a moment, then vanished. "I've learned a few things, and I'll manage."

He cupped her chin in his hand, tilted her face toward the light and studied her for a moment. He saw her radiance, and sensed the inner strength she had acquired. "Ah," he said. "You've got strength now, baby. And it looks beautiful on you."

A few tiny slivers of light slanted in through the closed venetian blinds, but it remained very dark in the master bedroom of the Park Avenue apartment. So Max, clad in pajamas, robe and slippers, moved with care as he made his way across the room, gingerly holding aloft two steaming mugs of coffee. Placing one on the small table at the near side of the king-sized bed, he went to the closest easy chair and lowered himself into it.

Sipping the hot coffee, he realized he had enjoyed his best night's sleep in months.

"Stell," he called softly. "It's late."

The tousled blond head on the pillow did not move.

"We have to get our passports renewed," he said, "and I want to get you some new luggage."

"I can't believe it. In eleven days from now is the grand

reopening of the London hotel. And in five days from now we sail."

He chuckled. "So what else is new?"

"Everything. Us. I said I'd marry you. Remember?"

There was a long silence and then Max said, "I've been thinking. We'd be smart not to have children, Stell."

"That's nonsense!" she retorted. "You want them as much as I do, and you know it!"

"Okay," Max said with a sigh, "I'll be honest with you. To some people these days it's probably a small thing. Others work it out. But there's something inside me that objects to my children becoming Catholics. Don't say a word!" he continued, raising a hand, "Let me finish. I know. I'm bigoted. I'm narrow. I'm selfish. I'm unreasonable. Granted. If you want to be a Catholic, that's up to you, naturally. But not the children. Not the Church the way it still is, the way it was when I was a boy in Europe. The Catholic Church of tomorrow that's just beginning to take shape, all right. But we don't have that Church yet."

Stella stubbed out her cigarette. "Max, I've been thinking, too. We've learned, the hardest way, that we can't live apart. We want and need marriage. And children. So, if I must, I'll give up my Church. Not my faith—nothing can change that. I can still go to Mass, even though I'll be denied the Sacraments. But I can do it and marry you outside the Church. I know I can, and I will."

Max stared at her. "Now I'll tell you something," he said. "I'm known as a very big, important man. Everybody says so. A very strong man, too. Universal opinion. So many people think it that I've come to believe it myself. But it's all a lie. You're the strong one, Stell. Not me. You have the real courage."

"When a woman loves a man—"

"I know you love me! But how do I prove that I love you?"

"You can prove it every day of your life, honey."

He gazed morosely down at the floor.

"Max," she called softly.

314

He made no move.

"Max." Stella became more insistent.

He looked at her, and their eyes met.

Stella gently patted the bed.

"I'm happy to oblige," Max said, and, his spirits lifting, went to her.